ALMOST
TOUCHING
THE SKIES

ALMOST TOUCHING THE SKIES

Women's Coming of Age Stories

Edited by
Florence Howe and Jean Casella

Introduction by
Marilyn French

The Feminist Press
at The City University of New York

New York

Published by The Feminist Press at The City University of New York
365 Fifth Avenue, New York, NY 10016
www.feministpress.org

First edition, 2000

Library of Congress Cataloging-in-Publication Data

Almost touching the skies : women's coming of age stories / edited by Florence Howe
and Jean Casella.—1st ed.
       p. cm.
     ISBN 1-55861-233-5 (alk. paper) — ISBN 1-55861-234-3 (pbk. : alk. paper)
     1. Women—United States—Fiction.   2. American fiction—Women authors.
  3. Coming of age—Fiction.   4. Young women—Fiction.   I. Howe, Florence.
  II. Casella, Jean.

  PS648.W6 A79 2000
  813.008'0352042—dc21

                                                                99-086368

Epigraph on p. v from poem 1176 by Emily Dickinson, written c. 1870, originally
published 1896.

The Feminist Press at The City University of New York would like to thank
The AT&T Foundation for a generous grant in support of this publication and of
the celebration of the thirtieth anniversary of The Feminist Press.

The Feminist Press also thanks Jan Constantine, Helene D. Goldfarb, Nancy
Hoffman, Joanne Markell, and Genevieve Vaughan for their generosity.

Text design and typesetting by Stratford Publishing Services, Brattleboro, Vermont
Printed on acid-free paper by RR Donnelley & Sons
Manufactured in the United States of America

07 06 05 04 03 02 01 00   5 4 3 2

We never know how high we are
Till we are asked to rise
And then if we are true to plan
Our statures touch the skies —
— Emily Dickinson

CONTENTS

Part Three
Work and the World

PREFACE

In the thirty-year history of The Feminist Press, perhaps no gesture was more significant than Tillie Olsen's insistence in 1971 that we reprint *Daughter of Earth* by Agnes Smedley. For faculty who had for decades taught such novels as *Sons and Lovers* by D.H. Lawrence, the rediscovery of Smedley allowed us to add to the curriculum a working-class novel that centered on a young woman. In Lawrence's novel, Paul Morel scoffs at a female character who claims she likes her job as a teacher. He rebukes her sharply, saying that work may be enough for men, but women need love (and a heterosexual marriage) more than anything else. Like Lawrence's Paul Morel, Smedley's Marie Rogers abandons her family, but unlike him, she channels the guilt she suffers into work for the world's poor and unknown. She knows she needs work more than marriage.

Just as important, the rediscovery of Smedley led us to imagine that we might spearhead the recovery of many more women writers. For more than a decade, The Feminist Press's publishing program focused on lost literary classics, both novels and collections of short fiction. Then, in the mid-1980s, long before memoirs had become as popular as novels, we began the Cross-Cultural Memoir Series. Both strands—fiction and memoir—have emphasized the lives of girls and young women growing to consciousness in a world not altogether friendly to their visions of themselves as autonomous, intelligent, creative, and responsible persons who know they need both love and work.

To celebrate our thirtieth anniversary, we have brought together a selection of this published work. We regret that we had to omit more than we were able to include. We also had to make the difficult decision to limit our texts to those written by American women writers, even though we had, by the 1980s, begun to publish international work. We chose to produce a volume that could be read as expressing a century of changing perceptions about both the possibilities and the realities of women's lives in this relatively privileged but vastly inequitable country. The earliest story was written in the 1870s; the most recent memoir in the 1990s. We wanted the collection to allow a reading of women as agents of their own change, as resisting uniform agendas, as caring for their sisters and brothers, as understanding the power of their awakened consciousness. Thus, despite many differences of race, class, ethnicity, sexual orientation, and physical ability, the volume also celebrates the common experiences of girls discovering what it means to be young, gifted, and female in the United States.

Like most good things that have emerged from the thirty-year history of The Feminist Press, this book is a product of collaboration. We want to thank, first, our authors, who have made this book possible by capturing brilliantly the experiences of young women, sometimes their own selves. We thank Marilyn French, who wrote a lovely introduction on a moment's notice. And we thank Vera B. Williams, who created and produced the sixteen watercolors that make up the cover art for this book, a true match for the literature inside the covers.

We thank The Feminist Press staff and volunteers who helped us complete the book in time for our gala anniversary celebration in April (which will feature readings from the volume): Amanda Hamlin assisted at every stage of the editorial and production process. Corinna Rodewald researched and outlined some of the head notes and assisted with copyright permissions. Dayna Navaro brought to the book a lovely design and high production values. The editorial staff took on many extra tasks so that we could focus on this book.

We extend our deepest thanks to the AT&T Foundation, and especially to our program officer, Marilyn Reznick, for support of this book and of other events and projects surrounding our thirtieth anniversary. They have been important partners in our work for some years now, and we appreciate their generosity.

Finally, we thank our readers, some of whom are also our donors, for your contribution to the survival and health of The Feminist Press. You have sustained us for three decades, and we know you will continue to do so for many decades to come.

Florence Howe
Jean Casella
New York City
January 2000

INTRODUCTION

When I reached eleven or thereabouts, my beloved old books suddenly seemed inadequate. I needed something I could not learn from fairy tales, myths, verse, and Frances Hodgson Burnett's novels. I disliked most children's books of my day, the sort my teachers lent me, finding them pious, moralistic, and sentimental (although I didn't yet know those words).

I needed, I thought, stories about someone like me, whatever that meant. I searched, but as a minor, was barred from the adult section of the library. I read and discarded in despair until one day, visiting the child of a family friend in Jamaica, Queens, I found in the Jamaica public library (far larger than the one in my neighborhood) *Sue Barton, Student Nurse.* This was the story of a girl who decides to choose a profession, and it excited me. It was one of a series my library did not possess. Whenever I visited my friend, we would go to the library for another Sue Barton book.

But it soon appeared that Sue Barton's true goal was not work but marriage. The books began to be about her relationship with a boyfriend. Since I was sure I didn't want to marry, ever, I abandoned Sue, and continued to seek books to help me grow up. I concluded they didn't exist.

They did. In fact, the books from which some of the selections in this volume are drawn were published when I was a girl. But I was ignorant, my parents were uneducated, most librarians were not interested in children, and most teachers knew only those gooey books about goody-goody little girls who learn from their moment of rebellion that parents are good, authorities right, and obedience required.

If only The Feminist Press had existed then! Then I might have had a teacher who would slip a book into my hand—this one, perhaps. Wallowing in luxurious plenty, I could have read accounts of girlhood from Mississippi to Brooklyn, of girls of varied colors, backgrounds, and sexual tendencies, all of whom faced, as youngsters, the same unspeakable problem—the rigid, narrow position of women in society. If in reading these tales I did not find myself exactly, I would certainly have found a wider perspective on womanhood, a sense of freedom.

Scholars have shown that most girls feel filled with power, able to "jump at de sun," as Zora Neale Hurston put it, until puberty. I remember the world beginning to constrict, borders to narrow, darkness to hover. The future no longer seemed a bright field of possibility, but a vague hovering emptiness. And indeed, whatever we were or were capable of, the future of most women of my generation was the same. We did not choose our lives; we were slotted into them, like the servant/porter class in Huxley's *Brave New World*. Perhaps many of us would have liked to marry and have children—in our own time, by our own volition, and accompanied by the ability to use other parts of ourselves. Some of us would have taken entirely different paths. But we did not feel we had a choice.

Even as adults, women may have trouble finding books that reflect the huge variety of female experience. Despite the tremendous inroads women have made in higher education, the professions, and the corporate world, they still face severe obstacles everywhere—including the world of literature and publishing. Women in the United States are the majority of readers; they buy two-thirds of all books. Yet fewer women are published than men, and women are far less likely to be reviewed. (Check out any issue of the *New York Times Book Review*.) Women authors are less likely to be well known, and are taken less seriously than male writers. So they are far less likely to be remembered. Each time another woman is rescued from oblivion, we are dismayed to realize (again) that a woman can be a master writer, and yet be dismissed and forgotten.

Jean Rhys's work was out of print when she was "discovered," and Edith Wharton was unread, considered passé when I was in college. In the 1970s, I asked a professor of French literature about the great George Sand, and was told she was unimportant. One of the great accomplishments of The Feminist Press has been to resuscitate female masters like Zora Neale Hurston, Kate Chopin, and Agnes Smedley. It has also published fine writers like Alice Walker, Bella Spewak, Louise Meriwether—well, and all the writers in this book, all of them published by The Feminist Press. So you can buy one book and read widely and take your pick, then go out and build yourself a library.

Most of the pieces in part one of *Almost Touching the Skies* are memoirs of childhood or early adolescence, grouped under the title "Family" because parents and siblings are the most powerful forces at this time of life. In all

Introduction

of them, the heroine's sex is a major factor, but not the only factor, complicating her move to maturity. Class, race, poverty, or rigid middle-class mores also affect her sense of self and seem to be barriers between her and a maturity chosen in freedom.

Zora Neale Hurston had the courage to write, in her 1942 memoir, *Dust Tracks on a Road*, about poor African Americans who speak in the vernacular and whose customs a white middle-class person might not consider respectable. It took courage to write about the poor when George Sand, in the nineteenth century, became the first writer in the world to do so. (She shocked Europe and influenced Walt Whitman, Karl Marx, and Mikhail Bakunin, among others.) It still took courage when Zora Neale Hurston did it in the early twentieth century, influencing every major black writer since—and many white writers, as well. Hurston writes grittily about real things, events we recognize, people we know we know. The genuineness of her writing stays with us, like a good meal, which feeds not just the body but the spirit, producing something triumphant that hovers above and around the edges of daily life.

The selection from the memoir of Estella Conwill Májozo, *Come Out the Wilderness*, set in the African American community of 1950s Louisville, is a scene of children at play, and offers two opposing worlds—the boys' world with its excitement, courage, cameraderie, and murderousness, and the grandmother's woman's world, nurturing, affectionate, moral, and pious. The girl, at the very moment of maturity, is ambivalent; half of her wants to stay with the boys and half wants to move on to a still mysterious womanhood.

Flavia Alaya's memoir, *Under the Rose*, describes an enchanted year in her childhood, 1942. Pursuing some private dream, her immigrant father takes his family to Arizona, a strange environment for these New York Italian Americans. Her mother, one of four sisters talented in fashion, all of whom give up promising careers to marry, is bewildered. Her father is a brilliant, possessive, domineering patriarch who suddenly falls ill, losing his power. Her siblings are a typical crew of mischief and fun, who skirt danger in this new world. The mother's glamorous sister comes to visit and stays to marry a soldier. Through it all, the eight-year-old girl watches and thinks and wonders and, intelligently, changes.

In her memoir, *I Dwell in Possibility*, Toni McNaron provides the other half of the American racial dichotomy—a white middle-class family in the industrial South during the Depression. There is nothing typical about this family. Her father calls Toni "Son" until she is six. Desperate to give him what he wants, she keeps trying to find ways to do so—trying to kiss her elbow, for instance, because a Southern maxim promises this will turn her into a boy. Her overwhelming mother, forty when she is born, is filled with anxieties for the new child. But she also imposes on her a discomfiting intimacy. Toni also has a sixteen-year-old sister who announces that she will never speak to the child unless she can name her.

The story by Toni Cade Bambara, "Raymond's Run," is recounted by a young African American girl who loves running and her brother Raymond. Raymond, who has a big head, has something wrong with him. He is her responsibility: in large families in past ages, girls were commonly burdened with rearing younger siblings. The children in the streets mock Raymond, but the girl sees inside him and understands his imagination, his longing to walk a tightrope or slosh in a puddle or climb a fence like a gorilla. Her tough silent love for her brother is interwoven with her ambitions at running (which she does very swiftly), and her fears of other girls, in particular a rival she'd rather were her friend. This is an awful lot for a girl to deal with on the busy streets of New York City.

A story by Hisaye Yamamoto, *Seventeen Syllables*, tells a moving, understated story of a Japanese American family living on a farm in California. Rosie, the daughter, on the edge of maturity, is given a surprise kiss by the son of the Mexican American family that helps her family pick the tomatoes. Unsure about this, unsure of her feelings, she is letting it mulch inside her when a family drama occurs. Its bearing on her confusion is unstated, but clear, and presents the girl with a rather bleak sense of future prospects.

Katharine Butler Hathaway wrote a memoir, *The Little Locksmith*, published in 1943, the year after her death, and forgotten until The Feminist Press republished it this year. Hathaway had tuberculosis of the spine. When she was five years old, she was strapped to a stretcher and kept immobile for ten years—the treatment at the time. When she was freed, however, her body was deformed. The vignette excerpted here describes the complex emotions between the sick child and her loving mother. It is profoundly observed, and profoundly felt: a beautiful piece.

In *Juggling*, Jane Gould describes her life as the daughter of a distinguished Jewish family in a suburb of New York City in the 1930s. The Depression has destroyed her father's business, and the family begins to slide downward economically. Her parents' struggle to survive shadows her adolescence: her father's inability to accept his failure (still, he works stubbornly, staunchly, to support the family) and her mother's resentment of it (still, she rallies staunchly and works hard to keep up domestic standards). But this struggle, a major one when seen from her maturity, is mere background to the girl, who is, like most young women, obsessed with trying to be popular, to be like the other girls.

Mary E. Wilkins Freeman is another woman writer esteemed in her own time—the mid-nineteenth century—and then forgotten. "Louisa" tells of a young woman courted by a man she doesn't want to marry. Her mother continually nags at her to marry him, suggesting that the intransigent daughter could save the family from starvation. The daughter triumphs when her mother recognizes her rightness.

Part two of the volume centers around "Teachers and Friends," the potent influences of young adulthood. Marjorie Agosín fled Chile with her family, and remained in exile from the dictatorship of Augusto Pinochet. But her parents' memories of Chile ran deep, and she captured them in two memoirs. Agosín's mother was a member of one of three Jewish families living—along with fifty Nazis—in a small Chilean town during World War II. In A Cross and a Star, Agosín writes in her mother's voice, recalling her life with the family cook, Carmen Carrasco, in a prose soaked in the magical, mystical climate of the Latin American imagination.

Shirley Geok-lin Lim is of Chinese heritage, born in Malaysia, one of ten children. But she was named for Shirley Temple, and received a British education after being abandoned by her mother. Among the White Moon Faces, her memoir, describes the child in school with Catholic nuns, whose "domineering secretive discipline" helped bring her to "rebellion and to literature." The child is constantly told she is sinning but does not know what her sin is—a familiar situation for those taught by nuns, I think—and concludes that her selfhood itself is the sin, grounds for rebellion in any culture.

Edith Konecky, author of the novel Allegra Maud Goldman, describes a summer at camp. Her heroine, Allegra, is at the age when crushes on camp counselors are de rigueur, and she manages to come up with one. It, in turn, leads her not just to romantic heartbreak, but to poetry and the literary life, in a charming piece done with great economy.

In The Changelings, nominated for a Pulitzer Prize, Jo Sinclair deals with the encounter between immigrant whites, Jewish and Italian, and a gradually encroaching African American community. Vincent, a twelve-year-old girl, has her own gang until she loses it when the boys rise violently against her. They strip and humiliate her. But she has an ally: a black girl, Clara Jackson, who has watched the attack and empathized with her. Although her background has taught Vincent to see blacks as the enemy, the "other," Vincent sees that Clara is exactly like her except for color, and the grounds are laid for friendship.

Helen Rose Hull, born in 1888, lived until 1971 and published widely. In "The Fire," Cynthia, a young woman, visits her art teacher to sever their relationship. Her mother, suspicious of a single woman living alone, will not permit her to continue the lessons. Not until Cynthia has done the sad deed and returned home does she comprehend how much—and what— the lessons and the relationship mean to her, that they offered a direction, freedom, an independent move toward beauty and meaning. But even as she becomes aware of this, she finds these things for herself.

Part three treats "Work and the World," the largest context of women's lives, and includes some of the finest writers in the book.

Canadian-born Edith Summers Kelley was, at one point in her life, a tobacco farmer. The knowledge this experience gave her is reflected in her first novel, *Weeds*, published in 1923 and forgotten. Republished in 1973, it was called "a major work of American fiction"—and forgotten again until it was rescued by The Feminist Press. In this section, Judith, as an infant and then a little girl, grows up in love with all the living things on the farm around her until, one terrible day, she discovers the inexorable laws of nature.

In the selection from Louise Meriwether's *Daddy Was a Number Runner*, about a girl growing up in Harlem in the 1930s, Francie is twelve when she gets her first period. At the movies shortly afterward, a man arouses her sexually with his hand, shocking her. She leaps up and runs from the theater, but the experience lingers—for her, not as a memory of victimization, but as proof of her bad character.

Bella Spewak lived as a child on the Lower East Side of New York just after the turn of the century. She grew up to become part of a husband-and-wife playwriting and screenwriting team, which wrote *Kiss Me Kate*, among other works. When, in 1990, I first read her book, *Streets*, I was desolate that my mother had died and could not read it. The New York streets Spewak brings to such vivid life were much like the Brooklyn streets my mother had trod in *her* childhood. Spewak's book helped me understand

Introduction

my mother's inarticulate, inexpressible fear, even horror, of the neighborhood she grew up in—although Spewak herself found life there.

Agnes Smedley was an international activist who worked to free India from Great Britain and sided with the Communists during the Russian and Chinese revolutions. She went to jail as a spy, and she wrote a great book, *Daughter of Earth*. This autobiographically based novel was published in 1929 and reissued six years later, yet did not receive full appreciation until The Feminist Press revived it in 1973. Now Smedley is beginning to get the respect she deserves. In this excerpt, she describes the great hardship and poverty of the Mexicans of New Mexico and the tough hardiness of sixteen-year-old Marie Rogers, who lives among them.

Meena Alexander was born in India, educated in the Sudan and England. In this excerpt from her memoir, *Fault Lines*, she recounts the feelings of a girl as she begins to fathom the enormous pressures on women in Hindu and Muslim cultures. Just as she is becoming aware of the beginnings of desire, she learns that "improperly" dressed women are stoned to death, that fathers push pregnant unmarried daughters into wells, drowning them, and that in marriage, everywoman's destiny, none of her student accomplishments will have any value. Understated and without bitterness, this is a sharp little piece.

Anzia Yezierska, a Polish Jew, immigrated to the United States in 1902, where she was educated and became a writer of some renown. In this story, "Children of Loneliness," she describes the gulf that opens up between uneducated peasant parents and their educated daughter, wounding to both, and perhaps fatal to their relationship. Many of us have forgotten the terrible alienation suffered by many immigrants and their educated children, but this story brings it to vivid life.

Kate Chopin, a nineteenth-century writer who was rediscovered and acclaimed in recent years, lived in the French-Creole communities of St. Louis and later New Orleans. She saw with great clarity the situation facing any woman who was also an artist: the impossibility of being a wife, who by law and custom owes her husband total duty and devotion, and being an artist, when art requires the same duty and devotion. This story, "Wiser Than a God," has an outcome unusual for its period.

Alice Walker is one of America's best-known and best-loved authors. The essay "Beauty: When the Other Dancer Is the Self" is structured poetically, like much of Walker's work, a composite of fragments from different moments of memory. The whole is a consideration of something that marred life, marred the self, felt like an unforgivable flaw, and then turned out to be a *world*, an entire universe unto itself, and a part of beauty.

I introduce this book to you with pleasure, hoping you will read it in pleasure, and will give it to the young women you know, especially girls on the cusp of maturity, seeking a way to be in the world; and to all mature women who seek in literature a reflection of their own unique experience; and to all men who wonder, "What do women want?"

Marilyn French
New York City
January 2000

Part One

Family

Zora Neale Hurston

From Dust Tracks on a Road

Zora Neale Hurston (1901?–1960), a novelist, journalist, folklorist, and critic, was, between 1920 and 1950, the most prolific African American woman writer in the United States. Today acknowledged as an intellectual and spiritual foremother to generations of African American writers, Hurston was a writer ahead of her time. Although her writing was praised by some when it appeared, she was also widely condemned for her audaciousness and independence.

With the publication in 1979 of the first volume of selections from her work, *I Love Myself When I Am Laughing . . . and Then Again When I Am Looking Mean and Impressive: A Zora Neale Hurston Reader,* edited by Alice Walker, The Feminist Press became one of the pioneers in the contemporary restoration of Hurston's legacy. This excerpt, from her 1942 autobiography *Dust Tracks on a Road,* describes her childhood in the all-black town of Eatonville, Florida, at the turn of the century. The piece reveals both Hurston's indomitable spirit and her ear for the beauty of African American expression. Hurston's mother encouraged her daughter's strength and creativity, even in a world determined to destroy them.

My Folks

. . . We lived on a big piece of ground with two big chinaberry trees shading the front gate and Cape jasmine bushes with hundreds of blooms on either side of the walks. I loved the fleshy, white, fragrant blooms as a child but did not make too much of them. They were too common in my neighborhood. When I got to New York and found out that the people called them gardenias, and that the flowers cost a dollar each, I was impressed. The home folks laughed when I went back down there and told them. Some of the folks did not want to believe me. A dollar for a Cape jasmine bloom! Folks up north there must be crazy.

There were plenty of orange, grapefruit, tangerine, guavas and other fruits in our yard. We had a five-acre garden with things to eat growing in it, and so we were never hungry. We had chicken on the table often; home-cured meat, and all the eggs we wanted. It was a common thing for us smaller children to fill the iron tea-kettle full of eggs and boil them, and lay around in the yard and eat them until we were full. Any left-over boiled eggs could always be used for missiles. There was plenty of fish in the lakes around the town, and so we had all that we wanted. But beef stew was something rare. We were all very happy whenever Papa went to Orlando and brought back something delicious like stew-beef. Chicken and fish were too common with us. In the same way, we treasured an apple. We had oranges, tangerines and grapefruit to use as hand-grenades on the neighbors' children. But apples were something rare. They came from way up north.

Our house had eight rooms, and we called it a two-story house; but later on I learned it was really one story and a jump. The big boys all slept up there, and it was a good place to hide and shirk from sweeping off the front porch or raking up the back yard.

Downstairs in the dining-room there was an old "safe," a punched design in its tin doors. Glasses of guava jelly, quart jars of pear, peach and other kinds of preserves. The left-over cooked foods were on the lower shelves.

There were eight children in the family, and our house was noisy from the time school turned out until bedtime. After supper we gathered in Mama's room, and everybody had to get their lessons for the next day. Mama carried us all past long division in arithmetic, and parsing sentences in grammar, by diagrams on the blackboard. That was as far as she had gone. Then the younger ones were turned over to my oldest brother, Bob, and Mama sat and saw to it that we paid attention. You had to keep on going over things until you did know. How I hated the multiplication tables—especially the sevens!

We had a big barn, and a stretch of ground well covered with Bermuda grass. So on moonlight nights, two-thirds of the village children from seven to eighteen would be playing hide and whoop, chick-mah-chick, hide and seek, and other boisterous games in our yard. Once or twice a year we might get permission to go and play at some other house. But that was most unusual. Mama contended that we had plenty of space to play in; plenty of things to play with; and, furthermore, plenty of us to keep each other's company. If she had her way, she meant to raise her children to stay at home. She said that there was no need for us to live like no-count

Negroes and poor-white trash—too poor to sit in the house—had to come outdoors for any pleasure, or hang around somebody else's house. Any of her children who had any tendencies like that must have got it from the Hurston side. It certainly did not come from the Pottses. Things like that gave me my first glimmering of the universal female gospel that all good traits and leanings come from the mother's side.

Mama exhorted her children at every opportunity to "jump at de sun." We might not land on the sun, but at least we would get off the ground. Papa did not feel so hopeful. Let well enough alone. It did not do for Negroes to have too much spirit. He was always threatening to break mine or kill me in the attempt. My mother was always standing between us. She conceded that I was impudent and given to talking back, but she didn't want to "squinch my spirit" too much for fear that I would turn out to be a mealy-mouthed rag doll by the time I got grown. Papa always flew hot when Mama said that. I do not know whether he feared for my future, with the tendency I had to stand and give battle, or that he felt a personal reference in Mama's observation. He predicted dire things for me. The white folks were not going to stand for it. I was going to be hung before I got grown. Somebody was going to blow me down for my sassy tongue. Mama was going to suck sorrow for not beating my temper out of me before it was too late. Posses with ropes and guns were going to drag me out sooner or later on account of that stiff neck I toted. I was going to tote a hungry belly by reason of my forward ways. My older sister was meek and mild. She would always get along. Why couldn't I be like her? Mama would keep right on with whatever she was doing and remark, "Zora is my young'un and Sarah is yours. I'll be bound mine will come out more than conquer. You leave her alone. I'll tend to her when I figger she needs it." She meant by that that Sarah had a disposition like Papa's, while mine was like hers.

Behind Mama's rocking-chair was a good place to be in times like that. Papa was not going to hit Mama. He was two hundred pounds of bone and muscle and Mama weighed somewhere in the nineties. When people teased him about Mama being the boss, he would say he could break her of headstrong ways if he wanted to, but she was too little that he couldn't find any place to hit her. My Uncle Jim, Mama's brother, used to always take exception to that. He maintained that if a woman had anything big enough to sit on, she had something big enough to hit on. That was his firm conviction, and he meant to hold on to it as long as the bottom end of his backbone pointed towards the ground—don't care who the woman was or what she looked like, or where she came from. Men like Papa who held to any other notion were just beating around the bush, dodging the issue, and otherwise looking like a fool at a funeral.

Papa used to shake his head at this and say, "What's de use of me taking my fist to a poor weakly thing like a woman? Anyhow, you got to submit yourself to 'em, so there ain't no use in beating on 'em and then have to go back and beg 'em pardon."

But perhaps the real reason that Papa did not take Uncle Jim's advice too seriously was because he saw how it worked out in Uncle Jim's own house. He could tackle Aunt Caroline, all right, but he had his hands full to really beat her. A knockdown didn't convince her that the fight was over at all. She would get up and come right on in, and she was nobody's weakling. It was generally conceded that he might get the edge on her in physical combat if he took a hammer or a trace-chain to her, but in other ways she always won. She would watch his various philandering episodes just so long, and then she would go into action. One time she saw all, and said nothing. But one Saturday afternoon, she watched him rush in with a new shoe-box which he thought that she did not see him take out to the barn and hide until he was ready to go out. Just as the sun went down, he went out, got his box, cut across the orange grove and went on down to the store.

He stopped long enough there to buy a quart of peanuts, two stalks of sugarcane, and then tripped on off to the little house in the woods where lived a certain transient light of love. Aunt Caroline kept right on ironing until he had gotten as far as the store. Then she slipped on her shoes, went out in the yard and got the axe, slung it across her shoulder and went walking very slowly behind him.

The men on the store porch had given Uncle Jim a laughing sendoff. They all knew where he was going and why. The shoes had been bought right there at the store. Now here came "dat Cal'line" with her axe on her shoulder. No chance to warn Uncle Jim at all. Nobody expected murder, but they knew that plenty of trouble was on the way. So they just sat and waited. Cal'line had done so many side-splitting things to Jim's lights of love—all without a single comment from her—that they were on pins to see what happened next.

About an hour later, when it was almost black dark, they saw a furtive figure in white dodging from tree to tree until it hopped over Clark's strawberry-patch fence and headed towards Uncle Jim's house until it disappeared.

"Looked mightily like a man in long drawers and nothing else," Walter Thomas observed. Everybody agreed that it did, but who and what could it be?

By the time the town lamp which stood in front of the store was lighted, Aunt Caroline emerged from the blackness that hid the woods and passed the store. The axe was still over her shoulder, but now it was draped with Uncle Jim's pants, shirt and coat. A new pair of women's oxfords were dangling from the handle by their strings. Two stalks of sugarcane were over her other shoulder. All she said was, "Good-evening, gentlemen," and kept right on walking towards home.

The porch rocked with laughter. They had the answer to everything. Later on when they asked Uncle Jim how Cal'line managed to get into the lady's house, he smiled sourly and said, "Dat axe was her key." When they kept on teasing him, he said, "Oh, dat old stubborn woman I married, you can't teach her nothing. I can't teach her no city ways at all."

. . .

Wandering

. . . It was not long after Mama came home [from Alabama] that she began to be less active. Then she took to bed. I knew she was ailing but she was always frail, so I did not take it too much to heart. I was nine years old, and even though she had talked to me very earnestly one night, I could not conceive of Mama actually dying. She had talked of it many times.

That day, September 18th, she had called me and given me certain instructions. I was not to let them take the pillow from under her head until she was dead. The clock was not to be covered, nor the looking-glass. She trusted me to see to it that these things were not done. I promised her as solemnly as nine years could do, that I would see to it.

What years of agony that promise gave me! In the first place, I had no idea that it would be soon. But that same day near sundown I was called upon to set my will against my father, the village dames and village custom. I know now that I could not have succeeded.

I had left Mama and was playing outside for a little while when I noted a number of women going inside Mama's room and staying. It looked strange. So I went on in. Papa was standing at the foot of the bed looking down on my mother, who was breathing hard. As I crowded in, they lifted up the bed and turned it around so that Mama's eyes would face the east. I thought that she looked to me as the head of the bed was reversed. Her mouth was slightly open, but her breathing took up so much of her strength that she could not talk. But she looked at me, or so I felt, to speak for her. She depended on me for a voice.

The Master-Maker in His making had made Old Death. Made him with big, soft feet and square toes. Made him with a face that reflects the face of all things, but neither changes itself, nor is mirrored anywhere. Made the body of Death out of infinite hunger. Made a weapon for his hand to satisfy his needs. This was the morning of the day of the beginning of things.

But Death had no home and he knew it at once.

"And where shall I dwell in my dwelling?" Old Death asked, for he was already old when he was made.

"You shall build you a place close to the living, get far out of the sight of eyes. Wherever there is a building, there you have your platform that comprehends the four roads of the winds. For your hunger, I give you the first and last taste of all things."

We had been born, so Death had had his first taste of us. We had built things, so he had his platform in our yard.

And now, Death stirred from his platform in his secret place in our yard, and came inside the house.

Somebody reached for the clock, while Mrs. Mattie Clarke put her hand to the pillow to take it away.

"Don't!" I cried out. "Don't take the pillow from under Mama's head! She said she didn't want it moved!"

I made to stop Mrs. Mattie, but Papa pulled me away. Others were trying to silence me. I could see the huge drop of sweat collected in the hollow at Mama's elbow and it hurt me so. They were covering the clock and the mirror.

"Don't cover up that clock! Leave that looking-glass like it is! Lemme put Mama's pillow back where it was!"

But Papa held me tight and the others frowned me down. Mama was still rasping out the last morsel of her life. I think she was trying to say something, and I think she was trying to speak to me. What was she trying to tell me? What wouldn't I give to know! Perhaps she was telling me that it was better for the pillow to be moved so that she could die easy, as they said. Perhaps she was accusing me of weakness and failure in carrying out her last wish. I do not know. I shall never know.

Just then, Death finished his prowling through the house on his padded feet and entered the room. He bowed to Mama in his way, and she made her manners and left us to act out our ceremonies over unimportant things.

I was to agonize over that moment for years to come. In the midst of play, in wakeful moments after midnight, on the way home from parties, and even in the classroom during lectures. My thoughts would escape occasionally from their confines and stare me down.

Now, I know that I could not have had my way against the world. The world we lived in required those acts. Anything else would have been sacrilege, and no nine-year-old voice was going to thwart them. My father was with the mores. He had restrained me physically from outraging the ceremonies established for the dying. If there is any consciousness after death, I hope that Mama knows that I did my best. She must know how I have suffered for my failure.

But life picked me up from the foot of Mama's bed, grief, self-despisement and all, and set my feet in strange ways. That moment was the end of a phase in my life. I was old before my time with grief of loss, of failure, and of remorse. No matter what the others did, my mother had put her trust in me. She had felt that I could and would carry out her wishes, and I had not. And then in that sunset time, I failed her. It seemed as she died that the sun went down on purpose to flee away from me.

That hour began my wanderings. Not so much in geography, but in time. Then not so much in time as in spirit.

Mama died at sundown and changed a world. That is, the world which had been built out of her body and her heart.

Estella Conwill Májozo

From Come Out the Wilderness

Estella Conwill Májozo (b. 1949), a poet, performance artist, community arts activist, single mother, and professor of English at Hunter College, City University of New York, writes in the preface of her 1998 memoir, *Come Out the Wilderness: Memoir of a Black Woman Artist*: "I am rooted in contradictions, so many that I find it no small wonder that I am often undone by them. As a poet, I have long tried to discover some state of grace beyond the wilderness, beyond the physical, spiritual, and cultural contradictions in my life."

Wilderness is a powerful symbol in Májozo's depiction of her early years, growing up as the only girl among five brothers in a deeply religious family in segregated Louisville, Kentucky, in the 1950s. This excerpt describes one tumultuous, watershed day in the life of nine-year-old Estella, when a loving mother and grandmother welcome her into womanhood.

I had climbed the walnut tree and swung my legs over the thick branch so I could see both gangs clearly. The Kirbys came unarmed into the jungle; the large weeded area that lay behind the sprawling yard that joined Momma's and Grandma's houses. The Conwills—my five brothers, Adolph, William, Houston, Spivey, and Joe—gathered into a crude semi-circle, and the Kirby gang—Emerson, Mike, and Marcus Manning, Bony and Raven—positioned themselves likewise to make the circle complete. I could see that Squeaks was missing. He was deaf and may not have heard the call. The Kirbys had not missed him any more than my brothers had missed me. From where I sat, I could see Constance, whom the boys called Redbone, stretching to watch from her porch across the street. She was the only other girl who dared come to our yard that summer.

Adolph and Raven moved to the center, each staring hard at the other. William removed a pocket knife from his pants and opened it. Marcus

Come Out the Wilderness

Manning struck a wood-stem kitchen match and held it to the edge of the blade. Then, together, William and Marcus held the knife to the extended finger of Adolph and then Raven. I did not see the blood, but I knew it was there because Bony swallowed hard and wiped his mouth with the back of his hand. I did not see the blood even when the two pressed their fingers high above their heads.

As Adolph and Raven turned in a small circle, they chanted, "Blood brothers, blood brothers," and the rest of them joined in. I said nothing but felt something strange happening in my own body, something gathering like rain—clouds. It wasn't the blood that was now visible on both their fingers. And it wasn't even the fact that nobody would ever call me "blood brother" that caused my anxiety. It was, I know, that between those pressed fingers I saw myself, and the canary that had fueled the war in the first place.

Nobody remembered how the seven-week war got started that summer of 1958, when I was nine years old. But we all knew that when Adolph strangled the Mannings' canary, the war intensified. From then on, both gangs were fighting about the bird. Even I, throwing rocks, apples, clumps of dirt, or whatever was at hand, thought only of the bird.

There remains a sort of confusion about that time. It seems that after Daddy died, the impulse toward violence heightened in all of us. His death was an accident. He fell from a third-story fire escape while trying to help a friend who had locked his key inside his apartment. He fell through the air as helpless as a feather. I was with him when it happened. Actually, I was waiting at the front of the house for him, so I didn't see it exactly. A woman who lived in the building came out and ushered me inside to protect me from the horror. But that didn't stop me from hearing whispers and then sirens. It didn't stop me from running to look through her bedroom window and seeing the medics bring out a covered body to the ambulance. Daddy, my daddy, was under that blanket. Daddy, who could stand six foot six inches high and ride me on his shoulders into the sky, was there. Daddy, who called me "princess" and never came home without something in his pockets for me, who played Bessie Smith albums at night and laughed when I tried to sing along, who always let me have a taste of his brown beans drenched in hot sauce knowing I'd have to hide the tears, who always told my brothers "take care of your sister, now, because she is your sister," was under that dark green blanket.

I felt powerless. I didn't even scream then. But the canary's death was different. I saw the canary in Adolph's grip. I could have pleaded for its life, even at the risk of being called a traitor, but I didn't. I felt like an accomplice.

Now, as Adolph and Raven moved within that circle, the others joining the chant and marking time, I could not control the flashing lights and shadows before my eyes. I clung to the branch beneath me with the backs of my knees and reached above for the security of a smaller branch. As I held on, I saw the bird in Adolph's hands again. He was vengeful, he said, because the Mannings had caught him outside the jungle, bloodied his nose, and smeared the purple clots into his eyes; because the Mannings had chased Houston, Spivey, and Joe, calling them "sissy-punk-Catholic-tiddy-teacher-sonsofabitch," through the park and all the way home; because they had come to make war on the Conwills after the gang of white boys stole the Kirbys' basketball and ran them out of Shawnee, the white folks' park, in the west end.

Shawnee had all the best things, bigger courts, newer swings, and an entrance to the Ohio River that was more shallow than the drop-off we had in Chickasaw Park. My brothers had stolen into Shawnee a week earlier to go swimming in the river and had been confronted by that same gang of white boys who appeared at the edge of the water, their BB guns cocked and daring. Spivey was so frightened he almost drowned. They had to save him first, they said, and then save themselves, fighting off the flying pellets that could sear the skin, blind an eye. They fought them, even without ammunition. Crawling through the mud, they came up on them, making their way through the barrage of nigger names, BBs, and sticks cracking against defiant bones, Adolph and William telling the little ones to run to the top of the hill. They fought them, the weaklings, and they won. Never mind that the white boys had brothers who were even bigger white boys and that they had cousins, uncles, and fathers who were part of a system that stretched from the Ku Klux Klan to the high courts of Kentucky and that could act as cannon against them. Never mind the possibility of their utter destruction. Never mind any of that. My brothers had triumphed over the attackers and had bonded with one another in a whole new way. They took a vow of secrecy to keep Momma and Grandma from ever finding out. Walking home that day, confidently, proudly, they refashioned the tale for themselves and, when they got home, they refashioned it again for me. By the time I had lent my voice to the telling, they were Igbos rising out of the water and marching, literally marching, across the idiotic unbelieving liquid faces of their foes. They had faced the enemy, but the Kirby gang had not. Instead, the Kirbys had used their rage against the white boys to come and take vengeance on the Conwills over some no-bouncing useless basketball, and had washed Chief Adolph's face in his own Conwill blood.

When Adolph got hold of the Mannings' canary, he said the bird in his hands had to be sacrificed because of those recent transgressions. Sacrificed, he said—not killed, murdered, choked to death, or any other word that would have defined it more accurately, but sacrificed. He repeated it over and over again, the words coming at the end of a longer, almost chantlike explanation of his duty to carry out the act. There was not a crack in his voice, nothing that smacked of those unexpected, almost Tarzan-like breaks in tone that had marked him earlier that summer. His voice sounded strong. Those words stormed forth as if to control reality.

The Mannings were holding my two older brothers, William and Houston, hostage for the bird. And Adolph was demanding that they be set free, never once letting up the pressure of his fingers on the bird's throat. I imagined the yellow puff of fear pulsating frantically in Adolph's hand, the little marble eyes bulging, begging for life. I bent down, my fingers clutching a fistful of weeds. Hearing Adolph repeat his vow to kill the bird, I knew that he meant for the bird to die. It didn't matter what the Kirby gang did—the bird would die. Their demand for the bird as ransom merely provided the occasion for Adolph to make the act a public one. Even William and Houston, the captives, demanded by their continued defiance that the bird die no matter what.

I wanted to summon a rush of energy and sweep the bird from Adolph's grip and set it free. But I didn't. I just sat there, saying nothing, feeling the power of Adolph's words and the tightening pressure in my own throat.

It was the same now, in the jungle. High above the ritual of blood brotherhood, I clung to the branches of the tree and could smell death, pitched back against the muscles of my throat, dripping hot and acrid into my lungs and stomach. I was dreaming of my father falling. I was the bird—alter ego and victim. The ritual of the blood brotherhood demanded my life. Below me, all my brothers danced and chanted and blended with the others. I could distinguish neither their forms nor their voices.

I found myself wishing that Grandma would call me in out of the jungle. Ever since the war between the Conwills and the Kirbys started, she had gotten into doing that more frequently. It was as if I was being banished from the activities out back. She and Momma believed, like my brothers, though surely for different reasons, that I should be seeking out my own separate territory that God had created for me. It didn't help that I grew breasts at age nine. "Mosquito bites," Spivey had called them. Spivey—who could not swim, who got everybody in even bigger trouble by having the nerve, after the water was coughed from his lungs, to mock the biggest white boy in the crowd with gorilla sounds that rivaled King Kong's—had begun riding me in offbeat moments by suddenly slapping himself across the chest as if swatting some worrisome insect. "Mosquito!" he'd yell, throwing up both his hands. No, it did not help that I grew breasts. Nor did it help that Squeaks, who could not talk, had begun just before the war to draw obscene pictures in the dust and scream wildly in a language only he understood whenever I showed up. Where I was concerned, my two oldest brothers became men overnight with no time or patience for girls. And even Houston, my third oldest brother and the one who always was on my side, took to offering me his slingshot or one of his june bugs to fly around instead of helping to defend me when Adolph or William said I had to go. Once it had gotten so bad that they had taken me by the arms and legs, screaming and kicking, back to the edge of the lawn, back to where it was mowed, trimmed, and whitewashed. It was only thirty yards away at most, but the very idea galled me. I begged Houston to come up front and play with me. We could play jacks, dodgeball, or racing like we always did. We could turn on the water and chase each other with the hose. We could play "close your eyes and read my mind." Anything at all. But the stakes had gotten too high for Houston, and despite what he said about why he couldn't come, I didn't want no slingshot and those green june bugs stunk when you kept them too long. That was their way of getting even. Who would want to have strings tied on their legs while they flew around in a circle? No, keep your june bugs and that little bug-eyed frog that looks just like all of you. "Mosquito bites!" I heard from somewhere deep in the weeds.

But, worse than all this, during the summer of the war Grandma and Momma conspired to just about do away with all the rest of the fun I had as a girl. Grandma would, out of the blue, call me into the house for piano lessons, to set the table, to crochet, or to have me sit down while she looked at me. Yes, simply looked at me. She said next to nothing directly. Rather, she told over and over the stories of her youth.

When she was three, her mother died. Her father, a preacher whose voice was thunder, died when she was a teenager and she had come to Louisville to live with Aunt Minnie. She worked two jobs for several years. Indeed, she would not work forever for folk who paid pennies for a day's labor, who demanded more bricks with no straw, who at five o'clock, just before the last bus was to leave, suddenly remembered one more thing that needed to be done. No, not forever for folk who thought you had nothing to celebrate or serve except their parties on Christmas Day and Easter, who demanded that you climb some rickety ladder, in your work dress, mind you, to wash the second-floor window "from the outside, girl! Junior, here, will be right underneath you helping to sturdy the ladder." Her father would have died again. No thank you, sir. I can do just fine. At twenty-one, not a day later, she opened her own storefront restaurant in the heart of the downtown Black community.

Her food was ambrosia. It could heal you. Make you fall in love. Make you remember parts you hadn't even learned yet. I'm talking about rolls that melted like manna in your mouth, mellow sauces that called you back long after dinner was over. She prayed and cooked and prayed again; then, in time, she converted to Catholicism, married my grandfather, and became Mrs. Estella Herndon.

Grandaddy was a loving, enterprising man, and together they worked out a scheme for selling pies. She baked them—apple, custard, lemon, and chocolate—and he distributed them every day to other restaurants and shops, and to folk throughout the city, especially those betting at Churchill Downs during Derby time. It worked, and over the years Grandma and, later, their four daughters—one of whom was Momma—baked, packaged, and had ready for delivery five hundred mini pies every morning before sunrise. They prospered and invested in real estate, renovating apartment houses and renting out the rooms. The houses that we helped paint each summer were gotten from that work. And from Grandaddy withstanding the scorching heat, Grandma said, for long hours hawking his wares with snatches of rhymes he created:

Pieman, Pieman, heah comes the Pieman.
Stuff's sweet as honey. Get out your money!

Eat my pies for goodness sakes.
They beat anything yo' momma can make!

The houses and land and even her own house that they had built to-gether also came in part from his strategizing and straining over racing forms at night, studying the histories of the horses and then going to the stables early in the morning to talk to the horses themselves sometimes, so he could pass on tips to the big-time gamblers from around the country who sought him out—but who would have to buy one of his pies to get the tip.

Why you always askin' credit?
All you do with money's bet it!

Grandma told me that once in a while he'd have to dodge those who had taken one of his not so accurate tips. (It wasn't that the horses had taken to lying but that they had taken to double-talking, riffing on the truth, and you had to listen hard to catch it.)

Grandma's stories were filled with giving and loving and forgiving and selflessness, and the more I heard them, the more I was convinced that there must be some skills involved in being a girl. But my nine-year-old heart was not in it, especially when she'd call me in from the thick of what-ever I was doing with my brothers.

Momma, who agreed with Grandma mostly all the time, had called me out of the jungle a few weeks before the war began to tell me, she said, something really special. Grandma got up from the porch to check on some rolls she had in the oven. Momma sat down in Grandma's chair and started telling me quite calmly about "periods" and woman's times. The only reason I was convinced that what she was saying was OK was because she kept smiling the whole time she was talking. No wonder Grandma got up to leave. She certainly wouldn't know anything about this. But Momma assured me that all women did it and every month, and that I would do it too when the time was right.

I wasn't sure what that meant. I was already feeling out of sync. Nobody in my class at school had breasts, not even my best friend, Betty Jo, and if my brothers ever knew that I had started my period they would probably try and banish me to the house. Momma assured me that it would be OK, that she would take care of my brothers. But, instead, she and Grandma started taking care of me.

The only time I remember being relieved to hear either of them call me was when Adolph was putting that final pressure on the canary's neck.

Adolph had killed the canary at the count of ten, nine, eight . . . but in reality I had not seen it. Grandma had called me in. With her almost perfect sense of timing, she for whatever reason had called me in. I was about to commit treason that would likely have lost me honor among my brothers. I wanted to save the bird—just let it go free. Killing it was taking a life, and I had wanted to shout that out in my clearest voice when Grandma called me in.

I was not so blessed on the day of the truce. Grandma did not sense my need of her. She was busy in her flower garden, bent low against weed seedlings. I had to let loose of my grip on my own, drop down to the ground, and lose my brothers, the Kirby gang, the chanting, and the danc- ing to the labyrinth of paths leading toward the front of the two houses.

I could see her in the distance, the shrubbery and flowers all around blending into the floral print of her dress, could almost hear her prodding the ground beneath the roses, and working her thoughts in prayer. Her soul was being tended. "Love is patient"—she would sometimes whisper— "Love is kind"—touching one of the roses. "Love is not jealous, it does not put on airs . . . neither does it brood over injuries. . . ." I knew she was prob- ably deep in meditation, but I wanted to tell her clearly that there was a war going on behind her. That it was all dressed up to look like peace but I, for one, didn't trust it. That they had knives out back and had sliced into each other's fingers and that it could well be their guts next round. That Adolph had said to William and Houston and me that there was such a thing as justice, and it's almost as great as the love you sing about, Grandma. That Joe was back there crying because Adolph told him that he was too little to get his finger cut open and Spivey was crying because he knew that he was next.

"Grandma," I said, meaning to go on and tell. But when she lifted her head, I could not go through with it. "Did you call me, Grandma?"

"No, girl, I didn't. What's the matter? Did Adolph put you out of that weed patch again?"

"No, Grandma," I said, trying to keep my voice from edging into a falsetto. And she turned on me that cut of her eye that signaled she already knew.

"Well, I told you and I told your Momma that you ought not be back out in all them weeds. . . . You feeling all right, girl? You look a little flushed. What they done to you this time, Stella Marie?"

I told her as much as I could without blowing it for them, knowing full well that she'd set her watery black eyes on me, listen as though in some kind of trance, and say, "But you're a little girl." That nervous feeling in my stomach returned. And instead of being feverish, now I was chilled. I didn't like this feeling that seemed never able to make up its mind. I still wanted answers: Why did my brothers and the Kirby gang carry almost everything to the point of blood? And why should I have wanted to save the canary even in the briar patch ritual? Grandma did not answer me right away. Instead, she turned her back and stooped to scoop soil up around the base of the tulip bed.

"In that back yard that your brothers are calling the jungle, they supposed to be coming up with something more to do than kill canaries," Grandma said. It had not occurred to me then that the jungle was something more than a male territory, a space that my brothers could claim for themselves. Neither I nor my brothers saw it as a space to recognize order or our own potential creativity. It was only later that I consciously realized that Grandma's own garden had come out of that jungle. My brothers, likewise failing to see this order, were imitating the disorder or wildness that they thought they saw.

"Adolph and William know how they supposed to act back there, and I done told them the consequences if they don't."

"He ain't said nothing about no consequences, Grandma."

"That's OK; he sure enough knows."

I wanted to ask about the consequences, but she had already put it behind her. Her turning at that moment has become a fixture in my mind and in my many dreams of her since. In her turning, I saw a smiling woman child in plaits and a floursack dress leaving Tennessee to come to Louisville. I had heard the story many times, but I saw it then for the first time. Then I focused in on her, wanted to see her face.

"I pruned the dogwoods today, see?" she said over her shoulder. "You remember, you helped me plant them. They about finished growing now." It was Grandma's voice, not a little girl's at all. But I knew the two were the same. The same plum-colored skin. The same dark mirror eyes. "See here," she said, looking at me. I sat next to her and could smell the earth. It was the same scent you pick up right before it rains, when only one or two drops have fallen but the earth is already rejoicing. It soothed me, calmed my stomach. And the lilacs, late roses, and petunias all lent their sweetness to the song.

"There was a time, though," Grandma continued, "when dogwood trees like these would have grown tall and would have spread their limbs near about the whole yard." The three dogwoods separated the lawn from the jungle. There were two white ones and a red one in the middle. They were small trees, their blossoms like butterflies. "Now, they won't grow much bigger than this. You know why?" she asked me, and before I could say anything she went on to answer herself. "Because it's the kind of tree they made the cross out of. This is the kind of tree Jesus was crucified on and its growth has been stunted ever since," she said. "Been stunted ever since."

I had known the answer. Grandma's whole yard was a garden, and she had stories about each of the varieties of plants—the roses, the tulips, the chrysanthemums; the catalpa, evergreen, and apple trees. The garden was a testament to her truths. To hear her stories, you'd believe that she let the briar patch grow for the contrast.

"I know," I said quietly. "The red one represents Jesus and the white ones are the two thieves." Grandma had impressed the catechism of her garden and I rendered the text. Each cluster of plants represented either the Ten Commandments, the Seven Sacraments, or the Eight Beatitudes. I knew them well and I recited them with the enunciation I knew would please her. The rose bush at the back entrance of the house I knew was the Blessed Mother. I had personally designated it so. She never appeared to me like Our Lady of Guadeloupe did to Juan Diego in Mexico or the Immaculate Conception did to Bernadette in Lourdes, but I knew when I stood there that she was always with me. And I loved her as much as any child would a mother so tender.

"Who taught you so well about the dogwoods—Adolph?" Grandma asked proudly.

"No, Houston," I said.

"That's good," she told me, "that's good. And Adolph, he teaches them all." I tried to forget about what was going on behind us.

"And these right here, what are they?" she asked, pointing to some beautiful purple flowers surrounded by dark sturdy leaves.

"Oh, Grandma," I whispered, kneeling closer. "Where, I mean how did you get these?"

She laughed. "They're yours, Stella Marie. They're African violets. I planted them for you."

"African violets," I said, repeating after her, already feeling the other question rising up in me. "But what are they for us?" I asked.

"They're gifts of the Spirit, child," she said. "Gifts that the Lord gives to people called to do something really special."

"Like me, Grandma?"

"Of course, baby. I told you that a hundred times. Now looka here. There're seven in all, see. This one here is wisdom, and there's understanding, and fortitude, and knowledge, and counsel and piety, and fear of the Lord. They're all there. Gifts of the Spirit. Now, wisdom," she said, "means having real good sense about things—like knowing how to judge the earth. And understanding is what we're doing here, standing up underneath a thing and seeking its meaning. And fortitude, why that means being strong—having inside strength," she said lifting her head. "It ain't got nothing much to do with muscles or being able to wrestle somebody if they gang up on you or try to throw you out of a place." I know I must have begun folding my arms defensively and tilting into myself. "And counsel," she continued, "that means that you can give advice lovingly, that you can look at people who might look to you like snakes, rats, or even bug-eyed frogs, Stella Marie, and still tell them the best way for unbugging, if that's what we're talking. That you can find a way to tell them true. The gift of counsel can help change a person into something really special, if you've got it. It does more good for a person than a kiss can for any frog."

"But Grandma," I said, meaning to defend myself for the name-calling she referred to—but she shushed me.

"But Grandma," I insisted, and she covered my mouth.

"And piety," she said slowly, deliberately, "piety means being holy. And that's really all that you were sent here to be." She smiled. "Now what did you want to say?"

"Grandma, I'm not trying to be a smart aleck, but what if that frog you talking about doesn't want to be kissed? Suppose he's just begging to be told how ugly he is?" A chuckle rose out of her and on into me.

"Listen, little girl," she said, "this last flower here, it's fear of the Lord. That means God don't take no mess so behave yourself, you hear?"

"Yes, Grandma. I will. But can I ask you something?"

She nodded.

"How come you don't ever answer whatever I ask you?"

Her face said, "Oh, child, please." But her words said, "Would it hurt your feelings if I told you I honestly don't know? Some things you don't say because you know the moment after you say them the meaning is already changed in your head, changed sometimes even before you say anything. You take that bird, now—you all talked about that canary bird so much you had your Momma crying about that thing. I said at the time that it was a shame she let you all go on about it so. And the way you talking about the bird, honey, you better let it go out your mind or it's gonna mess with you every chance it gets. Now everybody else done stopped talking about that bird. You told me yourself that the boys done made up over the thing 'cause it don't have one ounce of meaning between them anymore."

"But it ought to, Grandma."

"Well they're making peace now, girl."

"But they didn't have to choke it to death!"

"But the bird is dead, girl, dead. And you oughta leave it alone. You hear me?"

It was precisely at moments like this that I wanted Momma. I wished right then that she could just come home from work. The blunt edge of Grandma's authority had nailed me into the soil among the dogwoods. And suddenly I felt weighted with the memory of my father and was suspicious that Grandma herself had conjured his image into my mind. She did that sort of thing after I had worn down her tolerance. I was with my Daddy riding his shoulders again. He was a moving oak. Tall, graceful, strong. We were laughing and he was pulling something, maybe a bracelet, out of his pocket for me.

"Your daddy wouldn't have wanted to see you carry on like this," she said.

"I'll leave it alone, Grandma," I said, and turned to the path that my brothers and I had worn between her house and ours. Walking the path, I remembered Daddy and I was stepping, deliberately stepping, just like him. Working that hump-a-dip bluesman's walk that marked him the moment he set foot outside the house, whether on his way to the waiter job at the Brown Hotel or to the corner drugstore for a smoke. It was his "jitter juju," and I was doing it, the thing that transformed him into the aroma of strength and cool and readiness. But it wasn't working for me, not really. It just made me miss him more. So I went on to the front of our house and waited for Momma. If I could sit down next to her, put my head on her lap, maybe I would feel better. I pinched a little peppermint from the patch that grew at the bottom of the steps and chewed its leaves.

No sooner had I gotten the flavor juicy in my mouth when I heard the blood brotherhood coming out of the jungle. They were ready to play now, siding up for a game of baseball. A spot near the curb was first base, the rock in the center of the yard was second, third was a spot on the opposite side, and home plate was some magic spot one ran to and declared oneself safe.

I could see Constance across the street but kept my eyes staring at the spaces where the blood brothers swung their bats, popped their fists into empty palms, and rooted for their teams. Constance was everything Grandma seemed to want me to be. She dressed like a lady, sat out her summer days on the front porch in the green and white porch swing, sucker in hand or thumb in mouth. I knew I would go to her before the day was out, but I didn't want to talk just now. Constance knew things, and when we did talk, she told me things that Momma and Grandma wrapped in parables, axioms, and life stories. She said to me one day, out of the blue, "Stella, I do believe your grandmother wants to turn all your brothers into priests." Perhaps she was just fishing for information. Perhaps she knew about the Mass we held in the basement.

At the start of that summer, in an attempt to be strengthened or maybe just to play church, Adolph had gathered Momma's white linen tablecloth, her long white candles, and even a couple of her white summer dresses for robes, and we all had gone to the basement to hold Mass, the ceremony that we had come to accept as the blood rite of blood rites, as he called it. Adolph acted as priest and William and Houston concelebrated with him. Spivey and Joe were altar boys. We all had Communion made from regular slices of bread that I had pressed and clipped into wafers. We set up the basement like a church with an altar, candles, crucifix, chalice, Bible, and chairs.

Our house was already somewhat of a sanctuary. Momma had consciously designed it so. The crucifix and the statue of our Blessed Mother had their own special places in the front room. And we had the family ritual of coming together in the evening to say the rosary. Ella Fitzgerald, Nat "King" Cole, and whoever was on the radio would be silenced. The playing, laughing, and fighting would be stilled. During the holy seasons of Advent and Lent, our rituals intensified. The preparing, or "making ready the way," was serious, and sometimes the sacrifices or mortifications were considered for weeks in advance. Whatever you decided upon you announced before the first day. If you were giving up candy for forty days, refraining from bad language or thoughts, or from slapping somebody "upside the head," the commitment was made aloud. If the commitment was carried through, it would strengthen the others who witnessed it, and if it wasn't, then that person would endure a certain amount of hassle from the others. At church the sacrifices were written down and burned as offerings. They were considered to be between you and God. But at home, we made new offerings, and they were considered to be between you, God, and the family. Most of these sacrifices had to do with relationships, no doubt encouraged by Momma's insistence that if you can't recognize God in one another, then you're not going to be able to recognize God in Spirit.

That the focus was on relationships was especially important that year. Perhaps as part of the process of mourning my father, my brothers often came to knock-down drag-out battles in the house. In an attempt to keep the jungle from infringing upon her order, Momma made the across-the-board rule that no fighting would be allowed in the house. She would not necessarily stop the fights. She would simply say, "Take that chaos out of this house!" On the other hand, if you were taking a pretty bad beating in the jungle, you could always retreat to the house. But to avoid the shame of it, you would generally chance dying on the battlefield rather than retreating.

When we decided to have our Mass in the basement, we had put curtains on the window to keep the snoopers away, especially the Kirby gang. It was nobody's business what went on there. Constance wasn't even supposed to know about the Mass. It was private. With our heads bowed, we struggled through the Latin responses to Adolph's prayers. He started with the sign of the cross. "In Nomine Patris, et Filii, et Spiritus Sancti. Amen." We joined in and made up new responses if the real words failed us. "Hanna-hanna de hanna hanna," we mumbled the rhythm of the parts we didn't know.

When the consecration time came and all three of my older brothers extended their right hands over the bread, I joined in saying the sacred words with them. "Hoc Est Enim Corpus Meum": This Is My Body. You would have thought a sacrilege had been committed, that I had cursed heaven or strangled some precious belief so fiercely it left them all wasted. Houston's mouth fell agape. Adolph all but stopped the ceremony. William turned around as if to say, "Girl, you know you ain't supposed to be saying those words. You ain't hardly no man!" I bowed my head, retreated behind tear-filled eyelids, stayed there alone in the dark.

I had no problem knowing what I was supposed to do in a real church, but in the realm of play, especially play that was serious, something inside had been jolted. There they were, all five of my brothers at the altar playing priest, the representatives of God, each with a participant's role, and there I was on the other side, separated by a jump rope that they had strung to show the distinction, playing the congregation. All I understood then was that I was a girl and was being excluded from the ritual. Now I realize that what started happening there that summer had been happening in different ways all over the world for years. And that when we decide to stop playing church, we have a lot of coming out of the jungle to do.

As for Grandma, when she closed her eyes, I don't know if she saw what the future held for us at all, but heaven knows, we were anything but the royal priesthood she felt all people were called to be.

As for Constance, she probably didn't know everything about the Mass that day. She was probably following up on some tip. On the day of the truce, when I saw her get off her swing and start coming across the street, I got up to join her. I got up because Squeaks, who had no idea about the truce, come charging into the brotherhood. He leaped into the huddle and began clawing at my brothers. Everybody tried to stop him. I moved faster toward Constance because I knew that once they cleared it with Squeaks that the war was over. Adolph would want me to come join the Conwills in the game to make the teams even. I did not want to play. I almost made it across the diamond, but Squeaks saw me and let out a piercing holler, "Ah-ah-oh!" He rushed onto me, shimmying his haphazard hoodlum body across my backside. "Wa-a-ah!" he screamed. "Ah-o-o-oh!" he yelled again. I shoved him off and, at my back, heard my brothers yell in concert.

"Raven, you better tell that fool to be cool or I'll put a brick in his deaf skull!" Adolph shouted.

"Yeah," somebody else said, "you better get that no-talking devil before he start the whole damn war again."

Constance was on her feet, her hands balled into fists, the stem of a sucker twitching between her teeth. "Stella," she hissed in a voice that seemed sharp and guarded, "you get up here, girl. That dog'd attack his own mother. You hear that fool, honey. He's down there cussing. Tell me how a person who can't even hear learns to cuss. He can't even say two clear words of proper language and he's down there cussing blood up from the ground. Get him, Adolph, get him. Don't just stand there." Her voice carried only as far as the end of the porch, but I read her terror. My brothers had positioned themselves near Adolph, who stood with the bat cocked.

In front at the curb, Marcus held Squeaks in a full nelson, his fingers squeezed to knuckles at the back of Squeaks's head.

"He don't understand you, man. He don't know no better. He do what he see, man," Marcus said.

"Then somebody better teach the sucker some sense," William said, "or one day he gonna go picking his brains up off the sidewalk."

Then Constance started in. "If Adolph hauls off and hits him one, I bet he'll understand." I was almost crying. I knew the understanding she was talking about had nothing to do with anything except somebody getting hurt. Or maybe even killed like the bird. Or like my daddy, who said, "Wait right here, I'll be right back, this won't take but a minute, sweets." And Mr. Johnson taking me home and knocking at the door to face Momma's shock: "Where's my husband? Where is he? Boys, Adolph Junior, come and get your sister."

"Tell him the war is over," Adolph said. "Tell him we blood brothers now. Tell him no touch-feely on this street, least not my little sister. Or Adolph Conwill will pick his teeth with this baseball bat."

"Something terrible happened," I had said that day as Momma grabbed her coat to leave. My brothers stopped jumping from bed to bed long enough to look at me and ask, "What?" The stammering took too long, the search for how to say what never ended. "What is so terrible?" they asked. The discerning of things from their form. Knowing what was beneath the blanket by the contours of his face. Never finding the words to carry all that weight.

"Tell him the war is over," Adolph said. "Tell him and make him understand!" Marcus was restraining Squeaks, whose two arms were suspended like broken wings above the back of his head. One of his own gang, a voice I don't remember to name, declared that Squeaks wasn't even a member of the new brotherhood, having missed out on the ritual, and that he should be taught a lesson. I could not see Squeaks's face—but his body writhed under Marcus's hold.

"They oughta teach him a thing or two," Constance piped in, her voice edged with excitement.

"No," I said. "It won't do no good to hurt him. They should just let him go. Let him go on back home. Somebody can tell him that. Go home before he starts another war."

"He may be deaf and dumb, but he can't go around acting a fool all his life. I say he ought to have a lesson. That'll straighten him up," Constance insisted.

Squeaks was crying now. I could hear the chirping sounds from where I stood. Streaks of blood from the brotherhood's wounded fingers were all up and down his T-shirt. He began kicking, too, at first out at the air and then at my brothers and the members of his own gang. Bony caught one of his legs midair and held it. "Kick now, fool," he said. "Kick the other foot and gravity will have your ass."

Everybody was laughing, even Constance—and Squeaks's cries became louder. My own voice rose above his screams. "If y'all don't let him go, I'll call Grandma!" I yelled, knowing that it was treason and I'd suffer for it.

Contrary to the teasing I got for months afterward, I did not "like" Squeaks. I had just decided that I would not stand by and let them tease him to death. The new blood brotherhood had found a common victim, and I could see that they wouldn't stop until they had wrung out his last breath of air. Poor Squeaks would have hopped around on that one leg dragging Bony around with him until he dropped from exhaustion. Laughing all the while, the brotherhood would have then pounced upon him until there was blood.

The instant I said it, Bony dropped Squeaks's leg and Jimmy let go of his hold. Squeaks fell to the ground, drawing his knees up to his chest. It seemed that all eyes contorted toward me, and I felt unbelievably powerful. "Help him out of the street," I said to Adolph and Raven. And without hesitation, they did it, helped him to his feet, then stood there as if beaten. What was happening? Could mere words be that powerful? Could their very pronouncement command this kind of utter respect? Yes, indeed they could, if your very angry grandma suddenly appears at the screen door behind you exuding an almost stupefying rage.

"This. This don't make no sense," she seethed. "And you sure got pain to pay."

After staring for what seemed like hours at Adolph, William, Houston, and all of them and draining all the color from the summer sky, she turned like a sudden storm to sit down on the rocker.

"Grandma," Adolph tried to plead, but there was no need. We all knew that something vital had happened. That another war had been waged—though, for everybody except Adolph, it had not been named. And none of the rest of us dared to ask her what the consequences would be.

What I remember is that all of us, the Conwills, the Kirbys, and even Squeaks, were stretching to assume postures of normalcy. They were straightening out their clothes, then trying to pretend that there was no need at all to do so. They were stepping away (though surely not too far away) in pairs and bunches, whispering under stolen breaths about being sure enough in trouble this time. When William leaned in to ask Adolph what Grandma was going to do, Adolph shook his head as if in mourning.

"Get lost, Estella!" Adolph growled.

"Jerk!" William added.

"I can't believe she did that," Houston said.

"I wasn't trying to tell Grandma," I pleaded. "I was trying to tell you."

"Wasn't trying to tell Grandma, your butt," Spivey said.

"You done ruined everything now. How come you always gotta go tattling?" Adolph yelled.

"Me?" I said. "Me? How come you all always gotta carry things to the point of blood?" I yelled back.

"'Cause we ain't stupid like you!" he said, as if that made any sense. I walked away. There was no need to even try to explain. When Momma came home, Grandma's version would be all there was anyway.

Once when I got back to the steps, it was Constance who answered the question: "Old folk say boys carry on to blood like that because they can't bleed like a woman." Wait a minute, Constance knew about women bleeding? Constance knew that? This opened a whole new terrain.

She looked hard at me. "You do know about women doing that, don't you?"

"Of course I know," I told her fast, knowing that she was probably already doing it—that she knew how it felt and what "when the time is right" meant.

"That's what they say," she said, ready to go on about men's blood rites. But I didn't want to talk about them anymore, not then anyway. I wanted to know everything she knew about women's times. Do you have to do anything to make it happen? Is it something you eat that'll help make it start? If it doesn't have anything to do with age, like Momma says, then does it have something to do with the size of your breasts? I looked at Constance's breasts, and even though she was three years older, mine were almost as big.

"I'm starting mine real soon," I said softly. She looked at me and tried to keep from laughing. "I am, Constance. I even dreamed it. It's true."

She reached over, plaited one of the ends of my hair. "I used to dream I'd get mine, too. That's why you got to stop going out back with them," she said, stretching to see what was in the street. "It's a good thing you

Estella Conwill Májozo

didn't let them cut your finger, girl. Your period probably would never come." My eyes widened. I wanted to know more.

"Constance," I asked, swallowing hard, "did you feel kind of funny when it happened?"

"Yeah, a little bit, but I was glad to get it."

"I mean, did you feel a little something down in here?" I asked, touching just below my navel. She looked at me curiously and began shaking her head in denial.

"Naw, uh-uh. You don't feel nothing. Not no cramps, not nothing," she said. "It just comes."

"Not hot, I mean, or a little cold neither?" I asked.

"Nothing," she said with an air of finality.

"Nothing." I repeated behind her.

Then she leaned in a little closer. "And remember, it's like I was saying, they do it because they can't," and she nodded her head and swept her glance into the wind.

It sounded awfully strange, though even now, I cannot say it was not the answer my sense of things required. Had I not witnessed my brothers nurse a war wound like a badge of courage? Had they not pressed the edges to let the blood flow, as if the flow itself was the rite of passage? "It's because," Constance went on, "it's because they can't be like us." She tied her hair ribbon back into a tighter bow. "Just like we can't be like them."

Contrary to what Grandma said, I did not dislike Constance because she wore fine dresses and pretty colored ribbons; it was just that she always tied the knots too tight. So when William yelled, "Come on, let's play dodgeball," I didn't think twice about joining in. I went on out confident that Grandma would not call me back.

Dodgeball was my game, and though I could not play at full speed that day, I tried. But in all honesty, I was distracted. I guess everybody was. Constance's words were ringing in my ears and Adolph was still mad at me. My skin was wet, my shirt was clingy, and even my shorts felt strange. That earth smell that comes after rain was suddenly everywhere and there was not a cloud in the sky.

"Come on, Stella!" Houston yelled. "Pay attention or they gonna put you out!" Was that all the heck they knew?

"You already out when Grandma gets through with you, so pay your own attention!" I yelled back, dodging the ball as it whizzed by my legs.

"What she say?" Adolph asked butting in the conversation. "What's Grandma gonna do?"

"She gonna stare a hole in your behind from that porch!" I yelled. "She gonna stare at you like that forever!"

The ball almost caught Adolph right upside the head and he was getting an attitude. "I ain't playing, Stella. What's she saying!"

"I don't know," I answered. "She ain't saying nothing."

The ball handlers changed twice and I still hadn't been hit. The ball handler threw the ball at the easiest mark or to the one he wanted to absorb his frustrations. The two most likely targets were me and Squeaks. I had an advantage—I could hear the ball coming. And Squeaks, who had simmered down, also had an advantage. We all claimed he was good at the game because, not hearing, he could see better than any of us. No doubt now, Marcus was aiming strictly for the two of us. However, the ball struck Houston, and he rushed to the end to throw the ball before we had a chance to fully distance ourselves from his end.

Squeaks suddenly began taunting the ball handlers with screams, and I watched Bony wind up and go for him. "Ooo—eee-ah," Squeaks screamed out, dodging the ball. He screamed again and nobody had even thrown the ball. Squeaks wouldn't let up hollering, now pointing frantically at the seat of my pants. "Um mahee-fuhee!" he screamed. "Mahee-fuhee ha ha ha!" he laughed hilariously, grabbing members of his gang to join him.

"Ah, come on, man, cut it out!" Marcus said as he spit on the ground. Squeaks continued screaming.

"Come on, Houston! Throw the ball!" Adolph said. And that was when I felt it. A warm wetness between my thighs. I froze at first, then ran behind the house to check myself. And my whole body flushed from the recognition. I ran inside with my secret—a secret no one knew except for Squeaks and he, thank God, couldn't tell anybody.

"Man, cut it out," I heard Marcus say through the window. And Adolph added, "Man, we in enough trouble as it is."

I didn't know what else to do except wait for Momma. I looked at the clock, got a drink of water, then looked out the door at Grandma.

"You waiting for your Momma?" she asked. I stood there half-smiling. "She got plenty to know today."

She kept looking out toward the bus stop and I kept looking too.

Didn't I tell Constance I was going to start? Didn't I tell her I had dreamed it? And it was there just like it had appeared in the dream: the spread of a flower unfolding right there upon the cotton. As if someone had used watercolors to paint a little violet in that spot. I looked at Grandma and wondered if I looked any different or if I should put tissue in my pants. Then I worried that if I kept standing there, any moment now, there would be a labyrinth of trickles down my legs like the paths from the tree house throughout the jungle. I closed my eyes and tried not to think about it.

The screeching of Grandma's chair and the ticking of the clock on the mantel gave off a funny little rhythm. "Mary Luella gonna be tired when she gets home this evening, but she gonna want to know about this. And I ain't covering for them, either, not this time," she said. And while I waited for my Momma, I could hear them playing outside. I could hear our dog Bronda barking in the back. I could hear birds nesting right on the magnolia tree in front, but I could not hear the bus coming with my Momma standing at its back door. Suppose she missed it or decided to work overtime at that stupid post office? All year long she taught at Immaculate Heart of Mary, our school. Why did she have to work summers? When I grew up I would make all the money and she could stay home forever and nobody would have to be crying about where is she and what am I supposed to do and what if something horrible happened to her too on that stupid yellow canary bus. Then she was at the corner.

The playing outside quieted and Grandma's chair came to a halt. The breath I was holding inside raced out to the open air. I wiped my tears and waited, patiently.

My brothers greeted Momma, all but kissing her feet. "My finger didn't get cut," Joe said, and she lifted him up, unsuspecting, to kiss it. She moved past them and made her way to the porch and smiled into Grandma's eyes. "I'm exhausted. It's good to be home. Estella, come give Momma a kiss."

I was reluctant to come past Grandma so I stuck out my finger and curled it for her to come inside with me. "I'm beat, Estella," she said. "Come on and sit down with me a minute."

"She may be trying to plead their case before I tell you," Grandma said. "It ain't gonna do no good, Stella Marie," she called out over her shoulders.

I backed up farther into the house, and still within eyeshot of Momma I stretched both my arms out and pleaded with her to please come in.

Then I heard the back door open and I knew one of them was coming.

"What they saying?" Houston said, running up on me. "I want to know."

"They ain't saying nothing yet. She just got home."

"Stella, I know you didn't mean to tell," he said, moving too close for comfort.

"Just go away. I'll tell you what she says," I said, trying to keep myself at an angle so that the back of me wouldn't show.

"Naw, you won't. You still mad about what happened."

"Naw, I ain't, I'm just standing here, that's all. I ain't gonna tell on you."

"Well, I'm gonna stand here too," he said. "I'm gonna stand right here and see."

"You don't have to. Look, I'll let you have my jai alai bat if you just go on back outside," I said.

"What, you suddenly bearing gifts?"

"I ain't bearing no gifts, Houston," I said, straining not to intone in his voice. "Look, I just want to be by myself, that's all."

"Then why you standing here?"

"Because I want to be by myself standing here," I said—the same thing they had said to me that day I left the jungle but slipped back and found William and Houston with their pants down, seeing who could pee the farthest. "Pitiful," I said under my breath, but they heard me.

"I won't ever bother you again when you ask me to go," I pleaded.

"The heck if I believe you!" he said, looking at my jai alai bat. "You don't know the meaning of privacy."

"Yes, I do, Houston. I cross my heart," I said. "If you want to be alone, I will just let you be."

"I didn't say all the time," he said.

"I didn't say all the time neither."

"Let me see the jai alai bat."

I handed him my watch, too.

"Promise?" he asked, looking at me straight.

"Promise," I said, relieved. Then I watched him walk to the back door.

I heard Momma yell, "What?" and Grandma say, "They done gone too far." And I knew that I had now even less of a chance of capturing her attention; my timing was terrible.

"Momma," I signaled within her range, but she didn't want to hear it. "Momma," I signaled again. And Grandma, who maybe really did have eyes underneath the loose strand of hair, said, "Better go on and see what she wants. She been waiting long enough."

When I told Momma, she hugged me and held me there for a long, long time. Then she helped me with my necessities. For a few moments, it seemed none of what was happening outside even mattered. I had become a lady. And that was serious. I was even going to get a new dress. Momma was going to make it. And I could wear it every time I had a period and feel really pretty. She would start on it tomorrow, she said. But today she had to deal with my brothers.

She changed clothes and went outside and called out to them. "Adolph, William, Houston—come on," she said. "We gonna clear this out back here. The rest of you boys, good evening."

"We can't clear out the jungle, Momma!"

"Naw. Momma, uh-uh."

Momma's insistence became firmer against their defiant cries that surely they would be the laughingstock of the neighborhood, that they would be cursed as sissies the rest of their lives, that her demand that they love their rivals was as cold a command as death.

"How are we to grow into men of this house if we can't even demand respect?" William asked, and before Momma could answer, Adolph insisted, "Everybody listened to Daddy—even people who were bigger than him. They knew who he was!"

Momma stared unflinchingly into the eyes of her older sons, letting go a handful of weeds. "How many times," she asked, "did you ever see your father beat someone till he bled?" For a moment everything quieted. Adolph retreated, not out of submission but to recharge.

"He could, though," Adolph insisted. "He could have done it, just didn't have to."

"Why not?"

"He probably got it straight when he was growing up with all those dudes."

"He's not from here. You know your father was from Mississippi. When he came to this town, how'd he get all those people, those dudes, straight? Did he strangle all their canaries to get his bluff in?"

"I don't know," William said sternly, and Adolph backed him up: "He didn't tell us."

If Momma had been in mourning up to that point, she certainly wasn't crying now. She braced herself like a giant eagle having flipped her babes from the nest. "That's what you need to learn," she said "What you've got that you can use other than your fists." She handed the sickle to Adolph just as he began to speak. "Get to work," she told him. It was final. The rest of us chopped harder. I felt a mixture of horror and release. I knew Adolph was crying when he turned his back. We all cried a little that day. Bony rode by on his bike. "Hey, man, what y'all doing?" he asked, unable to believe what he was seeing. Nobody answered.

The Queen Anne's, ragweed, thistles, and twigs were all cut down and hauled to the back to burn—a public sacrifice. Of course the rabbits left, the robins scattered, and the fuzzy-tailed squirrels scurried away. But they did that, anyway, every time the "blood brotherhood" entered bringing their wildness into the jungle. Their presence was already disturbing and undermining its creative potential. Cutting down the jungle was an effort to help them to come out of the wilderness within.

Seeing the tiny snakes and salamanders and crickets and baby spiders scurry into the secret bosom of the earth was arresting. We stood there in the end in awed recognition of the order that had been there all along—of all that hidden life and possibility over which we had so recklessly trampled.

Flavia Alaya

From Under the Rose

Flavia Alaya (b. 1935) developed, at an early age, an appreciation for the "opera" of her culture—the passion and expressiveness she associates with being Italian American. In her 1999 memoir, *Under the Rose: A Confession,* she describes the vibrant atmosphere in her extended family's East Harlem tenement. A darker side emerges in her confrontations with her brilliant but volatile father, who is determined to control his daughter's life—and especially her nascent sexuality. Alaya's unconventional path to independence would include scholarship, community activism—and a twenty-year relationship with Father Harry Brown, a Roman Catholic priest with whom she had three children.

In this excerpt, Flavia—together with her parents, Mario and Maria, and her brothers and sister, Lou, Carlo, and Ann—leave New York for Tucson in 1942, following a vision of the "bright and beckoning west." For eight-year-old Flavia, it would be a "journey that altered, ever after, the way I read the universe."

Mario stayed behind to sell the fixtures in the North Avenue market; Maria packed us four for the scouting trip westward, and we headed to Tucson by train to search out a place to live. I remember my sister and me hugging the window seats, watching the states unroll beside us like a vast cloth on which the feast of America was spread, cupping our hands at night against the glass until our eyes ached, sleeping curled together in our plush seats (which felt like little rooms and smelled close and spongy) as the hum and click of the track set the rhythm of our heartbeats. I remember stepping off the train four days and nights later into the freshness of early morning Tucson amid a sweeping surround of sun and cactus. I felt as if I had been suddenly given the sky.

But Maria did not see sky. Faced with the four of us amid the stark green walls of a room in a motor court, she had discovered the limits of her bravado. Stopped in full flight, she lay plunk as a sopped towel in an armchair, the tears bleeding silently down her face, while we stood with our stupefied big-baby eyes frozen beside her.

Within days we were rattling again across the prairies, switching in Chicago to the Rock Island Rocket, blazing like a railroad movie into Grand Central Station, where Maria and Mario, in whose orbit of passion we lived and moved, turned the roar on the platform into a *crescendo appasionato*, and fell into each other's arms.

But for Mario there could be no stopping now, no changing, no turning back, whatever Maria's misgivings. He had never turned back, not since he'd left Sperone, not since the day in 1921 when, in a driving rain, he had stepped onto the ship in Santa Lucia, his beloved Naples behind him, drenched in the national grief of Enrico Caruso's funeral. Within weeks, we were packed and ready, on the road like Okies, all the stuff we could fit piled into an old Dodge and a pickup. And still my mother amazed us, driving a truck. We had never seen a woman drive a truck.

Spelling them both at the wheel was a friend who had joined them for the journey, Joe Detta, a tailor from New York, *paesano*, exhilarated like Mario by the romance of moving on. Joe was about my father's age, smart, lean, hardhanded. He was a kind of immigrant Tom Joad, no wife, no kids, just a caring anarchist heart and a pure, clean passion for the road. I know he struck out for parts even farther west soon after we arrived in Tucson. Throughout our marvelous journey, even if we called him Uncle Joe for respect, we privately invoked him as "JoeDetta," in one single, magical word. He stars in some of my vividest recollections of our first days in the Arizona desert, pointing the way like a shaman to the secrets of our astonishing new moonscape.

Above all else, that journey taught us the authority of the continent. We might pretend that we had conquered every mile as we went, but the truth was that we had also humbly yielded it up again behind us. It took our little caravan about two weeks to cross the country, counted out in Route 66 telegraph poles and Burma Shave signs with messages we kids memorized frame by frame and sang out in competitive ecstasy from the back of the car before we even got close enough to read them. Every night we seemed to drop into the very same E-Z Rest Motor Court with the railroad tracks alongside, the same fifty-five-car freight train passing at four every morning. There was the occasional wayside farmhouse that obligingly took guests, where breakfast was a full-course meal around an immense table, already surrounded by men in dungarees with the size and appetites of giants, who would gently help us load our plates from enormous bowls of potatoes and grits and chuckle about how four little kids could really eat.

Food was in every sense enormous that trip—a pure revelation of strangeness from day to day, like space itself, which seemed to have taken on a fourth dimension. I couldn't have known the metaphysics I was in the presence of; I knew only that there was something about earth and sky both perpetual and friendless. I can remember waking up in the truck after nightfall, on a black stretch of barren Texas prairie somewhere east of El Paso, to see Dad and JoeDetta wrestling some huge thing in a ditch alongside the road, my brothers standing by, their faces lit with wonder in the circle of pink and orange light thrown by a crude fire, and my mother, behind them, lit with a fainter glow, watching with shaded eyes, unmoving. Ann still slept beside me.

The boys toiled up the embankment to tell me with a hush of excitement that it was a steer the men had just pulled, torn and bleeding, off the roadside barbed wire, a fence that had for hundreds of miles marked the impassable boundary between ranch and road. A butcher's child, I could not yet hate this work by which my father lived, but I was at once captivated and bewildered by the almost wordless rhythm of the hard teamwork of butchering, which I had never yet been permitted to see. Survival seemed suddenly to be more amazing, extreme, and violent than I had ever imagined. For a few days after, we bypassed the Bar-B-Q stands and ate our well-carved sirloins over open campfires like the privileged children we were, digesting the ambiguities of meat and meaning together.

JoeDetta had a way of making freedom and love seem like nothing more than your plain two hands. He waited to move on until we'd found a little rented bungalow off the main road south of Tucson, hanging on maybe a month or so until we were settled, repairing the truck's broken axle and hunting wild quail and bringing a brace back for supper, all with that innocent, unthankable air of doing what needed doing. He taught us about the stars, when the sky that had hung so bright and hot and close all day seemed to curve indifferently away from us at night like a great black dome pricked with light holes.

The older three of us had started school (albeit reluctantly, sorry to leave the day school of JoeDetta) at a little two-room schoolhouse out beyond the desert flats, and were coming back from our first day when he met us at the porch, little wide-eyed Ann beside him. I was full of my first-day story. I had just set my dusty foot on the porch step, ready to announce that the teacher had said I counted so well I could move one row over to the second grade, when Joe said he'd killed a rattlesnake, and did we want to see it?

We'd been warned about rattlers; it was their desert, really. But none of us had actually seen or heard one, and we followed him eagerly, fearlessly, as we always did, and the instant he said, "There," we froze. Out of the brush came the chattering sound we'd been told of, and my first thought was that the creature Joe had killed had miraculously come back—the desert, to me, already full of miracles enough for such a thing—but no, there lay the dead snake, flat in the footpath. What we'd heard was another, a second one, and then we saw it, magnificently coiled and arched and hissing noisily two or three yards away, poised to strike if anyone dared to touch the poor dead thing lying stiff and papery in the dust. "She's his mate," Joe whispered simply, laying a firm hand on my arm, and we backed away, leaving the dead snake untouched.

I did not ask how he knew, or how he knew she was a she. JoeDetta knew such things, and the tone of sorrow and tenderness in his voice became a key, unlocking the snaky universe and all its tragedies forever.

Tucson, in those days, still at least a decade away from the Sun Belt, was nothing more than a cow town with a college. It had had its moment of Depression-era fame, when the Feds had caught Dillinger there in a famous bank-robbing shootout. That was before he'd become Public Enemy Number One, while he still had a grip on the popular mind as an outlaw hero. For us—as for him, I suppose—it was still the romantic Wild West, its few dusty intersections lying open to the unguarded chances of fate and adventure. But the romance had its menace. Around us stretched a bleak sand sea, harsh and hostile, the tall saguaro cactus marching away in files like an occupying army to a vanishing point in the flanks of the Catalina Mountains. And everything—and everyone—on this earth, under this new and inexorable sun, seemed blond or blonding: the houses built of adobe sand cakes, the tin-roofed cement squats hunkered down beside the runoff ditches along the roads, the roads themselves, the tanned hills holding up the sky like mounds of cornflakes, even the crouching little cacti looking bleached and crisp, disguising their pulpy innards. Only we were not blond, and the Chicanos, and the Indians who sought shaded street corners from which to sell their wares, the bracelets I loved that tumbled in rippling rivers of blue and silver across their blankets.

Was I feeling what my father felt? Ten years before this westward trek, the already reinvented Mario Salvatore had invented himself again as an American. Proud, even smug in the faintly accented but flawless grammar of his American English, he had become a citizen with the zeal of a newly baptized convert entering the Church. Everything—his studied knowledge of American politics, his dedication to Republican self-reliance, even his devotion to baseball—had seemed preparation for a future symbolized by the Golden West, had made the troubles of the Old World seem ancient and inconsequential.

And then Mussolini dragged Italy into the war on the Axis side and Mario felt the shame he couldn't escape. Even his shoulder hurt again, where the shrapnel still lodged from the Alto Adige campaign. Digging in, he declared himself an American, and went to a nearby defense plant looking for work. And now, after fifteen years proving he wasn't *gangster, anarchist, Mafioso, wop*, he was suddenly *belligerent, enemy alien*—new names to cut him with like a steer in the barbed wire. So much for the America of the beckoning future. He took up his pen. In righteous anger, in his fine hand and perfect grammar, he wrote his complaint to President Roosevelt. Then he went on, uncertainly tossing about for work. Maria seemed to feel even more displaced. Her naturally shadowed eyes had become deep pools of longing from which he knew tears fell at night in the dark. Should he go back? What was there for him now if he did? In his life-odyssey, you always went forward. Back meant failure. It was closed for him, closed as water.

The two of them schemed about another business they might begin independently, what they had perhaps hoped to do from the start. For a time he found work in town with a prosperous grocer who seemed to understand his plight. Afternoons, my mother would sometimes pile us into the truck and take us to visit him. We would prowl the store while she shopped, slipping comic books stealthily from the racks and sneaking off to read them because it was something he hated to see us do.

The day waned, the palm trees cast long shadows across the tiled front plaza. I waited eagerly for his workday to be done, sitting on a low little wall and watching him, the prince of my Oedipal romance, pushing the day's dust across the pink herringbone bricks with a long-handled broom.

I think it must have been then, more than ever, that he began to dream of Italy again—of mother, motherland, mother tongue—dreams that both salved and corroded his heart. We must learn to speak Italian, he told us. He schooled us with proper little black-and-white-bound composition books for vocabulary and verbs, and burst into rages when we came to our drills reluctant or unprepared. My mother would gladly have done this, and spared him by teaching us herself—she loved to teach—but no, her Italian was a despised Sicilian dialect bastardized by a generation in New York. She sewed instead, cocking an ear to our stormy lessons and attacking her machine more zealously than ever. A superb dressmaker, she had once vaulted to principal draper for Bergdorf Goodman in the palmy career days before her marriage. Now she had begun quietly to sell her sophisticated skills altering fine clothes for the wives of the rancher gentry.

And it was then that my father's Italy became a place imprinted on the platen of my soul. Forever after this, to go there meant a return somehow to a place already known and loved, a place we might have danced to on the airs of his cherished operas. His lessons were not always harsh. Sometimes he would forget to drill us and fill an hour instead with tales of home. He was a storyteller born. In a single sensual gesture of language or a hand lightly playing on the air, he could catch just that icy freshness of spring water in the heat of summer, the cool of overhanging chestnut trees, the burst of a succulent fig on the tongue, the scorch-scent of pinecones tossed on the fire to release their pearly nuts, the majesty of a long, snaking processional to the shrine at Montevergine as the village begged the Blessed Mother to intercede in illness or war. He could remember climbing the well-ribbed flank of Vesuvius to peer into her churning mouth, and he laid his boyish fear and courage on our hearts.

He would tell us about how it had been to be the first of fourteen children, run out of fingers counting them. Fourteen! I could not imagine being one of fourteen, when to be one of four already seemed so many. And he had not even been the first. Two infants had died before him. The wise women of his village had told his mother, the beautiful grandmother we had never known, that she'd lost them because she was too tender and hovering, too protective. *"Lascialo andá!"*—"Let him go!" they'd admonished her whenever he pressed his rubbery baby legs into her lap, eager to fly. And so, he said, she had finally "tossed him into the road" as soon as he could crawl, and he laughed, as if to say, "And so you see, now!" And so we saw.

And how proud he was of me, his smartest girl, when I said my Italian vowels roundly, and rolled my *rs* (and yet it came so easily to me!). How enchanting he was when he wasn't angry or dull or withdrawn into his grief, or boiling with some scheme that would pave his way—and ours— with gold. So I could not separate him from Italy or from love, the unresist- ing love of a girl-child for her father's sorrowing eyes.

But fuse that love with fear, even fear of love—a fusion like those wax images sealed between two disks of glass one sometimes sees in collections of Roman antiquities, the mysterious art that once welded them together now completely lost.

I am eight, and in love. It is dinnertime; the family is gathered around the table. Outside our house, in the yard, I know there is a desert wind rustling the cottonwood trees, but I can barely hear it because my brothers are taunting me, demanding that I tell the name of the boy I love. They do not mean this to torment me only. My father is already scowling. We can- not tell which of us is wounding his dark olive eyes.

The boy I love is not dark. He is as white and gold as moonlight on sand. Even his name is white: *Charlie White*. I tell it over to myself secretly, like a spell.

My father calls me to him after supper. "Who is this boy you love at school?" he asks, with just that crucifying touch of scorn on the word *love*. But the name fights back. It is as though there is a danger in my mouth, and only the whitest white silence can protect it. "Tell me his name," he says. All gentleness has been emptied from his voice, and he says, "If you won't tell, you must never speak to me again." I know this is a game. I look at him, astonished, trying to find the playful message in his face, in a twitch of mouth or eyebrow. But I am thinking, I cannot tell, and you cannot mean to shut me away with your silence—not for such a little thing! His indifference is enthralling. Near him in the dark, I read every curve of his body hungrily for a sign. I wish I had his pen now; I could so easily draw the face outlined by lamplight, the sinuous line easily embracing the fine, sad profile, the black hair silvering above the shapely ears.

A half-hour goes by. It is made of thirty separate and unbearable min- utes, I have counted them, and they are forever enough. I go to him, not daring to touch even his sleeve. When he lifts his head and turns it toward me his faraway glance is tender, and a delirious sense of salvation catches at my throat.

I ask him what he is writing. He shows me a letter in Italian, to his sister Irena in Striano, a village near Sperone. I think of Italy, the village, the aunt, his sister, I have never seen, her children, my cousins. But he has not forgotten his warning. "Now you have spoken," he says, with dark and terrible finality. My brain is blinded with disbelief. More than ever now I will not tell him. I am stunned by this new power my father's love has over me, dazed by the superb and violent cunning of his jealousy.

"Write it," he says calmly.

I take the pen from his hand, meaning to resist, but the tip presses itself to the white sheet. I tell myself it is a name, a silly name, *Charlie White*, but in the wind I can hear it fall and see it break into dust and scatter and lose itself among the trees.

Perhaps less guiltily than I later thought he should have, my father began to leave a book about the house, face down to mark his place, a book with a green baize library binding plainly imprinted in white and a straightforward title like *Managing the Squab Farm*, full of line drawings of various pigeon breeds and poor-quality photos exhibiting the layouts of sheds.

All this seemed to go from print to reality like the swift turning of a movie page. We moved from our little bungalow into a bigger one on a rather bald and dusty road, oddly named Fair Oaks Drive. The house itself seemed clattery and somewhat the worse for wear, but it had a pebbled horseshoe driveway in the front, bordered with great, green, shaggy rhododendrons and oleanders that lent it a sheltered look, and in the back, shading the barn and two long rows of tin-roofed pigeon sheds, a majestic phalanx of cottonwood and eucalyptus trees.

Soon enough we children learned of the miracle of bird and egg and how they did increase and multiply, and how suddenly and ruthlessly they died, got plucked, and on the third day were sent off to be eaten. And then it wasn't long before the pigeons were joined by ducks and chickens and turkeys, making an only slightly profitable enterprise slightly more profitable. And since, unlike the pigeons, these forlorn creatures wandered about the yard pecking at the gravel and playfully attacking us, and were as often accused of misdemeanors as we were, we inevitably endeared them with names and made them our friends.

But it was not a playful business. Squab farming was hard and dirty and demanding, and Lou and Carlo were soon recruited into the feeding and cleanup when they were not at school. Eventually the slaughter, too. At first they may have thought it a perverse adventure. But it was brutal work to break the necks of baby birds, and it didn't take long for the ugliness to spread itself, dreary and awful, on their souls. I am amazed to remember how the fall of a single infant sparrow from its nest in the porch roof was a catastrophe the four of us rushed to like a battlefield medical-surgical unit, how we would take turns wrapping it in warmed towels and nursing it with an eyedropper, and when it died, which it always did, bury it in the garden with a little Popsicle-stick cross, every one of us weeping, my brothers no less than my sister and me. But this childish reparation could not lift the stone of guilt from off their daily little murders. Denial soon passed into sullen resistance, and when this roused my father's anger to sterner discipline, the two boys began to scheme how they might run away.

I would not have known this except that I had taken refuge one afternoon in a favorite spot of mine for reading, a comfortable crotch in a branch of a great cottonwood tree at the back of the yard. Like some Nancy Drew storybook heroine, I simply overheard them, hunkered down together behind one of the pigeon sheds, conspiring. Their plans seemed already far advanced. They'd built small wagons out of old wooden crates and discarded baby-carriage wheels, crammed them with cereals and tins of soup and beans, and hidden them behind the barn. They even had rifles and gunpowder-makings (my genius brother Lou having researched the formula), and a supply of .22-caliber bullets, though they swore later they would not have killed a rabbit unless they were starving. Lou had talked a friend into joining them, Billy, a neighborhood kid who shared his dog-eared Zane Grey novels and seemed to have a natural hormonal reservoir of thirteen-year-old discontent. The three of them were wild when they realized I knew what they were up to. I cried desperately, not out of fear, but at the thought of their going forever. I swore I would never give them away, not even under torture, and I meant it.

But my honor was never put to the test, my father never dreaming I could be part of such a heinous plot. I lay in my bed on the screened porch, listening to the caravan creakily depart in the dark before dawn with my heart pounding so loud in my chest I thought it could wake the house. But the boys were miles away before my father missed them, and they were miles farther on before he understood what it meant. My mother begged

him to be calm, but she was no match for his bellowing rage. She herself
was caught between fear of his wrath and the plain, crushing truth that her
sons had also left *her*. Billy's father was drawn into the search. They headed
the old pickup into the Catalinas along the route he and the boys had
taken the previous Christmas, when they'd braved snow to cut trees to sell
on city street corners, guessing now that this was the familiar road the
boys would trust. And sure enough, by nightfall they found them, huddling around their campfire high in the mountains, some twenty miles
away.

Lou was thirteen, his voice just beginning to break. Carlo only ten, shy,
undergrown, with a sickliness that left him still a kind of baby. I could hear
the small, uneven duet of their strangled sobs even as the truck crunched
into the drive in the deep of the night, and my father pushed them out into
the yard and into the barn. Then their howls of pain, punctuated by his
choking staccato monotone of rage. He whipped Carlo first and sent him
into the house, then tied Lou to a post and flogged him again and again,
until the sun rose and lay full and plain over the desert and all one heard at
last was the silence, even of the birds.

I had lain through the night in a stupor of disbelief, struggling to
understand. How could he inflict a pain of which he seemed never to get
enough? How could he bear it? How could my mother, who would flinch
at the sight of a splinter in the palms of our hands? She must have drugged
herself, stoned herself to death with prayer, devised some lie of the mind,
some mercifully self-annihilating belief that this was happening to *her*, that
she was merely surrendering blindly to her own punishment. How did *I*
bear it? You could not drive the sobbing sound out of your head, no matter
how much noise you made crying into the pillow, no matter how you
stopped your ears with the sheets. It was as if I were there with them in
that dim-lit barn, had seen it happening. It wasn't possible, he would never
have let me, and yet I think I still see them there where we were not
allowed to go, not even to bring them water. I see her, whispering into her
rosary, her throat tight and dry with exhausted grief, the crystal beads
wedged between her thumbs, and her heart a lump of volcanic ash still too
hot for the tears she wept to be wet.

When you are a child, when you are told to step over and around the
corpse on the carpet, you do it. The corpse in this case was not just my
father's cruelty but his misery, the livid bestial frustration and selfish panic

at who knows what world lost, darkened still more by my mother's complex of self-sacrifice and guilt at somehow having dealt him this fate. The moral bearings of all these things escaped me. I needed to love my parents. I needed to forgive them. I began faintly to grasp at a solacing if still bewildering truth that there was a link between our family's lives, which had in earlier days seemed for all their tumult so much our own, and that mysterious, dim other universe of wars and national hatreds. This world, which came at us in wonderful alliterative warnings like "loose lips sink ships" and bloodthirsty jingles about Hitler and Mussolini and Tojo blithely sung in the school playground, in hearty exhortations to do your part for the war effort—which we kids translated into fishing through dirt heaps for scrap metal and turning in our brown copper pennies for white ones—had just that airy false optimism and dark undertow I still connect with the comic radio of Jack Benny and Fibber McGee. We didn't know enough to call it history, but whatever its name was, we knew we lived in it. It did not forgive. It did not explain. But it said, You don't understand, my dear little girl, because there is so much, so much, to understand.

And it seemed to speak sometimes in the nasal voice of President Franklin Delano Roosevelt, for even if he had not replied to my father's letter in his own person, there appeared the sudden fact that something in the war had changed, Italy had joined the Allies, and that the same Italians who'd been scorned on Wednesday were back on Thursday in the good graces of the American government. If with equal suddenness a place for Mario's fine Italian hand was found on the defense equipment finishing line in a plant just outside of Tucson, it did not seem so entirely amazing or far-fetched to think the president had personally interceded. Mario, vindicated, took his place painting insignias on warplanes, spending much of his day on his back or squirming around on elbows and hips, like Michelangelo under the Sistine ceiling.

Beware the wish granted, by gods or presidents. Unlike Michelangelo, Mario was steeped in a dense bath of chemical solvents and paint fumes. Within six months he was deathly ill. He wandered about the house at first, perplexed at the willful refusal of his own body. He worked intermittently, when his strength came. He sought out healers who were baffled by his illness, and got slowly thinner and weaker.

The chores of the pigeon farm had to go on without him. My brothers told me secretly that Lou had devised a way to anesthetize the birds before killing them with a thin needle inserted behind the skull. It was no more than a kind of delusionary triage. Even if he could get to the infant birds in time, the hapless chickens and ducks couldn't be spared, and at holiday market time dozens of them still squawked, in brutal scenes of madcap slaughter, headless and bleeding about the yard.

The most terrible death was that of a spangled Japanese Bantam rooster, whose dawn crowing had become as familiar a part of our lives as the cooing of the pigeons at twilight. We called him "Nip-on-knees" because if you got too close to his hens he would sneak-attack you with his beak at what it was funny to think of as the Pearl Harbor level of your anatomy. When his time came to die for somebody's fricassee, my sister and I suffered so vocally that my mother declared all Bantam-slaying over. She could make such ultimatums now, though she'd never have admitted—in deference to my father, would never have dared think—she ruled the roost. But he had taken to his bed, and though he still gave orders from his closed and unapproachable room, we could tell he was growing less and less able to police how well they might be filled.

Probably in response to a gloomy epistle of my mother's complaining that everything that could go wrong had, my Aunt Mildred, Spagnola sister number four, wrote us that winter. "I'm coming," she declared, and she did, arriving from the East one day like a sunrise. Maybe she was having her own life crisis, or had reached an impassable plateau in her career. Or maybe she had simply, selfishly, imagined that any visit out here, to the land of eternal sunshine, had to be a vacation. But that was Aunt Mildred; you could never tell, as she unpacked her seventy-seven halter tops, what she did to please you from what she did to please herself.

Like all her sisters, Mildred was in the fashion trades. Or like and unlike them. They say the eldest, May (really Gandolfa, the same who had never quite forgiven Maria the injury of catching a husband before her), had already destroyed her eyes beading by the time she married Dante, that improbably named pretty-boy of hers—a man I remember from my later years in East Harlem as always mysteriously pale and well-shaven, and never to be seen on the tenement stairs before noon on weekdays in his trademark soft fedora silk tie. Next came my mother, Maria—called Mary at home—with her promising berth at Bergdorf before Mario carried her away. And then Teresa, who had followed Mary into a similarly promising career before she'd met and married her fine, patrician-looking cousin, Louis. But Mildred, who had slapped a kind of movie star moniker over her own original Carmela and effectively passed, had outshone them all, going into fashion design and making it at the Seventh Avenue cutting edge. Not black-haired and Arab-African–looking like all the others, but sandy red-haired like Papa Calogero and hazel-eyed like nobody (in that anciently mixed-up, who-knows-what-you-will-get way of the children of Sicily, an island trod by every race since time began), she even had the high cheek-bones and air of cool command that could put you in mind of Dietrich in the right light. She knew what to wear, and how and when to wear it. On her own sewing machine, fitted on her own dressmaker's dummy, she made things rich women died for. And she was still single and flaunted it.

The relatively recent buzzword for this particular form of cool was *glamour*, which had begun to denote something, some irresistibly feminine, Coco Chanel sort of something that even women who were powerful and career-oriented could have—or maybe that *only* women who were power-ful and career-oriented could have. I knew she had it, whatever it was, the moment she stepped down off that transcontinental express in Tucson and set her open-toed sandals on the station platform. And I wanted it, too.

She also had a certain starry look in her eyes. My first thought was that the glamour and the starry look went together, not understanding that they were actually antithetical, as things often are that follow one another as cause and effect and so for a single confounding moment show up in the same place. We kissed and hugged and cried for joy, and Mildred said how amazed she was to see what a pack of four little Indians her sister was rais-ing, and so on. But it wasn't long before she let out that she had met her dream man on that train, someone by the totally southern American name of Ferril Dillard, a tall, blond, beautiful Alabama soldier-boy coming west with his platoon to be trained for combat in the Japanese theater of war.

If there was one being in those mid-war days who was even more glam-orous than a Seventh Avenue fashion plate, it was a man in uniform. And this Ferril Dillard turned out on sight to be really delectable, a kind of blond Elvis before there was an Elvis, with baby blues and a crooning sort of drawl and a funny joyous fatalism that was such a contrast with the rather dark kind we'd grown up with that I fell half in love with him myself. He came to visit on weekends before going overseas, and brought us things, and courted and cuddled up more and more to Aunt Mildred, and she, who was so tough and smart and self-possessed when he wasn't around, turned into a kind of backlit American Beauty rose at a garden show, and just smiled and smiled.

My father, I'm sure, had his dark doubts about what was afoot, or what might actually come of this whirlwind courtship. But he was already too sick and bed-bound to raise a fuss over somebody who had actually shown up to give Maria a hand. And if he didn't like to encourage marriage to this totally un-Italian Alabaman, even less did he like the idea of Mildred's having a fling without it. So he played resident patriarch as best he could, and Aunt Mildred, not especially chafed by his watchdogging, settled into Tucson "for the duration," as they said, or as much of it as it took.

There were moments of total misty absence of eye contact when you could tell she was thinking about *him*. But she not only loved us kids, but truly adored my mother, and most of the time Mildred was with us she was actually with us, a kind of celebrity big sister, dolled up and ready for her public, prancing around in shorts, showing off the trademark family good legs in bobby sox and platform heels. It was she who taught me about making a statement with lipstick, of which she had at least nine equally brilliant shades in expensive cases. And when she wasn't lending a hand with the shopping or the wash or the cooking, or conspiring with my mother over some fine seam on the sewing machine, she would slather herself all over in cocoa butter (the smell of it can still pull the memory of her, like a genie, out of a jar) and throw herself down in the sun in her glamorous red bare-midriff swimsuit for a good hour's tan.

And whenever Ferril had a short furlough, she dazzled him, and he dazzled her, and before you knew it she was pinning together a cream-colored satin dress on the mannequin, and they were married in a quick and simple ceremony that was part of what came in those days with men going off to war. And then he went off to war, and they had a baby on the way. Mildred never had another child. Thinking back, I can understand why. I was much too protected to be let in on the medical aspect of her condition when I was a girl, but I know she went a terribly long time giving birth. And I remember my sister and I being steered away from her until well after it was over.

She'd gone into labor the night before the night before Christmas. When we were finally allowed to see her, her face looking drained—and astonishingly lipstickless—there was all the same such a lustrous glory in her eyes that I thought her delight in her child must at least be proportional to her difficulty in getting it out of her body. It was a girl, a very tiny girl, born deep in the night of Christmas Eve, sleeping in a bassinet off to the side of her bed when we came enchanted and whispering into the room.

My mother and she had spent months playing with names, but Mildred threw it all over and completely surprised her. "Starr," she announced, when asked. Maria kissed her cheek and smiled her most winsome smile. We all smiled. The whole issue of naming, now that we had left the Old World with its heavy burden of the deaths of ancestors, seemed to be thrown wide open. And Starr, in this context, could arguably be said to have had a basis in scripture. But for Mildred as for her tribe, only the road of excess could lead to the palace of wisdom, and a single allusion to the triumph of giving birth on O Holy Night would never be enough. "Starr Carol," she corrected herself archly, looking a little, I thought, like a cat who has stuck her paw in the cream, again.

Maria expressed content by finding her least ironical smile and smiling it, and was just blowing her nose into a hankie when Mildred added, "Noel," and forced her black eyebrows to shoot up again. Ann and I laughed and then clapped our hands over our mouths. Our mother shot a glance our way and then turned back to Mildred. Jokingly, she asked, "Any *more* names?"

"Of course," said Mildred, wincing slightly as she shifted her weight in the bed. "Starr Carol Noel *Dillard*." She pronounced it as if she had just locked in her baby's claim to a platoon of harmonizing angels, and in that full, long, magical string you could hear the self-satisfaction of the Spagnola woman who has already got pretty much everything she ever wanted out of her man, and then some.

With a few exceptions, my sister Ann figures so little in the experiences I most remember about early Tucson that I have wondered if she was still too young to be part of them, apron-tied at home while every day my brothers and I adventurously (I thought) crossed a stretch of desert to our schoolhouse, a mile away. I am sure I strove to distance myself from her babyhood—even her girlness—in my longing to be taken seriously by my brothers, whose boy-freedom I envied and whose boy-daring I wanted to emulate.

But it was a continuous struggle: the more I sought them, the more they avoided me. As we followed the footpath home from school they would dart ahead or straggle behind, roaring for joy whenever an unpredictable finger of evolutionary anomaly called "jumping cactus" flung itself at my head and grabbed one of my thick black braids, or stuck me full on the backside through my shorts, driving me to tearful despair, as if the whole Arizona universe were conspiring to punish me for being a girl.

The family called me "Fluffy," to make matters worse. It was meant endearingly, a baby name that had hung on as such names do, and my mother used it with an especially tender affection that my little sister echoed. But still, it was a silly, lapdog sort of a name. And especially since my own body made itself laughable and awkward, it could be used against me. I could not seem to shed my baby fat no matter how tomboyishly I ran and played dodgeball and climbed trees. People might patronize me as "pleasingly plump," but I was never fooled. I had to face it. The plain fact was I loved to eat. Not all of it went to fat, of course. By the time I was eight or nine I was also bigger and stronger than Lou, who was actually rather scrawny and bookish, and I was a giant compared with Carlo, whose misery nickname was the Runt. But to my brothers, I was forever Fat Fluffky. And they knew that the moment they skewered me with that name, I would disappear, hurt and humiliated.

Only the movies brought us together. My father, who ranked Saturday matinees lower than comic books as moral minefields for the impressionable young, must have made an exception for Walt Disney's *Dumbo*, or else a restless, pregnant Aunt Mildred had prevailed over his house rule. He was right. Once we had seen that absurdly sweet and doleful, wing-eared circus elephant, we couldn't get him out of our minds or our bodies. All Lou had to do, when the four of us were cleaning up after supper, was give the signal, and we would jump together and stack ourselves acrobatically on the kitchen floor, me at the bottom holding up the other three.

My brothers made no secret of how impressed they were with this performance of supergirl strength. For a few heavenly weeks I was their buddy. Now and then they would cut me in on a devilish plot, just so I could display my quisling subjection.

Like the day we decided to poison my sister. It was really the silliest ploy in the book. Ann was six, nearly seven, and even if she was tiny and naïve, she was nobody's fool. The new bars of bluing my mother had begun to use for soaking the bed sheets out in the wringer-tub in the yard were stamped into break-off squares like a Hershey bar, but they were actually blue. When I told her this was a new kind of chocolate she was really going to like, she wasn't tricked in the least, and said firmly, "It is *not*."

Somebody, maybe my mother herself, had said that whatever those bluing cubes were made of could poison you, or at least make you blind, but I still urged Ann to try one. "Try it yourself," she said, pushing me away, sure that it if was candy and as tasty as all that, I wouldn't be in such a hurry to share it. But I held her and tried to force it to her lips, just as my mother abruptly came in from the yard and my brothers crawled sniggering from behind the couch and scurried out the door. Ann grabbed her around the knees. "They were trying to poison me!"

My mother glared at me hard, snatching the package out of my hand and reassuring Ann in a voice tight with banked anger. I had watched the boys disappear, and stood there, paralyzed, yet weirdly awake. Ann protested that I had really tried. She was right. I had, to buy an instant of my brothers' admiration. "They wouldn't have let you, darling," my mother had said. But I knew what I knew, and it was like sudden carnal knowledge. She lay now in the safe circle of my mother's arms, her hair stroked and kissed, as I slipped guiltily out and across the yard and scrambled into the familiar splayed branch of the cottonwood tree, my own gut tumbling and aching as if I had poisoned myself. Time passed. The screen door swung gently open from the enclosed back porch where Ann and I usually slept together. I could see her tiny shape, in her little blue and white pinafore, emerge tentatively into the yard. Her feet were bare. A mass of hair had escaped from her braids and sprung into irregular loose brown curls around her dusky face. Her face was all-wide-open eyes, searching the fading light.

I knew she was looking for me. It was as if I were seeing her for the first time.

I am glad not to have been a mother then. It was struggle enough to learn to be a motherly child. Nothing declared the impotency of parenting more than an apocalyptic Arizona rainstorm, when, after days—weeks—eternities of blanching and relentless blue skies and flaming sunsets, of long, blue-velvet nights flagrant with moonlight, a switch would be thrown on the universe, and rain and wind would flash across the desert, shutting down the world in a solid wall of water and erasing connection to anyone out of the reach of your arms.

My mother, who had a houndlike vigilance about danger (a sixth sense in her, literally, almost as overdeveloped as her sense of smell, which was legendary), would gladly have raised cowards, I think, just to be sure we'd hide safely under our beds like puppies when the power-rains came down. But her sons had just that bit of the blind, gambler's daring of their father that seemed to have got us to Arizona in the first place, and even something of his queer taste for rousing and then flouting her womanish terrors. When the rain exploded out of the skies that famous year of Aunt Mildred, as suddenly as the lightning plunged into that live radiant soup of September heat, the boys rallied against all cries and dove into the flashing water like crocodiles, disappearing from sight before they had left the horseshoe drive, even before the smashing rain had caromed their reckless whoops and yelps out of the air.

We women and girls stood by, arms helplessly outstretched. But not all of us wanted to stop them. I wanted to be with them, to leap barefoot and bare-chested into that air ocean and let my eyesight be shattered by the sheer force of water and the rain pelt my back like bullets, as I had seen it pelt theirs, and dart and dance into the running river of the road. Here in the house the rain hammered on the metal roof, the wind drove sudden gushes of water at the windows. We could imagine the birds in their screened refuges soaked right through their oily feathers, hunkered down into soft balls, huddling together for comfort as the rushing rain drove deep new freshets into the dirt floor of the sheds. But they were safe, and would not fly, like boys, into the wall of water.

Had she known Carlo was in danger of drowning in a gully before she knew he'd been rescued, my mother might have died, just from the sheer fact of being helpless to save him. Something just that quixotic lay between the two of them, a deep tenderness she felt for his vulnerable smallness, he with that seemingly inarticulate yearning to be her boy, her only boy—to be, in fact, her *man*. With so much of her family's strange witchcraft coded into acts of naming and renaming, perhaps there had been the magic of the patronymic he was blessed with as second son, singularly entitled to carry the name of her beloved Papa—or the elegant variation of it acceptable to my father. For Carlo, too, she would have stopped a bullet, a hundred times.

I think he knew he had this hold on her, that he lived and moved within the safety of its possession. Sickly and small, he had first survived pneumonia as an infant (one of our oft-repeated family miracles), then, with Lou, a scarlet fever that had left them both afflicted with the same fever-weakened eyesight. But Lou's owlish glasses made him look the genuine budding genius, while Carlo's lay as heavy and huge in his tiny face as the optics of a bottle fly. He clowned, he tricked, he teased, he ruthlessly taunted my sister and me, he did whatever he was told not to. He became ever more the mischievous little scapegrace as he grew. My father, his heart increasingly darkened and sore, felt baited, and even from his sickbed gave him the full brunt of a military, withering scorn. And the more he gave, the more Carlo seemed to want, to taunt him to give, as if it were a drug for which he had developed a habit, or as if it had become the dark side of my mother's unconditional and enabling love, which could deny him nothing, forgive him everything.

But that day, when they brought him home half-dead, the shriek she shrieked could have stopped your heart. The sun had already burst through the clouds again and was beating the soaked earth into smoke when the whole posse of them abruptly appeared at the bottom of the drive, Lou and the neighborhood boys leading the way. Behind them walked the gas station man from down the road, Carlo lying across his arms as limp as a bolt of wet muslin. We knew he was alive. As they drew closer, we could hear him grotesquely weeping against his chattering teeth in a parody of his own impish laughter, see him wanly waving his brown little legs as if he wanted to run, as if he'd been caught and not rescued. But he was safe, safe, *safe*, everyone reassured her! Yet she could not stop wailing in terror-exaggerated pain. And yet I knew she indulged her passion, her fury, and did not drop down dead at the sight of him, because by Jesus, Mary, and Joseph, and all the holy saints, even if he was half-dead, he was still alive.

The boys grabbed excitedly at their breath as they told us that the rain had already stopped pounding, and was just beginning to sift down straight through the sunlight, when Carlo had taken it into his head to breast the wild water flooding the drain ditches in streams as wide and boiling as rivers. He'd been caught, swept into a culvert pipe under the crossroad by the gas station. Lou had lunged forward and grabbed and held him by the wrists, screaming for help as he threw himself across the embankment, but without the strength to wrench him out against the force of the current. There was nothing to do but resist it, the two of them one body, arms tearing at shoulders, until the other boys came and made a chain and held them both back from the flood rushing into the great pipe. And then the garage man with his strong back and forearms had come and just reached down and yanked Carlo out.

For a few moments my mother simply took him in her arms, and, weeping, laid him across a blanket in her lap, took his head between her hands and kissed the streaky wet hair. His chest bled where it had been thrashed against the arch of the culvert, the fine brown-gold skin stripped away from throat to navel. He howled with pain coughing the foul, coffee-colored water out of his choking lungs, and she wept, we all wept, in pity for him. But he was *alive*. The saints had kept him alive.

Still, it was a deathblow, the last shimmering spike in my mother's feeling for this beautiful and cursed place—a feeling that from the beginning had never been love. Ever on the watch for signs, she lost no time in reading this one, as she had my father's slow decline, only without doubt or equivocation. Even as we moved through our own slow gulfs of childhood time, increasingly haunted by the thinning form we caught only in occasional scaring glimpses when the bedroom door was left ajar, we knew conferences were held, plans made; we felt a nameless danger, sensed a new horizon of hope.

Aunt Mildred, restless for independence, perhaps superstitious enough to be repelled by the morbid sadness of our house, had moved out and nested into special single blessedness at the back of her own shop in town until the Christmas baby arrived, and then into a special kind of madonna-with-child blessedness afterwards. She turned a small income from cutting and draping and stitching her artful fashions, drawing on Ferril's army pay and what was left of her savings, finding her niche, content to wait out her soldier in the Arizona sunshine.

She was still a mesmerizing sight for two little girls whenever she visited the squab farm. From the somewhat sprung-out armchair in the family room, our eavesdropping perch on the kitchen, we could see, as she moved the baby from shoulder to shoulder, that she was cultivating a slightly blowzy Rita Hayworth look now, self-consciously tossing her mass of brassy gold hair out of the way, and dodging carefully as my mother careered about the room. Both of them seemed caught in an instinctive dance of frenetic Spagnola energy, rapt in jolted, telegraphic conversation filled with hushed allusions to doctors in the East.

It snowed the following winter in Tucson, for the first time in fifty years. The snowflakes floated out of a lowering gray sky like fine volcanic ash and sublimed back into the air almost before they had dusted the earth.

In my anguished and misremembering mind's eye it is all one image—the vanishing snow, my father taken from the house on a stretcher that then lifts so lightly into the train it seems to be empty, the sighing train heaving itself away as if it could feel pain.

The farm vanishes, the birds, the splayed cottonwood tree. For a very little time we seem to be with my aunt and the Christmas baby with the lovely Disney name, my little sister and I, together, climbing up and down the dust pile in her parking lot, collecting bits of scrap metal for the war effort.

And then the lights behind the big blue sky go quietly dark.

Toni McNaron

From I Dwell in Possibility

Toni McNaron (b. 1937), now a writer, activist, and professor of English and women's studies at the University of Minnesota, grew up near Birmingham, Alabama. She witnessed the
savage attacks by local police and citizens against nonviolent civil rights activists, and
would later have to overcome her own demons in the form of the oppression that kept her
silent about her lesbianism through the 1950s and 1960s.

In McNaron's 1992 memoir, *I Dwell in Possibility*, she writes courageously of her alco-
holism and recovery, her blocked ambition, her coming out, and her personal and professional rebirth. This excerpt describing her early life and her relationships with her singular
father and mother is remarkably effective at presaging many of the issues she will contend
with later in life.

I grew up in a one-story white frame house, with living room, dining room,
and kitchen on one side of a long hall, three bedrooms and a bath on the
other. The house was in Fairfield, Alabama, home of Tennessee Coal and
Iron (TCI), a subsidiary of United States Steel. Called the Pittsburgh of
the South, TCI boasted a model steelworkers' town, with low-cost housing
and schools located near the plant. Nothing was said about the grit that
appeared on windowsills and furniture within hours of dusting. Because
the worst of the manual labor in the hellish blast furnaces was done by
blacks, they outnumbered whites. Everyone in Birmingham, the city to
which Fairfield was attached, worked directly for "the company" or for one
of its necessary feeder industries and services. It was the late thirties, and
the South had only just begun to pull out of the Great Depression.

My father progressed from working in the wire mill as junior book-
keeper to being chief accountant for TCI, and we lived where we did for
his convenience. He liked to come home for lunch, and the mill was only
about ten minutes from our house. Though an unpretentious house in a

working-class neighborhood, my home was full of antiques. A few of them, including a delicate drop-leaf, three-drawer sewing table, came down the Mississippi on a flat boat with my maternal great-grandmother. With her French Huguenot family, she had fled one of many persecutions and landed in Canada. Some of the other fine pieces were gifts to my mother, primarily from my sister but occasionally from my father. I remember a fishing trip from which he returned with a four-branch gas chandelier and no fish. He had spied it in the barn of a farm where he had stopped to get fresh eggs. Painted red, it was being used by the local chickens, attested to by wisps of straw still falling from the lamp bases. My father bought it for a couple of dollars, and we all watched as it became a gorgeous brass light that hung from then on in our living room.

Most of the antique furniture was acquired by my mother in her many jaunts to shops filled with old chests and tables, china, silver, and other bric-a-brac. In the forties, Alabama shopkeepers were not always aware of the value of their holdings, but my mother knew wood grains, silver markings, porcelain symbols. Often I accompanied her to serve as decoy. We would arrive at a shop and browse until the proprietor asked if he could help us. Somehow, Mamie (the name my sister had used as a baby that became what most people called my mother) turned the conversation to me, and I launched into one of my distracting recitals. Since I knew names of rivers, oceans, continents, and other phyla, I could charm adults fairly easily. While I spouted off something years ahead of my comprehension, my mother slipped into remoter rooms of unfinished furniture. Using the pearl-handled penknife always in her purse, she quickly chipped through some colored paint on a washstand or end table. When she found cherry or mahoghany, or, on rare occasions, rosewood, she returned to me smiling. At the next lull in whatever conversation the owner and I were having, she would say in all innocence, "Oh, I happened to notice the little painted piece in back—how much is that if I just take it with me now and not bother you with refinishing it?" If the price was right, a bargain was struck, and the piece piled into the back of our old black Plymouth. Once home, and the newest treasure in the basement, she and I stripped off the bad color, restoring the wood to its original beauty.

Perhaps had my mother lived in another age or been able to tell herself a different story, she might have opened an elegant little shop. Then she could have bought up old painted pieces, restored them, and sold them to people wanting the pleasure of owning them. Instead, we accumulated pieces of antique furniture as my schoolmates' parents might collect matchboxes or miniature china horses. Inside my house, I often felt overwhelmed by objects I had been told were priceless and feared I might accidentally knock to the floor at any moment.

My mother seldom did anything on a small scale. Though she was only four feet eleven inches tall, her imagination and energy formed a force field that lent her at least an additional foot. This commanding presence left me often feeling eclipsed, effaced, though Mamie clearly adored me. I still remember going into our house on Holly Court some five months after she had died and being met instantly by the smell of her perfume. It was as if she had just stepped out and would return at any moment.

When I first knew her, she was already forty, so I have very little sense of her as a girl or young woman. Old photos show her in typical twenties styles—tight-fitting black dresses with lace, low-slung wide belts, large ornamental pins on her equally large bodice, funny hats with feathers. One story from her youth that I heard repeatedly was about a dance in Montgomery to which she went, along with Zelda Sayre of whom my mother was an acknowledged look alike. She and Zelda reputedly decided to play a joke on Scott Fitzgerald, in town on furlough from the army. My mother was to "play" Zelda for a time to see if Scott could tell the difference. I listened as Mamie spun her tale about dancing with the dashing soldier who would become one of America's great writers. The joke seems to have worked, at least in her reminiscence.

But the person I knew in childhood had changed in some major ways from that storybook character. No longer svelte, my mother was always either on a diet or about to go on one. Given her frame, at 160 or so, she was twenty to thirty pounds overweight. Rising in the morning full of resolution, she ate her two squares of zwieback and drank a cup of tea while pointing out her virtue to us egg and toast munchers. By lunch, resolve had weakened to allow a taste of whatever dessert she had made for the rest of us; by dinner, caution had flown into the southern air. Mamie was a fine and proud cook, preferring French dishes with rich sauces and elaborate sweets of all sorts. Her cream puffs were legendary, shared with many townspeople when she had to make her contracted monies for the church coffers. Birthdays brought out all her creative talents, not only in the cake of one's choice but in the side dishes: sweet potatoes mashed and put into scooped-out orange halves complete with handles; fried chicken wings or pork chops dressed in paper "shoes" to keep fingers greaseless; tiny Parker House rolls shaped like miniature English pasties.

Her weight in no way obscured her elegance. Most weekdays, Mamie wore a housedress and a smock during the morning as she cleaned or cooked. In mid-afternoon, she took a leisurely bath and "dressed"—nice clothes over massive foundation garments, careful makeup to give her a certain old-world beauty. Her hair was brownish with auburn tints, often worn wrapped around a thick rat that lent a halo effect not unlike Greer Garson's. The wreath, which softened her face, also cast her backward in time.

Throughout my childhood, my mother wore tiny pince-nez glasses. Whenever she took them off, two bright red ellipses appeared on either side of her patrician nose. I called these "holes" and worried because they took so long to fade. When she finally succumbed to tortoise-shell glasses with regulation ear pieces, she lost some of her exoticism.

Early in the twentieth century, when she was nearing twenty, Mamie had won a scholarship to study piano outside the South. But before she could leave Selma, Alabama, she met, fell in love with, and married Mac, as she called my father. They carried on a brief courtship when he was on shore leave from Newport News, Virginia, and were married over Thanksgiving of 1917, because Daddy could get away at holiday time. Most of the photographs in their early years are of them in bathing suits or other casual wear at some beach with lots of relatives. A little later they appear with my sister, Betty, born about a year after they were wed.

My father was handsome in a craggy sort of way. About five feet six or seven, he had steel blue eyes that stare out of photographs much as they did in real life. He seems almost always to have worn his hair in a close crew cut. It was totally gray when I was born, the story being that it turned overnight after his father died. When I knew him, he too was overweight, though he never seemed to be doing anything to change that. My mother tried to get him to wear belts, but he insisted they cut him and so he preferred suspenders. They allowed him to buy trousers that were loose, that let him breathe. As a child I often watched in excited horror on those occasions when his trousers inched down over his stomach, lower and lower, until, suddenly recalling them, he hitched them back to his waist. He was the perfect antidote to Mamie, in her half-body girdles and massive brassieres.

But his laxity in the matter of fitted clothes was delusive. I was constantly surprised by the particular forms of his fastidiousness. One that seemed especially romantic to me as a child involved his donning a smoking jacket some weekday evenings after supper and on weekends for most of the afternoon. I thought him dashing and relaxed, especially in the silk one I gave him when I was twelve. The other manifestation felt much more oppressive. It involved forcing me to be letter and number perfect in school subjects. Nights often found me sitting on the cedar chest across from his favorite easy chair. We were there to go over my history or geography lesson, and Daddy defined that activity as follows: he would announce a topic heading; I would recite, word for word, the material underneath. If I missed even a preposition or conjunction, I had to do it over. Similarly, when I brought home tests graded 97 or 98, his only response was, "Well, why didn't you get 100?"

Of course I adored him, as my first memory of him shows: It is early Christmas morning, and I am nine months old. Warm in my flannel sack, I come out of sleep to see my father leaning over my baby bed. His face smiles, his eyes twinkle; his prematurely gray hair is cut unusually crew for the holiday. He calls to me: "Wake up, Jay Bird Blue, it's Christmas."

Daddy had another special name for me—Son—that he used in private for the first six years of my life. In the South, a saying went, "If you can kiss your elbow, you'll turn into a boy." One summer when I wanted desperately to be Daddy's son and was old enough to realize that I was only a daughter, I would sit in my back yard, alone, in my seersucker playsuit, contorting my arms, trying to get a lip over to an elbow. Once I even asked a girl friend to bend my arm further than I could. That night I lay awake in my canopied bed aching from my trial.

Failing the elbow trick, I tried other devices to pass. I asked for and got boys' toys: a jungle gym, chemistry sets, Lincoln logs, tinker toys, baseballs and gloves and bats, and all manner of guns during World War II. I wore cowboy shirts with my school skirts; I learned to run fast, to play hard ball, to shoot marbles, and to throw a pocketknife so that it landed blade in ground.

When Daddy stopped calling me Son, my attempts to be one merely became more subtle. To avoid being a "dizzy blond," I learned all I could as fast as I could. Because Daddy once showed me pictures of the Axis army's territories and chuckled when I tried to say the French or German names, I studied history with a passion. Because I heard him humming the tune to

"Ghost Riders in the Sky," I read cowboy books until I could spout the lingo like a native. Because my father once said he admired Alan Ladd in *Whispering Smith*, I wore two six-shooters and leather chaps even in the hottest summer weather. When I saw neighbor boys working in the yard or on the family car so their dads could read the Sunday funnies, I pretended to like mowing the grass and washing our old Plymouth. When I began menstruating, I denied my pain so I wouldn't be like "those silly girls" who stayed home from school the first day, lying under heating pads or hot water bottles. I carried books for boys I had crushes on in junior and senior high school, not even aware of how confused I was about my gender identity. Embarrassed in adolescence not to be able to shave my face, I took a razor to my underarms every morning, causing rashes that stung most of the day.

As I was growing up, I longed to hear my father call me Jay Bird Blue or some other term of endearment. But he stopped calling me pet names or any names as he and I got older. Something about me was causing my idol to fade from sight. Rare moments, to which I have attached tremendous importance, stand out. When I was four or so, he occasionally let me crawl up into his lap after supper and listen while he read me the daily funnies: "Major Hoople's Boarding House," "Gasoline Alley," "Hazel," "Dagwood and Blondie"—domestic strips in which well-meaning men were henpecked by imposing women.

In about 1943, I decided that my father bore some physical resemblance to Adolf Hitler—he too wore a small mustache in the center of his upper lip and had dark eyebrows. I would beg him to let me wet comb his crew cut over to the right. With his hair plastered down, the image was remarkably like the Führer's. When he indulged me in this fantasy, I imagined him powerful and assertive, full of words and passion.

Wanting desperately to spend time with him away from home, I asked to go fishing from the time I was about seven. Though he often promised—"The very next trip, you can go, but not just now"—I never got to go on one of these magical adventures. He preferred the company of his friend Mr. Kelton, a huge beefy man over six feet tall, whom my mother disliked intensely. On lucky Saturday afternoons, Daddy offered to take me for a treat, when he was not off fishing. What we actually did was go over to Mr. Kelton's house, and he and Daddy talked, while I played relatively unsupervised in a back yard, fenced in for Mr. Kelton's hound dog.

I Dwell in Possibility

Once when I was ten, Daddy took me to a professional baseball game at night under huge floodlights that attracted thousands of southern summer bugs. Birmingham had two baseball teams—the Barons and the Black Barons. The Barons were a farm team for the Boston Red Sox, while the Black Barons trained the earliest blacks who broke into major league baseball. Spectators for each team were absolutely segregated. Sitting in the bleachers with my father, I felt excited to be there. I ate a hot dog and drank Coca-Cola in a paper cup with Walt Dropo's picture on it. Walt was my hero since he, like I, was a left-handed first baseman. Near the end of play, Daddy bought me an ice cream sandwich. But he was annoyed by my questions: "Why do they fall onto the ground near home plate?" "Can we move down into those seats where nobody's sitting and we could see more?" "Why is that man with the red face yelling at the umpire?" "Wasn't that a strike, not a ball?" "Why can't I have a Popsicle?" He never took me to another ball game.

With his sudden death in 1954 when I was almost seventeen, my father became even more a mystery to me than his shadowy presence had caused him to seem. From that time until I entered therapy twenty-five years later, I made up stories about him and what he would think about his daughter/ "Son" as I matured.

Early memories of my mother are much more troubled. I see her face, moon-round, smiling but often slightly strained, coming closer than was comfortable for me. "Don't cross the street, honey, you'll get hurt." Hearing her say this, I feel instantly defiant and angry. Within half an hour, I've gone outside, toddled over to the curbing, looked across the road at nothing of interest, and crossed that street. No hurt comes to me, so I feel tricked.

Mamie seemed full of "don'ts," sentences telling me what not to do in order to avoid danger: "Don't go barefoot outside, you'll get impetigo." "Don't go swimming in public, you'll get polio." "Don't run and play, you'll get overexertion exhaustion." "Don't get your nice starched white pinafore wrinkled." "Don't go out of your yard, the stray dogs will get you." "Don't lie in the dirt, you'll get eaten by ants." "Don't play pitch, you'll hurt your fingers for piano practice." "Don't perspire, it's not nice." "Don't spit out your watermelon seeds, it's common." "Don't ever eat ice cream and watermelon on the same day or you'll die like Mrs. Munson did last Fourth of

July." I explored all these warnings and found only one true—when I played pitch frantically with a hard ball, I did sprain fingers, making piano playing virtually impossible.

My mother was acting out of her best sense of what was necessary for me to become only a slightly modernized version of the southern belle she had been. Two images of me clearly illustrate her hopes: All through childhood, I wore my golden blond hair waist long. Wanting me to look like someone in *Gone With the Wind,* my mother rolled hunks of my thick hair on worn-out boys' socks that she scavenged from neighbors with growing sons. Trying to sleep on eight or ten wads of hair was an ordeal, and I felt only relief when my locks were finally shorn as I entered junior high. All through childhood, I also wore a starched white pinafore each morning over my dotted swiss or polka dot piqué dresses. Mamie would get me ready for a morning presumably of play, put her hands lovingly on my shoulders, look me hard in the eyes, and say: "Now, go outside and have a good time, honey, but remember not to get your little pinafore wrinkled or dirty, in case we have company this afternoon."

My way of coping with so many don'ts was to lie, not merely to avoid trouble but as a way of life. Most of the time I wasn't found out, but fear haunted me. When I was caught, it was shameful and full of pain for us both. One summer between college terms, I insisted, when Mamie asked if I was bored with spending so much time with her, that I liked playing two-handed solitaire every afternoon and sitting in front of the TV trying to think of something other than the programs or her occasional contented snoring. I wrote my true feelings to my roommate and buried her answering letter in my underwear drawer. My mother periodically inspected my drawers, insuring that my clothes were neatly stacked. The day she met me at the front door, tears in her eyes and Jean's letter in her hands, I lied extra hard to calm her and to cover my rage. "There's only a month left till we can go back to Tuscaloosa and freedom" meant that Jean was unhappy with her home life, not that I had said anything about mine. "Your mom is like mine—they want their little girls close, just in case" was really saying how much we appreciated the loving watchfulness from our mothers as we got older. "Just put on a smiling face and count the days": I couldn't construct any other meaning for that one.

If I managed to get away with most of my lies, my disobedient acts were more flagrant and perceptible. Mamie's mode of dealing with me was effective. As an active child, I ran and played as many hours as possible.

Feeling trapped inside my house, I stayed outside except for lunch and occasional bathroom breaks, though I even preferred to squat in our back yard behind a hydrangea bush so as not to interrupt my play. Knowing all this, Mamie devised "Punishment." Never spanked, I was forced to sit perfectly still in a rocking chair in my parents' bedroom every time I disobeyed. There was a direct correlation between degree of defiance and number of minutes in that chair. The range was from five to thirty: five minutes can be a long time for puppies and little girls; thirty an eternity. I couldn't take anything of mine into the room—no crayons, paper, books, games. They would distract me from contemplating what a "bad girl" I had just been. My mother never understood that I was trying to be a bad girl, since that was the closest I could get to being a boy.

What I did, shut in that room without a clock to let me see how my confinement was progressing, was fantasize. Within a few months, I was able to become sufficiently involved so that sometimes, out of sheer spite, I refused to leave. Mamie would come to the still-closed door when the last minutes were passing and say, "Time's up, honey, you can go out and play now." Mostly I just sat out my fantasy, prolonging the last scenes while she waited for my appearance. Rarely, I said, "Just a minute, I'm busy." She'd stand it as long as she could and then burst into her own room and urge me out into family space. Once or twice she cried from sheer frustration, saying over and over, "I just don't know why you hurt me this way."

After one of my refusals to leave the room on her schedule, Mamie smarted around the house for the rest of that day overlooking smaller disobediences. I comprehended that I had won something; I felt smug and mean and lonely.

Most of my schoolmates lived in situations where at least the bathroom was private. I did not. The excuse went something like: "Oh, honey, excuse me, but we only have one bathroom and I just have to. . . ." There was a turn bolt on that door and my sister used it. When I tried, I was sharply reprimanded for inconveniencing Mamie who, after all, was responsible for dinner or lunch or whatever was currently important. More than I resented those intrusions, I disliked being called in while she bathed and dressed for the day. We talked there, or I was asked to help her into one of her several armoring garments—brassiere, massive girdle, tight-fitting slip. The intimacy and role reversals that surrounded these meetings several times a week for years seem even at this great distance to be troublesome.

I always sat on a little wicker clothes hamper, my eight-year-old feet barely touching the cool tile floor. I stayed very still, hoping my mother would forget I was there. Mouse quiet, I gazed at her, drying from her morning bath. She stood before me, huge and strong and all soft, rounded folds—layers of folds—face, breasts, stomach, thighs, ass, or as she insisted on calling it, "derrière."

Once dry, she would start all over, this time with a powder puff bigger than my whole hand. The powder made me want to sneeze, but I would hold fingers like a clothespin on my nose so she would go on, forgetting me. With short quick motions, she dusted under her melon bosoms, slowly so they poised between rise and flop. Then she moved down to her satin stomach with its big open space she called a navel—to me a cave. Then her puff-hidden hand moved down, but I have blocked that scene. At this point I would jump off the hamper and ask "why" about some silly thing. I wanted to make her dress; I could not watch her any more.

My question broke into her lazy ritual, and she started to pile on ladies' armor that crushed her lovely folds. First, a vest, soft but hiding. Then a brassiere one size too small so that her floppy breasts looked like iron ones. Was she really a lady knight in disguise? Then came the girdle I helped her close; I snapped the snaps—one . . . two . . . three . . . four— from waist to . . . Then came hooks and eyes over what I eventually learned was pubic hair. Then soft panties over that and a clingy slip over everything. At the very last, she smeared on Mum, a white cream for marble-shaved underarms, rouged her checks, and lined her full lips with a hard red stick.

Then she would loom over me—a statue in a mask—ready to fight her own dragons, I thought. I could not see any skin and had no hope for a soft hug; I would hurt myself on some new-made edge.

The other person living in our house was my sister, Betty. Sixteen and a half when I was born, she had been an only child until then. My first knowledge of her stems from a story Mamie told: when Betty found out that I was on the way, she is supposed to have replied, "If I can't name the brat, I won't speak to it." My mother recounted this to relatives, neighbors, friends. She found it humorous, but I did not like being called "brat" or "it." Betty was allowed to name me, and she chose Toni. Had I been a boy, I would have been called Tony. Many people do not understand the fine point of this gender-based spelling, so that all my life I have gotten mail addressed to Mr. McNaron. Once when I was going to church camp, I was mistakenly put into the boys' cabin, only to be moved immediately upon arrival.

My sister is essentially verbal. From the beginning, she taught me words that I at first had no idea about, which I remembered by sound or later by spelling: "postprandial divertissement" was one of my earliest phrases, along with "marsupials are indigenous to Australia" and "the prolixity of *lapins* is horrific." I see her sitting beside me rattling off these words, being amused and proud when I could repeat them to her latest swain.

. . .

My mother's mother died quite suddenly one summer in Foley, Alabama, in a movie house. Every year, my family vacationed there, staying in the cabin owned by Mamie's parents. Foley boasted a picture show among its more modern attractions and Mamie's mother took Betty and a boy cousin to afternoon matinees as often as the feature changed. There, in the darkened theater, my grandmother had a heart attack, and while my sister held her head her cousin ran for a doctor. My grandmother died, and my mother fell into a depression that lasted three years before my father intervened. At his insistence, they visited Dr. John, the family doctor. When my father asked what they might do to "cure Old Lady," Dr. John recommended having another child. Though my parents were almost forty, I was conceived. Whenever Mamie told the story of Dr. John's suggesting that she and Mac have a baby to "cheer Theresa up," I felt like running. I grew up in the shadow of that expectation, always trying to please, so often sensing that what I did was not quite enough.

I felt too important to the adults in my house. They kept close watch over me, encouraging me to be what they were not or could not be, reluctant to let me be myself. As a result, my childhood was full of instances in which I very much wanted their attention, but when it came in quantities, I would feel compelled to pull away. For instance, my junior high school teachers seemed intent on having us create "projects," assignments that caused me considerable consternation. Visual effects were to accompany our written reports, and we all knew that decorations determined whether our work received a B for competence or an A for "creativity." Part of me welcomed the help readily forthcoming from Mamie, with Betty as her assistant, since I was not particularly artistic. They would cheerfully volunteer to make my covers, correct my spelling, encourage me to do yet more reading and writing to insure the coveted A. Somewhere in the middle of this process, my gratitude would turn sour, and I would feel taken over, unable to own my work but equally unable to snatch it from them.

My family taught me to see myself as superior to virtually everyone and to isolate myself in the name of precocity or independence or some other large, empty word. One result was that I developed an extraordinarily active imagination, another was few companions my own age. Angry and confused, I took my feelings outside where I ran and played, day after day, to the point of exhaustion.

Toni Cade Bambara

Raymond's Run

Toni Cade Bambara (1939–1995), like many of her young protagonists, was raised by her mother in New York City. Bambara, a writer and teacher, was also a lifelong activist, deeply involved in both the civil rights movement and the women's movement. In 1970, Bambara broke new ground with her publication of the first African American feminist anthology, *The Black Woman*. She would go on to publish essays, criticism, a novel, *The Salt Eaters*, and several volumes of critically acclaimed and widely anthologized stories, including *The Sea Birds Are Still Alive* and *Gorilla, My Love*, which includes the story "Raymond's Run."

"Raymond's Run" also appeared, in 1979, in the Feminist Press anthology *Women Working*, edited by Nancy Hoffman and Florence Howe. The story reflects the consciousness of an African American girl growing up in Harlem—in this case, a young runner preparing for a school competition, who is charged with the care of her developmentally disabled brother. It offers a moving portrayal of a sister's devotion and an early homage to the empowering possibilities of women's sports—and also a timeless, inspirational model of female self-respect.

I don't have much work to do around the house like some girls. My mother does that. And I don't have to earn my pocket money by hustling; George runs errands for the big boys and sells Christmas cards. And anything else that's got to get done, my father does. All I have to do in life is mind my brother Raymond, which is enough.

Sometimes I slip and say my little brother Raymond. But as any fool can see he's much bigger and he's older too. But a lot of people call him my little brother cause he needs looking after cause he's not quite right. And a lot of smart mouths got lots to say about that too, especially when George was minding him. But now, if anybody has anything to say to Raymond, anything to say about his big head, they have to come by me. And I don't play the dozens or believe in standing around with somebody in my face doing a lot of talking. I much rather just knock you down and take my chances even if I am a little girl with skinny arms and a squeaky voice, which is how I got the name Squeaky. And if things get too rough, I run. And as anybody can tell you, I'm the fastest thing on two feet.

There is no track meet that I don't win the first place medal. I used to win the twenty-yard dash when I was a little kid in kindergarten. Nowadays, it's the fifty-yard dash. And tomorrow I'm subject to run the quarter-meter relay all by myself and come in first, second, and third. The big kids calls me Mercury cause I'm the swiftest thing in the neighborhood. Everybody knows that—except two people who know better, my father and me. He can beat me to Amsterdam Avenue with me having a two fire-hydrant headstart and him running with his hands in his pockets and whistling. But that's private information. Cause can you imagine some thirty-five-year-old man stuffing himself into PAL shorts to race little kids? So as far as everyone's concerned, I'm the fastest and that goes for Gretchen, too, who has put out the tale that she is going to win the first-place medal this year. Ridiculous. In the second place, she's got short legs. In the third place, she's got freckles. In the first place, no one can beat me and that's all there is to it.

I'm standing on the corner admiring the weather and about to take a stroll down Broadway so I can practice my breathing exercises, and I've got Raymond walking on the inside close to the buildings, cause he's subject to fits of fantasy and starts thinking he's a circus performer and that the curb is a tightrope strung high in the air. And sometimes after a rain he likes to step down off his tightrope right into the gutter and slosh around getting his shoes and cuffs wet. Then I get hit when I get home. Or sometimes if you don't watch him he'll dash across traffic to the island in the middle of Broadway and give the pigeons a fit. Then I have to go behind him apologizing to all the old people sitting around trying to get some sun and getting all upset with the pigeons fluttering around them, scattering their newspaper and upsetting the wax-paper lunches in their laps. So I keep Raymond on the inside of me, and he plays like he's driving a stagecoach which is O.K. by me so long as he doesn't run me over or interrupt my breathing exercises, which I have to do on account of I'm serious about my running, and I don't care who knows it.

Now some people like to act like things come easy to them, won't let on that they practice. Not me. I'll high-prance down 34th Street like a rodeo pony to keep my knees strong even if it does get my mother uptight so that she walks ahead like she's not with me, don't know me, is all by herself on a shopping trip, and I am somebody else's crazy child. Now you take Cynthia Procter for instance. She's just the opposite. If there's a test tomorrow, she'll say something like, "Oh, I guess I'll play handball this afternoon and watch television tonight," just to let you know she ain't thinking about the test. Or like last week when she won the spelling bee for the millionth time, "A good thing you got 'receive,' Squeaky, cause I would have got it wrong. I completely forgot about the spelling bee." And she'll clutch the lace on her blouse like it was a narrow escape. Oh, brother. But of course when I pass her house on my early morning trots around the block, she is practicing the scales on the piano over and over and over and over. Then in music class she always lets herself get bumped around so she falls accidentally on purpose onto the piano stool and is so surprised to find herself sitting there that she decides just for fun to try out the ole keys. And what do you know—Chopin's waltzes just spring out of her fingertips and she's the most surprised thing in the world. A regular prodigy. I could kill people like that. I stay up all night studying the words for the spelling bee. And you can see me any time of the day practicing running. I never walk if I can trot, and shame on Raymond if he can't keep up. But of course he does, cause if he hangs back someone's liable to walk up to him and get smart, or take his allowance from him, or ask him where he got that great big pumpkin head. People are so stupid sometimes.

So I'm strolling down Broadway breathing out and breathing in on counts of seven, which is my lucky number, and here comes Gretchen and her sidekicks: Mary Louise, who used to be a friend of mine when she first moved to Harlem from Baltimore and got beat up by everybody till I took up for her on account of her mother and my mother used to sing in the same choir when they were young girls, but people ain't grateful, so now she hangs out with the new girl Gretchen and talks about me like a dog; and Rosie, who is as fat as I am skinny and has a big mouth where Raymond is concerned and is too stupid to know that there is not a big deal of difference between herself and Raymond and that she can't afford to throw stones. So they are steady coming up Broadway and I see right away that it's going to be one of those Dodge City scenes cause the street ain't that big and they're close to the buildings just as we are. First I think I'll step into the candy store and look over the new comics and let them pass. But that's chicken and I've got a reputation to consider. So then I think I'll just walk straight on through them or even over them if necessary. But as they get to me, they slow down. I'm ready to fight, cause like I said I don't feature a whole lot of chit-chat, I much prefer to just knock you down right from the jump and save everybody a lotta precious time.

"You signing up for the May Day races?" smiled Mary Louise, only it's not a smile at all. A dumb question like that doesn't deserve an answer. Besides, there's just me and Gretchen standing there really, so no use wasting my breath talking to shadows.

"I don't think you're going to win this time," says Rosie, trying to signify with her hands on her hips all salty, completely forgetting that I have whupped her behind many times for less salt than that.

"I always win cause I'm the best," I say straight at Gretchen who is, as far as I'm concerned, the only one talking in this ventriloquist-dummy routine. Gretchen smiles, but it's not a smile, and I'm thinking that girls never really smile at each other because they don't know how and don't want to know how and there's probably no one to teach us how, cause grown-up girls don't know either. Then they all look at Raymond who has just brought his mule team to a standstill. And they're about to see what trouble they can get into through him.

"What grade you in now, Raymond?"

"You got anything to say to my brother, you say it to me, Mary Louise Williams of Raggedy Town, Baltimore."

"What are you, his mother?" sasses Rosie.

"That's right, Fatso. And the next word out of anybody and I'll be *their* mother too." So they just stand there and Gretchen shifts from one leg to the other and so do they. Then Gretchen puts her hands on her hips and is about to say something with her freckle-face self but doesn't. Then she walks around me looking me up and down but keeps walking up Broadway, and her sidekicks follow her. So me and Raymond smile at each other and he says "Gidyap" to his team and I continue with my breathing exercises, strolling down Broadway toward the ice man on 145th with not a care in the world cause I am Miss Quicksilver herself.

I take my time getting to the park on May Day because the track meet is the last thing on the program. The biggest thing on the program is the May Pole dancing, which I can do without, thank you, even if my mother thinks it's a shame I don't take part and act like a girl for a change. You'd think my mother'd be grateful not to have to make me a white organdy dress with a big satin sash and buy me new white baby-doll shoes that can't be taken out of the box till the big day. You'd think she'd be glad her daughter ain't out there prancing around a May Pole getting the new clothes all dirty and sweaty and trying to act like a fairy or a flower or whatever you're supposed to be when you should be trying to be yourself, whatever that is, which is, as far as I'm concerned, a poor Black girl who really can't afford to buy shoes and a new dress you only wear once a lifetime cause it won't fit next year.

I was once a strawberry in a Hansel and Gretel pageant when I was in nursery school and didn't have no better sense than to dance on tiptoe with my arms in a circle over my head doing umbrella steps and being a perfect fool just so my mother and father could come dressed up and clap. You'd think they'd know better than to encourage that kind of nonsense. I am not a strawberry. I do not dance on my toes. I run. That is what I am all about. So I always come late to the May Day program, just in time to get my number pinned on and lay in the grass till they announce the fifty-yard dash.

I put Raymond in the little swings, which is a tight squeeze this year and will be impossible next year. Then I look around for Mr. Pearson, who pins the numbers on. I'm really looking for Gretchen if you want to know the truth, but she's not around. The park is jam-packed. Parents in hats and corsages and breast-pocket handkerchiefs peeking up. Kids in white dresses and light-blue suits. The parkees unfolding chairs and chasing the rowdy kids from Lenox as if they had no right to be there. The big guys with their caps on backwards, leaning against the fence swirling the basketballs on the tips of their fingers, waiting for all these crazy people to clear out the park so they can play. Most of the kids in my class are carrying bass drums and glockenspiels and flutes. You'd think they'd put in a few bongos or something for real like that.

Then here comes Mr. Pearson with his clipboard and his cards and pencils and whistles and safety pins and fifty million other things he's always dropping all over the place with his clumsy self. He sticks out in a crowd because he's on stilts. We used to call him Jack and the Beanstalk to get him mad. But I'm the only one that can outrun him and get away, and I'm too grown for that silliness now.

"Well, Squeaky," he says, checking my name off the list and handing me the number seven and two pins. And I'm thinking he's got no right to call me Squeaky, if I can't call him Beanstalk.

"Hazel Elizabeth Deborah Parker," I correct him and tell him to write it down on his board.

Toni Cade Bambara

"Well, Hazel Elizabeth Deborah Parker, going to give someone else a break this year?" I squint at him real hard to see if he is seriously thinking I should lose the race on purpose just to give someone else a break. "Only six girls running this time," he continues, shaking his head sadly like it's my fault all of New York didn't turn out in sneakers. "That new girl should give you a run for your money." He looks around the park for Gretchen like a periscope in a submarine movie. "Wouldn't it be a nice gesture if you were . . . to ahhh . . ."

I give him such a look he couldn't finish putting that idea into words. Grown-ups got a lot of nerve sometimes. I pin number seven to myself and stomp away, I'm so burnt. And I go straight for the track and stretch out on the grass while the band winds up with "Oh, the Monkey Wrapped His Tail Around the Flag Pole," which my teacher calls by some other name. The man on the loudspeaker is calling everyone over to the track and I'm on my back looking at the sky, trying to pretend I'm in the country, but I can't, because even grass in the city feels hard as sidewalk, and there's just no pretending you are anywhere but in a "concrete jungle" as my grandfather says.

The twenty-yard dash takes all of two minutes cause most of the little kids don't know no better than to run off the track or run the wrong way or run smack into the fence and fall down and cry. One little kid, though, has got the good sense to run straight for the white ribbon up ahead so he wins. Then the second-graders line up for the thirty-yard dash and I don't even bother to turn my head to watch cause Raphael Perez always wins. He wins before he even begins by psyching the runners, telling them they're going to trip on their shoelaces and fall on their faces or lose their shorts or something, which he doesn't really have to do since he is very fast, almost as fast as I am. After that is the forty-yard dash which I used to run when I was in first grade. Raymond is hollering from the swings cause he knows I'm about to do my thing cause the man on the loudspeaker has just announced the fifty-yard dash, although he might just as well be giving a recipe for angel food cake 'cause you can hardly make out what he's saying for the static. I get up and slip off my sweatpants and then I see Gretchen standing at the starting line, kicking her legs out like a pro. Then as I get into place I see that ole Raymond is on line on the other side of the fence, bending down with his fingers on the ground just like he knew what he was doing. I was going to yell at him but then I didn't. It burns up your energy to holler.

Raymond's Run

Every time just before I take off in a race, I always feel like I'm in a dream, the kind of dream you have when you're sick with fever and feel all hot and weightless. I dream I'm flying over a sandy beach in the early morning sun, kissing the leaves of the trees as I fly by. And there's always the smell of apples, just like in the country when I was little and used to think I was a choo-choo train, running through the fields of corn and chugging up the hill to the orchard. And all the time I'm dreaming this, I get lighter and lighter until I'm flying over the beach again, getting blown through the sky like a feather that weighs nothing at all. But once I spread my fingers in the dirt and crouch over the Get on Your Mark, the dream goes and I am solid again and am telling myself, Squeaky you must win, you must win, you are the fastest thing in the world, you can even beat your father up Amsterdam if you really try. And then I feel my weight coming back just behind my knees then down to my feet then into the earth and the pistol shot explodes in my blood and I am off and weightless again, flying past the other runners, my arms pumping up and down and the whole world is quiet except for the crunch as I zoom over the gravel in the track. I glance to my left and there is no one. To the right, a blurred Gretchen, who's got her chin jutting out as if it would win the race all by itself. And on the other side of the fence is Raymond with his arms down to his side and the palms tucked up behind him, running in his very own style, and it's the first time I ever saw that and I almost stop to watch my brother Raymond on his first run. But the white ribbon is bouncing toward me and I tear past it, racing into the distance till my feet with a mind of their own start digging up footfuls of dirt and brake me short. Then all the kids standing on the side pile on me, banging me on the back and slapping my head with their May Day programs, for I have won again and everybody on 151st Street can walk tall for another year.

"In first place . . ." the man on the loudspeaker is clear as a bell now. But then he pauses and the loudspeaker starts to whine. Then static. And I lean down to catch my breath and here comes Gretchen walking back, for she's overshot the finish line too, huffing and puffing with her hands on her hips taking it slow, breathing in steady time like a real pro and I sort of like her a little for the first time. "In first place . . ." and then three or four voices get all mixed up on the loudspeaker and I dig my sneaker into the grass and stare at Gretchen who's staring back, we both wondering just who did win. I can hear old Beanstalk arguing with the man on the loudspeaker and then a few others running their mouths about what the stopwatches say. Then I hear Raymond yanking at the fence to call me and I wave to shush him, but he keeps rattling the fence like a gorilla in a cage like in them gorilla movies, but then like a dancer or something he starts climbing up nice and easy but very fast. And it occurs to me, watching how smoothly he climbs hand over hand and remembering how he looked running with his arms down to his side and with the wind pulling his mouth back and his teeth showing and all, it occurred to me that Raymond would make a very fine runner. Doesn't he always keep up with me on my trots? And he surely knows how to breathe in counts of seven cause he's always doing it at the dinner table, which drives my brother George up the wall. And I'm smiling to beat the band cause if I've lost this race, or if me and Gretchen tied, or even if I've won, I can always retire as a runner and begin a whole new career as a coach with Raymond as my champion. After all, with a little more study I can beat Cynthia and her phony self at the spelling bee. And if I bugged my mother, I could get piano lessons and become a star. And I have a big rep as the baddest thing around. And I've got a roomful of ribbons and medals and awards. But what has Raymond got to call his own?

So I stand there with my new plans, laughing out loud by this time as Raymond jumps down from the fence and runs over with his teeth showing and his arms down to the side, which no one before him has quite mastered as a running style. And by the time he comes over I'm jumping up and down so glad to see him—my brother Raymond, a great runner in the family tradition. But of course everyone thinks I'm jumping up and down because the men on the loudspeaker have finally gotten themselves together and compared notes and are announcing "In first place—Miss Hazel Elizabeth Deborah Parker." (Dig that.) "In second place—Miss Gretchen P. Lewis." And I look over at Gretchen wondering what the "P" stands for. And I smile. Cause she's good, no doubt about it. Maybe she'd like to help me coach Raymond; she obviously is serious about running, as any fool can see. And she nods to congratulate me and then she smiles. And I smile. We stand there with this big smile of respect between us. It's about as real a smile as girls can do for each other, considering we don't practice real smiling every day, you know, cause maybe we too busy being flowers or fairies or strawberries instead of something honest and worthy of respect . . . you know . . . like being people.

Hisaye Yamamoto

Seventeen Syllables

Hisaye Yamamoto (b. 1921), a Nisei (second-generation Japanese American) who grew up in southern California, was among the 110,000 Americans of Japanese descent imprisoned in internment camps during World War II. She became one of the first writers to write about the experience of internment, and also about the relationships between immigrants from Japan and their American-born children and grandchildren.

"Seventeen Syllables," the title story from Yamamoto's widely admired story collection *Seventeen Syllables and Other Stories*, reflects the tensions and misunderstandings between generations, and also serves as testament to a Nisei daughter's powerful love and respect for her immigrant mother. Published by the Feminist Press in the 1985 anthology *Between Mothers and Daughters: Stories Across a Generation*, edited by Susan Koppelman, the story also offers moving depictions of a girl's first love and of a woman artist struggling against—and thwarted by—the limitations placed upon her.

The first Rosie knew that her mother had taken to writing poems was one evening when she finished one and read it aloud for her daughter's approval. It was about cats, and Rosie pretended to understand it thoroughly and appreciate it no end, partly because she hesitated to disillusion her mother about the quantity and quality of Japanese she had learned in all the years now that she had been going to Japanese school every Saturday (and Wednesday, too, in the summer). Even so, her mother must have been skeptical about the depth of Rosie's understanding, because she explained afterwards about the kind of poem she was trying to write.

See, Rosie, she said, it was a *haiku*, a poem in which she must pack all her meaning into seventeen syllables only, which were divided into three lines of five, seven, and five syllables. In the one she had just read, she had tried to capture the charm of a kitten, as well as comment on the superstition that owning a cat of three colors meant good luck.

Hisaye Yamamoto

"Yes, yes, I understand. How utterly lovely," Rosie said, and her mother, either satisfied or seeing through the deception and resigned, went back to composing.

The truth was that Rosie was lazy; English lay ready on the tongue but Japanese had to be searched for and examined, and even then put forth tentatively (probably to meet with laughter). It was so much easier to say yes, yes, even when one meant no, no. Besides, this was what was in her mind to say: I was looking through one of your magazines from Japan last night, Mother, and towards the back I found some *haiku* in English that delighted me. There was one that made me giggle off and on until I fell asleep—

> *It is morning, and lo!*
> *I lie awake, comme il faut,*
> *sighing for some dough.*

Now, how to reach her mother, how to communicate the melancholy song? Rosie knew formal Japanese by fits and starts, her mother had even less English, no French. It was much more possible to say yes, yes.

It developed that her mother was writing the *haiku* for a daily newspaper, the *Mainichi Shinbun*, that was published in San Francisco. Los Angeles, to be sure, was closer to the farming community in which the Hayashi family lived and several Japanese vernaculars were printed there, but Rosie's parents said they preferred the tone of the northern paper. Once a week, the *Mainichi* would have a section devoted to *haiku*, and her mother became an extravagant contributor, taking for herself the blossoming pen name, Ume Hanazono.

So Rosie and her father lived for awhile with two women, her mother and Ume Hanazono. Her mother (Tome Hayashi by name) kept house, cooked, washed, and, along with her husband and the Carrascos, the Mexican family hired for the harvest, did her ample share of picking tomatoes out in the sweltering fields and boxing them in tidy strata in the cool packing shed. Ume Hanazono, who came to life after the dinner dishes were done, was an earnest, muttering stranger who often neglected speaking when spoken to and stayed busy at the parlor table as late as midnight scribbling with pencil on scratch paper or carefully copying characters on good paper with her fat, pale green Parker.

The new interest had some repercussions on the household routine. Before, Rosie had been accustomed to her parents and herself taking their hot baths early and going to bed almost immediately afterwards, unless her parents challenged each other to a game of flower cards or unless company dropped in. Now, if her father wanted to play cards, he had to resort to solitaire (at which he cheated fearlessly), and if a group of friends came over, it was bound to contain someone who was also writing *haiku*, and the small assemblage would be split in two, her father entertaining the non-literary members and her mother comparing ecstatic notes with the visiting poet.

If they went out, it was more of the same thing. But Ume Hanazono's life span, even for a poet's, was very brief—perhaps three months at most.

One night they went over to see the Hayano family in the neighboring town to the west, an adventure both painful and attractive to Rosie. It was attractive because there were four Hayano girls, all lovely and each one named after a season of the year (Haru, Natsu, Aki, Fuyu), painful because something had been wrong with Mrs. Hayano ever since the birth of her first child. Rosie would sometimes watch Mrs. Hayano, reputed to have been the belle of her native village, making her way about a room, stooped, slowly shuffling, violently trembling (*always* trembling), and she would be reminded that this woman, in this same condition, had carried and given issue to three babies. She would look wonderingly at Mr. Hayano, handsome, tall, and strong, and she would look at her four pretty friends. But it was not a matter she could come to any decision about.

On this visit, however, Mrs. Hayano sat all evening in the rocker, as motionless and unobtrusive as it was possible for her to be, and Rosie found the greater part of the evening practically anaesthetic. Too, Rosie spent most of it in the girls' room, because Haru, the garrulous one, said almost as soon as the bows and other greetings were over, "Oh, you must see my new coat!"

It was a pale plaid of grey, sand, and blue, with an enormous collar, and Rosie, seeing nothing special in it, said, "Gee, how nice."

"Nice?" said Haru, indignantly. "Is that all you can say about it? It's gorgeous! And so cheap, too. Only seventeen-ninety-eight, because it was a sale. The saleslady said it was twenty-five dollars regular."

"Gee," said Rosie. Natsu, who never said much and when she said anything said it shyly, fingered the coat covetously and Haru pulled it away.

"Mine," she said, putting it on. She mined in the aisle between two large beds and smiled happily. "Let's see how your mother likes it."

She broke into the front room and the adult conversation, and went to stand in front of Rosie's mother, while the rest watched from the door. Rosie's mother was properly envious. "May I inherit it when you're through with it?"

Haru, pleased, giggled and said yes, she could, but Natsu reminded her gravely from the door, "You promised me, Haru."

Everyone laughed but Natsu, who shamefacedly retreated into the bedroom. Haru came in laughing, taking off the coat. "We were only kidding, Natsu," she said. "Here, you try it on now."

After Natsu buttoned herself into the coat, inspected herself solemnly in the bureau mirror, and reluctantly shed it, Rosie, Aki, and Fuyu got their turns, and Fuyu, who was eight, drowned in it while her sisters and Rosie doubled up in amusement. They all went into the front room later, because Haru's mother quaveringly called to her to fix the tea and rice cakes and open a can of sliced peaches for everybody. Rosie noticed that her mother and Mr. Hayano were talking together at the little table—they were discussing a *haiku* that Mr. Hayano was planning to send to the *Mainichi*, while her father was sitting at one end of the sofa looking through a copy of *Life*, the new picture magazine. Occasionally, her father would comment on a photograph, holding it toward Mrs. Hayano and speaking to her as he always did—loudly, as though he thought someone such as she must surely be at least a trifle deaf also.

The five girls had their refreshments at the kitchen table, and it was while Rosie was showing the sisters her trick of swallowing peach slices without chewing (she chased each slippery crescent down with a swig of tea) that her father brought his empty teacup and untouched saucer to the sink and said, "Come on, Rosie, we're going home now."

"Already?" asked Rosie.

"Work tomorrow," he said.

He sounded irritated, and Rosie, puzzled, gulped one last yellow slice and stood up to go, while the sisters began protesting, as was their wont.

"We have to get up at five-thirty," he told them, going into the front room quickly, so that they did not have their usual chance to hang on to his hands and plead for an extension of time.

Rosie, following, saw that her mother and Mr. Hayano were sipping tea and still talking together, while Mrs. Hayano concentrated, quivering, on raising the handleless Japanese cup to her lips with both her hands and lowering it back to her lap. Her father, saying nothing, went out the door, onto the bright porch, and sat down on the steps. Her mother looked up and asked, "Where is he going?"

"Where is he going?" Rosie said. "He said we were going home now."

"Going home?" Her mother looked with embarrassment at Mr. Hayano and his absorbed wife and then forced a smile. "He must be tired," she said.

Haru was not giving up yet. "May Rosie stay overnight?" she asked, and Natsu, Aki, and Fuyu came to reinforce their sister's plea by helping her make a circle around Rosie's mother. Rosie, for once, having no desire to stay, was relieved when her mother, apologizing to the perturbed Mr. and Mrs. Hayano for her father's abruptness at the same time, managed to shake her head no at the quartet, kindly but adamant, so that they broke their circle to let her go.

Rosie's father looked ahead into the windshield as the two joined him. "I'm sorry," her mother said. "You must be tired." Her father, stepping on the starter, said nothing. "You know how I get when it's *baiku*," she continued, "I forget what time it is." He only grunted.

As they rode homeward, silently, Rosie, sitting between, felt a rush of hate for both, for her mother for begging, for her father for denying her mother. I wish this old Ford would crash, right now, she thought, then immediately, no, no, I wish my father would laugh, but it was too late: already the vision had passed through her mind of the green pickup crumpled in the dark against one of the mighty eucalyptus trees they were just riding past, of the three contorted, bleeding bodies, one of them hers.

Rosie ran between two patches of tomatoes, her heart working more rambunctiously than she had ever known it to. How lucky it was that Aunt Taka and Uncle Gimpachi had come tonight, though, how very lucky. Otherwise, she might not have really kept her half-promise to meet Jesus Carrasco. Jesus, who was going to be a senior in September at the same school she went to, and his parents were the ones helping with the tomatoes this year. She and Jesus, who hardly remembered seeing each other at Cleveland High, where there were so many other people and two whole grades between them, had become great friends this summer—he always had a joke for her when he periodically drove the loaded pickup from the fields to the shed where she was usually sorting while her mother and father did the packing, and they laughed a great deal together over infinitesimal repartee during the afternoon break for chilled watermelon or ice cream in the shade of the shed.

What she enjoyed most was racing him to see which could finished picking a double row first. He, who could work faster, would tease her by slowing down until she thought she would surely pass him this time, then speeding up furiously to leave her several sprawling vines behind. Once he had made her screech hideously by crossing over, while her back was turned, to place atop the tomatoes in her green-stained bucket a truly monstrous, pale green worm (it had looked more like an infant snake). And it was when they had finished a contest this morning, after she had pantingly pointed a green finger at the immature tomatoes evident in the lugs at the end of his row and he had returned the accusation (with justice), that he had startlingly brought up the matter of their possible meeting outside the range of both their parents' dubious eyes.

"What for?" she had asked.

"I've got a secret I want to tell you," he said.

"Tell me now," she demanded.

"It won't be ready till tonight," he said.

She laughed. "Tell me tomorrow, then."

"It'll be gone tomorrow," he threatened.

"Well, for seven hakes, what is it?" she had asked, more than twice, and when he had suggested that the packing shed would be an appropriate place to find out, she had cautiously answered maybe. She had not been certain she was going to keep the appointment until the arrival of her mother's sister and her husband. Their coming seemed a sort of signal of permission, of grace, and she had definitely made up her mind to lie and leave as she was bowing them welcome.

So, as soon as everyone appeared settled back for the evening, she announced loudly that she was going to the privy outside. "I'm going to the *benjo!*" and slipped out the door. And now that she was actually on her way, her heart pumped in such an undisciplined way that she could hear it with her ears. It's because I'm running, she told herself, slowing to a walk. The shed was up ahead, one more patch away, in the middle of the fields. Its bulk, looming in the dimness, took on a sinisterness that was funny when Rosie reminded herself that it was only a wooden frame with a canvas roof and three canvas walls that made a slapping noise on breezy days.

Jesus was sitting on the narrow plank that was the sorting platform and she went around to the other side and jumped backwards to seat herself on the rim of the packing stand. "Well, tell me," she said, without greeting, thinking her voice sounded reassuringly familiar.

"I saw you coming out the door," Jesus said. "I heard you running part of the way, too."

"Uh-huh," Rosie said, "Now tell me the secret."

"I was afraid you wouldn't come," he said.

Rosie delved around on the chicken-wire bottom of the stall for number two tomatoes, ripe, which she was sitting beside, and came up with a left-over that felt edible. She bit into it and began sucking out the pulp and seeds. "I'm here," she pointed out.

"Rosie, are you sorry you came?"

"Sorry? What for?" she said. "You said you were going to tell me something."

"I will, I will," Jesus said, but his voice contained disappointment, and Rosie, fleetingly, felt the older of the two, realizing a brand-new power which vanished without category under her recognition.

"I have to go back in a minute," she said. "My aunt and uncle are here from Wintersburg. I told them I was going to the privy."

Jesus laughed. "You funny thing," he said. "You slay me!"

"Just because you have a bathroom *inside*," Rosie said. "Come on, tell me."

Chuckling, Jesus came around to lean on the stand facing her. They still could not see each other very clearly, but Rosie noticed that Jesus became very sober again as he took the hollow tomato from her hand and dropped it back into the stall. When he took hold of her empty hand, she could find no words to protest; her vocabulary had become distressingly constricted and she thought desperately that all that remained intact now was yes and no and oh, and even these few sounds would not easily out. Thus, kissed by Jesus, Rosie fell, for the first time, entirely victim to a helplessness delectable beyond speech. But the terrible, beautiful sensation lasted no more than a second, and the reality of Jesus' lips and tongue and teeth and hands made her pull away with such strength that she nearly tumbled.

Rosie stopped running as she approached the lights from the windows of home. How long since she had left? She could not guess, but gasping yet, she went to the privy in back and locked herself in. Her own breathing deafened her in the dark, close space, and she sat and waited until she could hear at last the nightly calling of the frogs and crickets. Even then, all she could think to say was oh, my, and the pressure of Jesus' face against her face would not leave.

No one had missed her in the parlor, however, and Rosie walked in and through quickly, announcing that she was next going to take a bath. "Your father's in the bathhouse," her mother said, and Rosie, in her room, recalled that she had not seen him when she entered. There had been only Aunt Taka and Uncle Gimpachi with her mother at the table, drinking tea. She got her robe and straw sandals and crossed the parlor again to go outside. Her mother was telling them about the *haiku* competition in the *Mainichi* and the poem she had entered.

Rosie met her father coming out of the bathhouse. "Are you through, Father?" she asked. "I was going to ask you to scrub my back."

"Scrub your own back," he said shortly, going toward the main house.

"What have I done now?" she yelled after him. She suddenly felt like doing a lot of yelling. But he did not answer, and she went into the bathhouse. Turning on the dangling light, she removed her denims and T-shirt and threw them in the big carton for dirty clothes standing next to the washing machine. Her other things she took with her into the bath compartment to wash after her bath. After she had scooped a basin of hot water from the square wooden tub, she sat on the gray cement of the floor and soaped herself at exaggerated leisure, singing "Red Sails in the Sunset" at the top of her voice and using da-da-da where she suspected her words. Then, standing, still singing, for she was possessed by the notion that any attempt now to analyze would result in spoilage and she believed that the larger her volume the less she would be able to hear herself think, she obtained more hot water and poured it on until she was free of lather. Only then did she allow herself to step into the steaming vat, one leg first, then the remainder of her body inch by inch until the water no longer stung and she could move around at will.

She took a long time soaking, afterwards remembering to go around outside to stoke the embers of the tin-lined fireplace beneath the tub and to throw on a few more sticks so that the water might keep its heat for her mother, and when she finally returned to the parlor, she found her mother still talking *haiku* with her aunt and uncle, the three of them on another round of tea. Her father was nowhere in sight.

At Japanese school the next day (Wednesday, it was), Rosie was grave and giddy by turns. Preoccupied at her desk in the row for students on Book Eight, she made up for it at recess by performing wild mimicry for the benefit of her friend Chizuko. She held her nose and whined a witticism or two in what she considered was the manner of Fred Allen; she assumed intoxication and a British accent to over the climax of the Rudy Vallee recording of the pub conversation about William Ewart Gladstone; she was the child Shirley Temple piping "On the Good Ship Lollipop"; she was the gentleman soprano of the Four Inkspots trilling "If I Didn't Care." And she felt reasonably satisfied when Chizuko wept and gasped, "Oh, Rosie, you ought to be in the movies!"

Her father came after her at noon, bringing her sandwiches of minced ham and two nectarines to eat while she rode, so that she could pitch right into the sorting when they got home. The lugs were piling up, he said, and the ripe tomatoes in them would probably have to be taken to the cannery tomorrow if they were not ready for the produce haulers tonight. "This heat's not doing them any good. And we've got no time for a break today."

It *was* hot, probably the hottest day of the year, and Rosie's blouse stuck damply to her back even under the protection of the canvas. But she worked as efficiently as a flawless machine and kept the stalls heaped, with one part of her mind listening in to the parental murmuring about the heat and the tomatoes and with another part planning the exact words she would say to Jesus when he drove up with the first load of the afternoon. But when at last she saw that the pickup was coming, her hands went berserk and the tomatoes started falling in the wrong stalls, and her father said, "Hey, hey! Rosie, watch what you're doing!"

"Well, I have to go to the *benjo*," she said, hiding panic.

"Go in the weeds over there," he said, only half-joking.

"Oh, Father!" she protested.

"Oh, go on home," her mother said. "We'll make out for awhile."

In the privy, Rosie peered through a knothole toward the fields, watching as much as she could of Jesus. Happily she thought she saw him look in the direction of the house from time to time before he finished unloading and went back toward the patch where his mother and father worked. As she was heading for the shed, a very presentable black car purred up the dirt driveway to the house and its driver motioned to her. Was this the Hayashi home, he wanted to know. She nodded. Was she a Hayashi? Yes, she said, thinking that he was a good-looking man. He got out of the car with a huge, flat package and she saw that he warmly wore a business suit. "I have something here for your mother then," he said, in a more elegant Japanese than she was used to.

She told him where her mother was and he came along with her, patting his face with an immaculate white handkerchief and saying something about the coolness of San Francisco. To her surprised mother and father, he bowed and introduced himself as, among other things, the *haiku* editor of the *Mainichi Shinbun*, saying that since he had been coming as far as Los Angeles anyway, he had decided to bring her the first prize she had won in the recent contest.

"First prize?" her mother echoed, believing and not believing, pleased and overwhelmed. Handed the package with a bow, she bobbed her head up and down numerous times to express her utter gratitude.

"It is nothing much," he added, "but I hope it will serve as a token of our great appreciation for your contributions and our great admiration of your considerable talent."

"I am not worthy," she said, falling easily into his style. "It is I who should make some sign of my humble thanks for being permitted to contribute."

"No, no, to the contrary," he said, bowing again.

But Rosie's mother insisted, and then saying that she knew she was being unorthodox, she asked if she might open the package because her curiosity was so great. Certainly she might. In fact, he would like her reaction to it for, personally, it was one of his favorite Hiroshiges.

Rosie thought it was a pleasant picture, which looked to have been sketched with delicate quickness. There were pink clouds, containing some graceful calligraphy, and a sea that was a pale blue except at the edges, containing four sampans with indications of people in them. Pines edged the water and on the far-off beach there was a cluster of thatched huts towered over by pine-dotted mountains of gray and blue. The frame was scalloped and gilt.

After Rosie's mother pronounced it without peer and somewhat prodded her father into nodding agreement, she said Mr. Kuroda must at least have a cup of tea, after coming all this way, and although Mr. Kuroda did not want to impose, he soon agreed that a cup of tea would be refreshing and went along with her to the house, carrying the picture for her.

"Ha, your mother's crazy!" Rosie's father said, and Rosie laughed uneasily as she resumed judgment on the tomatoes. She had emptied six lugs when he broke into an imaginary conversation with Jesus to tell her to go and remind her mother of the tomatoes, and she went slowly.

Mr. Kuroda was in his shirtsleeves expounding some *haiku* theory as he munched a rice cake, and her mother was rapt. Abashed in the great man's presence, Rosie stood next to her mother's chair until her mother looked up inquiringly, and then she started to whisper the message, but her mother pushed her gently away and reproached, "You are not being very polite to our guest."

"Father says the tomatoes . . . " Rosie said aloud, smiling foolishly.

"Tell him I shall only be a minute," her mother said, speaking the language of Mr. Kuroda.

When Rosie carried the reply to her father, he did not seem to hear and she said again, "Mother says she'll be back in a minute."

"All right, all right," he nodded, and they worked again in silence. But suddenly, her father uttered an incredible noise, exactly like the cork of a bottle popping, and the next Rosie knew, he was stalking angrily toward the house, almost running, in fact, and she chased after him crying, "Father! Father! What are you going to do?"

He stopped long enough to order her back to the shed. "Never mind!" he shouted. "Get on with the sorting!"

And from the place in the fields where she stood, frightened and vacillating, Rosie saw her father enter the house. Soon Mr. Kuroda come out alone, putting on his coat. Mr. Kuroda got into his car and backed out down the driveway, onto the highway. Next her father emerged, also alone, something in his arms (it was the picture, she realized), and going over to the bathhouse woodpile, he threw the picture on the ground and picked up the axe. Smashing the picture, glass and all (she heard the explosion faintly), he reached over the kerosene that was used to encourage the bath fire and poured it over the wreckage. I am dreaming, Rosie said to herself, I am dreaming, but her father, having made sure that his act of cremation was irrevocable, was even then returning to the fields.

Rosie ran past him and toward the house. What had become of her mother? She burst into the parlor and found her mother at the back window, watching the dying fire. They watched together until there remained only a feeble smoke under the blazing sun. Her mother was very calm.

"Do you know why I married your father?" she said, without turning.

"No," said Rosie. It was the most frightening question she had ever been called upon to answer. Don't tell me now, she wanted to say, tell me tomorrow, tell me next week, don't tell me today. But she knew she would be told now, that the telling would combine with the other violence of the hot afternoon to level her life, her world (so various, so beautiful, so new?) to the very ground.

It was like a story out of the magazines, illustrated in sepia, which she had consumed so greedily for a period until the information had somehow reached her that those wretchedly unhappy autobiographies, offered to her as the testimonials of living men and women, were largely inventions: Her mother, at nineteen, had come to America and married her father as an alternative to suicide.

At eighteen, she had been in love with the first son of one of the well-to-do families in her village. The two had met whenever and wherever they could, secretly, because it would not have done for his family to see him favor her—her father had no money; he was a drunkard and a gambler besides. She had learned she was with child; an excellent match had already been arranged for her lover. Despised by her family, she had given premature birth to a stillborn son, who would be seventeen now. Her family did not turn her out, but she could no longer project herself in any direction without refreshing in them the memory of her indiscretion. She wrote to Aunt Taka, her favorite sister, in America, threatening to kill herself if Aunt Taka would not send for her. Aunt Taka hastily arranged a marriage with a young man, but lately arrived from Japan, of whom she knew, a young man of simple mind, it was said, but of kindly heart. The young man was never told why his unseen betrothed was so eager to hasten the day of meeting.

The story was told perfectly, with neither groping for words nor untoward passion. It was as though her mother had memorized it by heart, reciting it to herself so many times over that its nagging vileness had long since gone.

"I had a brother then?" Rosie asked, for this was what seemed to matter now; she would think about the other later, she assured herself, pushing back the illumination which threatened all that darkness that had hitherto been merely mysterious or even glamorous. "A half-brother?"

"Yes."

"I would have liked a brother," she said.

Suddenly, her mother knelt on the floor and took her by the wrists. "Rosie," she said urgently, "promise me you will never marry!" Shocked more by the request than the revelation, Rosie stared at her mother's face. Jesus, Jesus, she called silently, not certain whether she was invoking the help of the son of the Carrascos or of God, until there returned sweetly the memory of Jesus' hand, how it had touched her and where. Still her mother waited for an answer, holding her wrists so tightly that her hands were going numb. She tried to pull free. "Promise," her mother whispered fiercely, "promise." "Yes, yes, I promise," Rosie said. But for an instant she turned away, and her mother, hearing the familiar glib agreement, released her. Oh, you, you, you, her eyes and twisted mouth said, you fool. Rosie, covering her face, began at last to cry, and the embrace and consoling hand came much later than she expected.

Katharine Butler Hathaway

From The Little Locksmith

A recently rediscovered "lost" classic of women's writing and a pioneer work of disability literature, this luminous memoir by Katharine Butler Hathaway (1890–1942) was originally published, to enormous critical praise, a year after her death, and republished by The Feminist Press in 2000. At the age of five, suffering from a tubercular disease of the spine, Hathaway was strapped to a stretcher in an attempt to ward off "deformity." She remained immobile for ten years. Although her family was close and loving, a painful silence surrounded her disability.

This excerpt from *The Little Locksmith* reveals the young girl's remarkable insight into the unspoken feelings behind that silence, particularly on the day in 1910 when she finally rises to discover that in spite of the treatment, her back is hunched—like the "little locksmith" who had visited their home. (It is inspiring to note that later Hathaway would not only express, in writing, those thoughts and feelings she describes here as "locked inside," but would also have her own house on the coast of Maine, live among artistic circles in New York and Paris, and enter into a happy marriage.)

When I was fifteen this horizontal life of night and day was ended. In that year I was pronounced cured; I was to get up at last and see things from a perpendicular and movable point of view, after watching them for so long from a horizontal and fixed one. Everything would look different, of course. Also, I knew that I myself would look different standing up from the way I had looked lying down. Why, at the great age of fifteen I didn't even know how tall I was! And I had begun to wonder secretly about my back. There was that unknown territory between my shoulders where the tuberculosis had lodged and burrowed for so long. How much it had disfigured me I didn't know. As I had grown older there had been a baffling silence in regard to that side of my illness, and I never dared to ask. Nobody guessed that I was secretly worrying about it, and I could not tell them. Nobody guessed, because, I suppose, I gave the impression of being such a happy, humorous child. But when I was alone in the room I sometimes slid my hand up under me to explore that fateful part. But my hand always got strangely panic-stricken and came hurrying back without making me any wiser than before. My hand seemed to be mortally afraid of that place, which remained therefore unknown, waiting for the day when I should get up and stand plainly revealed.

Although my mother had so often told me, when I was little, how lucky I was, as I grew older she never spoke of my being lucky. Instead, quite a different feeling seemed to come over her whenever she or anybody else spoke of my "trouble" as it was called. I must first explain that when I was young my mother seemed to me dull and uninteresting compared with my father. He and I were conscious of each other, almost as lovers are. Everything he said held my attention, and was interesting and essential to me. In comparison, my mother seemed to have to think and talk about a lot of unessential things, and her real self, for me, was swamped and obscured by them. I had a feeling that she didn't like unessential things, but that she didn't quite know how to manage them easily and get them out of the way. So she labored awkwardly, directing the house and servants, and she worried, and had to go to bed with sick headaches. Sometimes I felt very maternal toward her, she had such a hard time doing things that I thought looked quite easy. My own hands were so much more skillful than hers, for instance, that if she tried to make a paper doll for me she seemed to me like a clumsy younger child. She was not an artist, or a craftsman, like the rest of us, and so she thought we were much more wonderful than we were. I never saw her eyes really shine with happiness as much as they did when she was admiring us as artists, and treasuring all the things we made. Then she made herself, in comparison, seem humble and unimportant. In matters of our conduct as human beings she was relentless, and we feared her as we feared God. We learned very young to be good and to obey and to respect our father and mother. But when she was admiring us as artists she gave us a feeling of absolute freedom from authority. We were all for weighing and criticizing each other's works. We knew to a hair's breadth which was better than another, and why. But she liked everything we did, our good things and also the ones we would have torn up and thrown away. She gathered them all together and kept and treasured them, and her eyes shone over us with a pride and a tenderness that I shall never see again.

Because of this humble uncritical attitude of hers toward art, I didn't notice her very much, and when I did I often wished that she were more exciting and knew how to do things herself. But once in a great while, when somebody spoke of my illness or she mentioned it herself, she was all changed. I couldn't very well not notice her then. A terrific wave of pain sprang up in her blue eyes, and it was evident suddenly that the pain was always there, controlled, inside her, like something terribly alive, always ready to leap up and hurt her all over again. She never cried, but her self-control was worse than crying.

"I ought never to have *let* it happen! It was wicked! Wicked!" she would burst out. And then, immediately after, I witnessed the silent and to me awful struggle as for some reason she fought against the physical symptoms of her grief. Not a tear ever succeeded in getting past the barrier of her will, and not a sob. But during those few seconds when she could not trust herself to speak, and her gentian-blue eyes were fiercely widened to prevent the tears from coming into them as she stared away from me, out of the window, anywhere, away from me, and swallowed back that great lump of sadness and forced it away down into the secret part of her being, I was awe-struck and shaken, much more than I would have been to see her yield to tears. Her secretive Spartan way made crying seem like an enemy that one must never submit to. The awesome struggle that it cost her affected me almost as if I had been forced to watch her from a distance struggling all alone with a savage animal and managing by sheer force of her will and character to keep it at bay.

When she was like that I could not very well not notice her or think she was uninteresting. Then her aliveness frightened me. And I loved her more than I could possibly have told. I felt a furious will to cherish her and protect her and never to let her suffer, when I got old enough to influence or control her. Yet I could not show her what I felt. Besides being inarticulate myself, I knew that I had seen something in her that she thought I was too young to see or even to know about, and I knew I must pretend I hadn't seen it. It was not her concern for me that made me love her so much then. It was because I saw her in the grip of essential things, and she became alive and fiery and very brave. I felt humble before her, for myself and for all the rest of us toward whom she had made herself seem unclever and unimportant.

Although I felt an almost unbearable tenderness and love for her in those moments, I felt hatred and rebellion too. I hated and rejected the idea that there was anything tragic about my illness, or that she was to blame. I was angry because when she battled with those terrible surging tears I had to battle too. Watching her, I felt a violent emotion suddenly throbbing against my throat, surging and aching in my chest. For she seemed to waken something in me that was a disgusting traitor to my conscious self, a sorrow over my own plight that leaped up out of the depth of me, and answered her with a grieving that seemed to understand and match her own. I could love her piteous sorrow for me, but I loathed and despised it in myself. And I pushed it away from me with an almost masculine strength and confidence in my own soundness and well-being. This rebellion made me appear hard and cold toward her, just at the moment when I loved her most.

Yet I always longed to know intimately and adore and caress that real fiery self of hers. Why did she hide it from her children and almost from herself? It seemed as if she thought that if she ever once let her emotion escape from under her control its poignancy would be unbearable, and would destroy her and destroy us all. Whatever the reason, when these moments arrived they passed in fierce silence and aloofness. The hearts of the mother and the child ached in pity for each other, each separate, stoical, and alone.

So, lying still and watching her, I was tense and fighting for her, helping her with all my might not to be overcome by the enemy that was trying to make us both cry and break out into sobs. I know that if anything could make her lose the battle it would be to have me be anything except the happy unconscious child she thought I was. And besides, except when she acted like this, I *was* happy. After all, what was there so sad about me and my illness? It was a mystery to me. I thought my mother's sadness must be just a phenomenon of mother love, which exaggerates everything.

When I got up at last, fifteen years old, and had learned to walk again, one day I took a hand glass and went to a long mirror to look at myself, and I went alone. I didn't want anyone, my mother least of all, to know how I felt when I saw myself for the first time. But there was no noise, no outcry; I didn't scream with rage when I saw myself. I just felt numb. That person in the mirror *couldn't* be me. I felt inside like a healthy, ordinary, lucky person—oh, not like the one in the mirror! Yet when I turned my face to the mirror there were my own eyes looking back, hot with shame. I had turned out, after all, like the little locksmith—oh, not so bad, nearly— but enough like the little locksmith to be called by that same word.

Katharine Butler Hathaway

What I felt that day did not fit in with the pleasant cheerful atmosphere of our family, any more than my horrors had fitted in. There was no place for it among us. It was something in another language. It was in the same language as my mother's suppressed panic-stricken grief, and I would have died rather than let that come to the surface of our cheerful life, for her to see and endure in me. And so from that first moment, when I did not cry or make any sound, it became impossible that I should speak of it to anyone, and the confusion and the panic of my discovery were locked inside me then and there, to be faced alone, for a very long time to come.

Here then was the beginning of my predicament. A hideous disguise had been cast over me, as if by a wicked stepmother. And I now had ahead of me, although I didn't know it, the long, blind, wistful struggle of the fairy tales. I had to wander stupidly and blindly, searching for I didn't know what, following fantastically wrong clues, until at last I might hit upon a magic that could set me free.

Jane Gould

From Juggling

In her 1997 memoir, Jane Gould (b. 1918) describes a life that paralleled and propelled many critical struggles in the contemporary women's movement. In the 1950s, despite the rewards of marriage and motherhood, Gould found herself plagued by a deepening sense that "something was missing." She took these feelings as inspiration, pioneering the middle-class "return to work" movement and becoming the first director of the history-making Barnard Women's Center.

In this excerpt from *Juggling: A Memoir of Work, Family, and Feminism,* Gould describes her adolescent struggles to break free of parental restraints, to fit in with peers, and to understand her own sexuality. In Gould's case, these struggles take place against a background of diminishing financial resources for her upper-middle-class Jewish family in the suburbs north of New York City, as the Great Depression takes hold.

After his father's death my father brought in a brother-in-law, a man with no business experience or aptitude, to be his partner. The two of them continued to run what had been a very successful business. Profits gradually began to decline, due no doubt to a combination of two inept partners and a generally deteriorating economic picture. By the time of the stock market crash in 1929, the business was in serious trouble.

The Great Depression dramatically affected our lives; yet there was never any discussion at home of our declining fortune or of what was happening in the larger world. Nevertheless, I could sense the rising tensions between my parents and could see the gradual change in the way we lived. The household staff was cut to a bare minimum, and my mother took on many of their tasks. By the time I was nine, we were sent to school on the school bus, and my mother and father started driving us to our after-school dates and other appointments.

The big change came in 1930, when I was twelve, and we transferred to public school. My father told us that this would only be for one year, until his business improved. I announced this proudly to my eighth-grade classmates. About six weeks into the first semester, a group from my class approached me saying that they had formed a club but that I was not invited to join since I was a snob. They told me they wished I would go back to private school. While this shook me up, it made me determined to adjust to this new school. By the end of the first year I would have resisted any attempt to move back to the Scarborough School, although, by then, it was also very apparent that I would remain in public school. At home there was still no discussion of the family's severe financial reversal.

Going to school in the community where we lived, within walking distance from our house, and making friends with classmates who lived in the houses that I passed every day were new and wonderful experiences for me. Although there was a "crowd" that I was never truly a part of, I did make a few close friends. One of these was Catherine Bellman, an easy-going, unpretentious girl. I spent hours at her house and loved the informal hospitality her family extended to me. She and I talked about school and also gossiped about who was popular and why. I never talked about my problems, and she didn't seem to have any, which I envied. The way Catherine's family accepted me—invited me to stay for dinner or to sleep over when they were going out—made it harder for me to understand the rigid rules in my own home. In our house, everything had to be arranged ahead of time. My mother would plan beautiful parties for special occasions like birthdays, but never encouraged the casual and often more spontaneous gatherings that I saw elsewhere.

During early adolescence and on through the next four years of high school, my goal was to be included in the social activities of the school. I did well enough in my studies, but academic success was not the key to popularity. My weekly trips to the public library continued but became secretive. God forbid that I should be called a bookworm! Being popular, being part of the mainstream, was almost all I cared about. I tried to look and sound like the other girls: to wear whatever was in vogue and to do everything I could to be accepted by the crowd. To be accepted became an obsession. I hated living in a big house at the top of a hill and wished we could live in a "regular" house with a front and backyard, surrounded by houses just like ours. I felt we were conspicuously different. My desperate need to be liked by everyone—to become like everyone else—was tantamount to waving a red flag in front of my mother. It signaled a war between us that was to last throughout my adolescence.

I must have been impossible as an adolescent. The lengths I went to in order to conform were ridiculous, but seemed deadly important. The girls I admired wore silk stockings and makeup. They even plucked their eyebrows. They went out on dates, and, by the time they were fifteen or sixteen, they went with boys who were old enough to have driver's licenses. They went to Sunday night church socials for teenagers. They had house parties when their parents were not home and stayed at school dances until midnight when their dates drove them home. Some of them even smoked.

By the time I started high school, I was very conscious of the opposite sex, and boys started asking me out to movies, parties, and various school functions. There was a new ingredient in my life: I began to experience strong new feelings that I didn't fully understand and felt like I couldn't talk about with anyone, least of all my mother. When I started to menstruate, my mother took me to see our family doctor and, in his presence, she talked a little about sex, but in a away that didn't invite further discussion. I could see how difficult it was for her to talk to me about this, and finally the doctor gave me a book about the birds and the bees. That was all the help I got from them about understanding sexuality.

I wasn't allowed to do any of the things that my friends were doing socially. Mother said she didn't care what other people did. She had her own standards and wasn't interested in keeping up with the Joneses. My father used to come and fetch me at school dances or house parties at 10:00 or 10:30 P.M., compounding the humiliation I suffered for being the only one in a short dress, so different from the grown-up, long gowns worn by all the other girls. Even when I was a senior in high school, I wasn't allowed to go out with the same boy more than once a month—anything more than this would signify "going steady," which my mother strongly disapproved of. I would sometimes get around this by having another boy come to the door to escort me and then switch dates when we got into the car.

I wore silk stockings under the lisle cotton stockings that my mother made me wear, and removed the outer stockings when I got to school. I also put on lipstick when out of sight of home, although I never plucked my eyebrows or used rouge or eye makeup. How chagrined I was when my mother drove by as I was walking home with friends, and she saw me wearing lipstick and silk stockings. For a couple of years the worse deprivation was not being permitted to go to the Sunday night church socials. It reinforced the confused feelings I had about religion and underscored that I was different.

I hated the endless pronouncements my mother made about "who we were" and about how she wasn't going to stoop to the standards of "ordinary people," even though we now went to school with the sons and daughters of local merchants, plumbers, and electricians. She placed a great weight on being an active member of the local chapter of the DAR (Daughters of the American Revolution) and was pleased to have her house and gardens used for occasional meetings. One day I came home from school and found a lively group of women, all in costumes dating back to the days of the American Revolution, having tea in the garden. At the time I didn't grasp the significance of being a member of the DAR and viewed this as further evidence of our difference. I thought my mother was a snob and linked her DAR affiliation with her general attitude of superiority. It took me many years to acknowledge that my family heritage was an interesting one.

Those years when I was growing up and rebelling were difficult for all of us. During that time my father was struggling just to eke out a living. My older brother was becoming more withdrawn and beginning to show symptoms of paranoia. These symptoms became more pronounced in his late teens, and, after a year and a half at the University of Michigan, Louis dropped out and then couldn't keep any of the several jobs my father found for him. At the age of twenty he was institutionalized in a private sanitorium. When it became clear that he was mentally ill, Louis was moved to a public institution, a good hour and a half from our home. My mother visited him weekly until he died.

During those years, my mother carried the enormous burden of keeping the house and garden going with very little household or outside help. How she managed, I will never understand. She seemed to have conquered all her earlier physical problems and showed amazing pluck, energy, and determination. She tried to sustain the style of living we had grown accustomed to. As long as we lived in the big house, appearances were important. We still used linen napkins and individual butter plates on which my mother placed perfectly made butter balls, which she had carefully rolled with wooden butter patters.

Neither of my parents ever talked to us directly about their financial problems, and I turned my back on what was happening at home. I was too self-involved to think about these changes and the meanings they held. I overheard arguments between my parents, mostly about money or about Louis, and this made me uncomfortable, but I never spoke about these feelings. I was seldom asked to help with household tasks; the message I always received was that these were grown-up matters.

The next few years brought major changes in our lives. The big house, once grand and palatial, became an albatross around my parents' necks. In 1934, when I was completing my junior year in high school and had just turned sixteen, my parents told us that we would have to move. The bank was foreclosing on the house. My mother was devastated and my father was clearly upset, but, in his usual manner, he said things would be all right very soon and that there was nothing to worry about. He had lost his business and was trying to make a living as a sales representative for a national cookie company—an unlikely occupation for this diffident, somewhat ineffectual man. He was to spend the rest of his working life tramping through city streets with a heavy bag of samples, trying to sell cookies to restaurants and to grocery stores. That this took place in the middle of a depression, which affected the lives of millions of people, didn't seem to reach us or to ease the pain in any way. I simply don't remember seeing other families in trouble. This was before the days of television, and the stories we read in the newspaper and heard on the radio about soup kitchens and long lines of unemployed seemed very remote.

By the time we were told the news, my parents had found a four-bedroom house in Briarcliff Manor, a small community a few miles from Pleasantville. I was perfectly happy to leave our house, but I was distressed that we were moving to a new community. This meant that I would have to spend my senior year at a different high school making new friends.

Our new house was, by normal standards, more than adequate, although my mother saw it as a large step down. It was situated on a pleasant, tree-lined, hilly street and was surrounded by other well-kept houses. At the top of the hill was an exclusive boarding school for girls. When school was in session, there was a constant parade of chattering young women walking up and down the street to the little village at the bottom of the hill. From time to time a few of them would stop and sit on the edge of our front lawn to listen to my brother Bob practicing and playing popular songs on his saxophone.

The rent was moderate enough to substantially reduce our living costs. We were to live there for six years, until our next move to an apartment in New York City, where we could live for considerably less money by giving up a car and cutting commuting expenses. My mother, for the first time, showed her feelings: her despair, her shame, and her displeasure with my father, whom she blamed for this change in fortune.

As an adolescent, I never understood the depth of my mother's distress or why my father was unable to honestly look at his finances. I knew that we were no longer rich and that life was difficult for both of my parents, but I connected wealth with all the values I hated and showed little sympathy for any of the changes our family was experiencing. In fact, I remember secretly vowing that I would never care about material possessions—a vow that, like many others, would become muted and modified over the years.

Mary E. Wilkins Freeman

Louisa

Mary E. Wilkins Freeman (1852–1930) began writing when financial problems in her New England family left her to support herself. The author of several novels and dozens of short stories, she became a success in her own time and, after a period of neglect, is now appreciated as a significant American writer. Freeman lived in a world where women were valued primarily as servants or ornaments. But her stories are remarkable for depicting often impoverished women whose ability to survive and flourish depends upon their creativity, intelligence, and most of all their strength of will: Freeman's heroines know their own minds.

The title character of "Louisa" is such a heroine. Determined, against all odds, to resist the pressures brought to bear by her mother, and by society at large, to marry a highly eligible suitor she does not love, Louisa will prevail through an astonishing feat of endurance.

"I don't see what kind of ideas you've got in your head, for my part." Mrs. Britton looked sharply at her daughter Louisa, but she got no response.

Louisa sat in one of the kitchen chairs close to the door. She had dropped into it when she first entered. Her hands were all brown and grimy with garden-mould; it clung to the bottom of her old dress and her coarse shoes.

Mrs. Britton, sitting opposite by the window, waited, looking at her. Suddenly Louisa's silence seemed to strike her mother's will with an electric shock; she recoiled, with an angry jerk of her head. "You don't know nothin' about it. You'd like him well enough after you was married to him," said she, as if in answer to an argument.

Louisa's face looked fairly dull; her obstinacy seemed to cast a film over it. Her eyelids were cast down; she leaned her head back against the wall.

"Sit there like a stick if you want to!" cried her mother.

Louisa got up. As she stirred, a faint earthy odor diffused itself through the room. It was like a breath from a ploughed field.

Mrs. Britton's little sallow face contracted more forcibly. "I s'pose now you're goin' back to your potater patch," said she. "Plantin' potaters out there jest like a man, for all the neighbors to see. Pretty sight, I call it."

"If they don't like it, they needn't look," returned Louisa. She spoke quite evenly. Her young back was stiff with bending over the potatoes, but she straightened it rigorously. She pulled her old hat farther over her eyes.

There was a shuffling sound outside the door and a fumble at the latch. It opened, and an old man came in, scraping his feet heavily over the threshold. He carried an old basket.

"What you got in that basket, father?" asked Mrs. Britton.

The old man looked at her. His old face had the round outlines and naïve grin of a child.

"Father, what you got in that basket?"

Louisa peered apprehensively into the basket. "Where did you get those potatoes, grandfather?" said she.

"Digged 'em." The old man's grin deepened. He chuckled hoarsely.

"Well, I'll give up if he ain't been an' dug up all them potaters you've been plantin'!" said Mrs. Britton.

"Yes, he has," said Louisa, "Oh, grandfather, didn't you know I'd jest planted those potatoes?"

The old man fastened his bleared blue eyes on her face, and still grinned.

"Didn't you know better, grandfather?" she asked again.

But the old man only chuckled. He was so old that he had come back into the mystery of childhood. His motives were hidden and inscrutable; his amalgamation with the human race was so much weaker.

"Land sakes! don't waste no more time talkin' to him," said Mrs. Britton. "You can't make out whether he knows what he's doin' or not. I've give it up. Father, you jest set them pertaters down, an' you come over here an' set down in the rockin'-chair; you've done about 'nough work to-day."

The old man shook his head with slow mutiny.

"Come right over here."

Louisa pulled at the basket of potatoes. "Let me have 'em, grandfather," said she. "I've got to have 'em."

The old man resisted. His grin disappeared, and he set his mouth. Mrs. Britton got up, with a determined air, and went over to him. She was a sickly, frail-looking woman, but the voice came firm, with deep bass tones, from her little lean throat.

"Now, father," said she, "you jest give her that basket, an' you walk across the room, and you set down in that rockin'-chair."

The old man looked down into her little, pale, wedge-shaped face. His grasp on the basket weakened. Louisa pulled it away, and pushed past out of the door, and the old man followed his daughter sullenly across the room to the rocking-chair.

The Brittons did not have a large potato field; they had only an acre of land in all. Louisa had planted two thirds of her potatoes; now she had to plant them all over again. She had gone to the house for a drink of water; her mother had detained her, and in the meantime the old man had undone her work. She began putting the cut potatoes back in the ground. She was careful and laborious about it. A strong wind, full of moisture, was blowing from the east. The smell of the sea was in it, although this was some miles inland. Louisa's brown calico skirt blew out in it like a sail. It beat her in the face when she raised her head.

"I've got to get these in to-day somehow," she muttered. "It'll rain to-morrow."

She worked as fast as she could, and the afternoon wore on. About five o'clock she happened to glance at the road—the potato field lay beside it—and she saw Jonathan Nye driving past with his gray horse and buggy. She turned her back to the road quickly, and listened until the rattle of the wheels died away. At six o'clock her mother looked out of the kitchen window and called her to supper.

"I'm comin' in a minute," Louisa shouted back. Then she worked faster than ever. At half-past six she went into the house, and the potatoes were all in the ground.

"Why didn't you come when I called you?" asked her mother.

"I had to get the potatoes in."

"I guess you wa'n't bound to get 'em all in to-night. It's kind of discouragin' when you work, an' get supper all ready, to have it stan' an hour, I call it. An' you've worked 'bout long enough for one day out in this damp wind, I should say."

Louisa washed her hands and face at the kitchen sink, and smoothed her hair at the little glass over it. She had wet her hair too, and made it look darker: it was quite a light brown. She brushed it in smooth straight lines back from her temples. Her whole face had a clear bright look from being exposed to the moist wind. She noticed it herself, and gave her head a little conscious turn.

Mary E. Wilkins Freeman

When she sat down to the table her mother looked at her with admiration, which she veiled with disapproval.

"Jest look at your face," said she; "red as a beet. You'll be a pretty-lookin' sight before the summer's out, at this rate."

Louisa thought to herself that the light was not very strong, and the glass must have flattered her. She could not look as well as she had imagined. She spread some butter on her bread very sparsely. There was nothing for supper but some bread and butter and weak tea, though the old man had his dish of Indian-meal porridge. He could not eat much solid food. The porridge was covered with milk and molasses. He bent low over it, and ate large spoonfuls with loud noises. His daughter had tied a towel around his neck as she would have tied a pinafore on a child. She had also spread a towel over the table-cloth in front of him, and she watched him sharply lest he should spill his food.

"I wish I could have somethin' to eat that I could relish the way he does that porridge and molasses," said she. She had scarcely tasted anything. She sipped her weak tea laboriously.

Louisa looked across at her mother's meagre little figure in its neat old dress, at her poor small head bending over the tea-cup, showing the wide parting in the thin hair.

"Why don't you toast your bread, mother?" said she. "I'll toast it for you."

"No, I don't want it. I'd jest as soon have it this way as any. I don't want no bread, nohow. I want somethin' to relish—a herrin', or a little mite of cold meat, or somethin'. I s'pose I could eat as well as anybody if I had as much as some folks have. Mis' Mitchell was sayin' the other day that she didn't believe but what they had butcher's meat up to Mis' Nye's every day in the week. She said Jonathan he went to Wolfsborough and brought home great pieces in a market-basket every week. I guess they have everything."

Louisa was not eating much herself, but now she took another slice of bread with a resolute air. "I guess some folks would be thankful to get this," said she.

"Yes, I s'pose we'd ought to be thankful for enough to keep us alive, anybody takes so much comfort livin'," returned her mother, with a tragic bitterness that sat oddly upon her, as she was so small and feeble. Her face worked and strained under the stress of emotion; her eyes were full of tears; she sipped her tea fiercely.

"There's some sugar," said Louisa. "We might have had a little cake."

The old man caught the word. "Cake?" he mumbled, with pleased inquiry, looking up, and extending his grasping old hand.

"I guess we ain't got no sugar to waste in cake," returned Mrs. Britton. "Eat your porridge, father, an' stop teasin'. There ain't no cake."

After supper Louisa cleared away the dishes; then she put on her shawl and hat.

"Where you goin'?" asked her mother.

"Down to the store."

"What for?"

"The oil's out. There wasn't enough to fill the lamps this mornin'. I ain't had a chance to get it before."

It was nearly dark. The mist was so heavy it was almost rain. Louisa went swiftly down the road with the oil-can. It was a half-mile to the store where the few staples were kept that sufficed the simple folk in this little settlement. She was gone a half-hour. When she returned, she had besides the oil-can a package under her arm. She went into the kitchen and set them down. The old man was asleep in the rocking-chair. She heard voices in the adjoining room. She frowned, and stood still, listening.

"Louisa!" called her mother. Her voice was sweet, and higher pitched than usual. She sounded the *i* in Louisa long.

"What say?"

"Come in here after you've taken your things off."

Louisa knew that Jonathan Nye was in the sitting-room. She flung off her hat and shawl. Her old dress was damp, and had still some earth stains on it; her hair was roughened by the wind, but she would not look again in the glass; she went into the sitting-room just as she was.

"It's Mr. Nye, Louisa," said her mother, with effusion.

"Good-evenin', Mr. Nye," said Louisa.

Jonathan Nye half arose and extended his hand, but she did not notice it. She sat down peremptorily in a chair at the other side of the room; Jonathan had the one rocking-chair; Mrs. Britton's frail little body was poised anxiously on the hard rounded top of the carpet-covered lounge. She looked at Louisa's dress and hair, and her eyes were stony with disapproval, but her lips still smirked, and she kept her voice sweet. She pointed to a glass dish on the table.

"See what Mr. Nye has brought us over, Louisa," said she.

Louisa looked indifferently at the dish.

"It's honey," said her mother; "some of his own bees made it. Don't you want to get a dish an' taste of it? One of them little glass sauce dishes."

"No, I guess not," replied Louisa. "I never cared much about honey. Grandfather'll like it."

The smile vanished momentarily from Mrs. Britton's lips, but she recovered herself. She arose and went across the room to the china closet. Her set of china dishes was on the top shelves, the lower were filled with books and papers. "I've got somethin' to show you, Mr. Nye," said she.

This was scarcely more than a hamlet, but it was incorporated, and had its town books. She brought forth a pile of them, and laid them on the table beside Jonathan Nye. "There," said she, "I thought mebbe you'd like to look at these." She opened one and pointed to the school report. This mother could not display her daughter's accomplishment to attract a suitor, for she had none. Louisa did not own a piano or organ; she could not paint; but she had taught school acceptably for eight years—ever since she was sixteen—and in every one of the town books was testimonial to that effect, intermixed with glowing eulogy. Jonathan Nye looked soberly through the books; he was a slow reader. He was a few years older than Louisa, tall and clumsy, long-featured and long-necked. His face was a deep red with embarrassment, and it contrasted oddly with his stiff dignity of demeanor.

Mrs. Britton drew a chair close to him while he read. "You see, Louisa taught that school for eight year," said she; "an' she'd be teachin' it now if Mr. Mosely's daughter hadn't grown up an' wanted somethin' to do, an' he put her in. He was committee, you know. I dun' know as I'd ought to say so, an' I wouldn't want you to repeat it, but they do say Ida Mosely don't give very good satisfaction, an' I guess she won't have no reports like these in the town books unless her father writes 'em. See this one."

Jonathan Nye pondered over the fulsome testimony to Louisa's capability, general worth, and amiability, while she sat in sulky silence at the farther corner of the room. Once in a while her mother, after a furtive glance at Jonathan, engrossed in a town book, would look at her and gesticulate fiercely for her to come over, but she did not stir. Her eyes were dull and quiet, her mouth closely shut; she looked homely. Louisa was very pretty when pleased and animated, at other times she had a look like a closed flower. One could see no prettiness in her.

Jonathan Nye read all the school reports; then he arose heavily. "They're real good," said he. He glanced at Louisa and tried to smile; his blushes deepened.

"Now don't be in a hurry," said Mrs. Britton.

"I guess I'd better be goin'; mother's alone."

"She won't be afraid; it's jest on the edge of the evenin'."

"I don't know as she will. But I guess I'd better be goin'." He looked hesitatingly at Louisa.

She arose and stood with an indifferent air.

"You'd better set down again," said Mrs. Britton.

"No; I guess I'd better be goin'." Jonathan turned towards Louisa. "Good-evenin'," said he.

"Good-evenin'."

Mrs. Britton followed him to the door. She looked back and beckoned imperiously to Louisa, but she stood still. "Now come again, do," Mrs. Britton said to the departing caller. "Run in any time; we're real lonesome evenin's. Father he sets an' sleeps in his chair, an' Louisa an' me often wish somebody'd drop in; folks round here ain't none too neighborly. Come in any time you happen to feel like it, an' we'll both of us be glad to see you. Tell your mother I'll send home that dish to-morrer, an' we shall have a real feast off that beautiful honey."

When Mrs. Britton had fairly shut the outer door upon Jonathan Nye, she came back into the sitting-room as if her anger had a propelling power like steam upon her body.

"Now, Louisa Britton," said she, "you'd ought to be ashamed of yourself—ashamed of yourself! You've treated him like a—hog!"

"I couldn't help it."

"Couldn't help it! I guess you could treat anybody decent if you tried. I never saw such actions! I guess you needn't be afraid of him. I guess he ain't so set on you that he means to ketch you up an' run off. There's other girls in town full as good as you an' better-lookin'. Why didn't you go an' put on your other dress? Comin' into the room with that old thing on, an' your hair all in a frowse! I guess he won't want to come again."

"I hope he won't," said Louisa, under her breath. She was trembling all over.

"What say?"

"Nothin'."

"I shouldn't think you'd want to say anything, treatin' him that way, when he came over and brought all that beautiful honey! He was all dressed up, too. He had on a real nice coat—cloth jest as fine as it could be, an' it was kinder damp when he come in. Then he dressed all up to come over here this rainy night an' bring this honey." Mrs. Britton snatched the dish of honey and scudded into the kitchen with it. "Sayin' you didn't like honey after he took all that pains to bring it over!" said she. "I'd said I liked it if I'd lied up hill and down." She set the dish in the pantry. "What in creation smells so kinder strong an' smoky in here?" said she, sharply.

"I guess it's the herrin'. I got two or three down to the store."

"I'd like to know what you got herrin' for?"

"I thought maybe you'd relish 'em."

"I don't want no herrin's, now we've got this honey. But I don't know that you've got money to throw away." She shook the old man by the stove into partial wakefulness, and steered him into his little bedroom off the kitchen. She herself slept in one off the sitting-rooms; Louisa's room was up-stairs.

Louisa lighted her candle and went to bed, her mother's scolding voice pursuing her like a wrathful spirit. She cried when she was in bed in the dark, but she soon went to sleep. She was too healthfully tired with her out-door work not to. All her young bones ached with the strain of manual labor as they had ached many a time this last year since she had lost her school.

The Brittons had been and were in sore straits. All they had in the world was this little house with the acre of land. Louisa's meagre school money had bought their food and clothing since her father died. Now it was almost starvation for them. Louisa was struggling to wrest a little sustenance from their stony acre of land, toiling like a European peasant woman, sacrificing her New England dignity. Lately she had herself split up a cord of wood which she had bought of a neighbor, paying for it in installments with work for his wife.

"Think of a school-teacher goin' into Mis' Mitchell's house to help clean!" said her mother.

She, although she had been of poor, hard-working people all her life, with the humblest surroundings, was a born aristocrat, with that fiercest and most bigoted aristocracy which sometimes arises from independent poverty. She had the feeling of a queen for a princess of the blood about her school-teacher daughter; her working in a neighbor's kitchen was as galling and terrible to her. The projected marriage with Jonathan Nye was like a royal alliance for the good of the state. Jonathan Nye was the only eligible young man in the place; he was the largest land-owner; he had the best house. There were only himself and his mother; after her death the property would all be his. Mrs. Nye was an older woman than Mrs. Britton, who forgot her own frailty in calculating their chances of life.

"Mis' Nye is considerable over seventy," she said often to herself; "an' then Jonathan will have it all."

She saw herself installed in that large white house as reigning dowager. All the obstacle was Louisa's obstinacy, which her mother could not understand. She could see no fault in Jonathan Nye. So far as absolute approval went, she herself was in love with him. There was no more sense, to her mind, in Louisa's refusing him than there would have been in a princess refusing the fairy prince and spoiling the story.

"I'd like to know what you've got against him," she said often to Louisa.

"I ain't got anything against him."

"Why don't you treat him different, then, I want to know?"

"I don't like him." Louisa said "like" shamefacedly, for she meant love, and dared not to say it.

"*Like!* Well, I don't know nothin' about such likin's as some pretend to, an' I don't want to. If I see anybody is good an' worthy, I like 'em, an' that's all there is about it."

"I don't—believe that's the way you felt about—father," said Louisa, softly, her young face flushed red.

"Yes, it was. I had some common-sense about it."

And Mrs. Britton believed it. Many hard middle-aged years lay between her and her own love-time, and nothing is so changed by distance as the realities of youth. She believed herself to have been actuated by the same calm reason in marrying young John Britton, who had had fair prospects, which she thought should actuate her daughter in marrying Jonathan Nye.

Louisa got no sympathy from her, but she persisted in her refusal. She worked harder and harder. She did not spare herself in doors or out. As the summer wore on her face grew as sunburnt as a boy's, her hands were hard and brown. When she put on her white dress to go to meeting on a Sunday there was a white ring around her neck where the sun had not touched it. Above it her face and neck showed browner. Her sleeves were rather short, and there were also white rings above her brown wrists.

"You look as if you were turnin' Injun by inches," said her mother.

Louisa, when she sat in the meeting-house, tried slyly to pull her sleeves down to the brown on her wrists; she gave a little twitch to the ruffle around her neck. Then she glanced across, and Jonathan Nye was looking at her. She thrust her hands, in their short-wristed, loose cotton gloves, as far out of the sleeves as she could; her brown wrists showed conspicuously on her white lap. She had never heard of the princess who destroyed her beauty that she might not be forced to wed the man whom she did not love, but she had something of the same feeling, although she did not have it for the sake of any tangible lover. Louisa had never seen anybody whom she would have preferred to Jonathan Nye. There was no other marriageable young man in the place. She had only her dreams, which she had in common with other girls.

That Sunday evening before she went to meeting her mother took some old wide lace out of her bureau drawer. "There," said she, "I'm goin' to sew this in your neck an' sleeves before you put your dress on. It'll cover up a little; it's wider than the ruffle."

"I don't want it in," said Louisa.

"I'd like to know why not? You look like a fright. I was ashamed of you this mornin'."

Louisa thrust her arms into the white dress sleeves peremptorily. Her mother did not speak to her all the way to meeting. After meeting, Jonathan Nye walked home with them, and Louisa kept on the other side of her mother. He went into the house and stayed an hour. Mrs. Britton entertained him, while Louisa sat silent. When he had gone, she looked at her daughter as if she could have used bodily force, but she said nothing. She shot the bolt of the kitchen door noisily. Louisa lighted her candle. The old man's loud breathing sounded from his room; he had been put to bed for safety before they went to meeting; through the open windows sounded the loud murmur of the summer night, as if that, too, slept heavily.

"Good-night, mother," said Louisa, as she went up-stairs; but her mother did not answer.

The next day was very warm. This was an exceptionally hot summer. Louisa went out early; her mother would not ask her where she was going. She did not come home until noon. Her face was burning; her wet dress clung to her arms and shoulders.

"Where have you been?" asked her mother.

"Oh, I've been out in the field."

"What field?"

"Mr. Mitchell's."

"What have you been doin' out there?"

"Rakin' hay."

"Rakin' hay with the men?"

"There wasn't anybody but Mr. Mitchell and Johnny. Don't, mother!"

Mrs. Britton had turned white. She sank into a chair. "I can't stan' it nohow," she moaned. "All the daughter I've got."

"Don't, mother! I ain't done any harm. What harm is it? Why can't I rake hay as well as a man? Lots of women do such things, if nobody round here does. He's goin' to pay me right off, and we need the money. Don't, mother!" Louisa got a tumbler of water. "Here, mother, drink this."

Mrs. Britton pushed it away. Louisa stood looking anxiously at her. Lately her mother had grown thinner than ever; she looked scarcely bigger than a child. Presently she got up and went to the stove.

"Don't try to do anything, mother; let me finish getting dinner," pleaded Louisa. She tried to take the pan of biscuits out of her mother's hands, but she jerked it away.

The old man was sitting on the door-step, huddled up loosely in the sun, like an old dog.

"Come, father," Mrs. Britton called, in a dry voice, "dinner's ready— what there is of it!"

The old man shuffled in, smiling.

There was nothing for dinner but the hot biscuits and tea. The fare was daily becoming more meagre. All Louisa's little hoard of school money was gone, and her earnings were very uncertain and slender. Their chief depen- dence for food through the summer was their garden, but that had failed them in some respects.

One day the old man had come in radiant, with his shaking hands full of potato blossoms; his old eyes twinkled over them like a mischievous child's. Reproaches were useless; the little potato crop was sadly damaged. Lately, in spite of close watching, he had picked the squash blossoms, pil- ing them in a yellow mass beside the kitchen door. Still, it was nearly time for the pease and beans and beets; they would keep them from starvation while they lasted.

But when they came, and Louisa could pick plenty of green food every morning, there was still a difficulty: Mrs. Britton's appetite and digestion were poor; she could not live upon a green-vegetable diet; and the old man missed his porridge, for the meal was all gone.

One morning in August he cried at the breakfast-table like a baby, because he wanted his porridge, and Mrs. Britton pushed away her own plate with a despairing gesture.

"There ain't no use," said she. "I can't eat no more garden-sauce nohow. I don't blame poor father a mite. You ain't got no feelin' at all."

"I don't know what I can do; I've worked as hard as I can," said Louisa, miserably.

"I know what you can do, and so do you."

"No, I don't, mother," returned Louisa, with alacrity. "He ain't been here for two weeks now, and I saw him with my own eyes yesterday carryin' a dish into the Moselys', and I knew 'twas honey. I think he's after Ida."

"Carryin' honey into the Moselys'? I don't believe it."

"He was; I saw him."

"Well, I don't care if he was. If you're a mind to act decent now, you can bring him round again. He was dead set on you, an' I don't believe he's changed round to that Mosely girl as quick as this."

"You don't want me to ask him to come back here, do you?"

"I want you to act decent. You can go to meetin' to-night, if you're a mind to—I sha'n't go; I ain't got strength 'nough—an' 'twouldn't hurt you none to hang back a little after meetin', and kind of edge round his way. 'Twouldn't take more'n a look."

"Mother!"

"Well, I don't care. 'Twouldn't hurt you none. It's the way more'n one girl does, whether you believe it or not. Men don't do all the courtin'—not by a long shot. 'Twon't hurt you none. You needn't look so scart."

Mrs. Britton's own face was a burning red. She looked angrily away from her daughter's honest, indignant eyes.

"I wouldn't do such a thing as that for a man I liked," said Louisa; "and I certainly sha'n't for a man I don't like."

"Then me an' your grandfather'll starve," said her mother; "that's all there is about it. We can't neither of us stan' it much longer."

"We could—"

"Could what?"

"Put a—little mortgage on the house."

Mrs. Britton faced her daughter. She trembled in every inch of her weak frame. "Put a mortgage on this house, an' by-an'-by not have a roof to cover us! Are you crazy? I tell you what 'tis, Louisa Britton, we may starve, your grandfather an' me, an' you can follow us to the graveyard over there, but there's only one way I'll ever put a mortgage on this house. If you have Jonathan Nye, I'll ask him to take a little one to tide us along an' get your weddin' things."

"Mother, I'll tell you what I'm goin' to do."

"What?"

"I am goin' to ask Uncle Solomon."

"I guess when Solomon Mears does anythin' for us you'll know it. He never forgave your father about that wood lot, an' he's hated the whole of us ever since. When I went to his wife's funeral he never answered when I spoke to him. I guess if you go to him you'll take it out in goin'."

Louisa said nothing more. She began clearing away the breakfast dishes and setting the house to rights. Her mother was actually so weak that she could scarcely stand, and she recognized it. She had settled into the rocking-chair, and leaned her head back. Her face looked pale and sharp against the dark calico-cover.

When the house was in order, Louisa stole up-stairs to her own chamber. She put on her clean old blue muslin and her hat, then she went slyly down and out the front way.

It was seven miles to her uncle Solomon Mears's, and she had made up her mind to walk them. She walked quite swiftly until the house windows were out of sight, then she slackened her pace a little. It was one of the fiercest dog-days. A damp heat settled heavily down upon the earth; the sun scalded.

At the foot of the hill Louisa passed a house where one of her girl acquaintances lived. She was going in the gate with a pan of early apples. "Hullo, Louisa," she called.

"Hullo, Vinnie."

"Where you goin'?"

"Oh, I'm goin' a little way."

"Ain't it awful hot? Say, Louisa, do you know Ida Mosely's cuttin' you out?"

"She's welcome."

Mary E. Wilkins Freeman

The other girl, who was larger and stouter than Louisa, with a sallow, unhealthy face, looked at her curiously. "I don't see why you wouldn't have him," said she. "I should have thought you'd jumped at the chance."

"Should you if you didn't like him, I'd like to know?"

"I'd like him if he had such a nice house and as much money as Jonathan Nye," returned the other girl.

She offered Louisa some apples, and she went along the road eating them. She herself had scarcely tasted food that day.

It was about nine o'clock; she had risen early. She calculated how many hours it would take her to walk the seven miles. She walked as fast as she could to hold out. The heat seemed to increase as the sun stood higher. She had walked about three miles when she heard wheels behind her. Presently a team stopped at her side.

"Good-mornin'," said an embarrassed voice.

She looked around. It was Jonathan Nye, with his gray horse and light wagon.

"Good-mornin'," said she.

"Goin' far?"

"A little ways."

"Won't you—ride?"

"No, thank you. I guess I'd rather walk."

Jonathan Nye nodded, made an inarticulate noise in his throat, and drove on. Louisa watched the wagon bowling lightly along. The dust flew back. She took out her handkerchief and wiped her dripping face.

It was about noon when she came in sight of her uncle Solomon Mears's house in Wolfsborough. It stood far back from the road, behind a green expanse of untrodden yard. The blinds on the great square front were all closed; it looked as if everybody were away. Louisa went around to the side door. It stood wide open. There was a thin blue cloud of tobacco smoke issuing from it. Solomon Mears sat there in the large old kitchen smoking his pipe. On the table near him was an empty bowl; he had just eaten his dinner of bread and milk. He got his own dinner, for he had lived alone since his wife died. He looked at Louisa. Evidently he did not recognize her.

"How do you do, Uncle Solomon?" said Louisa.

"Oh, it's John Britton's daughter! How d'ye do?"

He took his pipe out of his mouth long enough to speak, then replaced it. His eyes, sharp under their shaggy brows, were fixed on Louisa; his broad bristling face had a look of stolid rebuff like an ox; his stout figure, in his soiled farmer dress, surged over his chair. He sat full in the doorway. Louisa standing before him, the perspiration trickling over her burning face, set forth her case with a certain dignity. This old man was her mother's nearest relative. He had property and to spare. Should she survive him, it would be hers, unless willed away. She, with her unsophisticated sense of justice, had a feeling that he ought to help her.

The old man listened. When she stopped speaking he took the pipe out of his mouth slowly, and stared gloomily past her at his hay field, where the grass was now a green stubble.

"I ain't got no money I can spare jest now," said he. "I s'pose you know your father cheated me out of consider'ble once?"

"We don't care so much about money, if you have got something you could spare to—eat. We ain't got anything but garden-stuff."

Solomon Mears still frowned past her at the hay field. Presently he arose slowly and went across the kitchen. Louisa sat down on the door-step and waited. Her uncle was gone quite a while. She, too, stared over at the field, which seemed to undulate like a lake in the hot light.

"Here's some things you can take, if you want 'em," said her uncle, at her back.

She got up quickly. He pointed grimly to the kitchen table. He was a deacon, an orthodox believer; he recognized the claims of the poor, but he gave alms as a soldier might yield up his sword. Benevolence was the result of warfare with his own conscience.

On the table lay a ham, a bag of meal, one of flour, and a basket of eggs.

"I'm afraid I can't carry 'em all," said Louisa.

"Leave what you can't then." Solomon caught up his hat and went out. He muttered something about not spending any more time as he went.

Louisa stood looking at the packages. It was utterly impossible for her to carry them all at once. She heard her uncle shout to some oxen he was turning out of the barn. She took up the bag of meal and the basket of eggs and carried them out to the gate; then she returned, got the flour and ham, and went with them to a point beyond. Then she returned for the meal and eggs, and carried them past the others. In that way she traversed the seven miles home. The heat increased. She had eaten nothing since morning but the apples that her friend had given her. Her head was swimming, but she kept on. Her resolution was as immovable under the power of the sun as a rock. Once in a while she rested for a moment under a tree, but she soon

Mary E. Wilkins Freeman

arose and went on. It was like a pilgrimage, and the Mecca at the end of the burning, desert-like road was her own maiden independence.

It was after eight o'clock when she reached home. Her mother stood in the doorway watching for her, straining her eyes in the dusk.

"For goodness sake, Louisa Britton! where have you been?" she began; but Louisa laid the meal and eggs down on the step.

"I've got to go back a little ways," she panted.

When she returned with the flour and ham, she could hardly get into the house. She laid them on the kitchen table, where her mother had put the other parcels, and sank into a chair.

"Is this the way you've brought all these things home?" asked her mother.

Louisa nodded.

"All the way from Uncle Solomon's?"

"Yes."

Her mother went to her and took her hat off. "It's a mercy if you ain't got a sunstroke," said she, with a sharp tenderness. "I've got somethin' to tell you. What do you s'pose has happened? Mr. Mosely has been here, an' he wants you to take the school again when it opens next week. He says Ida ain't very well, but I guess that ain't it. They think she's goin' to get somebody. Mis' Mitchell says so. She's been in. She says he's carryin' things over there the whole time, but she don't b'lieve there's anything settled yet. She says they feel so sure of it they're goin' to have Ida give the school up. I told her I thought Ida would make him a good wife, an' she was easier suited than some girls. What do you s'pose Mis' Mitchell says? She says old Mis' Nye told her that there was one thing about it: if Jonathan had you, he wa'n't goin' to have me an' father hitched on to him; he'd look out for that. I told Mis' Mitchell that I guess there wa'n't none of us willin' to hitch, you nor anybody else. I hope she'll tell Mis' Nye. Now I'm a-goin' to turn you out a tumbler of milk—Mis' Mitchell she brought over a whole pitcherful; says she's got more'n they can use—they ain't got no pig now—an' then you go an' lay down on the sittin'-room lounge, an' cool off; an' I'll stir up some porridge for supper, an' boil some eggs. Father'll be tickled to death. Go right in there. I'm dreadful afraid you'll be sick. I never heard of anybody doin' such a thing as you have."

Louisa drank the milk and crept into the sitting-room. It was warm and close there, so she opened the front door and sat down on the step. The twilight was deep, but there was a clear yellow glow in the west. One great star had come out in the midst of it. A dewy coolness was spreading over everything. The air was full of bird calls and children's voices. Now and then there was a shout of laughter. Louisa leaned her head against the door-post.

The house was quite near the road. Some one passed—a man carrying a basket. Louisa glanced at him, and recognized Jonathan Nye by his gait. He kept on down the road towards the Moselys', and Louisa turned again from him to her sweet, mysterious, girlish dreams.

Part Two

Teachers and Friends

Marjorie Agosín

From A Cross and a Star

Marjorie Agosín (b. 1955), a poet, essayist, critic, international activist, and chair of the Spanish department at Wellesley College, left her homeland of Chile to settle with her family in the United States, in exile from the brutal dictatorship of Augusto Pinochet. The experience of exile and of political and cultural oppression, with particular sympathy for the experience of women, has informed much of her work: in poetry and prose, she has paid homage to women ranging from Anne Frank to the Mothers of the Disappeared. She has described her own family's journeys of exile in two memoirs: *Always from Somewhere Else: A Memoir of My Chilean Jewish Father* (1998) and *A Cross and a Star: Memoirs of a Jewish Girl in Chile* (1995).

In *A Cross and a Star,* Agosín tells the life story of her mother, who grew up, the daughter of European Jews, in a small Chilean town during the World War II era. Writing in the voice of her mother, she describes a childhood in "an unseemly and noisy house in southern Chile, [in] a town with fifty Nazis and three Jewish families." In this excerpt, she recalls the warm and mystical childhood world created by the family's cook, Carmen Carrasco.

Carmen Carrasco

After the dawn of the earthquake in 1930 the entire city of Chillán looked like a cemetery of the dead and the living, a real mixture of bones and corpses, only a howl of voices resembling a pack of hounds more than the sound of relatives entangled in those bundles of skin and bones. Carmen Carrasco spoke with the dignity of those who suffer and of those who love. We listened to her, shuddering from terror, and we felt a fear that was infinitely delicious.

Carmen Carrasco arrived at Osorno in one of those trains that the government provided to help relief victims. Among her only possessions was a chicken, Daniela, who had stayed tangled in one of her shawls, thus avoiding being split in two by the treacherous rubble of earth. She also carried with her a handful of salt, a candle, and sugar, the only elements necessary for survival and for making a home. With her belongings she ended up at the hospice of Holy Savior of the Tomb Hospital where she was able to rest, shut her eyes, and learn to pray for the living.

Her prayers were composed of a perpetual melody and rhythm that awoke the interest of Rosaura, our washerwoman, hospitalized for an infection of the jaw even though she barely talked. The two discovered each other to be wise and generous. Rosaura offered to share her bed with her in the small room in the back of the house of her employers, but Carmen Carrasco, with her usual generosity, asked her instead for a job.

I remember that Carmen Carrasco arrived in the month of September with her crimson-stained, bandaged arm and with some strange cigarette butts resting against her temples. At that time spring began to unveil itself and signs of happiness and of colors, like greens and yellows, began to appear along the countryside. Carmen curtsied before my mother, and she in turn remembered her first kiss on the hand by her husband, Joseph. It was then that she decided to accept her as a maid. However, both women came to love each other, to share memories, and to mix country herbs with Jewish recipes.

Carmen Carrasco lived with us for forty years. She protected me from evil spirits and from cadets, she was my confidante, she kept my lipstick hidden in the wooden electrical meter, she waited for my late arrivals next to the fireplace, and her hands slid over my skin practicing an exorcism that resembled matters of happiness more than of demons.

Carmen Carrasco protected me from love sickness. With her by my side, I learned to dry herbs and to convert them into special remedies used for curing ailments. I also learned to thrash trees on Saint John's Eve. Furtively she brought my brother and me to the town church, and with holy water she frightened us about evil omens. This is why she preferred to save me and carry me in her lap to the thresholds of a religion that I also loved, because I liked the sinister peace of the candles and the smell of death from burning incense.

Gazes

Carmencha will not stop looking at us; her eyes are like two strange, sharp-sighted fireflies, those fireflies that only shine with the arrival of the dead. It is so strange for me to see her squatting next to the water. I see her toss away some herbs to cure love sickness and I watch her prepare a potion of nuts, raisins, and meat juice, curled up and lost in her woolen shawls, soaked by a long sorrow resembling innundations and earthquakes.

My mother often tells us how Camencita lost her son Hector in the earthquake of Chillán when the earth constricted. It divided in two, creating fissures in the sidewalks and clouds of dust and awakening even the irascible dead. Wrapped up in her shawls and clothed in the rubble, she stooped over looking for them, her husband, Hector, and her son, Hector II. All she found was a fistful of earth which she carried in her apron pockets. All she found was a handful of sorrows before departing from the countryside in the solitude of the blood.

Baths

We loved the kitchen with its enormous wood-burning stove where we ceremoniously performed the ritual of our weekly baths. My brother, who always had grafts of earth, lizards, and eucalyptus in his hair, went first. Carmencha eagerly would throw wooden sticks under the unsteady and restless caldron and only after the water would make strange gurgling noises would we begin to enter the balsamic power of its tepid depths. In the distance, very close to the pantry, my mother would observe us. She always had an absent look about her and seemed like a lonely princess watching two savage children submersed in a grimy tub.

Carmencha would tell us that we should hurry to frighten away the always present bats that lived in the rear of the house, and we would only think about the next week's bath and the enormous caldrons of water. Our red and sweaty faces would drop into the profound sleep of children or insomniacs. Only then did I discover that my body was unlike that of my brother, filled with soft, docile, and smooth protuberances, shifting in step with the water's movements and to the rhythms of a flesh resembling sponges.

I wasn't afraid to look at myself because the rippling water elongated my forms and made me grow. Underneath the water I imagined a kingdom and a home without a leaky ceiling and without bats where the sun entered with rage, where the rain was merely a Sunday diversion, where my chores included reading stories to my brother, and where by looking at myself in the mirror, I could pretend to be a princess, distant like my mother, imagining happiness in a bathtub.

Blue Kitchen

The smoke entered flurrying through the blue room. Carmencita Carrasco liked to paint the kitchen in a shade of bluish blue not for reasons having to do with calm or melancholy but because she assured us that those colors drove away the flies. The thick mist of things at rest and cooking, the gigantic pieces of chicken, the profound sweetness of oregano and parsley, filtered through the terrifying and dazzling kitchen. The doors remained hermetically sealed because of that terrifying fear of air currents, which according to Carmen Carrasco, made the mouth sag and the neck permanently bend making love become a lament resembling the sadness of bereavement.

Filling ourselves with the luke-warmness of fear and delight, we would prepare to listen to her tales of ghosts and of princesses kidnapped on Saint John's Eve, on enormous white horses with two heads. There was a fireplace in the kitchen, restless and bare, making swirling noises similar to the sounds of birds and swallows. And there was also the never absent shared mate, to kill sorrows, accentuate deliriums, soothe the heart, and cure the misfortunes of love. And all of us, my sisters, the maids of the block in the obscurity of the blue room, with that half sharp and hoarse voice of Carmen Carrasco summoning the ghosts, the dead who floated scorched behind the earthquakes of Chillán, were numb with fear, a fear that made us slumber off to sleep to the vapor of the beautiful things. Sometimes Carmen Carrasco would pull out a chicken leg from among the bubbling vapors of the pot, and we would all chew on it together, ignorant of what are called foreign microbes, of colds bewitched in the delights of phantasmagoria; together we were submerged in a blanket of smoke, in a breath of mist, and the voice of Carmen Carrasco continued rocking back and forth like the deep rivers, like mirrors that end up tossing out our soul.

Carmencha Carmencha

Carmencha Carrasco liked Saint John's Eve because in the immensity of the Chilean sky and beyond all human frontiers, it was possible to invoke the spirit of the dead, making Hector, her son lost in the earthquake, approach to kiss her on the tip of the nose and making the night a pool filled with magical wonders.

A Cross and a Star

On the eve of the hallowed night, Carmen Carrasco would give herself a long bath. She perfumed herself with mint leaves and sprigs of anise and at this time would remove the potato peels that she always wore between her temples to cure the evil eye and fright.

My brother and I would accompany her to the countryside where she would thrash the trees in order to summon fertile growing seasons. After repeating the exorcisms of the night, we would go to her room in the most remote and dark corner of the house, where we would bathe in a festival of transparency and light. All the candles, all the tomatoes and oranges were placed around her beech wood bed. Then we would look at each other before the mirror and she would swear that she could see the shadow of death forecasting good luck.

Shawls

At dusk when the sky seemed like a veil of microscopic stars, we approached her small room always situated near the corner of the kitchen and dark zones. There she could be found in her roundness, bound to a toasty warm coal-burning stove with tenuous flames that reminded us of rituals and phantoms. She wore her familiar shawl, lead-colored and tattered by the many years of pleasure that had given it a color resembling life and the earth.

My brother and I entered her room and snuggled next to her smelling of cigarette smoke. We liked her pock-marked skin resembling dreams and children's illnesses that store and gather the secrets of sickness.

She also embraced us and we remained together in the disquieting darkness for a long time. Mama Carmencita was wrapped in her old, threadbare shawl. She placed little pieces of crumpled cigarettes on her temples and fine-tuned her voice like a doleful knife in the immense night as she prepared to tell us a very long and delicate story. She always began by telling us that we should preserve a respect and silence for the storyteller because if we didn't, her words would turn into black birds.

My brother and I also embraced each other and listened to her, silhouetted by the smoke and spellbinding words. We would fall asleep next to the coal stove, next to the cracked walls in the room of Mama Carmencita, the servant of my parents and of my Grandmother Helena, who was for us a light amid the mirrors of war.

Carmencita

Carmencita Carrasco appears behind the night with her enchanting scissors cutting scraps of life and making curtains resembling rainbows and incantations. She likes percale, poplin, and cobalt blue linen cloth and makes us clothes for traveling in imaginary and imagined carriages as she covers us with shawls to astound us before love and its splendors. Carmen Carrasco's clothing drapes itself over her tired body after sleep and long walks. We still preserve the red and greenish curtains, the shawls, and the apron filled with coriander, and sometimes when I am sleepy, I begin to dream about that wardrobe that protected all of my gazes, that helped me in despair and filled me with sunlight and clarity.

Shirley Geok-lin Lim

From Among the White Moon Faces

Shirley Lim (b. 1944), a fiction writer, poet, critic, activist, and professor of English and women's studies at the University of California, Santa Barbara, has also written often on the effects of emigration and exile, tracing the interactions between cultures in her native Malaysia and in the United States. Born of Chinese descent in a Southeast Asian country under British colonial rule (and under the American cultural influence that would lead her to be named after Shirley Temple), Lim was left to unravel the meaning of her complex cultural identity. She also faced the challenge of shaping her own female identity, after her mother's desertion of the family left her to travel the road to womanhood unaccompanied.

In this excerpt from her 1996 memoir, *Among the White Moon Faces: An Asian-American Memoir of Homelands*, Lim pays homage to the nuns at her all-girl Catholic school in Malacca, Malaysia. Providing both negative role models in the form of strict authoritarianism, and positive role models in the form of self-sufficiency and intellectual vigor, they are credited by Lim with having "brought me to rebellion and to literature."

A pomegranate tree grew in a pot on the open-air balcony at the back of the second floor. It was a small skinny tree, even to a small skinny child like me. It had many fruits, marble-sized, dark green, shiny like overwaxed coats. Few grew to any size. The branches were sparse and graceful, as were the tear-shaped leaves that fluttered in the slightest breeze. Once a fruit grew round and large, we watched it every day. It grew lighter, then streaked with yellow and red. Finally we ate it, the purple and crimson seeds bursting with a tart liquid as we cracked the dry tough skin into segments to be shared by our many hands and mouths.

We were many. Looking back it seems to me that we had always been many. Beng was the fierce brother, the growly eldest son. Chien was the gentle second brother, born with a squint eye. Seven other children followed after me: Jen, Wun, Wilson, Hui, Lui, Seng, and Marie, the last four my half-siblings. I was third, the only daughter through a succession of eight boys and, as far as real life goes, measured in rice bowls and in the bones of morning, I have remained an only daughter in my memory.

We were as many as the blood-seeds we chewed, sucked, and spat out, the indigestible cores pulped and gray while their juice ran down our chins and stained our mouths with triumphant color. I still hold that crimson in memory, the original color of Chinese prosperity and health, now transformed to the berry shine of wine, the pump of blood in test tubes and smeared on glass plates to prophesy one's future from the wriggles of a virus. My Chinese life in Malaysia up to 1969 was a pomegranate, thickly seeded.

When Beng and Chien began attending the Bandar Hilir Primary School, they brought home textbooks, British readers with thick linen-rag covers, strong slick paper, and lots of short stories and poems accompanied by colorful pictures in the style of Aubrey Beardsley. The story of the three Billy Goats Gruff who killed the Troll under the bridge was stark and compressed, illustrated by golden kids daintily trotting over a rope bridge and a dark squat figure peering from the ravine below. Wee Willie Winkie ran through a starry night wearing only a white night cap and gown. The goats, the troll, and Willie Winkie were equally phantasms to me, for whoever saw anything like a flowing white gown on a boy or a pointy night cap in Malaya?

How to explain the disorienting power of story and picture? Things never seen or thought of in Malayan experience took on a vividness that ordinary life could not possess. These British childhood texts materialized for me, a five- and six-year-old child, the kind of hyperreality that television images hold for a later generation, a reality, moreover, that was consolidated by colonial education.

At five, I memorized the melody and lyrics to "The Jolly Miller" from my brother's school rendition:

There lived a jolly miller once
Along the River Dee.

He worked and sang from morn till night,
No lark more blithe than he.
And this the burden of his song
As always used to be,
I care for nobody, no not I,
And nobody cares for me.

It was my first English poem, my first English song, and my first English lesson. The song ran through my head mutely, obsessively, on hundreds of occasions. What catechism did I learn as I sang the words aloud? I knew nothing of millers or of larks. As a preschool child, I ate bread, that exotic food, only on rare and unwelcome occasions. The miller working alone had no analogue in the Malayan world. In Malacca, everyone was surrounded by everyone else. A hawker needed his regular customers, a storefront the stream of pedestrians who shopped on the move. Caring was not a concept that signified. Necessity, the relations between and among many and diverse people, composed the bonds of Malaccan society. Caring denoted a field of choice, of individual voluntary action, that was foreign to family, the place of compulsory relations. Western ideological subversion, cultural colonialism, whatever we call those forces that have changed societies under forced political domination, for me began with something as simple as an old English folk song.

The pomegranate is a fruit of the East, coming originally from Persia. The language of the West, English, and all its many manifestations in stories, songs, illustrations, films, school, and government, does not teach the lesson of the pomegranate. English taught me the lesson of the individual, the miller who is happy alone, and who affirms the principle of not caring for community. Why was it so easy for me to learn that lesson? Was it because within the pomegranate's hundreds of seeds is also contained the drive for singularity that will finally produce one tree from one seed? . . .

I have seen myself not so much sucking at the teat of British colonial culture as actively appropriating those aspects of it that I needed to escape that other familial/gender/native culture that violently hammered out only one shape for self. I actively sought corruption to break out of the pomegranate shell of being Chinese and girl.

It was the convent school that gave me the first weapons with which to wreck my familial culture. On the first day, [our housekeeper,] Ah Chan took me, a six-year-old, in a trishaw to the Convent of the Holy Infant Jesus. She waited outside the classroom the entire day with a *chun*, a tiffin carrier, filled with steamed rice, soup, and meat, fed me this lunch at eleven-thirty, then took me home in a trishaw at two. I wore a starched blue pinafore over a white cotton blouse and stared at the words, *See Jane run. Can Jane run? Jane can run.* After the first week, I begged to attend school without Ah Chan present. Baba drove me to school after he dropped my older brothers at their school a mile before the convent; I was now, like my brothers, free of domestic female attachment.

The convent school stood quiet and still behind thick cement walls that hid the buildings and its inhabitants from the road and muffled the sounds of passing traffic. The high walls also served to snuff out the world once you entered the gates, which were always kept shut except at the opening and closing of the school day. Shards of broken bottles embedded in the top of the walls glinted in the hot tropical sunshine, a provocative signal that the convent women were daily conscious of dangers intruding on their seclusion. For the eleven years that I entered through those gates, I seldom met a man on the grounds, except for the Jesuit brought to officiate at the annual retreat. A shared public area was the chapel, a small low dark structure made sacred by stained-glass windows, hard wooden benches, and the sacristy oil lamp whose light was never allowed to go out. The community was allowed into the chapel every Sunday to attend the masses held for the nuns and the orphans who lived in the convent.

But if the convent closed its face to the town of men and unbelievers, it lay open at the back to the Malacca Straits. Every recess I joined hundreds of girls milling at the canteen counters for little plates of noodles, curry puffs stuffed with potatoes, peas and traces of meat, and vile orange-colored sugared drinks. The food never held me for long. Instead I spent recess by the sea wall, a stone barrier free of bristling glass. Standing before the sandy ground that separated the field and summerhouse from the water, I gazed at high tide as the waves threw themselves against the wall with the peculiar repeated whoosh and sigh that I never wearied of hearing. Until I saw the huge pounding surf of the Atlantic Ocean, I believed all the world's water to be dancing, diamond-bright surfaced, a hypnotic meditative space in which shallow and deep seemed one and the same. Once inside the convent gates, one was overtaken by a similar sense of an overwhelming becalmedness, as if one had fallen asleep, out of worldliness, and entered the security of a busy dream.

During recess the little girls sang, "In and out the window, in and out the window, as we have done before," and skipped in and out of arching linked hands, in a mindless pleasure of repeated movement, repeating the desire for safety, for routine, and for the linked circular enclosure of the women's community that would take me in from six to seventeen.

I also learned to write the alphabet. At first, the gray pencil wouldn't obey my fingers. When the little orange nub at the end of the pencil couldn't erase the badly made letter, I wetted a finger with spit, rubbed hard, and then blubbered at the hole I had made in the paper. Writing was fraught with fear. I cried silently as I wrestled with the fragile paper that wouldn't sit still and that crushed and tore under my palm.

My teacher was an elderly nun of uncertain European nationality, perhaps French, who didn't speak English well. She spoke with a lisp, mispronounced my name, calling me "Chérie" instead of Shirley, and, perhaps accordingly, showed more affection to me than to the other children in her class. Sister Josie was the first European I knew. Even in her voluminous black robes and hood, she was an image of powder-white and pink smiles. Bending over my small desk to guide my fingers, and peering into my teary eyes, she spoke my name with a tender concern. She was my first experience of an enveloping, unconditional, and safe physical affection. She smelled sweet, like fresh yeast, and as I grew braver each day and strayed from my desk, she would upbraid me in the most remorseful of tones, "Chérie," which carried with it an approving smile.

In return I applied myself to Jane and Dick and Spot and to copying the alphabet letter by letter repeatedly. Sister Josie couldn't teach anything beyond the alphabet and simple vocabulary. In a few years, she was retired to the position of gatekeeper at the chapel annex. When I visited her six years later, as a child of twelve, at the small annex in which a store of holy pictures, medals, and lace veils were displayed for sale, Sister Josie's smile was still as fond. But to my mature ears, her English speech was halting, her grammar and vocabulary fractured. It was only to a six-year-old new to English that dear Sister Josie could have appeared as a native speaker of the English language.

It was my extreme good fortune to have this early missionary mother.

Her gentle, undemanding care remains memorialized as a type of human relation not found in the fierce self-involvements of my family. My narrowly sensory world broadened not only with the magical letters she taught that spelled lives beyond what my single dreaming could imagine, but differently with her gentle greetings, in her palpable affection.

Nurturing is a human act that overleaps categories, but it is not free of history. It is not innocent. For the next eleven years nuns like Sister Josie broke down the domain of my infancy. Leaving the Bata shop and entering the jagged glass—edged walls of the convent, I entered a society far removed from Baba and Emak.

The nuns wore the heavy wool habit of the missionary, full black blouses with wide sleeves like bat wings, long voluminous black skirts, black stockings, and shoes. Deep white hoods covered their heads and fell over their shoulders, and a white skull cap came down over their brows. Inexplicably they were collectively named "the French Convent," like a French colony or the foreign legion, but they were not chiefly white or European. Even in the early 1950s, some were Chinese and Eurasian sisters.

Yet, despite their uniform habits and sisterly titles, a ranking regulated by race was obvious, even to the youngest Malayan child. Mother Superior was always white. A few white sisters, Sister Sean, Sister Patricia, and Sister Peter, taught the upper grades; or they performed special duties, like Sister Maria who gave singing lessons, or Sister Bernadette, who taught cooking and controlled the kitchen and the canteen.

Sister Maria was the only woman who was recognizably French. Her accent was itself music to us as she led us through years of Scottish and Irish ballads. No one asked why "Ye Banks and Braes of Bonnie Doon" or "The Minstrel Boy" formed our music curriculum, why Indian, Eurasian, Malay, and Chinese children should be singing, off-key, week after week in a faintly French-accented manner the melancholic attitudes of Celtic gloom. . . .

Of the nonmissionary teachers from Malacca, many were Eurasian, and a few were Indian and Chinese. The sole Malay teacher appeared only after the British ceded independence to the Federation of Malaya in 1957. Chik Guru taught us the Malay language in my last two years at the convent, just as now in the United States in many colleges and universities, the only African-American or Latino or Asian-American professor a student may meet teaches African-American or Latino or Asian-American studies. Up to the end of the 1950s, and perhaps right up to the violence of the May 13 race riots in 1969, the educational structure in Malaya was British colonial.

My first inkling of race preference was formed by these earliest teachers. In primary school, my teachers were almost all European expatriates or native-born Eurasian Catholics bearing such Iberian and Dutch names as De Souza, DeWitt, Minjoot, Aerea, and De Costa. They were the descendants of Portuguese soldiers and sailors who had captured Malacca from the Malay Sultanate in 1511, when Portugal was a small, poorly populated state. Expanding into the Spice Islands in the East, the governor-generals of the Indies encouraged intermarriage between Portuguese males and native women, thus seeding the loyal settler population with Portuguese mestizos. The Portuguese governed Malacca for 130 years. When the forces of the Dutch East India Company captured the port and its fortress in 1641, they found a garrison there of some 260 Portuguese soldiers, reinforced with a mestizo population of about two to three thousand fighting men. For over four hundred years, the mestizos of Malacca had identified themselves as Portuguese.

The Eurasian teachers were physically distinguished from me. I learned this in Primary Two with Mrs. Damien, a white-haired, very large woman whose fat dimpled arms fascinated me. While she demonstrated how to embroider a daisy stitch as we crowded around her chair, I poked my finger into the dimples and creases that formed in the pale flesh that flowed over her shoulders and sagged in her upper arms. She was a fair Eurasian who dressed as a British matron, in sleeveless flowered print frocks with square-cut collars for coolness. Her exposed arms and chest presented dazzling mounds of white flesh that aroused my ardent admiration. I do not remember learning anything else in her class.

A few Eurasian girls were among my classmates. While they were not as coddled as the white daughters of plantation managers, they had an air of ease and inclusion that I envied. Their hair, which often had a copper sheen to it, was braided, while we Chinese girls had black, pudding-bowl cropped hair. By the time we were twelve and thirteen, and still flat-chested, they had budded into bosomy women whose presence in Sunday masses attracted the attention of young Catholic males. The royal blue pleated pinafores that covered our prim skinny bodies like cardboard folded teasingly over their chests and hips. The difference between us and the early maturity of Eurasian girls was a symptom of the difference between our Chinese Malaccan culture and that dangerous Western culture made visible in their lushness. They were overtly religious, controlled by their strict mothers and the Ten Commandments that we had all memorized by preadolescence. But their breasts and hips that made swing skirts swing pronounced them ready for that unspoken but pervasive excitement we knew simply as "boys."

The convent held a number of orphans, girls abandoned as babies on the convent doorsteps, or given over to the nuns to raise by relatives too poor to pay for their upkeep. During school hours these "orphaned" girls were indistinguishable from the rest of us. They wore the school uniforms, white short-sleeved blouses under sleeveless blue linen smocks that were fashioned with triple overpleats on both sides so that burgeoning breasts were multiply overlayered with folds of starched fabric. But once school hours were over they changed into pink or blue gingham dresses that buttoned right up to the narrow Peter Pan collars. Those loose shapeless dresses, worn by sullen girls who earned their keep by helping in the kitchen and laundry, formed some of my early images of a class to be shunned.

Instead I longed to be like the privileged boarders, almost all of whom were British, whose parents lived in remote and dangerous plantations or administrative outposts in the interior. These girls wore polished black leather shoes and fashionable skirts and blouses after school. In our classes, they sang unfamiliar songs, showed us how to dance, jerking their necks like hieroglyphic Egyptians. In the convent classroom where silence and stillness were enforced as standard behavior, they giggled and joked, shifting beams of sunshine, and were never reprimanded. To every schoolgirl it was obvious that something about a white child made the good nuns benevolent.

The Chinese nuns and teachers looked like us, yet they had social status and power.

Even as some teachers acted badly, in ways that suggested they were not infallible, we were told that teachers were objects of reverence: they could do no wrong. Many teachers were openly unfair and harsh, yet at the same time we were ceaselessly indoctrinated with their moral superiority.

My lessons in the pedagogy of terror began in Primary Three, when our teacher, Mrs. Voon, asked if any of us had played the Ouija board. Ignorant of the game we all answered in the negative. She chose two of us, her best pupils, to report this to Sister Arthur who was investigating the matter. Pleased at being let out of the classroom even for a short errand, we ran to the Primary Five classroom, where Sister Arthur, a dark-complexioned Chinese nun with pronounced flat cheekbones and owlish glasses, was teaching. When I announced that no one in *our* class had ever played with a Ouija board, Sister Arthur's gaze bore down on me. "No, no," she exclaimed, "your teacher sent you here because you-oo are the one who has played the game!" I protested that it was not so; she only had to ask Mrs. Voon herself. "No, no, I know how wicked you are, I can see it for myself. You-oo are the one who has been playing this devil's board." I burst into tears, but Sister Arthur held firm. "You are not getting out of my class. You are a liar and you'll stay here until I decide what to do with you." She sent my companion to report to Mrs. Voon that I was detained, and I stood sobbing in front of the older children for the rest of the school day. It was only later in the afternoon that Sister Arthur sent me away. "I hope you have learned your lesson now," she said, and I worried for weeks about what that lesson could be.

Mrs. Voon never explained what had happened, and it seemed to me that only I knew that a horrible injustice had occurred. I hated Sister Arthur from then on, and remember hardening myself for years as her pupil. She taught art for all classes from Primary Four upwards, and there was no way convent girls could have avoided being in Sister Arthur's class at least once a week until they left the school.

Sister Arthur was vigilant against any form of talk during her class hours, and irrepressible child that I was, I could not help occasionally whispering words to the girls around me. Turning around quick as a gekko from the blackboard where she was writing directions, she would command me to stand up on the desk chair. Then, selecting a stick of chalk, she strolled up to me and asked me to place the chalk upright in my mouth. While the jaws ached from the forced open position, my saliva flowed copiously. To avoid the humiliation of slobbering over my pinafore, I worked my throat and kept swallowing my own bodily fluid. As the minutes changed into hours, the chalk disintegrated with the saliva and I kept choking down this foul combination of spit and gritty chalk, until such time as she allowed me down from my public perch.

My first meeting with Sister Arthur coincided with the year that my father lost his shop on Kampong Pantai, we lost our home, moved back to Grandfather's house on Heeren Street, and my mother left us for Singapore. In a year of such misery, I turned Sister Arthur into a joke, Old Battleax. Her penetrating voice was to be immediately exorcised with ridicule. Her myopic gaze allegedly unearthing evil thoughts in our faces taught me that the convent, like my own disintegrated family, held no certainty of trust or goodness.

In one sense Sister Arthur was correct. Though I had not used a Ouija board, I was full of questions that no known spirits in my family or in the convent could answer. I talked back to my teachers not because I was defiant but because my thoughts in response to their actions and statements appeared irresistibly logical. It always surprised me when teachers were offended by my answers and remarks, though they were frequently, it is true, unsolicited. I did not understand why they were angry, even inflamed, when I said something that appeared to me obviously correct. This pattern of punishment in the convent school for speaking what appeared transparently true continued for years.

The first time I understood fully that, unlike other children, I lacked the self-protective skill of silence, I had just turned fourteen. Until then I believed what the good nuns had repeated often, that I was a "naughty" child. The many disciplinary occasions that saw me standing for hours outside a classroom door or writing hundreds of lines of what I should or should not do, I believed, were directly related to my "stubborn" spirit. Although Sister Arthur was wrong to punish me for something I hadn't done, her act did not signify that I had not deserved punishment, since I was in any case a "naughty" child.

But at fourteen, one could become a "bad" girl. Mrs. Ladd, who was held in greater awe as one of the few British teachers in the secondary school, was upset because none of us had completed the class assignment. She was especially provoked by Millie, a timid Chinese orphan boarder, whom she accused of talking, and therefore not paying attention in her English-language class. Mrs. Ladd became so incensed that she left the classroom to call Mother Superior Paul to speak to us, a terrifying prospect.

In Mrs. Ladd's absence, a hubbub ensued. She had never assigned us the exercise she was now accusing us of not completing. Also, poor Millie, who was crying furiously, had not been talking. Too timid ever to break rules, she had been hushing us just as Mrs. Ladd had stalked through the door. We decided that we had to tell Mrs. Ladd the truth: she had made a mistake, and we all knew it. I asked for a show of hands of those who would stand up with me to offer this information to Mrs. Ladd when she returned with the Mother Superior, and every hand went up.

When Mother Superior walked in with Mrs. Ladd, whose square Irish jaw was set hard, I sprang to my feet and brightly made my little speech. Mrs. Ladd glared at the class and asked how many of the girls agreed with me. I was amazed when no one stood up.

"How dare you call your teacher a liar!" Mother Superior said, her face ruddy with rage. "What shall we do with her?"

The two white women talked above my head as if I were no longer present. I was banished from Form Two A to Form Two B, the second-rank class for weaker performing students.

I knew no one in Form Two B. For a whole month I kept my silence before the new teacher, who treated me with disdain, and with my new and former classmates for whom my disgrace had made me an untouchable. I was certain I would stay in the B class the rest of my life, but one day without any explanation I was asked to gather my books and to return to Form Two A where I picked up my position as class leader and scholar as if the entire episode had never happened.

This incident with its month-long banishment taught me again what I was learning at every stage of my life, that speaking what is evident to my senses as plain common sense can bring swift punishment. I was confused by the difference between what appeared manifestly correct to me and what adults with power—my parents and teachers—insisted on asserting or denying, and I was infused with outrage by this difference. As my teachers punished me daily for my brashness, what they called my talking back, the burn of defiance in my chest became a familiar sensation. My defiance made me an outcast and a social leader at the same time, and my clashes with authority became a source of amusement for my classmates.

These conflicts with teachers and reverend sisters continued throughout my years at the convent. With Sister Sean, Sister Patricia, and Sister Peter, my Form One, Form Four, and Form Five teachers, I enjoyed the most intense relationships and at the same time suffered the most abject treatment. All three responded to me with an affection, pride, and tenderness that I assumed I deserved because I was the funny student, the quick and bright one. All teachers loved bright students; that was a law of nature. Everything about my life testified to the fact that my value to the world lay in my demonstrated intelligence, and I took their keen interest as natural.

As with Sister Josie, I was Sister Sean and Sister Patricia's pet. "Shirley!" they would call out confidently each time a student answered a question incorrectly or floundered for a date. And so, when the sisters secretly punished me, I believed that they were simply participating in my secret life of the imagination.

I believed my mind held depths of associations, feelings, and understanding that effortlessly distinguished me from my peers. The one subject I could not or would not master was math. Because my math scores were a dismal D or C at best, I needed to compensate for its drag on the annual averaging of grade points that ranked us from first to last girl in the class. Thus I endeavored to score perfect hundreds on every other subject. History, geography, and scripture were study subjects in which my mathematically talented competitors could also achieve. But it was with English, a subject every Malayan student believed was mystically beyond mere study but was achieved as innate talent, that I hoped to overcome my self-imposed handicap. I marked myself as different from the brilliant math students whose scores I scorned with my contemptuous Cs and Ds: what I lacked in math I would make up for in imagination, the gift which is endowed neither by race, class, or religion.

One afternoon, Sister Sean, exasperated with something I had said, asked me to stay behind in the room after the rest of the girls had left for physical education class. There, her face contorted with passion, she slapped me hard across my face. I was astonished and dry-eyed. She was doing this for my own good, she said, blinking hard behind her thick glasses. I was never, never to talk back to her like that again.

So when Sister Patricia asked me two years later to follow her to an empty classroom and shut the door behind me, I knew what to expect. Sister Patricia had been called to a meeting just before our English period with her. I said "Hooray!" in what I thought was an imitation of British comic book characters. I only meant that her absence would relieve us of tedious English parsing, but her angry glance in response to my remark prepared me for the worst. Once in the classroom she spun around, her face a scowl of pain. I was rude, I didn't care for her feelings, how dare I suggest that we didn't care to have her as our teacher. She struck me hard on my right cheek, then told me to wait till the physical education period was over before joining my classmates.

After she'd hurried out, I wondered what it was about my mouth that always got me into trouble.

My badness, evident at every turn, seemed to be produced by my intelligence, which I also believed would have to save me from myself.

The next year with Sister Peter I was determined not to give her cause for grief. I would watch my mouth and concentrate on preparing for the O levels, the Overseas Senior Cambridge Examinations. The results of the exams would determine whether I would be accepted for the pre-university classes.

By then I was reading T. S. Eliot's *After Strange Gods*, D. H. Lawrence's *Sons and Lovers* and *Lady Chatterley's Lover*, Erskine Caldwell's *Tobacco Road*, even Henry Miller's *Tropic of Cancer*, banned volumes that my older brothers smuggled home, but which they discarded once they found their reputation as pornographic literature overrated. One hot afternoon while Sister Peter read us Henry V's stirring address, "Once more unto the breach, dear friends, once more," I pondered the vast gap between Shakespeare's language and that in the clandestine publications with their chatter of private organs, illicit sensations, and hidden and dangerous thoughts. Idly I wrote at the back of an exercise book all the dangerous words I had learned just that year: *cock, fuck, penis, cunt*. They formed a neat list of about seventeen words: then I forgot about them.

Two days later, Sister Peter asked me to remain behind after class: I had handed in an English essay in the same exercise book. Her long face paler than usual, she berated me for my wicked ways. Her disappointment was horrible to me. Among all the sisters who'd taught me, she was the one I wanted most to please. She was graceful, grave, reserved; the simple twinkle in her green-blue eyes was large reward for any witticism or eloquence, and I had striven to please her by flaying my mind to a high pitch in completing every writing assignment. Now she withdrew any warmth of approval, and for the rest of the year, her anger laid a cold glance on me.

I would rather she had slapped me and forgiven me, like Sisters Sean and Patricia.

My sense of possessing a reservoir of feelings and associations had every-thing to do with the misery of my everyday life and my withdrawal from it into books. At ten I learned to ride my father's discarded bicycle. Since its bar was too high to straddle, I rode it sideways by placing one foot under the bar, as if it were a pedicab. I must have looked a comic and awkward figure, but the bicycle permitted me an expansion of physical mobility that spelled greater freedom.

With my second brother I bicycled to the Malacca Library, about five miles from our home. Within the thick red-colored walls built by the Dutch in the 1640s, a room lined with shelves of children's books wel-comed me. Behind this front room was a larger chamber filled with shelves that narrowly divided the old red clay floor. This adult section was filled with hard-cover romances, detective thrillers, and books simply catego-rized "fiction." The librarian, perhaps out of boredom, for we never met more than another occasional visitor to the library, allowed us to sign up for a children's card, good for a book each time, and for an adult's card, which extended borrowing privileges to three books. Imagine the immedi-ate riches that fell into our hands! Four books a day, no questions asked, and another four the next day when we returned the first four. The world around me vanished into the voices, the colors, and the dance of language. I gazed, dazzled, into interiors that Malacca never held.

Even the external world became bathed in the language of imagination. Books in arms, I took to climbing a mango tree that grew a little ways up the lane to get away from my father's wife, Peng, and from the trapped sticky afternoon heat in our three-roomed shack. Leaning against the trunk with my feet securely hooked around a branch, I studied the resin oozing from a cut as tiny black ants trailed evenly up and down the grainy bark. The dark green leaves waved a cooling presence around and above me. In the distance, through the dust of the red laterite that separated me from my home, I could hear my brothers' shouts. This world, I understood dimly, was somehow connected to that world which I clutched in my hands. It had little taste of adventure, unlike the wars, princes, murders, and balls that took place regularly in books. But it was my world, red soil, green leaves, hot sun, cool shade, sturdy body, distant noises. What connected the two was myself, and I knew I would someday write this world down, finding a language that would do justice to it.

Discovering in books how large the world was outside of Malacca, I also began to see how large my own world was. As reader, I never surrendered my freedom to an author but always asked how what I was reading related to my observations, the people around me, and my surroundings. Knowing that children elsewhere read these books, I assumed that they would also want to know about someone like me. It was in this way that I took up pen-pal writing. The children's comics that Father bought as treats for us carried personals from children in Scotland or Wales or Exeter, who wished to correspond with children from other countries of the Commonwealth. I could not afford the stamps to take up these offers, but for a time I wrote letters to imaginary pen pals, writing details of my life and stories of school plays and exhibitions, and expressing a desire to hear from them.

In these letters, like children all over the world tracing home as the center of all arrivals, I sent the following address: Mata Kuching, Malacca, The Straits Settlements, Malaya, Asia, The Earth, The Milky Way, The Universe. Malacca was at the center of everything. It was what made the universe imaginable, the address which brought all the letters home.

Pumping my Schaeffer pen full of ink from an inkwell that winked a copper-green eye, I also considered writing a history of the world. It was convenient for me that Malacca was at the center of that crooked hunchbacked peninsula that filled an entire page, just as Australia or North America each filled a page. Malaya was in the middle of the earth, and everybody else fell out over the edges—China, cramped like a squeezed orange half, India, an inverted pyramid, leaking Ceylon as a teardrop.

This geography, placing me at the hub of the universe, was more than childish egocentrism. I felt the depth of my existence, and accepted that it was full of meaning. Meaning radiated from me, the subject on whom experience fell and the potential author on whom experience was dependent for sense. At the center of the world, of color, sound, sensation, touch, taste, movement, feeling, the shapes and forces of people and actions around me, I knew myself to be the agent of my world, my life, and the meanings that infuse both.

I was a child who never saw the universe as outside myself, but when I read Blake's line, "to see the universe in a grain of sand," I understood myself to be both that marvelous grain of sand and the speaker who made that image visible. Life's miseries dissipated into the sharp fertility of sense through my fixed idea that all I saw and felt would become words one day. The ambition for poetry, a belief in the vital connection between language and my specific local existence, was clearly irrational, even perhaps a symptom of small madness. By eleven I knew I wanted to be a poet, and nothing has changed that desire for me since.

My convent teachers had little directly to do with my emergent sense of self as a poet. After Sister Josie, every teacher-nun bore down on me with an attention as painful as the stinging red ants that overran Malacca. Their crushing devotion to my behavior, my misdeeds, and my psychology, as well as their occasional malevolence provided a counteruniverse for the diminishment of my family. Still, it was their domineering secretive discipline, together with the unspoken disintegration of my family, that brought me to rebellion and to literature.

Edith Konecky

From Allegra Maud Goldman

Edith Konecky (b. 1922), like the title character of her 1976 novel, grew up in an upper-middle-class Jewish family in Depression-era Brooklyn and was, from an early age, an aspiring writer and "a feminist before I ever had a name for it." Konecky, the author of poetry, short fiction, and two novels, has fashioned in Allegra Maud Goldman a funny, feisty, and much-beloved heroine, whom Tillie Olsen has called "a marvel of creation." Allegra must contend with parents who dote on her sickly, neurotic brother while they dismiss their precocious daughter's artistic yearnings, existential fears, and quest for the meaning of female identity: "Oh, you," her mother says. "You'll grow up and marry some nice man and have children."

In this excerpt, the preadolescent Allegra attends summer camp, where she finds alternative role models in her counselors—a group of hardy, intelligent young women who, unlike her mother and her mother's friends, have interests and aspirations that go beyond matchmaking, shopping, and playing mah-jong.

That summer at camp the girls in my age group were having crushes. That's what they called them: crushes. They never said the word love. I spent a lot of time in my favorite beech tree trying to figure out what was a crush and what was love. I will return to that.

Each girl had chosen a counselor on whom to have her crush. If you decided to have a crush, you had to choose a counselor who was not already taken. I made up my mind that if everyone else was going to have a crush, I had better have one, too. I made a list of all the counselors who were not yet taken and although I liked some of them well enough, there wasn't one on whom I wanted to have a crush. So then I asked myself which one I'd choose if I had complete freedom of choice and the answer was Hank, as I already admired everything about her: her smile, her looks, the way she moved, not only the way she played the violin, but the dreamy inward look on her face when she was playing it, the way she had with horses and the grace with which she rode them. Everything about her seemed worthy of emulation. Perhaps because she was a musician, even her voice was lovely, and she never used it to say anything vulgar, pointless, or silly. Although she had a sense of humor, she was a serious person with a great deal of reserve and dignity. The more I thought about her the more I had a crush on her. It was as though all I had to do in order to have a crush was to decide to have it. And at that point it was out of my hands.

There were two rainy weeks when, most of our regular activities curtailed, we sat around and talked. Bull sessions, we called them, although as far as I could see they were ordinary conversations.

"Do you realize that Legg is the only one here who hasn't got a crush on anyone?" Naomi Albrecht said one day when six of us were sitting around in a corner of the social hall. Legg had become my nickname that summer, thanks to an uncommon spurt of growth, most of it in that region.

"Maybe she isn't normal," Estelle Moscowitz kindly offered.

"There *is* someone," I said. "I just don't talk about it. I happen to think some things are private."

"You're making it up," Mitzi Swerdlow taunted.

"No, I'm not."

"Who is it, then?"

"Well, all right," I said. "It's Hank."

"*Hank!*" Mitzi shrieked. "But she's *my* crush."

"I can't help that. She's the one I love."

"*Love?*" they all screamed. They were as shocked as though I'd said something obscene.

"Yes," I said. "She's the one I'm in love with."

"*In love with!*" they chorused, outraged. "You can't be in love with her. She's a woman. She's the same sex."

"All right, then," I sighed. "She's the one I've got a crush on."

"Well you can't," Mitzi said. "She's *my* crush."

"For heaven's sake," I said, "I'm not planning to marry her or anything." In fact, I had no idea what you were supposed to do with a crush once you had it. "I can't help my feelings."

"It isn't fair," Naomi said.

"Why don't you have a crush on Judson?" Jennifer Berg suggested. "Nobody's using her."

"I don't happen to feel that way about Judson. Listen, who made up the rules? Where is it written?"

They thought about that for ten seconds and then Naomi, who was a few months older than the rest of us and had, therefore, in matters of the heart, assumed a certain leadership, said, "That's just the way it is. That's the way it's always been."

"Not as far as I'm concerned," I said firmly.

They looked at me with what I thought was a certain amount of respect, so I went on. "You can't legislate your feelings." Where had I read that? "If you like someone you like them, and the devil take the hindmost."

"Well, I'm going to tell Hank that I had a crush on her first," Mitzi said in an aggrieved voice. "And not to pay any attention to yours."

"Tell her whatever you like," I said. "Do you *really* tell them you have a crush on them?"

"How else would they know?"

"What do they say?"

"They act embarrassed, or they say don't be silly, or something like that."

"I pick blueberries for Aitch and leave them at her place at dinner every night," Naomi said.

"I make funny valentines for Casey," Estelle said. "I mail them to her with actual stamps."

"What do you do, Jennifer?" I said.

"I just sort of follow Horsey around," she said. "I go swimming whenever I can." Horsey was the swimming instructor. "I haven't been able to think of anything else to do. But I'm getting to be a marvelous swimmer."

"What do you plan to do about Hank?" Mitzi asked acidly.

"I don't plan to do anything," I said. "I didn't know you were supposed to."

"Oh, well, then, that's all right."

I escaped to my beech tree as soon after that as I could, though the leaves were still damp from the rain. My beech tree had a crotched bough that was as comfortable to lie in as a hammock. Although it was right outside the social hall and had a bench circling its trunk, no one had ever yet looked up and spied me in it, so it was still a secret place. I have never been able to figure out why people so rarely do look up. Although I had no intention of eavesdropping, people sat beneath me under that tree many a time and had long and possibly private conversations without ever once suspecting that there might be someone right above them in that tree.

It was midway through my first summer at Camp Stowe and I had long since stopped hating it. I hadn't wanted to go, and when the subject first came up I resisted fiercely. They had tried both David and me out at camp the summer I was eight and it hadn't worked. I had lasted out that summer, miserable and homesick, but David, after less than two weeks, managed to get stricken with acute appendicitis. My father had to charter a private plane and he and Dr. Wise flew to New Hampshire to get David. When they got back to Floyd Bennett Airport an ambulance was waiting to rush David to the hospital for his operation, and there was a story about it in the *Brooklyn Daily Eagle* headed: LOCAL DRESS MAN FLIES STRICKEN SON FROM N.H. CAMP. Imagine something like that making the newspapers today.

"I don't see why I have to go," I protested. "David doesn't, and he's already had his appendix out."

"David is too sensitive to go to camp," my mother said.

"I'm sensitive, too," I said. "I just try not to show it."

"I made a mistake when I sent you to Camp Caribou. You were too young. You'll like this camp."

"I'll hate it," I said.

My father was always pointing out how expensive Camp Stowe was and telling my mother that there were plenty of perfectly good camps that cost half as much, but for once my mother was adamant. So now my mother was the one to remind me that Camp Stowe was expensive and that I should therefore be grateful. I couldn't see what possible difference the cost could make, but it turned out she was right.

For one thing, it was a beautiful camp in the Massachusetts Berkshires. I hadn't been there long before I fell in love with the countryside—the woods, the lake, the gentle green mountains, the special blue of the sky, the sunlight and sunsets and the rolling meadows dotted with wildflowers.

Then, too, because Camp Stowe could afford to pay its counselors decent salaries, they weren't just kids looking for a free summer, but older women in their twenties, many of whom taught in New England women's colleges and specialized in something like painting or dramatics. My counsellor, whose name was Henrietta but whom everyone called Hank, was a professional violinist, one of the camp's chamber group. The group gave candlelight recitals two evenings a week. We weren't required to go, and if we did we could sit on the floor and read or write letters if we liked. I went to all of them. It was a new kind of music for me and, though I always brought along a book to read and didn't realize I was listening to the music, I really was.

As an added inducement to get me to go to camp willingly, I was allowed to take horseback riding, even though it was extra. Ever since my Zane Grey period I had been wild to get up on a real live horse, and as soon as I did I knew that was where I belonged and I would never again mourn not having a bicycle. I had a big chestnut mare named Sally. I rode her three times a week all that summer and I loved her. She had a silver mane and tail and a nose as soft and smooth as a mushroom and eyes as deep and gentle as mountain pools. I think she loved me, too. Once Hank had pointed out how to hold the reins and what to do with my knees and toes and heels and elbows, there wasn't anything else she had to teach me, because Sally herself showed me exactly how to handle her. We understood each other. I loved everything about riding, not only the sense of power it gave me, and the close wordless communion between Sally and me, and the motion and speed, but also the special way of seeing places you rarely get any other way. The trails led through woods, through dark, leafy, damp-smelling places and sun-dappled ones, and then out onto a road in full sunlight, past farms and across wooden bridges over gurgling brooks or roaring gorges, and from your height on a horse you could see much more than if you had been merely walking.

When I first got to camp, I didn't know anyone. It was an all-girls' camp, and that first night in the dining room there were more girls gathered in one place than I had ever seen before. Furthermore, since there was a camp uniform, we were all wearing the same green and white garb. Because it was such a good camp, many of the girls came back year after year. It was easy to spot the repeats, because they bubbled over with the joy of seeing each other again and being back at dear old Camp Stowe. Those few whose first summer it was were even easier to pick out, since we all looked glum and apprehensive and didn't know the words to the songs all the others began singing lustily the minute we sat down to dinner. One of these, Eleanor Marx, an unsmiling, sharp-featured girl with shrewd eyes, whom I had already met since she was in my bunk, sat beside me. While I was observing that this camp, unlike any I had ever heard of, had regular waitresses, and that the food, which looked good, was brought to the table on platters and set before the counselor at the head of each table, who then served us, Eleanor leaned to ask me a question in a low, confidential tone.

"Do you smoke?" is what I thought I heard her say.

"Do I what?" I asked in my normal voice.

"Shhh!" she said. "Smoke."

"Smoke what?" I said.

"Cigarettes, dummy. Wha'd you think, salmon?"

I giggled. "I'm too young," I said.

"What do I look like? Your great-aunt?"

"You could be any age," I said. "You have that kind of face."

"I'll teach you how to smoke," she said. "I've got a pack of Luckies in the bottom of my trunk."

"Okay," I said.

"And let's french the counselor's bed."

"Okay," I said.

We stole off into the woods the following afternoon, armed with Eleanor's Luckies and some other equipment she deemed necessary for furtive smoking: peppermints to sweeten our breath should anyone chance to kiss us afterwards, and Band-Aids to secure our index and middle fingers against telltale nicotine stains. However, once we had gotten deep into the woods and settled in a safe spot with our fingers bandaged, we discovered that the matchbook Eleanor had brought contained only three matches, and as there was a breeze and we were inexperienced, we never did get one of the cigarettes lit. It was too late to try again, but we did french Hank's bed that night and the next. She never said a word about it, but on the fourth morning we were told that we had been invited to sleep that night in Auntie (pronounced in the English way) Beck's bunk. Although I was to spend five summers at Camp Stowe, I never discovered what Auntie Beck's position was, but it must have been administrative, as she had nothing at all to do with the campers. She was a straight-backed, elderly woman, not much more than four feet high and splinter-thin, with a severe, sharply lined face and eyes as small and black and cold as a bird's. She appeared at most meals and functions, but at other times only rarely, usually striding across the campus as though it were a moor, invariably dressed in riding breeches and boots and a funny, narrow-brimmed felt hat that covered all of her head and her ears. She had a brown leather riding crop, one end of which was permanently wound around her right hand, while from time to time she snapped the whip end against the calf of her boot. She was an intimidating little woman.

Auntie Beck's bunk was in a secluded clearing in the woods, set apart from the rest of the camp. Clutching pajamas and toothbrushes, Eleanor and I approached it feeling very much as Hansel and Gretel might have felt had they had advance knowledge that the lady of the house was a witch. We were only too well aware that this invitation was a form of punishment, though no one had mentioned our crimes.

"They won't even be able to hear our screams," Eleanor said in a hoarse whisper. She was pale with fear, but I couldn't help suspecting that she was also thrilled. We had speculated all day on what Auntie Beck was going to do to us. Eleanor's imaginings ran to physical torture but my own guess was that we were in for a sharp tongue-lashing, which, coming from Auntie Beck, might be far more to be feared.

She opened the door to our timid knock as the bugle sounded taps off in the distance where our peers were settling in. It was the only time I was ever to see her with neither hat nor riding crop. She smiled a small, thin-lipped smile and said, "Come in, children. Welcome to my castle." It was a snug one-room cottage, all darkly varnished logs, with lots of books, a table in the center with a kerosene lamp already lit on it, a pair of cushioned rocking chairs, a primly made-up bed in one corner and, diagonally across from it, bunk beds in a curtained alcove.

"I guess we better go straight to bed," Eleanor suggested hopefully, her eyes darting nervously from the floor to Auntie Beck's face. "The bugle blew."

"Get your pajamas on," Auntie Beck said, "and then we'll sit down and have a little chat."

We bolted for the curtained alcove, Eleanor and I, and, shivering from the cold night coming on as well as from nervousness, we dawdled over undressing as long as we dared. When we were in our pajamas we neatly and painstakingly folded our clothes and laid them on the foot of the bottom bunk bed and then, with mathematical precision, lined up our four shoes under the bed. When there was nothing more we could think of to do, we stood for a moment regarding each other, while I wondered at the intimacy of our shared plight. I hardly knew Eleanor. I wasn't even sure if I liked her.

"You go first," Eleanor hissed, giving me a shove that sent me reeling through the curtains and nearly into Auntie Beck's lap. Auntie Beck, a book open before her, was seated at the table to which she had drawn up a third chair. She looked up at my abrupt entrance and I tried an embarrassed smile. She closed her book and smiled back. The light of the oil lamp softened her face and I saw that her smile, if not exactly kind, was genuine. She patted the chair beside her and I sat down in it and, glancing at her book, saw that it was something called *Sonnets from the Portuguese*. Eleanor appeared and slid into the third chair.

"I do covet my privacy," Auntie Beck said crisply, "but once in a while it's nice to have company." A plate of cookies and three glasses of milk had materialized on the table, and she passed these around. "I always like a little bedtime snack," she said. "I don't know why it isn't a regular part of camp policy. Help yourselves."

With the first sip of milk, my nervousness subsided and I began to be curious about Auntie Beck, about what kind of person she was and what her life was like. It was at this moment that she herself said, "Tell me a little something about yourselves, girls. Tell me about your lives. Eleanor?"

Eleanor looked up, startled. "My life?" she mumbled. "What about my life?"

"Do you like it? Are you happy?"

Eleanor stared at her and then burst into tears.

"Why are you crying?" Auntie Beck asked after a while.

"Because my mother has migraines," Eleanor sobbed. "She has them all the time. Ever since I was born."

Auntie Beck nodded at her.

"And insomnia," Eleanor added on a fresh wave of sobs. "She feels terrible all the time."

Eleanor blew her nose and stopped crying. "She's seen every kind of doctor there is," she said. "Nothing helps."

"Finish these up," Auntie Beck said, passing the cookies around again. "Would you like some more milk? What about you, Allegra? What about your life?"

I thought for a while. "It's a complicated question," I said.

"Life is complicated," Auntie Beck said.

"Yes. But maybe it will turn out all right. Is that a book of poetry?"

"Yes."

"Is it in Portuguese?"

"No, English. You may borrow it if you like." Then, apparently satisfied, Auntie Beck bustled us off to bed. No scolding, no lecture. I climbed into the top bunk bed and sank into a soft cloud. It must have been a feather mattress, because it folded itself about me like a warm embrace and I was instantly asleep.

"That was some punishment," Eleanor grumbled next morning as we headed away from Auntie Beck's cabin towards the dining hall and breakfast.

"This is a pretty good camp," I said, clutching Auntie Beck's book. "I may even end up liking it."

More than half the summer had gone by between then and the day I made public my crush on Hank, and, afterwards, reclining in my beech tree, I sat looking up at the sky through the glistening leaves. Clouds scudded by and between them the sky showed blue, that miracle-pure blue that comes after days of rain when you've almost forgotten blue. I had a lot to think about. The girls' horror at my use of the word *love* in connection with Hank had started me thinking. I'd forgotten that, except for a couple of men who worked on the grounds, we at Camp Stowe were all of the same sex. Not forgotten it so much as simply not thought about it. I tried to understand why. Without boys or men, except in group singing, the range and variety seemed pretty much what it was in the outside world. We had the doers and the dreamers, the leaders and followers, the tough and the gentle. I wondered if we were different because of the absence of men, different than we would have been with them, or whether it might be that we were in some way freer to be more ourselves. I was certainly beginning to feel better about myself than I did around my father and David and even my mother, who was so much my father's wife that, if not the disease itself, she was its carrier. It was as though I were growing a new personality, one that had nothing to do with whose daughter or sister I was. The tone was set by the directors and the counselors, women who took themselves ≠seriously, and who took us seriously as well; we were looked upon as real people with real potentials, real futures, real problems. They were the first group of women I knew who *did* things, things other than bridge and golf and shopping and hiring houseworkers. These women painted, played music, sang, acted, danced, taught, read. One was a theatrical director; another a botanist; a third, our camp physician, did medical research the other months of the year.

I wondered what kind of person my mother would have been in a setting like this. Although she hadn't gone to college, as the only thing she was expected to do was to make a good marriage, she had been the smartest and most popular girl in her graduating class in high school, and I knew she was intelligent, because she was a wizard at word games and puzzles. I couldn't help feeling sorry for her. It had simply never occurred to her, having married a successful businessman, as had most of her friends, to do anything with her own life.

So it was something of a surprise to me to come upon this new kind of women, women who were doing interesting and maybe even valuable work, doing what they loved and found exciting. Most of the campers were from families similar to mine, so I was sure they must all have been made as hopeful as I by all these proofs that our horizons might not after all be so limited. But not at all.

"They're still pretty young, remember," Naomi Albrecht pointed out. "In their twenties. How much do you want to bet that in the next five years they'll be married and have babies and have forgotten all about their careers."

"Not Dr. Allison," I said. "Not Hank. Not Aitch or Judson."

"The ones who don't get married will just become dried-up old maids. Who wants to be one of them?"

The scorn in her voice was nothing new to me. I had been hearing it all my life in connection with old maids or spinsters. As far as I could see, there was nothing more shameful to a girl than not to have her hand chosen (or to surrender it) in marriage. It meant that you weren't good enough, or that you were unnatural; in either case you were a failure.

"Why do they have to be 'dried-up' old maids?" I said. They all seem pretty attractive to me."

"*Now*," Naomi said. "While they have their youth."

I thought of a conversation I had had that spring with my cousin Sonia. As a rule I avoided conversations with her, but I'd gotten trapped into this one by having carelessly let fall the information that instead of marrying when the time came, I thought I might have a series of interesting affairs.

"You'll never be really happy as a woman," Sonia said, "until you have your own sweet baby at your breast."

I recognized this as something her mother, my Aunt Gertrude, was always saying to her, but I refrained from throwing up.

"What a disgusting notion," I said. "You mean, because of being female nothing else will ever make *you* happy?"

"Not really happy. Not in the same way."

"How about if you became the world's most famous tap dancer and a Hollywood star and got to do love scenes with Robert Taylor and Tyrone

Power and never had another pimple and could eat all the candy you wanted?" I said, cruelly playing on all her weaknesses.

"That would be nice, too," she admitted. "But I could do both."

"And what's so great about nursing a baby?" I said. "You feed it and then you have to hold it up and burp it and then it falls asleep and wets its diaper and you have to change it and then it wakes up and cries because it's hungry again. All you're doing is keeping the machinery going until it can run itself."

"You're just not normal," Sonia said, shaking her head sadly. "There's no point even talking to you."

In the social hall, not far from my tree, I could hear the quartet practicing. It made me feel good to know that Hank was near and to have the sound of her violin drift up into my treetop. I thought about love, about different kinds of love. I was pretty sure that in spite of everything I loved my mother and David and Grandma. It was even possible that I loved my father. Still, wasn't that because they had always been there and were so familiar? But what was a crush? I had done enough reading to know about passion, and even lust, and I wondered if it was that that was beginning to grow in me. But it was too hard to think about. I wanted to feel whatever it was I was feeling without complicating and spoiling it with words. I drifted back into a state I had been in so often that summer, a vague, restless, not entirely happy euphoria.

I was supposed to be at fencing, but as fencing and archery were my two worst activities, I avoided them as often as possible, although this was against the rules. I did have some free periods during the week, but not enough for all the thinking and reading I had to do that summer. Since the night in Auntie Beck's bunk I had been reading a lot of poetry. Although we had read some poems in school, I felt as though I had made a new discovery. The poems in school had been either too long and told stories, or too short and inspirational. They were not like the poems I was finding now, medium ones, like sonnets. They were more personal and seemed like a new kind of language to me: pure crystals formed out of ecstasy, or out of an equally unbearable agony, the pearl in the oyster, the butterfly bursting free of the cocoon and trembling in its first flight. Poems spoke to me in an entirely new way.

It came to me then, in the tree, that the finest thing I could do about my crush would be to write a poem to Hank. I began to struggle with it in my head, and then on paper during rest period. I had to stop for tennis and, after that, volleyball, but my mind continued to work on it. I skipped swimming that afternoon and escaped with my pad and pencil to the woods where I finally finished it. Here is the poem:

TO HANK

When first I did perceive you with my eye,
I saw you were a fair and comely maid.
And next I did perceive you through my ear
When Bach and Mozart in the Social Hall you played.
Lest eye and ear should not suffice, dear friend,
Know that it is my heart as well you now invade.

When I had polished it and copied it out in print, I read it through about ten times. Nothing I had ever done had been as satisfying, but how would it seem to Hank? I decided not to sign it, slipped it into an envelope, and a few minutes before the dinner bugle, I stole into the dining room and left it propped against Hank's water glass. When we filed in for dinner, I was already sorry about the whole thing because I was so nervous. What a stupid thing to have done. Now, of course, I had to compose myself into a picture of purest innocence and nonchalance, which I tried to accomplish by chattering away with Eleanor and never once looking in Hank's direction, though I was aware all the same of every move she made. It was as though instead of the two hundred and more souls in that big dining room, Hank and I were the only ones present. As soon as we had taken our seats after singing the predinner song to celebrate our gratitude for the joyous day that was drawing to a close and for the serene and gentle night that lay ahead, Hank reached for the envelope and opened it. Even though my heart was pounding so hard that I was sure everyone could hear it, I couldn't help stealing furtive glances at Hank's face while she read the poem. At first she looked surprised, and then just for a flash, amused, and then as I saw her eyes go up to the top of the page to read the poem again, her face showed nothing at all. When she had finished reading it for the second time she carefully refolded it, put it back in the envelope, and patted it into her sweater pocket. She looked over at Mitzi Swerdlow for about one second, and then she looked at me and smiled, a wonderful smile, and I knew it was all right.

After dinner, when we were walking back to the bunk, she took my arm. "Thank you, Legg," she said. "That's a good poem."

"How did you know I wrote it?"

"I just did," she said, smiling.

Then we went on to have a conversation about whether I was going to write more poems, and whether I had a talent, and it turned into a literary discussion with no mention at all of the subject matter of my poem. I didn't realize this until later that night when I was falling asleep. The important thing seemed to be that I had written a poem, not what it was about. I wondered if Hank had been trying to save us both from embarrassment, and then I thought how clever she had been.

But I did go on writing poems, first on the theory that one good poem deserves another, and then because writing poems is like eating salted peanuts; there is no turning back. Most of my poems were about Hank, or about Restless Yearning, but some were about Death and Nature. That summer Nature was unusually important to me; my new feeling for it was connected to the way I felt about Hank and poetry and Tchaikovsky's *Pathétique*, and it was getting to be almost more than I could stand. Once, for absolutely no reason, I burst into tears watching the sun set across the lake while the swallows wheeled and dipped. Another time, the sun came out after a shower and made a rainbow and the air had such a softness and smelled so sweet and piney that it made me drunk and I had to run off into the woods, where I fell asleep for over an hour. And another night, during a candlelight recital, listening to Schubert and looking through the windows at the stars, I suddenly felt that I was going to explode and I had to go outside and run around the social hall about a dozen times before the feeling went away.

I knew there was something the matter with me, some kind of severe mental illness, but I couldn't talk to anyone about it because I wouldn't have known how to explain it. Writing poems helped. It was taking the feeling and putting it somewhere outside myself, making a neat, manageable package of it. I spent more and more time in my beech tree.

I was up there one day while the quartet was practicing, working on a difficult poem that I couldn't get right. The lake had had an unusual infestation of leeches that week and I was trying to use this as a metaphor for love: how, aware of the pitfalls, you go swimming anyway because you have to take your chances, and, sure enough, when you come out you find one or more of these strange, uninvited creatures attached to you. They're hard to get off, sometimes the only way is to burn them off, but even so they take a part of you with them, your very blood.

I was vaguely aware that someone had come along and sat down on the bench beneath me. I looked down and I could tell by the short, prematurely gray hair that it was Judson. I went back to my poem, then, wondering why I couldn't get it to work, and my mind wandered off. Maybe the trouble was with the leeches. Grandma had told me that in the olden days barbers used to keep leeches for medical purposes. If you were sick they "leeched" you. The leeches were supposed to draw the impurities out of your blood. But did they really separate out the impurities; or did they merely take whatever blood they happened to get? And why should barbers have qualified as doctors? Except for the scissors, what did one thing have to do with the other?

These were some of the thoughts my mind was wasting itself on while below me Judson stamped out one cigarette and immediately lit another. It was late afternoon, a quiet time, as most of the camp was down at the lake. In a little while they would all come trooping back up the hill to shower and dress for dinner. It must have been a free time for Judson, whose specialty was nature walks. She knew a lot about mushrooms and ferns and the Latin names for all the trees. Tall and lanky, with a swinging athletic walk, she was one of those whom, at summer's end, it would be jarring to see wearing a dress and lipstick. She had a thin, pale face with features so regular that they left her face almost blank.

The Brahms Piano Quartet came to an end for the third time and, as the players all reached the end at the same time and without any discussion, I knew the rehearsal was over. One by one they came out and strode off in different directions. I watched for Hank. She was the last to come out, and when she appeared, Judson jumped to her feet and waved to her. Hank came over and they both sat down, Hank carefully putting her violin case and music on the bench beside her. I was just beginning to think about making my presence known, or coming down out of the tree, when I saw them turn and smile at each other, and then I saw Judson's hand close over Hank's. Neither of them said a word.

They just sat that way until we heard voices coming up from the road to the lake. Hank withdrew her hand from Jud's and they both got up and walked off in the direction of the bunks.

I stayed in the tree for a while after that, thinking about Hank and Judson and how quiet they had been, and then I tore up the poem because it was a lousy idea and when I got to the dining hall dinner was half over.

Jo Sinclair

From The Changelings

Jo Sinclair (Ruth Seid, 1913–1995) emerged from a working-class childhood in Cleveland to become an award-winning novelist and playwright whose work deeply explores issues of gender, ethnicity, race, and social class. Her novel *The Changelings*, first published in 1955 and nominated for a Pulitzer Prize, tracks both the growing racial tensions in a midwestern city around 1950, as African Americans move into an area long occupied by Jewish and Italian American families, and the growing friendship between two girls who courageously defy the racism and anti-Semitism of their respective communities. Sinclair created a particularly memorable character in Judith Vincent, a determined tomboy who dresses in her brother's clothes, calls herself "Vincent," and has succeeded in becoming the ringleader of the neighborhood gang of boys.

The events in this excerpt take place in a patch of urban woods frequented by Vincent's gang on a night when smoldering hostilities—over the fate of "empties" (vacant neighborhood homes vulnerable to occupation by African Americans), and over Vincent's authority in the gang—suddenly flare. On this tumultuous night, twelve-year-old Vincent will confront the enmity of her friends—and then make friends with "the enemy."

"Hey, girlie," [Dave] said, "what about that rule? No girls in the gang, huh?"

Not one of the gang said a word for Vincent. Their silence made her scalp feel prickly with apprehension.

"Hey, who the hell do you think you are?" Dave went on scornfully. "A guy?"

It was an accusation. She had never actually called herself a boy, but neither had she ever thought of herself as one of the girls she despised for their soft, plaintive weakness. She was simply Vincent, with the proud right to walk with the strong. She had proved it—in a thousand ways. As she turned away, with her old disdain, she was stunned to see that the other faces reflected Dave's ugly laughter.

"Who's eating potatoes with me?" she said gruffly, but the apprehension was choking and dry in her throat by now.

"Hey, girlie," Dave called, his tone like an insult. "Who's eating potatoes with this girlie, huh?"

Suddenly a wild shout pushed out of her. "Shut up, you dirty liar!"

"Ha ha," Dave said insolently. "Hey, gang, did you hear girlie?"

"Know what?" Santina said. "Bet she thinks she's a guy!"

Angelo rocked with laughter. "Vincent thinks she's a guy!"

Even Becky was staring at her, the dull eyes as unbearable as all the bright, excited ones. With difficulty, one of the old, working statements came from Vincent: "What's the matter, Dave, looking for trouble?"

"Trouble from a girl?" Dave's arms were crossed over his chest. "Because you wear pants when you don't go to school? That make you a guy?"

"You brother Nate's old pants," Leo said, like a dirty betraying enemy. "You copped 'em when he went to New York."

"What do you have to wear in school?" Dave went on inexorably. "Dresses—ha ha. Middy blouse, skirt. What do you get called in school, huh?"

"Judith," Alex said derisively. "Judith Vincent."

"What does your mother call you?" Dave said.

"Judy, Judy!" Dan's taunting voice answered.

But the gang had always called her Vincent, she thought numbly. Her friends, Jules—it was her name! With a carelessness she had to fight for, she began walking toward the clubhouse. "Who wants a butt?" she said.

"Where you going?" Dave said. "No girls in this gang—get it?"

She turned, shouted, "Lay off! Get home to your empty, you rat. This is my gang."

"The hell it is," he said. "No girl's going to be my boss."

"Me, either," Angelo said.

Alex said suddenly, "What you got under Nate's pants, girlie?"

An excited laugh burst from Santina. "Go on, Dave," she cried, "show her what guys got under their pants, huh?"

A wave of snickers and howls came from the gang, but Dave said airily, "You cop a sneak, will you?"

"Aw, come on, Dave," Santina said. "Show her what you got and she ain't. Come on."

"Save it," he said. "Save it for that guy they got all lined up to marry you, hot pants."

"Hey, lemme show her!" Alex said, and unzipped his pants, began to grope inside.

"That a boy, Blacky!" Santina cried.

Dave pushed Alex, so hard that he fell. "Show hot pants," he said. "If she wants to see so bad."

"What the hell?" Alex shouted, getting up.

"Button up or I'll bust you one," Dave said coldly, moving away. "Come on, gang."

They all assembled in a tight group, leaving the outsiders at the other side of the fire. After a second, Alex came, too, smoothing his pants shut.

"All right," Dave said with assurance. "So we prove it's a girl. Nothing dirty. All we do is pull off her clothes and prove it, see?"

There was an outburst of admiring whistles and catcalls. Across the three or four yards separating her from the gang, Vincent said unbelievingly, "You dirty bastards. You touch me and I'll kill you."

Another wave of whistling and taunting laughter came floating across, and Vincent's hands began to sweat in her pockets. It was as if they smelled her hidden fear, as if the whole summer of waiting had ripped her open suddenly and they knew—before she did—that she was no longer the fastest, the smartest.

. . .

"Let's go," Dave said, his voice clipped, and the gang moved behind him. Vincent saw a wedge of sullen faces and big, hunched bodies. Suddenly they all looked towering as men, lumpy with muscle.

Her hands came out of her pockets in fists. For the first time, she felt like the youngest. There had always been an agelessness about the gang before, a magic stretching to fit the particular adventure. When they had leaped from garage roof to tree, run the slopes and hills, they were kids. When they had entered a store, cool and full of distracting talk to make the snitch easier, they were adults. When they had sat in the candle-lit clubhouse, watching their cigarette smoke in the air and the shadows thrown by the flickering candles, they were dreamers—young or old enough to match any wish.

But now, as she watched the slow, deadly advance, she knew she was only twelve: to Dave's almost and Alex's full fifteen, to Angelo's and Leo's fourteen, to Dan's and Joey's over-thirteen.

"Surround her," Dave ordered, and the gang fanned out, and inside of her Vincent was saying her prayer with every ounce of her faith: Dear

Lord, kind Lord, gracious Lord, I pray Thou wilt look on all I love tenderly tonight. . . .

"Grab her arms first," Dave said.

"How about if I dive for her legs?" Leo said.

Weed their hearts of weariness, Vincent prayed. Scatter every care, down a wake of angel wings winnowing the air.

"Show her what she ain't got!" Santina screamed joyously. She, too, pressed Vincent's sudden youth back on her. She was Dave's age, Alex's; her outcry was full of mysterious knowledge, like their expressions.

And with all the needy, Vincent prayed, oh, divide, I pray, this vast treasure of content that was mine today. Amen.

The wedge came closer. Her prayer began again, faster, more dogged in its reaching for a miracle; but the slitted eyes and the taunting men's grins came closer.

Amen, amen! she called in her head, and Dave jumped into her flailing fists. Then the other bodies hit, on all sides of her, so that she could not see single members of the gang but felt all their knobby hardness at once. She was punching one gigantic face, one chest, one belly taut and solid.

"You got her!" Santina cried, a wild exultant voice.

Then every precious memory she had been hugging turned anonymous for Vincent, as if she had never had a Manny or Shirley, a Jules, a Nate, a prayer. One pair of hands with the strength of a hundred had her pinned to the ground. Gigantic hands—strangely powerful but still smelling of the Levine kids—were tearing off her blouse, peeling Nate's pants off her, down her thighs, down her legs and past her socks and shoes.

She went on fighting, with the automatic fury and skill of the old Vincent. Lying on the jagged stones of the ground, she kicked and buckled against the grabbing weight, cursed like the old Vincent, until they had her underwear pants off. The sensation of unshielded softness was so new and terrifying that she could not move suddenly. A weeping, so shrill with weakness that it sickened her, dinned through her head.

Then she felt that gigantic pair of hands seize her undershirt and tear it off, over her head. The weight lifted, the smell went away. She felt the hot Gully wind on her closed eyes as she lay twisted into herself, her thighs pressed together convulsively. The wailing inside her head made her think of Manny, that time he had been sick.

She recognized Dave's voice, breathless and gulping, above her: "All right! Still think you're a guy?"

It thrashed her to her feet. She leaped for her clothes, fumbled on her underpants. When she straightened, holding the other pieces against her, she was unable to think what to do with them.

Everybody stared at the whiteness of her skin next to the tanned arms and neck and the triangle of brown pointing into the small, beginning breasts. Her hair looked curly and soft; her naked back and the long legs, the slim waist, the rounded thighs, all were of a strange and pretty girl they had just been fighting.

Suddenly blood started like pinpricks near one corner of Vincent's mouth. Leo mumbled frantically, "Hey, I got to go!"

He ran to the fire, seemed to tap Anna and Louis, and the three disappeared as if wind had carried them out of the Gully. Dan backed off. Then Joey and Angelo moved, as if at a signal, slouched out of sight. Alex went to the fireplace and took Becky's hand.

"Come on home," he said shakily. "Ma'll give you eat."

"Alex!" Santina whispered. "Wait for me, Alex."

They were gone. Vincent and Dave stared blindly at each other. "Hey, Vincent," he said painfully, "you got blood on your mouth. Wipe it off, for Christ sake."

"Go to hell," she said dully.

He winced. "Does your face hurt?"

Her eyes looked wide and empty. There was such a ghastly loneliness about her that he felt scared. He turned away, almost falling as he ran.

Slowly, Vincent began to feel the quiet, the heat of the air on her bare skin. The first of the dusk was creeping into the Gully, the misty blue color she loved. It'll be dark soon, she thought, time to light the candles, start the meeting, plan tomorrow's snitch, and . . .

Suddenly, as if she had just walked into a room, she smelled the burnt potatoes in the fireplace. Her face was wet, forehead and upper lip, and she felt the heaviness in her arms, aching bruises all over her body. Quickly, she dressed herself, wiped the blood from her face, smoothed back her hair. She brushed leaves and dirt from her pants. Then she did not know what to do, so she stumbled back to the fire. Bits of wood were still smoldering, and she leaned numbly and tucked in some paper, made a latticework of thin wood to catch the first flame. The reek of burnt potatoes was smothering.

Little flames jumped up. Across the area, the clubhouse was just a blotch of shadow and she wished the candles were lit, but she was too tired to walk over and do it. She sat down in front of the fire, hugging her knees. The blue color was all different today; it made a lost place of the Gully, and she could not bear it. She hid her face against her knees.

And then, as she fought to keep herself from sobbing, a girl's voice behind her said scornfully, angrily, "Hey, if you're crying, you're a jackass."

Vincent jumped up, shouting, "Who's crying?"

Turning quickly, she saw the girl, standing with her hands in the pockets of her slacks. She was colored.

There was a mechanical tensing for action in Vincent, weight on her toes, arms ready to fly up at the first move from the enemy. In one flashing instant, her heart thudding heavily at the abrupt danger, she took in everything about the girl: brown pants, white blouse, tennis shoes, a chain or cord of some kind around her neck and the ends disappearing inside the front of her blouse. They were as tall as each other, and the girl's straight, black, shining hair was ear length too, parted on the side.

For a fantastic second, it was like staring into a mirror—except for the brown color of the face. Then Vincent became aware of the girl's direct, angry eyes, and she said, "Who the hell do you think you are?"

"I don't think—I know," the girl retorted. "Clara Jackson, that's who. If you don't like it, lump it."

All the words she had heard at home, and up and down the street, tangled in Vincent's mind. The suspicion and hatred, the fear, which had made strident echoes all the past summer, clanged through her like a warning. Should she run, fight? Should she walk away airily, holding her nose?

"What do you think you're doing in this Gully?" she said roughly.

"You own it? Is it private property or something?"

"It's my gang headquarters. That private enough?"

"No," the girl said. Then, with that intense anger, she said, "What do you mean, your gang? That blond guy just took it away from you, I'll bet. I saw the whole thing. I wanted to kill him! Why'd you let them do it?"

Vincent flushed. "Six to one?" she said bitterly.

The girl stamped her foot, making a savage, insulted gesture of it. "Why didn't you use your knife? Cut the bastards to pieces? I hate guys like that. They think a girl is a punk! I've been watching you for a long time— the whole bunch of you. Ever since I moved around here. Why'd you let them get you that way?"

"I don't know," Vincent said with desperate anger. "I was dumb—I should've been ready for it. Boy, dumb!"

In the blue light, they stared at each other, sharing fury and bitterness, a mutual intense pride. Vincent forgot this was her first close encounter with the enemy. "Where'd you move?" she asked.

"Over on East 112th," Clara said, then she came a few steps closer and said with a new surge of anger, "Why didn't you take your knife and cut off that damn thing they're always talking so big about?"

"I haven't got a knife!" Vincent shouted, overwhelmed by frustration.

"Stripping you! Next time they'll do it all—the works. That's all they ever want. You got to show them who's boss."

Clara was shaking a fist, as if it had been she thrust to the ground, undressed, humiliated. Her outrage encompassed both of them. Abruptly, she pulled something out of her pocket and thrust it at Vincent.

"Here," she said, "I'll lend you mine. Cut that blond guy to pieces. Cut it right off of him."

It was a small but thick knife. Vincent did not take it, and Clara said, "It's got two blades. Good and sharp. Go on—give it back in a couple of days. I'll meet you here."

"I'm not coming here any more," Vincent said. "The hell with it."

"Scared?" Clara cried, scorn lacing through her anger. "If you let that bastard get away with—" Again she stamped her foot in that proud, outraged way. "Show him you're better. I can't stand it if you don't! You hear me? See if you can get up enough nerve to show him."

"What do you mean, nerve?" Vincent demanded.

Clara looked her up and down. "No guy'd undress me," she said, her voice smoldering. "No twenty guys."

She threw the knife at Vincent's feet. "I'm lending it to you," she said contemptuously. "If that guy grabs you again you'll need it, hear? Bring it back. Monday night—that gives you three days. Meet me here, in your fancy, private place—I'm not scared."

As she turned, began to walk away in a leisurely way, Vincent said, "Hey, wait a minute."

Clara looked back at her. "Make it Tuesday," Vincent said, flushing. "My sister and her baby come every Monday night."

"Tuesday, sure," Clara said, "I don't care. Same time as now, huh? Cut him good—where he'll know it, you. You, Vincent," she added, giving the name a powerful, fisted sound.

Vincent watched her long, casual stride until she disappeared into the turning. Then she picked up the knife and put it in her pocket. In a daze, she went to the clubhouse to shut the door before she realized that it was no longer hers.

The knife lay in her pocket like a present, and she thought with amazement: But why did she lend it to me?

It was almost dark when she started out of the Gully. As she walked toward the slope leading up to the dead end of her street, she remembered the brown skin, the way the nostrils had flared, a sharply etched line of upper lip.

She remembered the shared bitterness and fury. This was the enemy, described from house to house all summer with fear? She had never stood as close to a Negro, or talked to one. On lower Woodlawn they were black faces to walk past. In school she had passed them in corridors without looking for the color of eyes or the shape of a face. One or two of them sat in some of her classes, but they had never focused for her outside of vague names. What color were Clara's eyes? She remembered only the blazing shade of anger.

As she approached the beginning of the slope, she groped to touch back to the way things had been before today. It was not the abrupt savagery of the act of violence that came with her out of the Gully but the protecting fierceness of the girl she had met there. And again the realization came of how alike they were—not only the pants, the way of standing on guard with their bodies, but the whole inner reflection of pride and arrogance. Had she dreamed Clara Jackson? No: her hand felt the knife in her pocket.

Vincent climbed the shallow slope, stepped onto the curving sidewalk of the dead end. It was always a little like stepping over a boundary line, one country into another, but tonight both countries were unreal.

She stood under the lamppost, trying to get her bearings. Kids were playing near the next lamppost, and a dog barked somewhere. The street smelled hot and used, and she was so lonely suddenly that she began to run toward the Golden house. Jules would help her. He always did.

Helen Rose Hull

The Fire

Helen Rose Hull (1888–1971) was a prolific and widely published writer in her time, author of more than a dozen novels as well as short stories, essays, and articles. Her fiction is noteworthy for its profound exploration of family dynamics, in particular of conflicts between parents or between generations and the effects of such conflicts on sensitive, intelligent girl characters. Several of her novels—which include *Quest* and *Islanders*, both reprinted by The Feminist Press—are also remarkable for their depictions of happy, stable lesbian relationships. Hull herself maintained a partnership with a woman for forty years.

This 1917 story, selected by Susan Koppelman and published in *Between Mothers and Daughters*, centers around the relationship between seventeen-year-old Cynthia Moriety and her painting teacher, Miss Egert. The relationship is not without an erotic charge, which may be what most threatens Cynthia's mother. For Cynthia, Miss Egert represents freedom from sexual orthodoxy, but also the freedom to think, to explore, to make art, and to aspire beyond the narrow, conventional life represented by her family.

Cynthia blotted the entry in the old ledger and scowled across the empty office at the door. Mrs. Moriety had left it ajar when she departed with her receipt for the weekly fifty cents on her "lot." If you supplied the missing gilt letters, you could read the sign on the glass of the upper half: "H. P. Bates. Real Estate. Notary Public." Through the door at Cynthia's elbow came the rumbling voice of old Fleming, the lawyer down the hall; he had come in for his Saturday night game of chess with her father.

Cynthia pushed the ledger away from her, and with her elbows on the spotted, green felt of the desk, her fingers burrowing into her cheeks, waited for two minutes by the nickel clock; then, with a quick, awkward movement, she pushed back her chair and plunged to the doorway, her young face twisted in a sort of fluttering resolution.

"Father—"

Her father jerked his head toward her, his fingers poised over a pawn. Old Fleming did not look up.

"Father, I don't think anybody else will be in."

"Well, go on home, then." Her father bent again over the squares, the light shining strongly on the thin places about his temples.

"Father, please,"—Cynthia spoke hurriedly,—"you aren't going for a while? I want to go down to Miss Egert's for a minute."

"Eh? What's that?" He leaned back in his chair now, and Mr. Fleming lifted his severe, black beard to look at this intruder. "What for? You can't take any more painting lessons. Your mother doesn't want you going there any more."

"I just want to get some things I left there. I can get back to go home with you."

"But your mother said she didn't like your hanging around down there in an empty house with an old maid. What did she tell you about it?"

"Couldn't I just get my sketches, Father, and tell Miss Egert I'm not coming any more? She would think it was awfully funny if I didn't. I won't stay. But she—she's been good to me—"

"What set your mother against her, then? What you been doing down there?"

Cynthia twisted her hands together, her eyes running from Fleming's amused stare to her father's indecision. Only an accumulated determination could have carried her on into speech.

"I've just gone down once a week for a lesson. I want to get my things. If I'm not going, I ought to tell her."

"Why didn't you tell her that last week?"

"I kept hoping I could go on."

"Um." Her father's glance wavered toward his game. "Isn't it too late?"

"Just eight, Father." She stepped near her father, color flooding her cheeks. "If you'll give me ten cents, I can take the car—"

"Well—" He dug into his pocket, nodding at Fleming's grunt, "The women always want cash, eh, Bates?"

Then Cynthia, the dime pressed into her palm, tiptoed across to the nail where her hat and sweater hung, seized them, and still on tiptoe, lest she disturb the game again, ran out to the head of the stairs.

She was trembling as she pulled on her sweater; as she ran down the dark steps to the street the tremble changed to a quiver of excitement.

Suppose her father had known just what her mother *had* said! That she could not see Miss Egert again; could never go hurrying down to the cluttered room they called the studio for more of those strange hours of eagerness and pain when she bent over the drawing-board, struggling with the mysteries of color. That last sketch—the little, purpling mint-leaves from the garden—Miss Egert had liked that. And they thought she could leave those sketches there! Leave Miss Egert, too, wondering why she never came again! She hurried to the corner, past the bright store-windows. In thought she could see Miss Egert setting out the jar of brushes, the dishes of water, pushing back the litter of magazines and books to make room for the drawing-board, waiting for her to come. Oh, she had to go once more, black as her disobedience was!

The half-past-eight car was just swinging round the curve. She settled herself behind two German housewives, shawls over their heads, market-baskets beside them. They lived out at the end of the street; one of them sometimes came to the office with payments on her son's lot. Cynthia pressed against the dirty window, fearful lest she miss the corner. There it was, the new street light shining on the sedate old house! She ran to the platform, pushing against the arm the conductor extended.

"Wait a minute, there!" He released her as the car stopped, and she fled across the street.

In front of the house she could not see a light, up-stairs or down, except staring reflections in the windows from the white arc light. She walked past the dark line of box which led to the front door. At the side of the old square dwelling jutted a new, low wing; and there in two windows were soft slits of light along the curtain-edges. Cynthia walked along a little dirt path to a door at the side of the wing. Standing on the door-step, she felt in the shadow for the knocker. As she let it fall, from the garden behind her came a voice:

"I'm out here. Who is it?" There was a noise of feet hurrying through dead leaves, and as Cynthia turned to answer, out of the shadow moved a blur of face and white blouse.

"Cynthia! How nice!" The woman touched Cynthia's shoulder as she pushed open the door. "There, come in."

The candles on the table bent their flames in the draft; Cynthia followed Miss Egert into the room.

"You're busy?" Miss Egert had stood up by the door an old wooden-toothed rake. "I don't want to bother you." Cynthia's solemn, young eyes implored the woman and turned hastily away. The intensity of defiance which had brought her at such an hour left her confused.

"Bother? I was afraid I had to have my grand bonfire alone. Now we can have it a party. You'd like to?"

Miss Egert darted across to straighten one of the candles. The light caught in the folds of her crumpled blouse, in the soft, drab hair blown out around her face.

"I can't stay very long." Cynthia stared about the room, struggling to hide her turmoil under ordinary casualness. "You had the carpenter fix the bookshelves, didn't you?"

"Isn't it nice now! All white and gray and restful—just a spark of life in that mad rug. A good place to sit in and grow old."

Cynthia looked at the rug, a bit of scarlet Indian weaving. She wouldn't see it again! The thought poked a derisive finger into her heart.

"Shall we sit down just a minute and then go have the fire?"

Cynthia dropped into the wicker chair, wrenching her fingers through one another.

"My brother came in to-night, his last attempt to make me see reason," said Miss Egert.

Cynthia lifted her eyes. Miss Egert wasn't wondering why she had come; she could stay without trying to explain.

Miss Egert wound her arms about her knees as she went on talking. Her slight body was wrenched a little out of symmetry, as though from straining always for something uncaptured; there was the same lack of symmetry in her face, in her eyebrows, in the line of her mobile lips. But her eyes had nothing fugitive, nothing pursuing in their soft, gray depth. Their warm, steady eagerness shone out in her voice, too, in its swift inflections.

"I tried to show him it wasn't a bit disgraceful for me to live here in a wing of my own instead of being a sort of nurse-maid adjunct in his house." She laughed, a soft, throaty sound. "It's my house. It's all I have left to keep me a person, you see. I won't get out and be respectable in his eyes."

"He didn't mind your staying here and taking care of—them!" cried Cynthia.

"It's respectable, dear, for an old maid to care for her father and mother; but when they die she ought to be useful to some one else instead of renting her house and living on an edge of it."

"Oh,"—Cynthia leaned forward,—"I should think you'd hate him! I think families are—terrible!"

"Hate him?" Miss Egert smiled. "He's nice. He just doesn't agree with me. As long as he lets the children come over—I told him I meant to have a beautiful time with them, with my real friends—with you."

Cynthia shrank into her chair, her eyes tragic again.

"Come, let's have our bonfire!" Miss Egert, with a quick movement, stood in front of Cynthia, one hand extended.

Cynthia crouched away from the hand.

"Miss Egert,"—her voice came out in a desperate little gasp,—"I can't come down any more. I can't take any more painting lessons." She stopped. Miss Egert waited, her head tipped to one side. "Mother doesn't think I better. I came down—after my things."

"They're all in the workroom." Miss Egert spoke quietly. "Do you want them now?"

"Yes." Cynthia pressed her knuckles against her lips. Over her hand her eyes cried out. "Yes, I better get them," she said heavily.

Miss Egert, turning slowly, lifted a candle from the table.

"We'll have to take this. The wiring isn't done." She crossed the room, her thin fingers, not quite steady, bending around the flame.

Cynthia followed through a narrow passage. Miss Egert pushed open a door, and the musty odor of the store-room floated out into a queer chord with the fresh plaster of the hall.

"Be careful of that box!" Miss Egert set the candle on a pile of trunks. "I've had to move all the truck from the attic and studio in here. Your sketches are in the portfolio, and that's—somewhere!"

Cynthia stood in the doorway, watching Miss Egert bend over a pile of canvases, throwing up a grotesque, rounded shadow on the wall. Round the girl's throat closed a ring of iron.

"Here they are, piled up—"

Cynthia edged between the boxes. Miss Egert was dragging the black portfolio from beneath a pile of books.

"And here's the book I wanted you to see." The pile slipped crashing to the floor as Miss Egert pulled out a magazine. "Never mind those. See here." She dropped into the chair from which she had knocked the books, the portfolio under one arm, the free hand running through the pages of an old art magazine. The chair swung slightly; Cynthia, peering down between the boxes, gave a startled "Oh!"

"What is it?" Miss Egert followed Cynthia's finger. "The chair?" She was silent a moment. "Do you think I keep my mother prisoner here in a wheel-chair now that she is free?" She ran her hand along the worn arm. "I tried to give it to an old ladies' home, but it was too used up. They wanted more style."

"But doesn't it remind you—" Cynthia hesitated.

"It isn't fair to remember the years she had to sit here waiting to die. You didn't know her. I've been going back to the real years—" Miss Egert smiled at Cynthia's bewildered eyes. "Here, let's look at these." She turned another page. "See, Cynthia. Aren't they swift and glad? That's what I was trying to tell you the other day. See that arm, and the drapery there! Just a line—" The girl bent over the page, frowning at the details the quick finger pointed out. "Don't they catch you along with them?" She held the book out at arm's-length, squinting at the figures. "Take it along. There are several more." She tucked the book into the portfolio and rose. "Come on; we'll have our fire."

"But, Miss Egert,"—Cynthia's voice hardened as she was swept back into her own misery,—"I can't take it. I can't come any more."

"To return a book?" Miss Egert lowered her eyelids as if she were again sizing up a composition. "You needn't come just for lessons."

Cynthia shook her head.

"Mother thinks—" She fell into silence. She couldn't say what her mother thought—dreadful things. If she could only swallow the hot pressure in her throat!

"Oh. I hadn't understood." Miss Egert's fingers paused for a swift touch on Cynthia's arm, and then reached for the candle. "You can go on working by yourself."

"It isn't that—" Cynthia struggled an instant, and dropped into silence again. She couldn't say out loud any of the things she was feeling. There were too many walls between feeling and speech: loyalty to her mother, embarrassment that feelings should come so near words, a fear of hurting Miss Egert.

"Don't mind so much, Cynthia." Miss Egert led the way back to the living-room. "You can stay for the bonfire? That will be better than sitting here. Run into the kitchen and bring the matches and marshmallows—in a dish in the cupboard."

Cynthia, in the doorway, stared at Miss Egert. Didn't she care at all! Then the dumb ache in her throat stopped throbbing as Miss Egert's gray eyes held her steadily a moment. She did care! She did! She was just helping her. Cynthia took the candle and went back through the passageway to the kitchen, down at the very end.

She made a place on the table in the litter of dishes and milk-bottles for the candle. The matches had been spilled on the shelf of the stove and into the sink. Cynthia gathered a handful of the driest. Shiftlessness was one of her mother's counts against Miss Egert. Cynthia flushed as she recalled her stumbling defense: Miss Egert had more important things to do; dishes were kept in their proper place; and her mother's: "Important! Mooning about!"

"Find them, Cynthia?" The clear, low voice came down the hall, and Cynthia hurried back.

Out in the garden it was quite black. As they came to the far end, the old stone wall made a dark bank against the sky, with a sharp star over its edge. Miss Egert knelt; almost with the scratch of the match the garden leaped into yellow, with fantastic moving shadows from the trees and in the corner of the wall. She raked leaves over the blaze, pulled the great mound into firmer shape, and then drew Cynthia back under the wall to watch. The light ran over her face; the delighted gestures of her hands were like quick shadows.

"See the old apple-tree dance! He's too old to move fast."

Cynthia crouched by the wall, brushing away from her face the scratchy leaves of the dead hollyhocks. Excitement tingled through her; she felt the red and yellow flames seizing her, burning out the heavy rebellion, the choking weight. Miss Egert leaned back against the wall, her hands spread so that her thin fingers were fire-edged.

"See the smoke curl up through those branches! Isn't it lovely, Cynthia?" She darted around the pile to push more leaves into the flames.

Cynthia strained forward, hugging her arms to her body. Never had there been such a fire! It burned through her awkwardness, her self-consciousness. It ate into the thick, murky veils which hung always between her and the things she struggled to find out. She took a long breath, and the crisp scent of smoke from the dead leaves tingled down through her body.

Miss Egert was at her side again. Cynthia looked up; the slight, asymmetrical figure was like the apple-tree, still, yet dancing!

"Why don't you paint it?" demanded Cynthia, abruptly, and then was frightened as Miss Egert's body stiffened, lost its suggestion of motion.

"I can't." The woman dropped to the ground beside Cynthia, crumpling a handful of leaves. "It's too late." She looked straight at the fire. "I must be content to see it." She blew the pieces of leaves from the palm of her hand and smiled at Cynthia. "Perhaps some day you'll paint it—or write it."

"I can't paint." Cynthia's voice quivered. "I want to do something. I can't even see things except what you point out. And now—"

Miss Egert laid one hand over Cynthia's clenched fingers. The girl trembled at the cold touch.

"You must go on looking." The glow, as the flames died lower, flushed her face. "Cynthia, you're just beginning. You mustn't stop just because you aren't to come here any more. I don't know whether you can say things with your brush; but you must find them out. You mustn't shut your eyes again."

"It's hard alone."

"That doesn't matter."

Cynthia's fingers unclasped, and one hand closed desperately around Miss Egert's. Her heart fluttered in her temples, her throat, her breast. She clung to the fingers, pulling herself slowly up from an inarticulate abyss.

"Miss Egert,"—she stumbled into words,—"I can't bear it, not coming here! Nobody else cares except about sensible things. You do, beautiful, wonderful things."

"You'd have to find them for yourself, Cynthia." Miss Egert's fingers moved under the girl's grasp. Then she bent toward Cynthia, and kissed her with soft, pale lips that trembled against the girl's mouth. "Cynthia, don't let any one stop you! Keep searching!" She drew back, poised for a moment in the shadow before she rose. Through Cynthia ran the swift feet of white ecstasy. She was pledging herself to some tremendous mystery, which trembled all about her.

"Come, Cynthia, we're wasting our coals."

Miss Egert held out her hands. Cynthia, laying hers in them, was drawn to her feet. As she stood there, inarticulate, full of a strange, excited, shouting hope, behind them the path crunched. Miss Egert turned, and Cynthia shrank back.

Her mother stood in the path, making no response to Miss Egert's "Good evening, Mrs. Bates."

The fire had burned too low to lift the shadow from the mother's face. Cynthia could see the hem of her skirt swaying where it dipped up in front. Above that two rigid hands in gray cotton gloves; above that the suggestion of a white, strained face.

Cynthia took a little step toward her.

"I came to get my sketches," she implored her. Her throat was dry. What if her mother began to say cruel things—the things she had already said at home.

"I hope I haven't kept Cynthia too late," Miss Egert said. "We were going to toast marshmallows. Won't you have one, Mrs. Bates?" She pushed the glowing leaf-ashes together. The little spurt of flame showed Cynthia her mother's eyes, hard, angry, resting an instant on Miss Egert and then assailing her.

"Cynthia knows she should not be here. She is not permitted to run about the streets alone at night."

"Oh, I'm sorry." Miss Egert made a deprecating little gesture. "But no harm has come to her."

"She has disobeyed me."

At the tone of her mother's voice Cynthia felt something within her breast curl up like a leaf caught in flame.

"I'll get the things I came for." She started toward the house, running past her mother. She must hurry, before her mother said anything to hurt Miss Egert.

She stumbled on the door-step, and flung herself against the door. The portfolio was across the room, on the little, old piano. The candle beside it had guttered down over the cover. Cynthia pressed out the wobbly flame, and, hugging the portfolio, ran back across the room. On the threshold she turned for a last glimpse. The row of Botticelli details over the book-cases were blurred into gray in the light of the one remaining candle; the Indian rug had a wavering glow. Then she heard Miss Egert just outside.

"I'm sorry Cynthia isn't to come any more," she was saying.

Cynthia stepped forward. The two women stood in the dim light, her mother's thickened, settled body stiff and hostile, Miss Egert's slight figure swaying toward her gently.

"Cynthia has a good deal to do," her mother answered. "We can't afford to give her painting lessons, especially—" Cynthia moved down between the women—"especially," her mother continued, "as she doesn't seem to get much of anywhere. You'd think she'd have some pictures to show after so many lessons."

"Perhaps I'm not a good teacher. Of course she's just beginning."

"She'd better put her time on her studies."

"I'll miss her. We've had some pleasant times together."

Cynthia held out her hand toward Miss Egert, with a fearful little glance at her mother.

"Good-by, Miss Egert."

Miss Egert's cold fingers pressed it an instant.

"Good night, Cynthia," she said slowly.

Then Cynthia followed her mother's silent figure along the path; she turned her head as they reached the sidewalk. Back in the garden winked the red eye of the fire.

They waited under the arc light for the car, Cynthia stealing fleeting glances at her mother's averted face. On the car she drooped against the window-edge, away from her mother's heavy silence. She was frightened now, a panicky child caught in disobedience. Once, as the car turned at the corner below her father's office, she spoke:

"Father will expect me—"

"He knows I went after you," was her mother's grim answer.

Cynthia followed her mother into the house. Her small brother was in the sitting-room, reading. He looked up from his book with wide, knowing eyes. Rebellious humiliation washed over Cynthia; setting her lips against their quivering, she pulled off her sweater.

"Go on to bed, Robert," called her mother from the entry, where she was hanging her coat. "You've sat up too late as it is."

He yawned, and dragged his feet with provoking slowness past Cynthia.

"Was she down there, Mama?" He stopped on the bottom step to grin at his sister.

"Go on, Robert. Start your bath. Mother'll be up in a minute."

"Aw, it's too late for a bath." He leaned over the rail.

"It's Saturday. I couldn't get back sooner."

Cynthia swung away from the round, grinning face. Her mother went past her into the dining-room. Robert shuffled upstairs; she heard the water splashing into the tub.

Her mother was very angry with her. Presently she would come back, would begin to speak. Cynthia shivered. The familiar room seemed full of hostile, accusing silence, like that of her mother. If only she had come straight home from the office, she would be sitting by the table in the old

Morris chair, reading, with her mother across from her sewing, or glancing through the evening paper. She gazed about the room at the neat scrolls of the brown wall-paper, at a picture above the couch, cows by a stream. The dull, ordinary comfort of life there hung about her, a reproaching shadow, within which she felt the heavy, silent discomfort her transgression dragged after it. It would be much easier to go on just as she was expected to do. Easier. The girl straightened her drooping body. That things were hard didn't matter. Miss Egert had insisted upon that. She was forgetting the pledge she had given. The humiliation slipped away, and a cold exaltation trembled through her, a remote echo of the hope that had shouted within her back there in the garden. Here it was difficult to know what she had promised, to what she had pledged herself—something that the familiar, comfortable room had no part in.

She glanced toward the dining-room, and her breath quickened. Between the faded green portières stood her mother, watching her with hard, bright eyes. Cynthia's glance faltered; she looked desperately about the room as if hurrying her thoughts to some shelter. Beside her on the couch lay the portfolio. She took a little step toward it, stopping at her mother's voice.

"Well, Cynthia, have you anything to say?"

Cynthia lifted her eyes.

"Don't you think I have trouble enough with your brothers? You, a grown girl, defying me! I can't understand it."

"I went down for this." Cynthia touched the black case.

"Put that down! I don't want to see it!" The mother's voice rose, breaking down the terrifying silences. "You disobeyed me. I told you you weren't to go there again. And then I telephoned your father to ask you to do an errand for me, and find you there—with that woman!"

"I'm not going again." Cynthia twisted her hands together. "I had to go a last time. She was a friend. I couldn't not tell her I wasn't coming—"

"A friend! A sentimental old maid, older than your mother! Is that a friend for a young girl? What were you doing when I found you? Holding hands! Is that the right thing for you? She's turned your head. You aren't the same Cynthia, running off to her, complaining of your mother."

"Oh, no!" Cynthia flung out her hand. "We were just talking." Her misery confused her.

"Talking? About what?"

"About—" The recollection rushed through Cynthia—"about beauty." She winced, a flush sweeping up to the edge of her fair hair, at her mother's laugh.

"Beauty! You disobey your mother, hurt her, to talk about beauty at night with an old maid!"

There was a hot beating in Cynthia's throat; she drew back against the couch.

"Pretending to be an artist," her mother drove on, "to get young girls who are foolish enough to listen to her sentimentalizing."

"She was an artist," pleaded Cynthia. "She gave it up to take care of her father and mother. I told you all about that—"

"Talking about beauty doesn't make artists."

Cynthia stared at her mother. She had stepped near the table, and the light through the green shade of the reading-lamp made queer pools of color about her eyes, in the waves of her dark hair. She didn't look real. Cynthia threw one hand up against her lips. She was sucked down and down in an eddy of despair. Her mother's voice dragged her again to the surface.

"We let you go there because you wanted to paint, and you maunder and say things you'd be ashamed to have your mother hear. I've spent my life working for you, planning for you, and you go running off—" Her voice broke into a new note, a trembling, grieved tone. "I've always trusted you, depended on you; now I can't even trust you."

"I won't go there again. I had to explain."

"I can't believe you. You don't care how you make me feel."

Cynthia was whirled again down the sides of the eddy.

"I can't believe you care anything for me, your own mother."

Cynthia plucked at the braid on her cuff.

"I didn't do it to make you sorry," she whispered. "I—it was—" The eddy closed about her, and with a little gasp she dropped down on the couch, burying her head in the sharp angle of her elbows.

The mother took another step toward the girl; her hand hovered above the bent head and then dropped.

"You know mother wants just what is best for you, don't you? I can't let you drift away from us, your head full of silly notions."

Cynthia's shoulders jerked. From the head of the stairs came Robert's shout:

"Mama, tub's full!"

"Yes; I'm coming."

Cynthia looked up. She was not crying. About her eyes and nostrils strained the white intensity of hunger.

"You don't think—" She stopped, struggling with her habit of inarticulateness. "There might be things—not silly—you might not see what—"

"Cynthia!" The softness snapped out of the mother's voice.

Cynthia stumbled up to her feet; she was as tall as her mother. For an instant they faced each other, and then the mother turned away, her eyes tear-brightened. Cynthia put out an awkward hand.

"Mother," she said piteously, "I'd like to tell you—I'm sorry—"

"You'll have to show me you are by what you do." The woman started wearily up the stairs. "Go to bed. It's late."

Cynthia waited until the bath-room door closed upon Robert's splashings. She climbed the stairs slowly, and shut herself into her room. She laid the portfolio in the bottom drawer of her white bureau; then she stood by her window. Outside, the big elm-tree, in fine, leafless dignity, showed dimly against the sky, a few stars caught in the arch of its branches.

A swift, tearing current of rebellion swept away her unhappiness, her confused misery; they were bits of refuse in this new flood. She saw, with a fierce, young finality that she was pledged to a conflict as well as to a search. As she knelt by the window and pressed her cheek on the cool glass, she felt the house about her, with its pressure of useful, homely things, as a very prison. No more journeyings down to Miss Egert's for glimpses of escape. She must find her own ways. Keep searching! At the phrase, excitement again glowed within her; she saw the last red wink of the fire in the garden.

Part Three

Work and the World

Edith Summers Kelley

From Weeds

Edith Summers Kelley (1884–1956) moved from her native Toronto to New York City in 1903. She participated in the rich intellectual life of Greenwich Village's artistic and radical circles before venturing to Kentucky in 1914 in an effort to "go back to the land." Struggling to farm tobacco through years of hardship and drought, Kelley found the seeds of her first novel, *Weeds*, which was published in 1923—and soon forgotten. Its republication, fifty years later, won Kelley comparisons to the great Naturalist writers of her time; the *New York Times Book Review* called *Weeds* "unquestionably a major work of American fiction . . . a book that will astonish and enrich anyone who reads it."

Weeds tells the story of Judith Pippinger, a hard-working, spirited young woman who finds herself in a soul-destroying battle with the imprisoning duties of raising a family and managing an impoverished household. In this excerpt, a very young Judith begins to learn about the ways of the world.

From early babyhood Judith had shown signs of an energy that craved constant outlet. From the time that she began to creep about on an old quilt spread on the kitchen floor, she was never still except when asleep. She soon passed the boundaries of the quilt, then of the kitchen, and began bruising her temples by pitching head first from the rather high doorstep. After two or three accidents of this sort, she mastered the art of crawling down the steps backward, and could soon do it with surprising agility. She did not creep on her knees, but went on all fours like a little bear, her small haunches high in the air. Soon, with this method of locomotion, she was going all over the yard and even following her father out into the cow lot, sticking close to his heels like a small dog. After she learned to walk the farm could no longer contain her, and she was many times brought back home by neighbors who happened upon her as she strayed away along the roadside.

As she grew older, she showed a strong interest in all living things about the farm. She followed after her mother when she went to feed the chickens, slop the pigs, and milk the cows. She watched her father hook up the mules; and when he plowed trotted along behind him in the furrow for hours together. She was great friends with Minnie, the big Maltese cat, and gave an excited welcome to each of her frequent litters of kittens. Perhaps more than any other animal on the farm she loved old Bounce, the dog, a good-natured and intelligent mongrel, mostly shepherd, brindle of color and growing with age increasingly lazy of habit. She was jubilant when a hen that had stolen her nest would come proudly out from under the barn or behind the pigpen clucking to a dozen or so fluffy little yellow-legged chickens, all spotless and dainty. Once she came upon a turkey's nest in a weed-shaded corner of the rail fence and, stooping with breathless excitement, saw that the little turkeys had just that day come out of the shell. They peeped at her from under the old turkey hen, not with the bright, saucy looks of little chickens, but with shy, wild, frightened eyes, like timid little birds. Even better than the turkeys and chickens, Judith liked the little geese. They were so big and fluffy when they came out of the shell, and such a beautiful, soft green; and they waddled and bobbed their heads so quaintly, as they moved in a little, compact band over the bluegrass that they loved to eat. They were prettier still when they sailed, like a fleet of little boats at anchor, in some quiet corner of the creek, the sun flecking their green bodies with pale gold as it blinked at them through the boughs of the overhanging willow tree.

She was absorbed in all the small life that fluttered and darted and hopped and crawled about the farm. The robins and finches that sang and built their nests in the big hickory tree by the gate; the butterflies, white, yellow, and particolored, that fluttered among the weeds and grasses; the big dragonflies with gauzy wings iridescently green and purple in the sunlight, that darted back and forth over the brook: these little creatures, with their sweet voices, their gay colors and shy, elusive ways, entered into Judith's life and became a part of it. The grass and the bare ground, too, were alive for Judith, alive with the life of beetles, crickets, ants, and innumerable other worms and insects. The toads that hopped about in the evening were her friends; and when she happened upon a snake she did not scream and run as Lizzie May would have done, but stood leaning forward on tiptoe admiring its colors, the wonder and beauty of its pattern and the sinuous grace of its movement until it wiggled out of sight in the grass.

She loved fish, too: the long, slinky pickerel that live where the pond is full of reeds and water lilies, the whiskered catfish and the beautiful perch, banded with light and dark green, as though they had taken their colors from the sun-flecked banks along which they lived. Better than these big pond fish, because they were smaller and nearer and so more intimately hers, she liked the little "minnies" that lived in her own creek. From time to time she had been lucky enough to secure a minnow, which she would bring home triumphantly in a salmon can. She would set the can down on the doorstep, fill it up with fresh water from the cistern and sprinkle the water lavishly with bread crumbs for the minnow's refreshment. Then she would sit with the can in her lap and lovingly watch the little dark, sinuous body slipping about beneath the bread crumbs.

The next morning she would find the little fish that only yesterday had been so dark and graceful and lively, lying inert and white-bellied among the sodden bread crumbs at the top of the water.

Then the pitiless grip of self-accusing horror and remorse would tighten on Judith. It made her leaden-hearted to think that she had been the cause of the death of this happy little creature that had seemed to love its life so well. Anguished in spirit, she would make frantic efforts to revive the minnow by supplying him with fresh water and bread crumbs and restoring him to his living position in the water, valiantly opposing her eager endeavors and warm pity against the iron inexorableness of death. But all in vain! The fresh water and bread crumbs always failed to interest him; and as soon as the anxious fingers that held him back upward were removed, he would turn up his little white, pink-veined belly to the fresh morning sunshine that would never gladden him again. Sadly Judith would own her defeat at last and, sick at heart with a sorrow too deep and real for childish tears, she would bury her hapless victim in a tiny, flower-lined grave, resolved that she would never again be so cruel as to catch a minnow. But in a few days, with the easy forgetfulness of childhood, she would slip away to the creek, salmon can in hand; and the old rapture and the old agony would sway her too eager soul all over again.

It seemed to Judith at such times, as she would sit on the doorstep staring dismally into vacancy, that not only in relation to minnows, but to everything else in life, she was foredoomed to failure—failure disastrous not only to herself but still more so to the objects that she tried to befriend and benefit. Mud turtles brought from the swampy land near the creek and kept in a soap box in the yard always died. Butterflies imprisoned in an old, rusty bird cage, though watched and tended ever so carefully, always died. Grasshoppers that she tried to domesticate by keeping them in a paste-board box with holes punched in it, even though tempted with raisins filched from her mother's pantry and called by the most endearing of pet names, always died. Beautiful, fuzzy, amber-colored caterpillars, treated in like manner, always died. The little girl, sitting meditatively chin on hand, wondered vaguely why all her efforts should be followed by such a curse of blight and disaster. One day she heard, coming nearer and nearer, the sound of sharp, shrill voices and harsh, staccato laughs which she recognized at once as those of boys. Peering through the tall weeds, she saw coming along the road the two Blackford boys, Jerry and Andy, who lived about half a mile farther along. They had with them a small, forlorn, white kitten, which, after the manner of boys, they were amusing themselves by torturing. Just as Judith looked, Andy gave its tail a sharp tweak; and the miserable little thing whined piteously and looked about in a feeble, watery-eyed fashion, for a way of escape. Then Jerry caught up the little creature by its limp tail and whirled it around and around in the air, shouting inarticulately, like the young savage that he was.

When Judith saw the hapless plight of the kitten, a spirit of uncontrollable horror and rage born of horror entered into her. The mother feeling, an instinct which rarely showed itself in her, would not let her see this little animal tortured. Her face blazed scarlet, her eyes flashed with a wild glitter, her long arms and legs grew strong and tense. She dropped her basket, leapt the picket fence and rushed upon the boys like an avenging Fury, her knife in her hand.

"You let that cat alone! Give it up to me! How dare you hurt a poor little helpless cat? By gollies I'll cut you! I'll kill you! Oh! Oh! Oh! Oh!"

The "Oh's" that Lady Macbeth uttered as she walked in her sleep were not more full of tragic horror than were Judith's as she brandished her knife to right and left in a frenzy of tumultuous emotions. Her long black pigtails, tied at the ends with bits of red grocer's twine, bobbed wildly in the air. Barefooted and bareheaded and wearing a faded and torn blue calico dress, she was yet in spirit a very queen of tragedy as she lunged with her kitchen knife and called down imprecations upon the heads of Jerry and Andy.

Her fury daunted the boys. They had had differences of opinion with Judith before and they knew how she-devilish she could be when angry. They had had experience of her biting, scratching, kicking, and hair-pulling as well as of the hard blows of her strong little clenched fists. While dodging one of the lunges of the knife, Jerry let go of the cat; and Judith instantly snatched it up and stood at bay, the knife poised in one hand, the cat in the other.

"Naow then, one of you jes dass come near here an' I'll run this knife right in yer guts! See if I don't!"

Jerry and Andy showed some sense of the value of discretion. They made no step forward, but stood where they were and bandied compliments.

"You wait till we git ye comin' home from school, ye little slut!" threatened Andy.

"Guess I'll wait a spell, too," retorted Judith, sticking out a viperish red tongue. "I'm not a-skairt of you ner ten more like ye. I can lick any kid in yer family; an' my father can lick yer father, too."

"Oh, can he so?" mocked Jerry. "Mebbe he'd better come over an' try!"

"He don't need to. He wouldn't dirt his hands to touch yer greasy ole dad. But he could if he had a mind to."

"I know sumpin 'bout you! Ah ha, I know sumpin 'bout you!" caroled Jerry derisively.

Judith had begun to lose interest in the verbal encounter.

"Aw shet up yer dirty mouth!" she snapped disgustedly, as she crawled back into her own yard through a hole in the picket fence.

The boys went on down the road walking backward, their fingers to their noses, calling after her in diminishing chorus.

"Cowardly kids! Cowardly kids! Cowardly kids!" returned Judith scornfully, until the enemy voices could no longer be heard.

When she got back to the house she set down her basket by the kitchen door, carried the kitten into the kitchen and got it a saucer of milk. Its eyes were bleared and abject in expression, its sharp little bones almost stuck through its dingy white fur; and its discouraged little tail, tangled with burrs, drooped pitifully.

Judith examined the frail joints of its legs and was immensely relieved to find that none of them were broken. Their intactness seemed to her a miracle; for they were so thin and small and delicate that it seemed as though the slightest blow or pressure would crush them. She shuddered as she felt these fragile joints; and through her whole body there surged a great ocean of tenderness and pity for this defenseless little creature. She experienced a vague, but overwhelming sensation of its pitiful helplessness against all the great, cruel powers of nature, which seemed to be conspiring against it. A clumsy foot, a slamming door, the fall of a flatiron from her mother's ironing board: these and a thousand such could cruelly mangle its frail body and even crush out its tiny spark of life. With a blank, painful, discouraged ache in her heart, Judith wondered vaguely why the whole world should be so rough and cruel and hazardous a place for kittens and minnows and all small, unbefriended things. She did not know that she was precociously experiencing the feeling of many a young mother who, with the birth of her helpless firstborn, feels in one overwhelming rush all the tragedy of weakness in a world where the weak must acquire strength or perish.

The very ugliness of the little thing endeared it to her; for it was a pitiable ugliness, an ugliness born of hunger and ill-treatment. Tenderly she stroked its mangy little head and vowed that she would take care of it and stand between it and the cruel world all the days of its life.

In the morning as soon as she awoke her thoughts flew to the kitten. She scrambled into her clothes and ran out into the yard, glancing about the empty kitchen as she passed through. For a long time she searched in vain and was beginning to think that the kitten had wandered away when of a sudden down at the foot of the hill she stopped in amazement and horror. Here in the heavy clay land beside the creek was a little pool that she had hollowed out the day before and into which she had put four live minnows. The flowers that she had planted around it had all wilted and fallen over. Some were lying flat on the muddy ground, some trailing lifeless in the water. Their bright yellows and purples and pinks had all faded into a common drab. On the edge of the water sat the white kitten. And even as she gazed with horror-dilated eyes it fished up a live minnow with its paw and crunched it mercilessly between its small, strong jaws. In a dazed, half-hearted way Judith looked down into the water of the pond and saw that there was now nothing there—nothing alive—only the pebbles and mosses and half dead water plants.

Silently she turned and ran away, far, far away from the unspeakable kitten and the dead flowers and the empty pool and all the hideous horror of it.

From that day she never again felt the same poignancy of distress at the sight of suffering and death among animals. As she grew more intimately into the life of the woods and the fields and the barnyard she learned to take for granted certain laws of nature which at first had seemed distressingly harsh and cruel. She became resigned to the knowledge that the big fishes eat the little ones, that the chickens devour the grasshoppers, that Bounce, the gentle and affectionate, would kill rabbits and groundhogs whenever he could get hold of them: that in all the bird and animal and insect world the strong prey continually upon the weak. It was hard at first to see Minnie's whole litter of kittens but one dropped into a bucket of water and drowned and to watch her father lead off to the butcher the calf that for two months she had been feeding and petting. But these things happened so often, and the law of the survival of the fittest was so firmly established a part of the life of the farm that she soon learned to accept it with equanimity. She might have been slower in learning this lesson if she had been given to self-deception. But she could never lull her sensibilities with this so commonly used opiate. She insisted upon standing over the bucket in which the kittens were drowned and upon knowing exactly what was going to happen to the calf. Soon she discovered that however many little fishes were eaten there were always plenty more; that an endless number of birds and butterflies and grasshoppers sang and fluttered and jumped through the summer days regardless of the depredations of their enemies; that there were always more kittens and calves being born. Without putting the thought into words or even thinking it, but merely sensing it physically, she knew that in the life of nature death and suffering are merely incidentals; that the message that nature gives to her children is "Live, grow, be happy, and obey my promptings." The birds and chickens and grasshoppers all heard it and Judith knew they heard it. Judith heard it too. As she trotted to school in the clear, sun-vibrant air of the early morning, or brought up the cows through the sweet-smelling twilight, or picked blackberries on the edge of the sunny pasture, nature kept whispering these words in her ear. It is given to few civilized human beings to ever hear this message. Perhaps in that generation Bill Pippinger's girl was the only human being in the whole of Scott County who heard and heeded these words: "Live, grow, be happy, and obey my promptings."

Louise Meriwether

From Daddy Was a Number Runner

Louise Meriwether (b. 1923), author of two novels and several books for children, grew up in Depression-era Harlem, a place she vividly re-creates in *Daddy Was a Number Runner*. Meriwether's rich portrait reveals a community where the daily grind of poverty, violence, and hopelessness is interrupted by moments of celebration and incidents of deep human kindness. Her twelve-year-old heroine, Francie Coffin, has a father who has lost his job and must run numbers for the mob and a mother who, in defiance of his wishes, secretly does domestic work—and they still have to accept "relief" in order to feed their family. With a blend of street smarts, vulnerability, and humor, Francie and her friends learn to cope.

In this excerpt, Francie passes a milestone in her coming-of-age—and learns more than she might wish about what it means to be poor, black, and female in 1930s America.

The first thing Sunday morning when I went into the bathroom I saw blood in my bloomers. I stared at it in disbelief for a moment and then started to holler: "Mother, Mother. I'm bleeding."

Mother came running. "Shut up that screaming, Francie. You ain't dying. You're just starting your period. Wait, I'll get you a clean rag."

I had heard about this, that when you was twelve you started to bleed every month, but nobody had given me any more details and I had halfway forgotten about it. Now Mother would have to tell me everything.

She returned with a torn piece of sheet and two safety pins. She folded the rag into a pad and slipped it between my legs, pinning the ends to my undershirt.

"Guess I'll have to buy you a brassiere, too," she said.

186

I stuck out my chest proudly. I had noticed lately that I wasn't so flat anymore.

"Francie, this means you're growing up."

"Yes, Mother." I looked up at her and waited.

Her eyes met mine. "It means . . ." she hesitated. Her eyes dropped and her voice became crisp. "It means don't let no boys mess around with you. Understand?"

"Yes, Mother."

"Change this pad every couple of hours. There's an old raggedy sheet in the closet I'll tear up for you to use. Understand?"

"Yes, Mother."

Then she was gone, but I didn't understand any more about the period now than I had before, and what did messing around with boys have to do with it?

That night everybody was home and we sat around in the living room. Junior and Sterling were beating each other at checkers and Daddy was playing the piano.

Mother was sewing on a nineteenth-century coat her Jewish lady had given to her for me. It had leg-of-mutton sleeves, it was that old, and I swore I wouldn't wear it. Mother said it was good wool, and she had dug up a piece of fur from the trunk—saved from some other hand-me-down-special—and she was sewing it on the collar. This ratty fur collar was supposed to make the coat more glamorous to me. My protests were loud but useless. We all knew that when the wind got to whipping around those corners I'd be glad to put that coat on to keep my butt from freezing.

Suddenly Daddy swung around on the piano stool. "Y'all listen to me," he said. "The social worker is gonna interview us tomorrow so we can get on relief. Now this ain't nothing to be ashamed of. People all over the country are catching hell, same as we are and . . . well, what I want to say is never forget where you come from."

Sterling groaned and Daddy shot him a threatening look. We knew what was coming. Daddy was going to tell us again about our great-great-grandmother Yoruba. We had heard this story before, and to tell the truth, none of us believed it much, not even Mother.

I looked at her to exchange a wink like we usually did when Daddy got to talking about Yoruba, but she was looking at Daddy now with something like sorrow in her eyes. I knew it was no time to be winking and laughing at Daddy's stories.

"Your great-great-grandmother Yoruba was the only daughter of Dana-kil, the tribal king of Madagascar," Daddy began.

"How many greats was that again?" Sterling asked.

Daddy usually rose to the bait going into lengthy detail as to who begat who until we were all laughing and cracking up about our energetic ancestors who sure knew how to begat. But tonight he wasn't in a laughing mood.

"To be exact," he said, "she was my mother's grandmother, so you figure it out."

According to the story, Danakil had outfitted Yoruba with a trunkful of gold and sent her to England to be educated.

Richard Sommers, the son of a Charleston planter, was in England on business and fell madly in love with beautiful Yoruba. He married her and took her home with him. Yoruba was a proud spitfire of a woman and refused to allow her spirit to be crushed by her in-laws' scorn. She and Richard started a rice mill in Charleston (with her gold) and she bore him four children. When Richard died, the white Sommers wouldn't even bury him in the family graveyard or have anything to do with his colored family, but they did take over the mill, which is still thriving down there.

"What I'm trying to tell you," Daddy said, "is you should be proud to be Yoruba's children. That's what my mother told us down there in Bip. 'Don't take nothing from these crackers,' she used to say, ' 'cause you're no piece of dirt with nothing to be proud of, you're one of Yoruba's children.' "

Daddy's voice trailed off as though he had forgotten his lines. The silence grew gloomy.

"Tell us about your father, Daddy," I said, hoping this might cheer him up.

Daddy began to speak, his voice still listless. His father's father was a runaway slave who lived in the swamps for seven years eating roots and berries and things, and maybe his wife sneaked him some food sometime from the big house, I don't know, but he did have a wife 'cause she had a baby boy just at the time the Civil War started. Anyway, they was escaping in a rowboat one night with a group of other slaves to the Union side. Just as they were gliding past the enemy lines on shore, the baby started to cry. His mother rocked him frantically, patting his little back, kissing his little face, but he wailed on.

"Throw that baby overboard," the leader of the rowboat commanded, "he'll get us all killed."

The baby screamed loudly. With desperate haste the mother ripped her dress open and pushed her breast into the baby's mouth. He gurgled, sputtered, and then became still. The boat glided past the Confederate post on shore and the slaves reached the Union lines safely.

That baby, Daddy's father, grew up to be captain of a fishing boat. During a hurricane off the Charleston harbor his boat capsized and he and all eight of his men were drowned. Their bodies were never recovered.

"Your grandfather was a fearless captain, who went down with his ship," Daddy said, his voice growing stronger. "See that you don't forget it. Now times ain't always gonna be like this, and when the breaks come you gotta be prepared to take them. That's why me and your mother want you to stay in school and get a good education. Both of us only went to the fifth grade down south but you all got a better chance up here in the north. James Junior, you listening to me?"

"Yes, Daddy, I'm listening."

Daddy turned to stare at him. "What's this I hear about Sonny peeing in the classroom just before school let out? I just heard about it."

"He asked the teacher could he leave the room," Junior said, "and the teacher said no, so . . ."

"So he just stood up and pissed in a corner, huh?"

"Yeah, Daddy, that's just what he did." Junior giggled.

"Them boys are so bad the teacher spends most of her time just trying to keep order," Sterling said, frowning at Junior as if the whole mess was his fault. Junior stopped giggling.

Daddy shook his head in dismay. "You better prepare yourself for the future, I'm warning you. Times gonna get better and you ain't gonna be ready."

"Y'all better listen to your father," Mother said.

"I'm listenin'," I said. "I like school."

"You're a girl," Sterling said, siding with Junior now. "You don't know from nothing."

"I do so."

"Okay," Daddy interrupted, "enough of that. I just want you to know we got a past to be proud of." He added softly, defiantly, "Relief ain't nothing to be ashamed of."

. . .

Rebecca didn't want to go. She was ashamed to be seen in the street lugging that shopping bag filled with prunes, butter, and the gold-can jive the relief people were handing out.

"Let's go early in the morning," she told me.

"The place don't open until nine, Becky."

"Let's be at the door then, Francie. I tell you what I'll do. I'll take you to the movies tomorrow night and pay your way. Ken Maynard's playing. Ask your mother if you can go."

We were talking through the dining-room window. It was too hot to sleep and we had just come down from the roof. It was after twelve, but the midnight heat was just as stifling as the noonday sun. I turned away from the window and went to find Mother, who was in the front room.

"Mother, can I go to the show with Becky tomorrow night?"

"Francie, come on and let's pull your bed away from the wall, and you get on in it. How do I know what you can do tomorrow night? Ask your father when he comes home."

"Where is he?"

"Playing poker, I expect." She mumbled something under her breath. They had argued last week about Daddy staying out so late every night playing cards. Daddy said he won most of the time so what was she griping about. Mother answered she never saw no extra money and God knows they needed every dime they could lay their hands on instead of throwing it away on cards.

I really didn't want to ask Daddy about going to the movies with Rebecca because he always said she was too old for me to be hanging around with, so I asked Mother again, and she said yes and to come on now and get to bed.

The next morning Becky and I were first in line at the relief place and now I knew why Becky had promised to take me to the show. We were on our way home and Becky was strutting ahead of me, her head held high, nodding good morning to everyone like she was a queen on parade. I followed a respectful distance behind her, bent almost double to the ground, lugging *her* shopping bag *and* mine. That gold-can jive weighed a ton.

Becky stopped at 119th Street to talk to three boys sitting on the stoop, who were up suspiciously early. I stopped, too, putting down the shopping bags and wiping my sweating palms. Rebecca sent a fierce look in my direction and I grabbed up the bags and stumbled on.

"Morning, Becky," I said as I passed her.

"Hello, Francie. Where you been so early?"

Without waiting for an answer she turned back to the boys and they all burst out laughing. I trudged on. Damn if the movies was worth all this shit.

By the time I got inside my hallway, Becky caught up with me and took her shopping bag.

"You didn't have to pretend as if you barely knew me," I complained as we continued up the stairs together.

"Don't be silly. I spoke to you, didn't I?"

"We still going to the movies tonight?"

"Maybe. That Duke, the one I was talking to, asked me to go to the Rennie with him. There's a barn dance tonight."

"Becky. You promised."

"Okay, we'll go early, about three o'clock and maybe Mama will still let me go to the dance. Watch me over the roof."

We climbed up the last flight and went through the roof door and I watched her as she crossed over the divider separating our two houses and pulled open her door.

"You be ready by three o'clock," she said, "and if you come over early I'll curl your hair."

"I'll be over early," I yelled as she disappeared through the door. That Becky sure was handy with a curling iron. I was glad she was my friend. I don't care what Daddy said.

I took the shopping bag into the kitchen and Mother put the food on the drainboard, looking rather hard at the canned meat wrapped so gaily in its yellow paper. I knew what she was thinking, what recipe would she use to doctor it up with this time?

The labels on the cans read "Choice Cuts of Beef," but everybody in Harlem swore it was really horsemeat, and no matter how our mothers sliced it, baked it, or stewed it, nobody would eat the mess, which we named the gold-can jive.

Mrs. Maceo had come up with a southern recipe, deep fried in batter, but her family wouldn't even break the crust. Mrs. Caldwell added plantains for a West Indian specialty, but her kids said it smelled funky. My mother baked it with tomatoes and green peppers, but none of us would touch it, except Daddy, who we jokingly called the human garbage can. Finally, our mothers stopped exchanging those delicious recipes and that gold-can jive started stacking up in everybody's cupboards, making the shelves buckle.

Rebecca didn't take me to the movies that afternoon after all. Her mother asked her if she was losing her mind. It was either the movies *or* the barn dance. Naturally Becky chose the dance, but she gave me a dime for the movies, so I wasn't mad at her. I had been waiting for Becky all day to make up her mind, so I got to the movies just before the prices changed at five o'clock.

I hadn't been there ten minutes before that fat little white man with the bald head who used to try to get me to come up on the roof slid into the seat next to me. I had to giggle. He sure was crazy about Westerns. Almost every time I came to the show by myself he would sit next to me, hand me a dime, and start feeling me under my skirt. We never said a word to each other, he would just hand me the money and start feeling.

I never let him get his hands too far inside my bloomers, though. By the time he worked his way up inside the elastic leg and got too close, I would shift my butt and he would have to start all over again, or I would change my seat.

Today, though, I guess I got too carried away with the picture and almost forgot all about him. Ken Maynard was my favorite. He and the rangers had just butchered a whole tribe of Indians to rescue this girl Ken Maynard liked, and now, in the moonlight, in his shy, sweet way, he was about to kiss her.

I felt a stirring in my stomach. Then I realized that this fat little man had gotten his fingers all the way inside me. I was throbbing down there like a drum. I squirmed. My legs opened wider, and his fingers moved higher. My flesh seemed to rush to meet him. I groaned. I was caving in, all of my insides straining toward that center where his fingers were making me melt. My God. I was on fire.

His hand touched a raw nerve and a streak of pain ripped through me. I snapped my legs shut, imprisoning his fingers. Violently, I tore his hand away and flung it back at him. I stood up, and stumbled down the aisle and into the street.

I went flying down 116th Street, that strange throbbing between my legs. It was wet down there. I could feel it collecting in my bloomers. I turned the corner at Fifth Avenue and raced home.

Mother was in her bedroom talking to Mrs. Caldwell through the window. I tiptoed into the bathroom and pulled down my bloomers with shaking fingers. It was wet all right. Goopy. Mother would kill me. I pulled off the bloomers and dabbed at the goop with a wet washcloth.

Why had I felt like that? That man was always following me because he knew he could make me feel that way. The memory of my opening my legs wider filled me with shame. That's the way those girls acted in the *True Con-*

fessions magazines, and they always came to a bad end. When I read about them kissing and messing around, it always made me tingle down there— that's why I read that stuff—but it was nothing like when that man was feeling me. If Mother saw these dirty pants she'd know I'd been doing something bad and she'd whip me with the thick end of the razor strop.

I scrubbed my bloomers harder. The fear came that somehow my guilt would show. Then I had a stupid thought: Maybe that's the way babies were made. My mind dashed about madly but I made it stop. I knew good and well you had to fuck to make a baby. Sukie said they put their thing inside you. It was a nasty, filthy thing to do, and I decided then and there that no man was ever going to put his thing inside me.

When I went to bed that night I couldn't sleep. I scratched and smashed bedbugs by the hundreds and finally gave in to my latest day-dream.

I was standing downstairs on the stoop and he came thundering down Fifth Avenue on his great white horse. Ken Maynard. I ran out into the street and without even slowing up, he bent down and swooped me up in his arms, setting me on the saddle behind him. I took one last look at the bell tower in Mt. Morris Park before we rode out of Harlem and into the sunset.

Just before I fell asleep, the memory of that man's hand inside me knot-ted up my stomach again, and I wondered sadly if I was gonna come to a bad end.

Bella Spewack

From Streets

Bella Cohen Spewack (1899–1990) was born in Bucharest and arrived in New York in 1903, where she settled, with her mother, in the impoverished slums of the Lower East Side's Jewish ghetto. Keeping barely a step ahead of starvation and homelessness, they moved from tenement to tenement, working when they could, taking charity when they could get it. Spewack wrote her witty and gritty memoir of her immigrant childhood when she was twenty-three years old—but it would not become a book until after her death nearly seventy years later, when her literary executors brought the unpublished manuscript to The Feminist Press. During her lifetime, Spewack worked as a foreign correspondent and a press agent, then won success as the author of more than thirty-five plays and screenplays in collaboration with her husband.

In this excerpt from *Streets: A Memoir of the Lower East Side*, the curious and daring Bella is learning what she can about the world—about religion, about books and ideas, about life and death.

Stanton Street has no personality of its own for me. It is just a street of the East Side for me—not gutterish enough nor yet clean enough to warrant distinct remembrance.

My recollection has this street bound up with the house we lived in on the corner of Lewis and Stanton Streets. It was a unique house. You could come up through the Stanton Street side and then go out through Lewis Street side or vice versa. And always there would be the candy store on the corner where on cold winter nights, I would cajole my mother into buying me sweet, watery hot chocolate.

There were four apartments in a row on each floor. In the middle, there was a square, high, wooden fence built around a hole in the floor so as to permit the light from the roof to give itself to the kitchens whose single windows faced the hall.

We children used to poise ourselves in the spaces between the wooden spikes of the fence and spit over and down on the floor below. Those of us who were too small to reach to the top would content ourselves by spitting down through the chinks.

Out of our hall, which was quite spacious—we sometimes danced in it—stretched another—a narrow, lightless strip that always smelled of conscienceless cats.

I spent one year in this house adventuring in friends and religion.

GOD
God.
god.
gOd.
goD.

I wrote these down and then looked earnestly at my mother's back as she sat sewing at the machine. She was singing.

I turned back to my list and added exclamation points.

"Don't sing," I said to my mother.

"Don't listen," my mother replied without turning around.

I took my paper and pencil into the hall. But there was not enough light near the fence so I went over to the stocking peddler's side. A stocking peddler and his family of wife and three daughters lived on the extreme left where light trickled in through an airshaft. In the summer, at times they would all come out into the hall and sit around several small laundry baskets of stockings and examine them for damages and resultant pricings. The father would take the black stockings, the mother, the men's socks; the girls would divide the brown silk stockings and children's socks among themselves.

But the light was just as poor on the stocking peddler's side so I returned to the fence and seated myself on the floor.

"God," I said aloud.

I repeated it.

I thought of the day my mother had sat with one of her countrymen discussing a third person of whom our visitor had said, "He grabs God by the feet but he's not to be trusted with a penny." God!

Feet!

I had stared at the man as if he had committed murder and waited momentarily for an exhibition of God's wrath. But it did not come, and for days afterward I grew moody over the man's impiety. Even if God had feet, how had he the temerity to mention it?

The man had violated not so much the tenets of the religion around me, as my own private religion that was an odd mixture of superstition, paganism, and myths of my own making—a part of the inchoate thing I called God.

A few examples. I disliked roaches not because they were creeping things and repugnant to the senses but because they destroyed food. And food was good. God wanted us to eat and be healthy.

I disliked washing my head in kerosene oil. It was slimy to the touch, even though the hair did acquire a certain silky sleekness after the ablution. So I imagined, after I had washed my head in the smelly solution and was lying in bed, that the angels sent from God smiled down upon me. They usually stuck their heads through the hall window, because it was cleaner than the narrow one that faced the skylight. Sometimes I substituted the head of a mythical lover. But I felt just as sure that God was pleased with me for having washed my head in kerosene water.

God to me was a Thing who liked to be pleased—a fatherly, formless, vague body whom one should please.

There was the other element: fear, but that played a secondary if important part in my religious fervor.

I crossed out gOd. I didn't like the way it looked. The wooden fence hurt my back. I slumped down until only the back of my head rested against it.

I wondered whether God was angry with me for leading Margaret into temptation. Margaret was a classmate of mine, a truly religious girl whose father was quite a dignitary in the synagogue—something like a trustee—and owned a milk store.

Before sundown on Friday, on my suggestion, Margaret had put five cents into the corner of her handkerchief. On Saturday afternoon, when we were standing near the flaring boards that marked the entrance to the moving-picture theater, she had looked off into the distance, first at the Williamsburg Bridge (better known on the East Side as the Delancey Street Bridge) and then at the white-flecked sky while I had put my hands into her pocket and drawn out the money in the handkerchief.

Neither of us had questioned the righteousness of our acts, for Margaret had silenced her religious conscience before she had decided to fall, and I had had no compunction whatever. We were complying with the rules of her God, I had argued. I was sinning and she was not.

But somehow sitting in the half light with that list before my eyes and the fence prodding my back, I began to think that perhaps my God wouldn't be pleased at Margaret's defection.

I punctured the edges of the paper with the point of my pencil.

He was probably very sad. Hurt.

I felt the tip of a shoe kick against my upturned sole. I looked up, startled. It was the rustic-looking pants presser.

"What's the matter. Mourning?" he asked in his soft voice.

One night my mother took me to Brooklyn and we sat in a vacant store that was filled with chairs. There were a few people—very few. Sitting on the platform were a few other men and women. One of them was sweet-faced, I remember, and sad. At intervals we rose and sang to the chords that a blond, pink-cheeked, round-shouldered man expelled from a small organ. We sang of Jesus.

I asked my mother why she went there and she laughed. I suspected my mother of not being frank with herself.

I had decided to wait at the Rivington Street Church until I would meet someone who looked as if he could lead me out of my religious maze. I did not choose the synagogue because I could not imagine the bearded Jews entering or emerging from it stopping to talk to a little girl who questioned their faith. Besides, my connection with the synagogue was one of holidays only, as on Yom Kippur and Rosh Hashanah when I would go to see my mother as she wept into her prayer book, sitting on the bench among many other crying, red-nosed women. I felt no everyday kinship with the synagogue. I had an idea that it belonged to the menfolk only.

My decision to wait outside of the church for my leader-out-of-the-wilderness rose from two sources. First, a little girl I had known for a short time had told me that she had gone to a kind of summer play school there and that she had also gotten ice cream and cake on several occasions. No, they hadn't made crosses on her back or her heart. They didn't even say Jesus Christ or make you say Jesus Christ.

And second, I had once seen a man enter that church who had greeted me with patient eyes and soft smile. It had come to me in a flash, then, that that man might perhaps be able to set me straight, religiously speaking.

I did not wait regularly, but each day that the feeling urged me I would hurry down to Rivington and Cannon streets. And one afternoon, I met him. He greeted me with the same patient eyes and soft smile. I remember him as a tall, slightly stooping man with gray side whiskers.

He would have passed me by, but I held up a wavering, restraining hand. "You want to talk to me?" His voice was melodiously soft and wonderfully pitched.

I don't know how I began telling him of my religious difficulties but I remember asking him why Jews are called Sheenies.

"Sheen means bright," he assured me and I was comforted somewhat.

I told him of the day we had gone to a wedding in Brooklyn and how we had lost our way coming home. We walked for many unfamiliar hostile blocks, my mother, the rustic-looking pants presser (the least offensive boarder), old man Lefkowitz, whose beard almost reached to his bosom, his daughter, Sarah, a blond, cow-eyed girl of twenty who laughed at everything, and myself. Finally we struck a trolley car line. Where that car line led, we did not know. My mother began wishing that someone would pass our way, of whom she could inquire the right direction. Over and over again. . . .

As if in response, several gentile boys—not one more than fifteen—came our way. At the sight of us, they began to snicker and lurch against each other. Before we were aware of what was happening, one of them pulled at the hem of my white cashmere coat while a second seized hold of old man Lefkowitz's beard and made as if to cut it.

A sheepish smile spread over the pants presser's face.

My mother made free with her hands and feet and the boys scattered. Gathered together at a safe distance from us, they began to shout derisively:

"Sheenies, ya damn Sheenies!"

They gesticulated wildly with their hands and mimicked among vile epithets: "For vot? For vot, I esk you?"

Away into the darkness they sped like leering shadows of the night, but the pain they left for me tortured me even after I had received comfort.

"They were not true Christians," observed the man sadly, after I had finished speaking.

At parting, he gave me a dime which I spent on a corned beef sandwich with mustard.

Here at this house, while I was getting religion on and off my mind, I made new friends. Margaret was still coming to see me and I her, but our relations were rather strained. She had asked me for a "fancy pin," a brooch which my mother wore exclusively. She knew this. After a deal of bickering with myself, I told her that I couldn't give her my mother's "fancy pin." Margaret became a little cooler, but I didn't mind. I was ready for a change in friends.

There was a thin little girl, whose narrow chest and large brown eyes had won my compassion. She had a large nose and a very weak little mouth with a tiny chin. Her hair was always sleekly drawn back from her forehead, and she always wore clean ribbons and clean aprons. In my mind there were two kind of girls, the kind who wore clean starched aprons and the kind who didn't. I belonged to the latter class but my friends were recruited from the former.

I liked Dinah very much. She would come on Saturdays and help me clean the sideboard of its lemonade sets and soiled doilies.

She begged to do the washing, but I always refused. She dried much better than I ever could. She was a perfect companion for one who wanted an echo—but I wanted someone to disagree with me, someone who could lead me. So one day I dispatched a note by her sister Becky, saying that I was "mad" on her.

I received a letter back in which Dinah implored me to still remain her friend. What had she done to deserve such treatment? I did not reply and she came to plead her cause. She left in tears, for I had not replied once to her.

I was relieved when she left.

There was May Weiss. I liked May for one reason. She could, by a twist of her tongue, elicit a little shower on any place you indicated. It was a trick worthy of emulation. Since I could not do it myself, I cultivated May. Outside of this sole accomplishment, May was not especially my kind. True, she could play the Fairy Wedding Waltz with a dash and vigor that always won admiring remarks from company, but she could not fool me. I had detected false notes in her playing.

May kept coming to my house at all hours and I was beginning to tire of her attentions. One day, as we sat in the hall, she asked me whether she couldn't wear the same dresses that I wore . . . the same hair ribbons . . . the same shoes. The request sickened me.

Where was May Weiss's self-respect?

To escape from her pleading little "cat's eyes," I turned away my head. May caught at my hand. I wrenched it away.

But the gods punished me, for I myself was eaten up with admiration for others. One whom I worshiped lived not far from me. Miriam wore her blonde hair in little Egyptian curls all over her head, and at other times, straight with a big plaid ribbon on the top. She had a little, slightly turned-up nose and a fretful little mouth. Her sister gave piano lessons. This fact alone would have given her caste had she been as ugly as she was remarkably pretty. Miriam ruled us all, friends and teachers.

I idolized her. I would offer her everything I had. I would help her in her lessons and in every way I could, especially in her geography. Margaret, she who had cast fond glances at my mother's brooch, helped her with her arithmetic, practically doing everything for her. And Miriam played favorites with us all.

When I watched her dance I would grow sick with love for her. She was so pretty, so graceful—so everything I wanted to be. Sometimes we would sing together; Miriam could harmonize well with me. The song we usually sang was "Sweet Molly Malone." We could sing it fourteen times during the day and never tire.

One day, Miriam took me to the house to show me that she could play the piano with her back turned to it. She did it and then we sang together. As we came out of the house a boy of eighteen rushed by us, out of breath.

"Who's that?" I asked curiously.

"My brother," Miriam said shortly.

The boy's face stayed with me, as if anxious to be located. I knew I had seen him before and I tried to think where. Finally, my thoughts went back to the days we had lived on Cannon Street . . . little Sadie . . . new lavender dress . . . moving pictures. Oh yes! My mind leapt eagerly upon the memory only to recoil in fear and disgust. No, I did not want to think of the time little Sadie's painted face was streaked with tears.

It sounds sentimental. But wet, painted faces are so poignantly helpless.

The day of the lavender dress started out very happily for Sadie. She had made it with the help of my mother, and when it was finished she could not resist showing it off immediately on the street. It was made in the coat-dress fashion—a straight panel, a shaped waist and a skirt with pleats starting a little above the knees. Sadie was like a child when she was happy. She made me help her pull the narrow black ribbon through the insertion at the neck and sleeves and where the pleats joined the body of the skirt. Then as a reward, she announced that she would take me to the "movies." It was then known as the "nickel show" and if we children came early, we could gain admittance "two for a nickel" and sometimes "two and a baby for a nickel." It depended on the place we patronized.

Sadie and I went to the Victoria Music Hall where moving pictures and Yiddish and English sketches were presented. We were just about to enter when Miriam's brother stepped up to Sadie and suddenly put his mouth to her ear. He did not whisper but voiced his demand so loudly that people passing on the sidewalk stopped to gape. For a moment, I thought Sadie was going to faint. A gray line formed around her mouth. Her eyes closed. When she opened them, she cried out so all who had stopped could hear.

"You dirty, rotten bum!"

At the same time she opened the door to the theater with a vehemence that almost knocked me off my feet and banged it tight behind her.

To my prediction of what Miriam's brother (I did not know then that he was) would do to her, Sadie merely bit her lower lip harder and harder. Then she began to cry. Luckily it was dark. I tried to say something to soothe her but I could not understand. She had been so brave in the beginning. The tears dropped into the lap of her lavender dress.

"To think that such a thing should have happened to me just when I was so happy with my new dress. It ain't right!" she muttered fiercely.

Then she gave herself up determinedly to looking at the screen.

But I could not forget. I plucked at her sleeve until I could feel that she was looking at me. "Supposing he's outside when we go home?" I offered.

Again Sadie drew in her lips, this time with a decision that added much to my respect for her. "I'll call a policeman," she replied. "Now, shut up. I'm gawna see this picture. Didn't I pay a nickel?"

I tried to smile at her witticism but failed.

When we came out, Miriam's brother was still leaning against one of the billboards, his hands in his pockets, a cynical, loose-lipped smile on his old-young face. As we approached the front of our house, Sadie asked me to look around and see if he was following us.

"Look yourself," I answered and rushed up the stairs.

In the playground one noon (I must have been in the fifth grade), Miriam took me aside and said she wanted to tell me something. She was "busting from laughing," and without cause, childlike. I joined heartily.

"You know what it is?" Miriam asked me. She seemed disappointed.

"No," I shook my head. "Honest, I don't."

Miriam began to laugh again uncontrollably.

"Hurry up," I said, "the bell'll ring."

She took me to a farther corner and told me a conundrum whose answer had something to do with the nuptial night. Miriam finished and waited expectantly for my applauding laugh, but I merely stared stupidly at her.

"What's the matter with you?" she demanded irritably, prodding me in the side. "Why don't you laugh?"

The bell saved me from replying. I don't know what I should have said to Miriam if it had not.

I swung to the other extreme in the choice of my next friend. Edith was uniformly unobtrusive. She was happiest when inconspicuous. Her whole bearing was as indicative of this as was her soft, low-pitched voice.

Edith Felk had a low, broad, slightly bulging forehead—the more since her mother believed in drawing every strand of hair tightly into two braids at the back. Then her two wide gray eyes set far apart always looked at one with such queer one-sided intensity that I could swear at times that Edith was cross-eyed. She was not. It was the effect of her inward vision. Because we were as unlike temperamentally and physically as could be, our friendship took a long time to assert itself.

For a time Edith could only visit me. Her mother, a rigorously religious woman, did not know whether to admit me to her home. She capitulated finally and I became a frequent visitor at the house. Besides Edith, there was Mary, an older girl who was downright ugly, but whose thick brown hair fell down to her knees; two silent, older boys, who always appeared to be harboring some grudge that they could not get rid of, and three younger children. It was a decidedly silent house—and more so on Friday and Saturday when religious observance forbade everything that would tend to introduce noise. On Friday before sundown, the four girls of the family would comb their hair, the mother helping the youngest who had to wear hers in curls. Before going to bed each would draw a cap over the freshly combed and plaited hair. In the morning, the cap was removed but no comb touched the hair until Sunday morning.

Gravely and quietly Edith explained the reason for this process. The hair might break while being combed. In that case, the child sinned for having torn something on the Sabbath.

I could not help snickering. "Supposing the rubber band in the cap busts when you're sleeping. Is it a sin too?" I queried wickedly. Edith, sweet-natured, did not take offense but tried very hard to mold her mournful mouth into a smile.

My friendship with Edith is one of the truly beautiful things I have to look back upon. And yet our relations consisted simply of going to the library together, to school together, and sometimes doing our lessons together. I liked doing my lessons in Edith's house. There was the quiet that I had come to welcome as a blessed relief to the noise that always seemed to infest our house. At night the Felks used candle and lamplight, and that too made it restful.

Adventures Edith and I never met, but we both had fertile imaginations. Together we would weave tales of startling episodes, and Edith's gray eyes would recede under her brows and become far away in their vision.

We visited every public library in the section and far beyond when we learned that our cards were transferable. Seward Park Branch, Tompkins Park Branch, Bond Street Branch, Rivington Street Branch, and the Second Avenue Branch saw us both, eyes alight.

It is a tradition, I suppose, among all the bookworms of eleven and twelve on the lower East Side that one public library at one time in its life is superior to the others in having available particular kinds of books. For instance, the Tompkins Park Branch had all the Gypsy Breynton series; the Bond Street Branch the Hildegarde books; and the Second Avenue or Ottendorfer Branch all the Patty series.

Edith and I found this out and would traipse all over the city in search of say, *The First Violin*. Sometimes one of us would be left on guard at one branch where it would be likely that *The First Violin* would be on the shelves later in the day. Most of the time we worked together. We would curve our bodies and bob our heads every which way when a girl who looked as if she might have a "good" book came to exchange it for another. Sometimes it would be the book we wanted, and then it would behoove me, as the older of the two, to step up to the astounded "teacher's" back and say, "Please, could we have that book?"

The librarian's back would stiffen. She was by this time stamping another group of books.

"What book?" she would snap.

"The book the girl brought back—the girl with the blue ribbon."

Edith would be sibilantly whispering the name of the book to me, frantic with anxiety.

"The book's name is *The First Violin*, by Fothergil," I would repeat from Edith's hurried prompting.

If the line stopped here, and there were no more books to stamp, the librarian would relax her back and give us the book. Then there would be exultation in our camp. Usually all the way home we would say nothing to each other. Sometimes our good fortune would be unparalleled and we would get two books we had been hankering for these three weeks and more. Then, all we would do was to look into each other's eyes and burst out into hysterical lilts of laughter.

But I grew tired of having to wait for the books we wanted from one day to another and I decided to join another library so as to have a second card. Edith when she heard shook her head obstinately. No, she wouldn't do that. It was wrong.

"But how is it wrong?" I argued with her. "What does a lib'ary care if you have a hundred cards, so long as you don't tear or dirty the books?"

Edith admitted the sanity of my arguments but refused to join me. So it was I alone who got the first typewritten letter we had ever seen. It had the letterhead of the New York Public Library, and it addressed me as Dear Madam. Me, Dear Madam!

Edith read the letter over. She was duly impressed by the regard the New York Public Library showed for me by its salutation, but being a little more practical than I, she immediately acquainted me with the facts.

"You can belong only to one lib'ary," she announced with the air of one who has scored a point, "it says so in this letter."

"But what's the diff'rence?" I demanded.

"It says so in the letter," repeated Edith.

"But anyway I got out books on the second card," I could not help saying.

"Yes, but you can't do it any more," Edith gently insisted.

"They can't arrest me if I do," I hazarded boldly.

Edith was silently weighing this new angle. "How do you know?" she asked without any particular emphasis on any word.

I lapsed into silence.

Suddenly we looked at each other and burst into laughter.

"Dear Madam!"

Just about the ages of ten and twelve, and even much more before them, there burns brightly in every ghetto child's brain the desire to see what lies without the ghetto's walls. For there are very definite high walls on all sides of us. Edith and I had already walked as far as Second Avenue and Third Street—which was quite a distance from Lewis and Stanton streets, but we had always stifled the wish to go on further. I had once been lost when I was about six following a May party to Seventh Street Park. And I had been taken to Fourteenth Street by my mother who had bought me a coat there.

For a week, Edith and I talked much of Paris, California, Coney Island, the country, London, and Fifth Avenue before we finally decided that we would walk to Andrew Carnegie's home. I don't know how we happened to hit on the residence of the late steel king, but we had heard that it was on Madison Avenue and Sixty-seventh Street. We were first to go to the library and then to "rubberneck" Andrew Carnegie's home.

That Saturday, Edith and her sister and I landed at Greenhut-Siegel's Department Store on Fourteenth Street—just to rest. As soon as we found ourselves there, we began to wander around on the main floor. We could merely stare . . . the ribbons, the silk petticoats, the ladies' lace jabots, the perfumes and powders. We could merely stare at the circular candy counter that surrounded the fountain. In the midst of the fountain was a huge figure of a woman that shone like gold. Its belly, we concluded, must be filled with candy.

When the moving stairs gripped our eyes, we could do nothing but advance toward them in a trance. We boarded them, icy with fear. We had never before been on escalators. The sensation, after a while, proved exceedingly pleasant. We looked at each other with congratulating eyes. We decided to "do" the rest of the building on the moving stairs. On the third or fourth floor, we decided to take an elevator and go down—but here Edith and Mary objected. That would be riding.

"Moving stairs is riding," I suggested wickedly.

"No," replied the gentle-voiced Edith. "The stairs move but they can't ride."

We walked down to the main floor and began our Jacob-like ascendancy. All went well until we reached the third floor where a man in uniform grabbed us by the arms.

"You just walk yourselves down and get out o' here just as quick as you know how," he said. "If I see you here again, I'm gawna have you arrested." He frowned threateningly.

We giggled.

On the main floor again, we regarded each other stoically and decided to continue our walk to Andrew Carnegie's house. Outside, however, we found that it was nearly five and Edith and Mary demurred. They had to be present at the havdalah ceremony which takes place in every Jewish home on Saturday at sundown. It consists of pouring a little brandy or wine on the table and lighting it with a special kind of braided candle. Then each would sip of the remainder. The prayer is one that falls under the heading of holy differentiations.

As we got nearer home, we could barely exchange goodnights. Each of us had received an insult in the presence of the other; also we were tired and disappointed. We had not seen Andrew Carnegie's home, and we knew despite earnest protestations to the contrary that we would never attempt to walk to it again.

But the moving stairs had been a discovery!

Helen was another of my brief flames. She had a small, very dark pointed face and little black curls to which she usually added a red ribbon. When we girls quarreled with her, we called her Pennyface. Her father owned the thriving candy store on the corner. Since she had a stepmother, I forthwith presented her with my pity although there was no need for it. Her stepmother was a very kind, hopelessly fat young woman with deep-set blue eyes and rough black hair that stood out about her head as if she had just arisen from bed.

Helen was several years older than myself and had already read *Tess of the D'Urbervilles*. She had renamed it "Tess of the Dumpyvilles." On her prompting, I had read it, but I am afraid I did not understand it very well— all except "Out of the frying pan into the fire." It made no lasting impression on me except that I felt Tess had not been given a square deal.

The thing that attracted me to Helen was that she was causing a young man to suffer. He was sixteen and was already in his third year of high school. I saw him trying to make her listen to him one night. He was well built but curiously short-legged, partly because of their tendency to go outward at the knees. He wore glasses and spoke like a gentleman. But Helen did not want to listen to him and walked away in the middle of his speech.

I felt matronly sympathy for that boy for I was in the throes of a domestic attack. My mother had been taken sick one day and it fell upon me to purchase the fish, the vegetables, and chicken. When my mother was better I still continued going to Delancey Street Bridge Fish Market where I would with a dexterous movement of my finger lift up the gills to see whether the fish had red blood. Besides that, I who had always scorned any kind of needlecraft began to knit a cape.

I scrubbed my three floors dutifully every Friday, although my mother didn't think I should. She sensed it wouldn't last however and so let me have my own way. It did not, but while my domestic fervor lasted, my sympathy for Helen's high school boy was acute and deep.

On Friday nights, I would meet all the girls—Helen and Fanny Rapp, whom we facetiously called Fanny-Rap-Me-in-the-Eye, May Weiss, and two or three others whom I can't recall—and we would engage in a screaming game of tag called "Help." Sometimes it would be Chinese Tag and sometimes it would be "Colors" or "Did you find a rat in your milk today?" Frequently, we would vary these games by daring bits of mischief. One of us would innocently approach a passerby and ask how to get to Cannon Street. The man or woman, if a stranger to this innocent trick, would seriously stop and explain. The asker would listen just as seriously, but the rest of us would be huddled together rocking or pinching each other with glee.

"She's fooling you, mister!" another of us would suddenly shout. And the man would go on his way, cursing us audibly for wasting his time and credulity.

In the case of a woman, one of us would step up to her and say in a shy whisper, "Missus, you're losing your petticoat!"

The woman—she was usually hatted, for we knew a bareheaded woman did not always care about such matters—would then run swiftly to the nearest hallway to correct her refractory apparel.

As soon as she was out of sight, we would burst out into hilarious laughter.

Other means of spending our Friday evening time would be to settle ourselves comfortably into a corner of a store doorway or on empty milk cans and sing school and street songs. I sustained the second part indiscriminately called tenor or alto during these impromptu recitals. Afterwards, I would be called on to render my imitations of my teachers or of a woman buying a pair of stockings on the street, or I would tell melodramatic tales of adventure, disguised thinly as dreams.

Later in the evening, Helen and I would naturally draw away from the rest and seat ourselves on the little stone doorstep in front of the watch and clock repair shop. And Helen would talk of her high school boy.

One night I assured her that if she continued in her heartless fashion the high school boy would forget her.

"Well, I don't believe in 'stick to me kid, you'll get diamonds,'" Helen replied with a birdlike flirt of her head.

I had never heard that phrase before and asked Helen to repeat it. I said it after her word for word and then we both said it together with individual intonations. For no reason, we both commenced laughing without ceasing, trying our best to say connectedly, "Stick to me kid, you'll get diamonds."

A family living next door included a very old woman and a very old man, several grown children and several young ones—the youngest a girl of my own age. If she had not been white, she would have been easily taken for a Negro girl. So she was called Niggerte. My interest did not lie in her—she was too servile and at the same time displayed a certain obstinacy at times that was not to my liking. I kept up an appearance of pleasure in her company for the sake of getting information, an inkling of which had kindled my imagination.

Her older sister, who had been abandoned by her husband for another woman, was trying to get him back by magic. I had heard my mother talking of midnight ceremonies wherein candles and mirrors figured extensively. I was anxious to know more. I'm afraid the Niggerte was stupid, for to all of my questions, delicate or straightforward, she would shrug her shoulders and elevate her thick lips. "I dunno," she would say.

"You're a dope," I finally told her one day and gave her up entirely.

One day, the eldest sister came in to talk to my mother.

As usual, I had a book before my eyes. To my mother, that was proof enough that my ears were not functioning.

They talked in whispers. I could barely hear them, as now and then my mother would set the wheel of the sewing machine going. She stopped suddenly, started, and rose excitedly. "But you know, you mustn't," she cried.

The eldest sister nodded and her sullen face grew dark and bitter. "Don't worry, I didn't. I remembered in time," she assured my mother with the smile of a cynic. Her face was one of those pointed sallow kinds that never fatten even with the best of foods. She had the weariest brown eyes that I had ever seen and I felt very sorry for her. (I have since seen eyes to which hers might have been likened to wedding lights.)

My mother set her work aside and gave herself up to listening to the eldest sister. I, likewise, but unnoticed, put my book down. It seems that through a friend the eldest sister had reached a woman who practiced witchcraft, a not uncommon practice, especially mimetic magic, on the lower East Side. To her she had told the story of her husband's desertion and her subsequent failures to locate him. The witch (I called her that then) had given her nine candles, one of which she was to light every midnight for nine days. She was to set the candle before the mirror and stand in front of it naked. She was to call the name of her husband three times and watch the mirror.

If she screamed, she would go crazy.

"My teeth wanted to tear at each other," wailed the eldest sister, "but I held myself in. I didn't scream but the tears came to me. I saw him, Fanny, I saw him the second night. He was getting out of bed and was dressing. But when I stopped calling, he went back to sleep. I saw it in the looking glass. Oh, he looked so bad as if he had come out of the ground. He is drinking. I know. I can do nothing. I can't hold him back from his devils."

If the eldest sister wanted her husband to come to her that same night, the witch told her to go down to the edge of the water—that would have been the pier of the East River—and turn a rock over and call his name out loud. Her husband would come to her that night from whatever place he happened to be in at the time.

"But I'm afraid. If someone could go with me, I would not be afraid so much, but nobody can come with me. That's what makes it so terrible." The eldest sister began to wipe her eyes. I do not know when she ceased crying during those nine days.

My mother comforted her in the sympathetic way she had.

"It's only two days more," she assured the woman.

"I wish I were dead," returned the eldest sister.

There was a baby's weak cry and she rose. "I stayed home from the shop on account of her," she said. "She is so sickly. She's always crying. Her head doesn't move from the hole it made in the pillow. Oh God, how much longer will you plague me?"

Such an exit could not fail but arouse me—but strangely enough it was only the part of me that loved the melodramatic. I was too young to feel any real pity for the eldest sister.

From the Niggerte I managed to elicit enough to fill the gaps in my story. The little baby's name was Mirele and because her grandmother, the Niggerte's mother, disliked the noise, the eldest sister had had to leave her in the nursery on Cannon Street. During the night the baby had improved a little and so the eldest sister had gone to work (she was a tacker on men's coats) and brought the baby to the nursery.

Last night had been the eighth night. Tonight would be the ninth. Would the husband come back? I lay back on my side of the bed and imagined the eerie scene: the nude woman standing in front of the mirror, a single candle flickering in the dark—and then the little moving picture in the mirror.

I longed to keep awake until after midnight but I could not. It was not necessary. At two o'clock in the morning, we were awakened by a loud rapping on the wall. For a moment, we could not locate it. I felt my mother breathing hard next to me. The rapping commenced again, this time accompanied by a loud wail that was recognized as that of the eldest sister.

"My baby is dead. People, my baby is dead!"

My mother slipped out of bed, cautioning me not to move out of it until she came back. The wailing rose higher and higher and then died down gradually. I fell into a semi-slumber, and then a shriek louder than I had ever heard before seemed to throw down the wall that separated our bedroom from that of the eldest sister.

"Now you're already here! He's here. He's here. Look on him. Here he is. Oh, my baby is dead. And my husband is back. God gives and God takes."

"God gives and God takes," settled down into the mourner's chant and lulled me back to sleep.

Agnes Smedley

From Daughter of Earth

Agnes Smedley (1894–1950) was a lifelong social activist. She worked for India's liberation from Britain, observed the Russian Revolution, and identified with the Chinese Communist movement. She was also a teacher, a journalist, and a writer; she wrote her first short piece (*Cell Mates*) while imprisoned as a spy during World War I. Smedley rendered her experience of growing up in a rural, dirt-poor, often brutal family through the autobiographical character of Marie Rogers in her masterpiece, *Daughter of Earth*.

Daughter of Earth was first published in 1929, republished in 1935, and subsequently went out of print until it was "rediscovered" by The Feminist Press in 1973. The novel depicts a young woman's struggle to live independently—which to her means doing without love in order to escape the forces that imprisoned most women, including her own mother. In this excerpt, Marie, at age sixteen, has gone off to teach in the New Mexico desert, where she meets a tough, resilient group of women who live in the kind of freedom she has longed for. Yet her family will pull her in once more.

Had it not been for the wanderlust in my blood—my father's gift to me—and had I not inherited his refusal to accept my lot as ordained by a God, I might have remained in the mining towns all my life, married some working man, borne him a dozen children to wander the face of the earth, and died in my early thirties. Such was the fate of all women about me. But settled things were enemies to me and soon lost their newness and color. The unknown called.

Within a year after we moved to Tercio, I found myself a school teacher—I, who had not finished the grammar school, who could not add one figure to another without mistakes, who could not remember one rule in grammar. And I was teaching children of six and boys of my own age: far out in New Mexico, on top of one of the purple-green-red mesas that suddenly rear themselves from the great plains and plateaus, a broad, flat mesa above the timber-line, surrounded by perpendicular rim-rocks that caught the lightning in the fierce storms sweeping over the mountain ranges.

There, out near the edge of the rim-rock, I lived in isolation in a two-room school house, the front room serving as my class-room, the back room as my living-room where I slept, cooked my food and corrected my school papers. It was May when I arrived, but at night the snow still flew before the wind and beat the rope hanging from the school bell against the side of the house: a dull, ghostly sound mingling with the hoarse wailing of the wind and the creaking of the bell above.

From the broad sweeping mesa, little boys and girls come to school; from the deep canyons below, Mexicans and half-breed Indians came; from the plains that stretched as far as eye could reach to the south, a few boys and girls from the ranches came riding on cow-ponies. I was ignorant, yes, but I was learned compared with those about me. And I possessed a native cunning. When a smaller child could not do a problem in arithmetic, and I saw that I also could not do it, I called upon one of the older boys to demonstrate his knowledge before the classroom. He did it proudly, and all of us learned something.

I was "teacher," and it was considered an honor to have me in a ranch house. Children brought me food as presents, a horse was always at my disposal, and I rode through a rough but kindly land—and I rode safely, as all women rode safely, for it was a land not only where strong men lived, but it was a land where women were strong also; or, if not, where the gun slung at their sides could answer their needs. But neither physical force nor guns were necessary. I recall now the years of my girlhood and youth amongst the men of the far West—unlettered, rough working-men who had tasted the worst of life: and with but one exception—that of a barber in a small town—I had never suffered insult and not one man had tried to lay a hand on me in violence. Perhaps I was too young or too ignorant. I had many suitors for marriage, for there were few women in that land. But I was wiser than most girls about me. My intellect, rough and unshod as it was, was wiser than my emotions. All girls married, and I did not know how I would escape, but escape I determined to. I remember that almost without words, my mother supported me in this.

There in New Mexico I rode with men far and wide, singly and in groups, at midday, or to and from dances at night. I danced with them in ranch houses down in the dark canyons or on the plains. They were honorable men, and I was safer with them than are girls within convent walls—

far safer. Of sex I thought not at all, for not only was I little more than a child, but I was too busy. There were so many other things to think about; and then, I had no intention of marrying.

I now recall with joy those hearty, rough, hairy-chested, unshaven men. I recall the rougher, unhappy men in the mining camps, and their silent, unhappy wives. It is with a feeling of sadness and of affection that I think of them now. But there were years when, in search of what I thought were better, nobler things, I denied these, my people, and my family. I forgot the songs they sung—and most of those songs are now dead; I erased their dialect from my tongue; I was ashamed of them and their ways of life. But now—yes, I love them; they are a part of my blood; they, with all their virtues and their faults, played a great part in forming my way of looking at life.

Back in Tercio I had, by the purest chance, met the camp school teacher, a woman from a normal school. At first I was resentful and suspicious of her because she was an educated woman. At last we became friends. We borrowed horses from the camp and rode and hunted together in the hills. She had urged me to study with her, take the county teachers' examination, and become a teacher. Before the year was finished she had loaned me one of her blouses and skirts, and I rode across the Divide to a New Mexico town where the teachers' examination was held.

"Say you are eighteen," she warned. "Lie—it won't hurt anybody."

"I'm not afraid of lyin'," I replied.

"Lie!" Big Buck later exclaimed when I told him of it. "Why, you can lie quicker'n a jackrabbit can jump!"

In fear and trembling I sat among older, better-educated women and took the examination. Two days passed and the County Superintendent of Schools sent for me. He was a tall, lean, black-eyed Mexican, intelligent and kindly.

"You have low grades in arithmetic, and grammar, and school law, and a few more things," he announced, "but if you can speak a little Mexican, here is a school. It is lonely. It is so cold that school is held only in the summer. It is rough and far from town. You will have to cook your own food and wash your own clothes. The life is rough . . . cattle men, you know!"

I didn't understand, but wisdom taught me to listen and look intelligent; it was news to me that there were people who did not cook their own food; and I thought that everybody except rich people washed their own clothing. Then "rough people" . . . what could he mean, I wondered . . . he must mean people who hang around saloons . . . yet that was not possible, for he said it was a lonely place. I would just wait and see; it never occurred to me that I myself belonged to just such rough people as he referred to.

So it was that I became a teacher. I had no fear of loneliness or the cold or wild animals . . . and as for roughness . . . well, I waited to see what it would be like. I never saw any of it. Everybody acted just like I did. Even when, up there on the mesa, I was stunned by lightning that struck the rim-rock a short distance from my house, and I was left lying stretched unconscious across my doorway for hours, it really never occurred to me to be either afraid or give up the school. I merely dragged myself into my room, crept to bed, and waited to get better. The school was the best thing I had ever known. I was making forty dollars a month and sending part of it to my mother. And she, delicate and gentle, proudly made shirts and skirts and sent them to her school-teacher daughter! She had always known I would become "edjicated." Now, when she met the wife of the Superintendent of the camp at Tercio, she did not try to hide her big-veined hands and pass by without being seen; she raised her head proudly and said:

"Howdye do, Mis' Richards . . . it's a nice day t'day, ain't it?"

Up there on the mesa I found a cheap, monthly, housewife's magazine that contained continued love stories, patterns for dresses, recipes for cooking, beauty hints, and odds and ends of a thousand kinds. There was also a list of names and addresses of men and women who wished to exchange picture post cards. From this list I chose the name of a man—the most beautiful name there—a Robert Hampton, whose address was Columbus, Ohio. That was a city far back East, and I had great ideas of the beauty and learning and culture of cities. I sent him a post card. He replied, and as the summer wore on one card gave way to two, then to four in an envelope. He wrote that he was finishing high school—a learned man, in my eyes! He began sending me his old books to read—history, literature, botany—and I studied them, even the things that were dry and uninteresting. Then I sent them on to my mother; for I wanted her to study also. When the school closed and I went home in the autumn, I found my mother sitting by the kitchen window patiently studying one of the books. It had taken her weeks and she was not yet half finished. It was so very new and difficult for her, yet she, as I, felt that it was necessary to know these things.

That was a great home-coming for me . . . I, the triumphant, conquering daughter of sixteen! I was now one of the chief supports of our family.

My father was working on a far-away ranch. He came to Tercio, where my mother now lived, while I was there. I still remember how he came. My mother was sitting by the window, her face enthusiastic as I told of my teaching and of the new school I was to have during the winter. I told her of Robert Hampton, who had sent me a picture of himself—how he was handsome and learned like the men in books. She replied nothing; perhaps she thought it best that I fell in love with a distant hero rather than a near-by reality. As we talked, her eyes wandered to the hillside beyond and I saw her face become suddenly miserable. I noticed how gray her hair had become, although she was but in her late thirties. My eyes followed her, and there from beyond the Company store came my father, walking heavily, his big shoulders stooped, his head down, his hands moving as if talking to some imaginary person.

I went almost immediately to my other school. It lay in a canyon far back of Primero, another of the C. F. & I. Company camps. There, for four months, I heard no English except that spoken in my school; even my students talked to me in Mexican. At night I went to my room in a Mexican adobe house. The man of the house was a Mexican on the school board and he felt it his right, as a man and as an official, to talk at length with the most intellectual woman in the countryside. And that woman was I! His wife was a broad, good-natured Mexican with no ambitions and no ideas. He always ate his supper with me and she waited table, moving back and forth from the kitchen to the room which was the dining-room, the living-room, and my bedroom, all in one. Later, she and her child ate their supper in the kitchen. Her husband spoke a remarkable jargon that was half Mexican and half English, although he led her to believe that he spoke perfect and fluent English. His contempt for her was great and he was always trying to let me see how humiliating it was for a man of his position and intelligence to be married to such a woman. I dared show no sympathy with the woman . . . such would have been a deadly insult to the man and perhaps I would have lost my position.

I wearied of his talk. But he thought a woman should always listen to a man and improve her intellect . . . a woman always knew less than a man; it mattered not who or what she was. I longed for the comfort of silence in which I could read the new book and the letter that had come from Robert Hampton in the East. Those letters were the most important things in my life; they were written in a handwriting that was perfect. While I was in my school the Mexican read them, without my permission, then questioned me about their contents. He understood little, but he knew the handwriting was incomparable and he respected me more for having learned friends. At night I sat for hours with them propped before me, trying to learn to write like that, and to this day my handwriting bears a similarity to them. I knew that if I could ever learn to write so beautifully my education would be complete.

My distant correspondent became the ideal who guided my life. He must have felt like a god, he, sitting back there reading the humble, groping, scrawling letters from a lonely canyon in the Rocky Mountains. Over my little table stood his picture and on the table his old books; if my emotions ever wandered to some dark, handsome Mexican-Indian boy in the neighborhood—as they often did, for I was a wanderer in all things—I fought them, and felt ashamed of myself at night when I went home. But it was not easy. There was an Indian boy just my age in school; he watched me with worshipful eyes, not daring to approach so learned a person as I. His homage to me was the discipline he exercised over all the other pupils—a blink of an eyelash against me from one of them and he escorted them to the edge of the forest at recess time!

One day as I was standing before my classroom and trying to induce my school to talk to me in English—my chief occupation—the door opened and my Mexican host appeared. A telephone call had come from beyond the hills, from Tercio; my mother was sick and I must go home. I stood staring at him, as if he were a messenger of death. He repeated the message. I turned without a word, took my hat and coat hanging in the corner and left the school building. It never occurred to me to dismiss the school. I only knew that my mother was dying . . . had I not dreamed it the night before?

The man caught up with me at his house. He would drive me over the hills tomorrow, he said, for now his team was up in the timber hauling props for the mines. Only one train a day came up the canyons from Trinidad and stopped at all the coal camps. It would reach Primero at two in the afternoon and Tercio in another hour. It was now eleven. I said I would walk to Primero. No, he protested, the snow was deep in the canyons and it was freezing cold. . . . It was dangerous. I hardly heard him. I went into my room, strapped my gun tightly about my waist beneath my coat, and started. He and his wife stood in the door watching in amazement as I started up the canyon road and turned to take the short-cut across the Divide. The snow was heavy, but a herd of sheep had been driven that way and had beaten it down. I climbed the slippery slope, pulling myself up here and there with the tough scrub oak that fastened itself in the frozen ground. If I could only reach the top of the Divide, the rest would be easy, for there I would reach the road. The cold, the possibility of meeting wild animals, the danger of slipping and falling and lying with a broken leg—nothing came to my mind except the top of the hills. Thinking nothing, feeling nothing, seeing nothing, I climbed.

At last I reached it. It had been swept clear of snow by a fierce wind, and was rutty and frozen. I hid my head in my coat collar for a second to warm my lungs. Then I began a slow, easy, steady trot that makes it possible to cover long distances and still not be too exhausted. My mind watched my body as if the two were separate units. My body was tough and strong—as tough as the mountain oak. My mind knew that when the body was so exhausted that it seemed unable to go further, a new energy would flow through it—the "second wind" would come. My mind was I, down that long hard road with the wind lashing my back—my body was a foreign thing. I—my mind—as clear as the winter air, was concentrated on one point—to reach the mining camp by two o'clock; my body was a foreign thing that must be coaxed and humored into doing it. The chief thing, I assured myself over and over again, was to keep the legs steady until the second wind came. There was a time when my legs trembled, weak and faltering. I turned a bend and there, far beyond and below, I saw the smoke of Primero. I lifted my chin—a new warm energy was coursing through my blood, and down the slope, my mouth buried in the neck of my coat to warm the air entering my lungs, my hands free to catch myself in case I should fall, I swung along, running in that slow, steady trot.

I reached the outskirts of Primero, turned to run past the Company store and take the road, black with coal dust, leading to the station. But I was not the only one running—other people, with horror-stricken faces, were rushing through the streets, and I saw that the windows in the Company store were shattered to bits . . . across the street the windows of other houses were also broken. A woman with a plaid shawl over her head stumbled by, weeping in wild terror and crying out in some foreign tongue.

Without faltering in my trot, I turned the corner of the store to pass the mouth of a mine on the hillside that lay before the station. The road was filled with people. Two working men met and ran toward the mine, one shouting at the other:

"They're shuttin' the air-shafts, the God damned . . ."

The mine was belching black smoke, like some primeval Fafnir. Men were drawing ropes around the base of the slag dump and were trying to beat back the struggling women, who fought with the savageness of wild beasts. Their men were penned in the mines, I heard . . . the air-shafts were being closed to save the coal . . . but the fumes would smother the men to death. Such was the burden of their cries. Coal was dear . . . life was cheap.

I ran on. I stumbled onto the station platform and up the steps of the train without even thinking of a ticket. I threw myself face downward on a seat. My lungs were tight and cold. Beyond . . . miles beyond the other side of the humming . . . humming . . . came the scream of a woman.

For three days and nights I watched by her bedside. A movement would awaken me as I dozed. Her blue-black eyes were tender as they followed me back and forth. The doctor who made his weekly rounds from mining town to mining town was out of patience . . . there seemed nothing wrong with her as he could see. Yes—pains in the stomach, of course . . . that was from bad food and from too little . . . what else could you expect, he said, if she insisted on living on potatoes and flour-and-water gravy! She must have better food . . . she was under-nourished. I wondered what "under-nourished" could mean. No, he answered my question, even if she wanted it, she could have no more bicarbonate of soda to ease the pain.

During the first two days she talked with me. Annie had died two weeks before . . . that she had written me. She had gone to her, away down on the desolate plain of western Oklahoma where Annie and Sam worked like animals on their homestead. Annie had left the baby . . . a tiny thing, lying in the next room. I warmed milk and fed it, and it watched me with wistful blue eyes; strange it was that its coming should have caused my sister's death.

My mother was very happy as I sat by her. But I think she knew that death was near, for she said strange things to me—things touching the emotions that she would never have dared say otherwise, for affection between parents and children was never shown among my people. She called me "my daughter"—a thing she had never said before in her life.

"I don't know how I could of lived till now if it hadn't been fer you," she said once, as if the words were wrung from her.

Once in the middle of the night she woke me to say: "Promise me you'll go on an' git a better edjication." Her hand closed upon mine, steady and strong, as if asking for a pledge. A wave of unfamiliar emotion swept over me. I clasped her hand.

When the doctor came the next day I said, "Please give her somethin' . . . she's goin' to die." He was disgusted . . . he had a lot to do and was sick of my telephoning down for him to come all the way up there when there was nothing wrong with my mother except that she needed decent food for a while, he said.

I watched him go. Then, standing by my mother's bedside, I realized that we faced death alone . . . and that I was helpless. She pleaded for the forbidden bicarbonate of soda. I would not give it. But she pleaded again and again and the look in her eyes apalled me. Then in my ignorance, I gave it. But when I did it, I turned and ran up the alley to the school building, burst into the schoolroom and, without thinking, called aloud to Beatrice, George and Dan.

When we reached her bedside, my father, who had come home that morning, was there. He had fallen on his knees and had buried his face in the covers. My mother's eyes were large and glistening, and she turned them on me in an appeal beyond all speech. I bent over the bed and, for the first time in my life, took her in my arms and held her close to my trembling body. "Marie!" My name was the last word she ever uttered.

The lids closed down over the glistening eyes. The body grew limp. I tore back the covering and listened to her breast, so flat, so thin, so poor. The heart throbbed twice, stopped . . . throbbed once more. I listened an eternity . . . intensely yearning . . . but no sound came. My father pulled me to my feet. With difficulty I could stand on my feet. But there were no tears in me. I only knew that I stood by the body of the woman who had given me life. I understood nothing except that this thing I could not understand. In my mind a brilliant light ran in circles, then contracted until it was a tiny black spot, then became lost in nothingness, and nothingness throbbed in beats, like the waves of a sea against a cliff.

Meena Alexander

From Fault Lines

Meena Alexander (b. 1951) was christened Mary Elizabeth but decided, at age fifteen, to change her name to Meena—a first step toward finding "some truer self, stripped free of the colonial burden." She grew up in India and the Sudan and received her Ph.D. from Nottingham University in Great Britain. She is currently Distinguished Professor of English and creative writing at Hunter College and the Graduate Center, City University of New York, and is the author of two novels and seven volumes of poetry in addition to her memoir, published in 1993.

In *Fault Lines*, Alexander explores the process of forging a cultural identity in spite of a patchwork past, and a female identity in spite of a need to integrate the differing expectations of her traditional South Asian heritage and her modern education. In this excerpt, Meena, on the brink of womanhood and living in the restrictive atmosphere of the Sudan, is torn between sensuality and shame as she becomes newly aware of her own female body.

When I open the journals I kept as a teenager in Khartoum, the thin cardboard of the covers slips through my hands. I see lines of bold, upright script scrawled in between the pages of poetry and quotes from Marcel Proust, Albert Camus, Wallace Stevens. These lines tell of the misery I went through:

"If you want me to live as a woman, why educate me?"

"Why not kill me if you want to dictate my life?"

"God, why teach me to write?"

The invocation to God in the last was not to any idea of God, but rather a desperate cry aimed at my mother. The fault lay in the tension I felt between the claims of my intelligence—what my father had taught me to honor, what allowed me to live my life—and the requirements of a femininity my mother had been born and bred to.

Essential to the latter was an arranged marriage. It was the narrow gate through which all women had to enter, and entering it, or so I understood, they had to let fall all their accomplishments, other than those that suited a life of gentility: some cooking, a little musical training, a little embroidery, enough skills of computation to run a household. In essential details and with a few cultural variants, the list would not have differed from Rousseau's outline for Emile's intended, the young Sophie. Indeed, I was to be a Malayalee version of Sophie, or so it sometimes seemed to me. There was a snag though. Amma was living quite far from the decorum of her Syrian Christian peers, and the expatriate life of Khartoum set up singular difficulties in her path. How was she to cope with the parties to which I went in the company of Sarra or Samira, where I met boys, even danced with boys? And what of the University where she knew I read out poems I had written in secret, hiding out in the bathroom at home? What was I learning there? How would I live?

I poured my pain into my journals. I sensed that my sexual desires—which were budding at the time, though they had hardly been satisfied in the flesh—were essential to my poetry. But how did they fit within the rational powers that enabled me to think, pass exams, maintain some independence of thought? I had no answer here. I knew I could not live without passion; but passion burnt me up. That was the forked twig that held me. In dreams I was the snake struggling in that grip. The snake about to be beaten to death.

One night, filled with longing for a young man, a Gujarati whose parents lived in Omdurman, on the other side of the river, filled too with despair at the memory of a dead body, tortured, swollen, lifted out from the Nile River, I walked out into the garden at night. The brilliant desert stars came close, swooping down towards me. I lay down on the grass. I put my cheek to the ground, took the blades of grass into my mouth. I put out both my hands and ran them across the ground till I reached a slight crack in the soil. I was convinced by the evidence of my touch and of my beating heart, that there was a crack in the earth nothing could heal, a fault in the very nature of things, treachery in creation.

. . .

They sit around the long dining table that almost fills the room, appa and amma, side by side. Behind them, the long windows of the Khartoum house edged with white shutters. Through the windows the sky and the acacia hedge are visible. The sky is white hot. There they are, appa and amma, male and female, the beginning of me, discussing their daughters' clothing.

"They can't travel to Kozencheri like this."

Amma was worried. The lines on her forehead were just beginning to form. She was approaching forty. I sensed in her a heaviness of flesh, a settling in, a being there. A mother with freckles and small lines on the face, never picture perfect. So close at hand that she shut the light out. The fine bones in her face were growing coarser, as she put on a little weight, as mothering troubles rose up.

Appa sat there, arms crossed, looking grim.

"Of course they can't." The words seemed to be torn out of him.

"Why not?" I was being daring now, foolhardy even.

I leant across the polished tabletop. The sunlight from the window was in my eyes. I was squinting, trying hard to see. There didn't seem to be anything terribly wrong in what I was asking.

"Why on earth not?" I persisted, hearing my voice in my ears, as if it were going nowhere, as if it could not be heard.

He straightened up. He was an honest, decent man, but one who held in his passions with great effort.

"Know what they do with women? If you go sleeveless in the marketplace, they stone you."

Amma was appalled in spite of herself.

"Shh, Mol." She was trying to calm me down. "You're too headstrong. Just like Sosamma and see what shame she's brought the family. Of course you won't wear sleeveless blouses. You'll cover your arms up. You'll dress well."

The trouble was persistent, and it involved dressing well. It might have been simple if dressing well could work for all times and all places. But while one could dress without long sleeves in Tiruvella, in Kozencheri, twelve miles to the south, it was impossible.

How exaggerated it all grew in my fifteen-year-old mind, all hot and feverish and blurred. The thick-skinned grapefruit from the garden, the taut lemons, the slippery dates, shone with an internal heat. The blue painted ceramic bowl in which they sat grew heavy, bearing the naked fruit. I pulled myself round.

"So what am I going to wear? Are you going to make a new set of clothes for us, all over again?"

Amma nodded, mutely. I knew she was worried. Her mind was on Sosamma, a close relative who had contravened all the family dictates and married a Brahmin doctor. The man, however, was already married, and since he had a high government position, the double bond put him in trouble with the civil authorities. But they were wealthy, had a large house, several Alsatian dogs who were fed meat and raw eggs, more than the beggars got when they called at their gates. They had two lovely sons. Then the quarrels started. Sosamma left her husband to return to her father's protection. That was thirty years ago and it must have seemed to her like leaping from the frying pan into the fire. In order to live in the ancestral home, she had to be accepted back into the church; she had to sign an apology saying she had sinned. Her tall majestic back, her loud shouts of disdain, the bitter recriminations that passed between her and my veliappechan were vivid in my mind. Appa, too, was deeply involved. He was very close to Sosamma and even as he was dead set against her ways, he seemed to understand the will that drove her. But for amma, Sosamma with her proud self-determination, her car and driver that she commanded at will, was much too much. In secret, amma scolded me, crying out, behind locked doors, "You too will be perachathe like Sosamma, bringing shame on us. I can tell even now, how strong your will is."

That morning, at the dining table in Khartoum, I felt amma's nervousness and gave in. In my mind's eye I saw my arms, bare all the way from Khartoum to Tiruvella, covered up in cotton sleeves for Kozencheri consumption; my skirts suddenly two inches longer; the necks of the blouses cut so high I could hardly breathe.

It was only in Kozencheri, appa's ancestral place, that we had to be careful. Elsewhere women from the family dressed in diaphanous saris and revealed all the plumpness of their tender forearms. And who cared? Some even wore backless blouses at dinner parties on Pedder Road. But Malabar Hill in Bombay was one thing, the ancestral home in Kerala was another.

. . .

Clearly, how one dressed was a problem. I was at Khartoum University at this time, and my girlfriends were caught up in the enormous excitement of shedding the tob. They were dressing in skirts and dresses and some of them, driving fast cars down the main street, behaved as if they were fit to turn into those women one had seen on international flights: at the drop of a seat belt they slipped out of their elaborate burkhas and, clad like liquid butterflies in fine Parisian costumes, sat downing drinks and sucking up cigarette smoke through ivory holders.

But Kozencheri and its demands could not be evaded. Watching a woman in a skimpy dress, her burkha shed to the side as she relaxed on a plane, was one thing; getting suitable clothing to gain permission to enter Kozencheri was another. Once puberty had set in, my returning home was fraught with anxiety. Ilya had been dead for four years and the Tiruvella house was locked up. Grandmother Mariamma was growing old and would soon herself die, quite peacefully in her sleep, dressed in her pure white garments. I wanted to lie with her in her great four-poster bed, learn the trick of silence, of female invisibility. How else could women protect themselves? Sometimes I felt it would be easiest for me, if I stood utterly still and disappeared.

In Kozencheri I had to learn all over again that girls could not walk out-side the compound without appropriate escorts. It was hard to get the scary image of women being stoned out of my mind. Did appa get it from the Bible? From the Koran? Hunched over the dining table, staring at his stern, handsome face, I decided it probably came from his raw experience. Such things did indeed happen to women in the marketplaces of Kerala, in the inner courtyards of the ancestral houses. And sometimes women took it upon themselves to do away with their own shameful bodies: they jumped into wells. The image of women jumping into wells was constantly with me during my childhood.

. . .

Born under the sign of Aquarius, I gravitate towards water: well water, pond, lagoon, river, sea. But the bond is uneasy. I am gripped by fear. I do not know what would become of me if I fell in. Perhaps I would dissolve, flesh devolving back into its own element, only my eyes remaining. Well water is most local, most domestic. Set at the threshold of the house, it calls all the girl-children to it. As a young child growing up in Tiruvella I heard countless stories of young women, beautiful as lotus blossoms in bud. At dawn they were discovered, black hair streaming, stretched fine as spider's filament over the well's mouth, bodies blanched and swollen.

Who discovered them? Why did they leap in? Eyes turned downwards, Marya would never tell. Nor would Chinna. Finally Bhaskaran blurted:

"The shame of it, Meenamol. The utter shame," and he gulped. He poked with a little stick at the ash that lay at his feet, at the shining fish scales Govindan the cook had lopped off the parrot fish we had for dinner two nights earlier.

"They were found with child," Chinna told me firmly, looking at me straight in the face. "They could not carry the dishonor."

We were standing beside the well as she spoke. Marya of the beautiful breasts had a bar of Sunlight soap in her hand. She was soaping up the clothes, before beating them on a rock set by the well. Bhaskaran stared at her uncontrollably as he gulped. He could not help himself.

"Kaveri, the blind girl who lived by the schoolhouse. They couldn't clean out the well after that! Who would drink from the water where his child had drowned? Some say the father pushed her to it."

"Pushed?" Chinna spoke up. "Listen, I think it's time we checked the mangoes. Come with me."

She pulled me away. As I walked with Chinna towards the tapioca patch I saw in a blur of light those great star-shaped leaves poised on the crimson stalks, high, higher than my face. But my pleasure was blotted out. Instead of feeling the stalks brush against my cheeks, I kept seeing the well. Over and over, like a mad flashback, I saw the well. First the wall, the brick painted over with gray mortar, streaked with moss, damp with monsoon rain, and then, as if the film had jerked, the inside.

Inside lay a woman. Once she must have been a girl-child like me. Now she was full grown, though she still had the slightly plump cheeks of a girl. I could see the tip of her nose, a fine pointed shape. Her oval face and floating hair framed by water were perfectly posed, like one of those calendar pictures sold in the marketplace. The water was a cloud on which she floated, hair splashing a little as the well frogs leapt. But this woman wasn't Paravati or Lakshmi. She didn't have four golden arms. Nor was she a film star like Nutan or Saira Banu, cheeks pink with paint. She was an ordinary Kerala woman, once girl-child, now full grown, skin wrinkled with water. Her eyes were wide open, staring shamelessly.

The almond-shaped eyes were huge, black, lidless. Under the face, tangling the black hair, was the mound of belly covered in floating cloth. Doubled up inside it like the baby dolphin I had seen in Trivandrum Zoo, was a creature, skinless, face blotched out. What manner of thing was it, forcing the poor woman to leap into water? Was her heart beating wildly as mine did now, this Kaveri or Mariamma, Meena or Munira? Had she locked her eyes so tight as she leapt over the hibiscus fence by the outhouse the servants used? Had she forced herself into the well, both hands clutching her nest of hair? Did she know that in well water her eyes would swing open wide, so shamelessly?

"Ah, the shame of it!" I glanced at Chinna. She was repeating herself, pointing to the golden coconuts on the miniature trees that grew by the hedge. The globes, heavy as a child's head, were tinged with green. They rolled in the sunlight. When I squinted my eyes they made glorious beads you could string together, clear, hard fruit, on a thread of sight. Gazing at the coconuts, I figured out how to freeze them in an instant of looking so the sun wouldn't blind me, so the poor pale thing in the well would flee from me.

Years later, when I read Wyatt's lines: "They flee from me that sometimes did me seek / With naked foot stalking in my chamber," I understood the poem immediately. The beloved, fleet of foot, was racing into water, and the lover was quite confused, bewildered by desire, but deciding not to do very much except stand where he was and make his poem. All dressed up in frills and furbelows and hose of apple green, the rage at the time, he stood his ground in his stately house, while she, poor thing, filled with shame, fled into the nearest tarn.

Sex and death were spliced and fitted into each other, quite precisely: like the milk-white flesh curved into the shell of the tender coconut as it hung on the tree; like the juicy flesh of the love apple rippling inside the purple husk that shone if you rubbed it against skirt or thigh. And shame lit the image. It was what women had to feel. Part of being, not doing. Part of one's very flesh.

Anzia Yezierska

Children of Loneliness

Anzia Yezierska (1885–1970) was born in a small village in Russian-controlled Poland and left home at age seventeen to start a new life in the United States. In a way, Yezierska personified the American dream: she worked hard in sweatshops on the Lower East Side in order to get an education, because education was the key to freedom. Her first story was published in 1915, and she became a renowned writer in her time, best known for depicting the Jewish women's immigrant experience. Up until 1932 she published steadily and even got a Hollywood contract. But fame alienated her from the very life she had been describing so effectively; she published little after the early 1930s, and fell into obscurity until her work was "rediscovered" decades later.

"Children of Loneliness" is the title story of a collection published in 1923. It was reprinted by The Feminist Press in 1981 in *Woman's "True" Profession: Voices from the History of Teaching*, edited by Nancy Hoffman. The story develops a theme that runs through all of Yezierska's work: a young immigrant woman's desire to become a "person," and to reconcile her conflicting worlds.

I

"Oh, Mother, can't you use a fork?" exclaimed Rachel as Mrs. Ravinsky took the shell of the baked potato in her fingers and raised it to her watering mouth.

"Here, *Teacherin* mine, you want to learn me in my old age how to put the bite in my mouth?" The mother dropped the potato back into her plate, too wounded to eat. Wiping her hands on her blue-checked apron, she turned her glance to her husband, at the opposite side of the table.

"Yankev," she said bitterly, "stick your bone on a fork. Our *teacherin* said you dassn't touch no eatings with the hands."

"All my teachers died already in the old country," retorted the old man. "I ain't going to learn nothing new no more from my American daughter."

He continued to suck the marrow out of the bone with that noisy relish that was so exasperating to Rachel.

"It's no use," stormed the girl, jumping up from the table in disgust; "I'll never be able to stand it here with you people."

"'You people?' What do you mean by 'you people?'" shouted the old man, lashed into fury by his daughter's words. "You think you got a different skin from us because you went to college?"

"It drives me wild to hear you crunching bones like savages. If you people won't change, I shall have to move and live by myself."

Yankev Ravinsky threw the half-gnawed bone upon the table with such vehemence that a plate broke into fragments.

"You witch you!" he cried in a hoarse voice tense with rage. "Move by yourself! We lived without you while you was away in college, and we can get on without you further. God ain't going to turn his nose on us because we ain't got table manners from America. A hell she made from this house since she got home."

"*Shah!* Yankev *leben*," pleaded the mother, "the neighbors are opening the windows to listen to our hollering. Let us have a little quiet for a while till the eating is over."

But the accumulated hurts and insults that the old man had borne in the one week since his daughter's return from college had reached the breaking-point. His face was convulsed, his eyes flashed, and his lips were flecked with froth as he burst out in a volley of scorn:

"You think you can put our necks in a chain and learn us new tricks? You think you can make us over for Americans? We got through till fifty years of our lives eating in our own way—"

"Wo is me, Yankev *leben!*" entreated his wife. "Why can't we choke ourselves with our troubles? Why must the whole world know how we are tearing ourselves by the heads? In all Essex Street, in all New York, there ain't such fights like by us."

Her pleadings were in vain. There was no stopping Yankev Ravinsky once his wrath was roused. His daughter's insistence upon the use of a knife and fork spelled apostasy, anti-Semitism, and the aping of the Gentiles.

Like a prophet of old condemning unrighteousness, he ran the gamut of denunciation, rising to heights of fury that were sublime and godlike, and sinking from sheer exhaustion to abusive bitterness.

"*Pfui* on all your American colleges! *Pfui* on the morals of America! No respect for old age. No fear for God. Stepping with your feet on all the laws of the holy Torah. A fire should burn out the whole new generation. They should sink into the earth, like Korah."

"Look at him cursing and burning! Just because I insist on their changing their terrible table manners. One would think I was killing them."

"Do you got to use a gun to kill?" cried the old man, little red threads darting out of the whites of his eyes.

"Who is doing the killing? Aren't you choking the life out of me? Aren't you dragging me by the hair to the darkness of past ages every minute of the day? I'd die of shame if one of my college friends should open the door while you people are eating."

"You—you—"

The old man was on the point of striking his daughter when his wife seized the hand he raised.

"*Mincha!* Yankev, you forgot *Mincha!*"

This reminder was a flash of inspiration on Mrs. Ravinsky's part, the only thing that could have ended the quarreling instantly. *Mincha* was the prayer just before sunset of the orthodox Jews. This religious rite was so automatic with the old man that at his wife's mention of *Mincha* everything was immediately shut out, and Yankev Ravinsky rushed off to a corner of the room to pray.

"*Ashrai Yoishwai Waisabuh!*"

"Happy are they who dwell in Thy house. Ever shall I praise Thee. *Selah!* Great is the Lord, and exceedingly to be praised; and His greatness is unsearchable. On the majesty and glory of Thy splendor, and on Thy marvelous deeds, will I mediate."

The shelter from the storms of life that the artist finds in his art, Yankev Ravinsky found in his prescribed communion with God. All the despair caused by his daughter's apostasy, the insults and disappointments he suffered, were in his sobbing voice. But as he entered into the spirit of his prayer, he felt the man of flesh drop away in the outflow of God around him. His voice mellowed, the rigid wrinkles of his face softened, the hard glitter of anger and condemnation in his eyes was transmuted into the light of love as he went on:

"The Lord is gracious and merciful; slow to anger and of great loving-kindness. To all that call upon Him in truth He will hear their cry and save them."

Oblivious to the passing and repassing of his wife as she warmed anew the unfinished dinner, he continued:

"Put not your trust in princes, in the son of man in whom there is no help." Here Reb Ravinsky paused long enough to make a silent confession for the sin of having placed his hope on his daughter instead of on God. His whole body bowed with the sense of guilt. Then in a moment his humility was transfigured into exaltation. Sorrow for sin dissolved in joy as he became more deeply aware of God's unfailing protection.

"Happy is he who hath the God of Jacob for his help, whose hope is in the Lord his God. He healeth the broken in heart, and bindeth up their wounds."

A healing balm filled his soul as he returned to the table, where the steaming hot food awaited him. Rachel sat near the window pretending to read a book. Her mother did not urge her to join them at the table, fearing another outbreak, and the meal continued in silence. The girl's thoughts surged hotly as she glanced from her father to her mother. A chasm of four centuries could not have separated her more completely from them than her four years at Cornell.

"To think that I was born of these creatures! It's an insult to my soul. What kinship have I with these two lumps of ignorance and superstition? They're ugly and gross and stupid. I'm all sensitive nerves. They want to wallow in dirt."

She closed her eyes to shut out the sight of her parents as they silently ate together, unmindful of the dirt and confusion.

"How is it possible that I lived with them and like them only four years ago? What is it in me that so quickly gets accustomed to the best? Beauty and cleanliness are as natural to me as if I'd been born on Fifth Avenue instead of the dirt of Essex Street."

A vision of Frank Baker passed before her. Her last long talk with him out under the trees in college still lingered in her heart. She felt that she had only to be with him again to carry forward the beautiful friendship that had sprung up between them. He had promised to come shortly to New York. How could she possibly introduce such a born and bred American to her low, ignorant, dirty parents?

"I might as well tear the thought of Frank Baker out of my heart," she told herself. "If he just once sees the pigsty of a home I come from, if he just sees the table manners of my father and mother, he'll fly through the ceiling."

Timidly, Mrs. Ravinsky turned to her daughter.

"Ain't you going to give a taste the eating?"

No answer.

"I fried the *lotkes* special for you—"

"I can't stand your fried, greasy stuff."

"Ain't even my cooking good no more either?" Her gnarled, hard-worked hands clutched at her breast. "God from the world, for what do I need yet any more my life? Nothing I do for my child is no use no more."

Her head sank; her whole body seemed to shrivel and grow old with the sense of her own futility.

"How I was hurrying to run by the butcher before everybody else, so as to pick out the grandest, fattest piece of *brust!*" she wailed, tears streaming down her face. "And I put my hand away from my heart and put a whole fresh egg into the *lotkes*, and I stuffed the stove full of coal like a millionaire so as to get the *lotkes* fried so nice and brown; and now you give a kick on everything I done—"

"Fool woman," shouted her husband, "stop laying yourself on the ground for your daughter to step on you! What more can you expect from a child raised up in America? What more can you expect but that she should spit in your face and make dirt from you?" His eyes, hot and dry under their lids, flashed from his wife to his daughter. "The old Jewish eating is poison to her; she must have *trefa* ham—only forbidden food."

Bitter laughter shook him.

"Woman, how you patted yourself with pride before all the neighbors, boasting of our great American daughter coming home from college! This is our daughter, our pride, our hope, our pillow for our old age that we were dreaming about! this is our American *teacherin!* A Jew-hater, an anti-Semite we brought into the world, a betrayer of our race who hates her own father and mother like the Russian Czar once hated a Jew. She makes herself so refined, she can't stand it when we use the knife or fork the wrong way; but her heart is that of a brutal Cossack, and she spills her own father's and mother's blood like water."

Every word he uttered seared Rachel's soul like burning acid. She felt herself becoming a witch, a she-devil, under the spell of his accusations.

"You want me to love you yet?" She turned upon her father like an avenging fury. "If there's any evil hatred in my soul, you have roused it with your cursed preaching."

"Oi-i-i! Highest One! pity Yourself on us!" Mrs. Ravinsky wrung her hands. "Rachel, Yankev, let there be an end to this knife-stabbing! *Gottuniu!* my flesh is torn to pieces!"

Unheeding her mother's pleading, Rachel rushed to the closet where she kept her things.

"I was a crazy idiot to think that I could live with you people under one roof." She flung on her hat and coat and bolted for the door.

Mrs. Ravinsky seized Rachel's arm in passionate entreaty.

"My child, my heart, my life, what do you mean? Where are you going?"

"I mean to get out of this hell of a home this very minute," she said, tearing loose from her mother's clutching hands.

"Wo is me! My child! We'll be to shame and to laughter by the whole world. What will people say?"

"Let them say! My life is my own; I'll live as I please." She slammed the door in her mother's face.

"They want me to love them yet," ran the mad thoughts in Rachel's brain as she hurried through the streets, not knowing where she was going, not caring. "Vampires, bloodsuckers fastened on my flesh! Black shadow blighting every ray of light that ever came my way! Other parents scheme and plan and wear themselves out to give their child a chance, but they put dead stones in front of every chance I made for myself."

With the cruelty of youth for everything not youth, Rachel reasoned:

"They have no rights, no claims over me like other parents who do things for their children. It was my own brains, my own courage, my own iron will that forced my way out of the sweatshop to my present position in the public schools. I owe them nothing, nothing, nothing."

II

Two weeks already away from home. Rachel looked about her room. It was spotlessly clean. She had often said to herself while at home with her parents: "All I want is an empty room, with a bed, a table, and a chair. As long as it is clean and away from them, I'll be happy." But was she happy?

A distant door closed, followed by the retreating sound of descending footsteps. Then all was still, the stifling stillness of a rooming-house. The white, empty walls pressed in upon her, suffocated her. She listened acutely for any stir of life, but the continued silence was unbroken save for the insistent ticking of her watch.

"I ran away from home burning for life," she mused, "and all I've found is the loneliness that's death." A wave of self-pity weakened her almost to the point of tears. "I'm alone! I'm alone!" she moaned, crumpling into a heap.

"Must it always be with me like this," her soul cried in terror, "either to live among those who drag me down or in the awful isolation of a hall bedroom? Oh, I'll die of loneliness among these frozen, each-shut-in-himself Americans! It's one thing to break away, but, oh, the strength to go on alone! How can I ever do it? The love instinct is so strong in me; I can not live without love, without people."

The thought of a letter from Frank Baker suddenly lightened her spirits. That very evening she was to meet him for dinner. Here was hope—more than hope. Just seeing him again would surely bring the certainty.

This new rush of light upon her dark horizon so softened her heart that she could almost tolerate her superfluous parents.

"If I could only have love and my own life, I could almost forgive them for bringing me into the world. I don't really hate them; I only hate them when they stand between me and the new America that I'm to conquer."

Answering her impulse, her feet led her to the familiar Ghetto streets. On the corner of the block where her parents lived she paused, torn between the desire to see her people and the fear of their nagging reproaches. The old Jewish proverb came to her mind: "The wolf is not afraid of the dog, but he hates his bark." "I'm not afraid of their black curses for sin. It's nothing to me if they accuse me of being an anti-Semite or a murderer, and yet why does it hurt me so?"

Rachel had prepared herself to face the usual hail-storm of reproaches and accusations, but as she entered the dark hallway of the tenement, she heard her father's voice chanting the old familiar Hebrew psalm of "The Race of Sorrows":

"Hear my prayer, O Lord, and let my cry come unto Thee.

"For my days are consumed like smoke, and my bones are burned as an hearth.

"I am like a pelican of the wilderness.

"I am like an owl of the desert.

"I have eaten ashes like bread and mingled my drink with weeping."

A faintness came over her. The sobbing strains of the lyric song melted into her veins like a magic sap, making her warm and human again. All her strength seemed to flow out of her in pity for her people. She longed to throw herself on the dirty, ill-smelling tenement stairs and weep: "Nothing is real but love—love. Nothing so false as ambition."

Since her early childhood she remembered often waking up in the middle of the night and hearing her father chant this age-old song of woe.

There flashed before her a vivid picture of him, huddled in the corner beside the table piled high with Hebrew books, swaying to the rhythm of his Jeremiad, the sputtering light of the candle stuck in a bottle throwing uncanny shadows over his gaunt face. The skull cap, the side-locks, and the long gray beard made him seem like some mystic stranger from a far-off world and not a father. The father of the daylight who ate with a knife, spat on the floor, and who was forever denouncing America and Americans was different from this mystic spirit who could thrill with such impassioned rapture.

Thousands of years of exile, thousands of years of hunger, loneliness, and want swept over her as she listened to her father's voice. Something seemed to be crying out to her to run in and seize her father and mother in her arms and hold them close.

"Love, love—nothing is true between us but love," she thought.

But why couldn't she do what she longed to do? Why, with all her passionate sympathy for them, should any actual contact with her people seem so impossible? No, she couldn't go in just yet. Instead, she ran up on the roof, where she could be alone. She stationed herself at the air-shaft opposite their kitchen window, where for the first time since she had left in a rage she could see her old home.

Ach! what sickening disorder! In the sink were the dirty dishes stacked high, untouched, it looked, for days. The table still held the remains of the last meal. Clothes were strewn about the chairs. The bureau drawers were open, and their contents brimmed over in mad confusion.

"I couldn't endure it, this terrible dirt!" Her nails dug into her palms, shaking with the futility of her visit. "It would be worse than death to go back to them. It would mean giving up order, cleanliness, sanity, everything that I've striven all these years to attain. It would mean giving up the hope of my new world—the hope of Frank Baker."

The sound of the creaking door reached her where she crouched against the air-shaft. She looked again into the murky depths of the room. Her mother had entered. With arms full of paper bags of provisions, the old woman paused on the threshold, her eyes dwelling on the dim figure of her husband. A look of pathetic tenderness illumined her wrinkled features.

"I'll make something good to eat for you, yes?"

Reb Ravinsky only dropped his head on his breast. His eyes were red and dry, sandy with sorrow that could find no release in tears. Good God! never had Rachel seen such profound despair. For the first time she noticed the grooved tracings of withering age knotted on his face and the growing hump on her mother's back.

"Already the shadow of death hangs over them," she thought as she watched them. "They're already with one foot in the grave. Why can't I be human to them before they're dead? Why can't I?"

Rachel blotted away the picture of the sordid room with both hands over her eyes.

"To death with my soul! I wish I were a plain human being with a heart instead of a monster of selfishness with a soul."

But the pity she felt for her parents began now to be swept away in a wave of pity for herself.

"How every step in advance costs me my heart's blood! My greatest tragedy in life is that I always see the two opposite sides at the same time. What seems to me right one day seems all wrong the next. Not only that, but many things seem right and wrong at the same time. I feel I have a right to my own life, and yet I feel just as strongly that I owe my father and mother something. Even if I don't love them, I have no right to step over them. I'm drawn to them by something more compelling than love. It is the cry of their dumb, wasted lives."

Again Rachel looked into the dimly lighted room below. Her mother placed food upon the table. With a self-effacing stoop of humility, she entreated, "Eat only while it is hot yet."

With his eyes fixed almost unknowingly, Reb Ravinsky sat down. Her mother took the chair opposite him, but she only pretended to eat the slender portion of the food she had given herself.

Rachel's heart swelled. Yes, it had always been like that. Her mother had taken the smallest portion of everything for herself. Complaints, reproaches, upbraidings, abuse, yes, all these had been heaped by her upon her mother; but always the juiciest piece of meat was placed on her plate, the thickest slice of bread; the warmest covering was given to her, while her mother shivered through the night.

"Ah, I don't want to abandon them!" she thought; "I only want to get to the place where I belong. I only want to get to the mountain-tops and view the world from the heights, and then I'll give them everything I've achieved."

Her thoughts were sharply broken in upon by the loud sound of her father's eating. Bent over the table, he chewed with noisy gulps a piece of herring, his temples working to the motion of his jaws. With each audible swallow and smacking of the lips, Rachel's heart tightened with loathing.

"Their dirty ways turn all my pity into hate." She felt her toes and her fingers curl inward with disgust. "I'll never amount to anything if I'm not strong enough to break away from them once and for all." Hypnotizing herself into her line of self-defense, her thoughts raced on: "I'm only cruel to be kind. If I went back to them now, it would not be out of love, but because of weakness—because of doubt and unfaith in myself."

Rachel bluntly turned her back. Her head lifted. There was iron will in her jaws.

"If I haven't the strength to tear free from the old, I can never conquer the new. Every new step a man makes is tearing away from those clinging to him. I must get tight and hard as rock inside of me if I'm ever to do the things I set out to do. I must learn to suffer and suffer, walk through blood and fire, and not bend from my course."

For the last time she looked at her parents. The terrible loneliness of their abandoned old age, their sorrowful eyes, the wrung-dry weariness on their faces, the whole black picture of her ruined, desolate home, burned into her flesh. She knew all the pain of one unjustly condemned, and the guilt of one with the spilt blood of helpless lives upon his hands. Then came tears, blinding, wrenching tears that tore at her heart until it seemed that they would rend her body into shreds.

"God! God!" she sobbed as she turned her head away from them, "if all this suffering were at least for something worthwhile, for something outside myself. But to have to break them and crush them merely because I have a fastidious soul that can't stomach their table manners, merely because I can't strangle my aching ambitions to rise in the world!"

She could no longer sustain the conflict which raged within her higher and higher at every moment. With a sudden tension of all her nerves she pulled herself together and stumbled blindly down stairs and out of the house. And she felt as if she had torn away from the flesh and blood of her own body.

III

Out in the street she struggled to get hold of herself again. Despite the tumult and upheaval that racked her soul, an intoxicating lure still held her up—the hope of seeing Frank Baker that evening. She was indeed a storm-racked ship, but within sight of shore. She need but throw out the signal, and help was nigh. She need but confide to Frank Baker of her break with her people, and all the dormant sympathy between them would surge up. His understanding would widen and deepen because of her great need for his understanding. He would love her the more because of her great need for his love.

Forcing back her tears, stepping over her heart-break, she hurried to the hotel where she was to meet him. Her father's impassioned rapture when he chanted the Psalms of David lit up the visionary face of the young Jewess.

"After all, love is the beginning of the real life," she thought as Frank Baker's dark, handsome face flashed before her. "With him to hold on to, I'll begin my new world."

Borne higher and higher by the intoxicating illusion of her great destiny, she cried:

"A person all alone is but a futile cry in an unheeding wilderness. One alone is but a shadow, an echo of reality. It takes two together to create reality. Two together can pioneer a new world."

With a vision of herself and Frank Baker marching side by side to the conquest of her heart's desire, she added:

"No wonder a man's love means so little to the American woman. They belong to the world in which they are born. They belong to their fathers and mothers; they belong to their relatives and friends. They are human even without a man's love. I don't belong; I'm not human. Only a man's love can save me and make me human again."

It was the busy dinner-hour at the fashionable restaurant. Pausing at the doorway with searching eyes and lips eagerly parted, Rachel's swift glance circled the lobby. Those seated in the dining-room beyond who were not too absorbed in one another, noticed a slim, vivid figure of ardent youth; but with dark, age-old eyes that told of the restless seeking of her homeless race.

With nervous little movements of anxiety, Rachel sat down, got up, then started across the lobby. Half-way, she stopped, and her breath caught.

"Mr. Baker," she murmured, her hands fluttering toward him with famished eagerness. His smooth, athletic figure had a cock-sureness that to the girl's worshipping gaze seemed the perfection of male strength.

"You must be doing wonderful things," came from her admiringly, "you look so happy, so shining with life."

"Yes,"—he shook her hand vigorously,—"I've been living for the first time since I was a kid. I'm full of such interesting experiences. I'm actually working in an East Side settlement."

Dazed by his glamourous success, Rachel stammered soft phrases of congratulation as he led her to a table. But seated opposite him, the face of this untried youth, flushed with the health and happiness of another world than that of the poverty-crushed Ghetto, struck her almost as an insincerity.

"You in an East Side settlement?" she interrupted sharply. "What reality can there be in that work for you?

"Oh," he cried, his shoulders squaring with the assurance of his master's degree in sociology, "it's great to get under the surface and see how the other half live. It's so picturesque! My conception of these people has greatly changed since I've been visiting their homes." He launched into a glowing account of the East Side as seen by a twenty-five-year-old college graduate.

"I thought them mostly immersed in hard labor, digging subways or slaving in sweatshops," he went on. "But think of the poetry which the immigrant is daily living!"

"But they're so sunk in the dirt of poverty, what poetry do you see there?"

"It's their beautiful home life, the poetic devotion between parents and children, the sacrifices they make for one another—"

"Beautiful home life? Sacrifices? Why, all I know of is the battle to the knife between parents and children. It's black tragedy that boils there, not the pretty sentiments that you imagine."

"My dear child,"—he waved aside her objection,—"you're too close to judge dispassionately. This very afternoon, on one of my friendly visits, I came upon a dear old man who peered up at me through horn-rimmed glasses behind his pile of Hebrew books. He was hardly able to speak English, but I found him a great scholar."

"Yes, a lazy old do-nothing, a bloodsucker on his wife and children."

Too shocked for remonstrance, Frank Baker stared at her.

"How else could he have time in the middle of the afternoon to pore over his books?" Rachel's voice was hard with bitterness. "Did you see his wife? I'll be she was slaving for him in the kitchen. And his children slaving for him in the sweat-shop."

"Even so, think of the fine devotion that the women and children show in making the lives of your Hebrew scholars possible. It's a fine contribution to America, where our tendency is to forget idealism."

"Give me better a plain American man who supports his wife and children and I'll give you all those dreamers of the Talmud."

He smiled tolerantly at her vehemence.

"Nevertheless," he insisted, "I've found wonderful material for my new book in all this. I think I've got a new angle on the social types of your East Side."

An icy band tightened about her heart. "Social types," her lips formed. How could she possibly confide to this man of the terrible tragedy that she had been through that very day? Instead of the understanding and sympathy that she had hoped to find, there were only smooth platitudes, the sightseer's surface interest in curious "social types."

Frank Baker talked on. Rachel seemed to be listening, but her eyes had a far-off, abstracted look. She was quiet as a spinning-top is quiet, her thoughts and emotions revolving within her at high speed.

"That man in love with me? Why, he doesn't see me or feel me. I don't exist to him. He's only stuck on himself, blowing his own horn. Will he never stop with his 'I,' 'I,' 'I'? Why, I was a crazy lunatic to think that just because we took the same courses in college, he would understand me out in the real world."

All the fire suddenly went out of her eyes. She looked a thousand years old as she sank back wearily in her chair.

"Oh, but I'm boring you with all my heavy talk on sociology." Frank Baker's words seemed to come to her from afar. "I have tickets for a fine musical comedy that will cheer you up, Miss Ravinsky—"

"Thanks, thanks," she cut in hurriedly. Spend a whole evening sitting beside him in a theater when her heart was breaking? No. All she wanted was to get away—away where she could be alone. "I have work to do," she heard herself say. "I've got to get home."

Frank Baker murmured words of polite disappointment and escorted her back to her door. She watched the sure swing of his athletic figure as he strode away down the street, then she rushed up-stairs.

Back in her little room, stunned, bewildered, blinded with her disillusion, she sat staring at her four empty walls.

Hours passed, but she made no move, she uttered no sound. Doubled fists thrust between her knees, she sat there, staring blindly at her empty walls.

"I can't live with the old world, and I'm yet too green for the new. I don't belong to those who gave me birth or to those with whom I was educated."

Was this to be the end of all her struggles to rise in America, she asked herself, this crushing daze of loneliness? Her driving thirst for an education, her desperate battle for a little cleanliness, for a breath of beauty, the tearing away from her own flesh and blood to free herself from the yoke of her parents—what was it all worth now? Where did it lead to? Was loneliness to be the fruit of it all?

Night was melting away like a fog; through the open window the first lights of dawn were appearing. Rachel felt the sudden touch of the sun upon her face, which was bathed in tears. Overcome by her sorrow, she shuddered and put her hand over her eyes as though to shut out the unwelcome contact. But the light shone through her fingers.

Despite her weariness, the renewing breath of the fresh morning entered her heart like a sunbeam. A mad longing for life filled her veins.

"I want to live," her youth cried. "I want to live, even at the worst."

Live how? Live for what? She did not know. She only felt she must struggle against her loneliness and weariness as she had once struggled against dirt, against the squalor and ugliness of her Ghetto home.

Turning from the window, she concentrated her mind, her poor tired mind, on one idea.

"I have broken away from the old world; I'm through with it. It's already behind me. I must face this loneliness till I get to the new world. Frank Baker can't help me; I must hope for no help from the outside. I'm alone; I'm alone till I get there.

"But am I really alone in my seeking? I'm one of the millions of immigrant children, children of loneliness, wandering between worlds that are at once too old and too new to live in."

Kate Chopin

Wiser Than a God

Kate Chopin (1850–1904), born Catherine O'Flaherty, grew up in St. Louis, and as a young married woman moved to New Orleans. In both cities she was part of a privileged French-Creole community that features prominently in her writing. A mother of six, she began writing after her husband died in 1882, partly to come to terms with her husband's and her mother's deaths and partly to support herself and her children. Kate Chopin's female characters are often trapped between limiting choices; many must choose between the life of an artist and the life of wife and mother. Chopin herself did not judge one superior to the other; she simply drew attention to the restrictions put upon women in her time, which made it impossible for them to live full lives.

These irreconcilable choices, which are at the heart of Edna Pontellier's dilemma in Chopin's acclaimed novel *The Awakening* (1899), can already be found in the early short story "Wiser Than a God" (1898), published by The Feminist Press in the 1974 collection *The Storm and Other Stories*, edited by Per Seyersted. Unlike Edna, however, Paula Von Stoltz is able to make a decision that she does not regret.

"To love and be wise is scarcely granted even to a god."—*Latin Proverb*

I

"You might at least show some distaste for the task, Paula," said Mrs. Von Stoltz, in her querulous invalid voice, to her daughter who stood before the glass bestowing a few final touches of embellishment upon an otherwise plain toilet.

"And to what purpose, Mutterchen? The task is not entirely to my liking, I'll admit; but there can be no question as to its results, which you even must concede are gratifying."

"Well, it's not the career your poor father had in view for you. How often he has told me when I complained that you were kept too closely at work, 'I want that Paula shall be at the head,'" with appealing look through the window and up into the gray, November sky into that far "somewhere," which might be the abode of her departed husband.

"It isn't a career at all, mamma; it's only a make-shift," answered the girl, noting the happy effect of an amber pin that she had thrust through the coils of her lustrous yellow hair. "The pot must be kept boiling at all hazards, pending the appearance of that hoped for career. And you forget that an occasion like this gives me the very opportunities I want."

"I can't see the advantages of bringing your talent down to such banale servitude. Who are those people, anyway?"

The mother's question ended in a cough which shook her into speechless exhaustion.

"Ah! I have let you sit too long by the window, mother," said Paula, hastening to wheel the invalid's chair nearer the grate fire that was throwing genial light and warmth into the room, turning its plainness to beauty as by a touch of enchantment. "By the way," she added, having arranged her mother as comfortably as might be, "I haven't yet qualified for that 'banale servitude,' as you call it." And approaching the piano which stood in a distant alcove of the room, she took up a roll of music that lay curled up on the instrument, straightened it out before her. Then, seeming to remember the question which her mother had asked, turned on the stool to answer it. "Don't you know? The Brainards, very swell people, and awfully rich. The daughter is that girl whom I once told you about, having gone to the Conservatory to cultivate her voice and old Engfelder told her in his brusque way to go back home, that his system was not equal to overcoming impossibilities."

"Oh, those people."

"Yes; this little party is given in honor of the son's return from Yale or Harvard, or some place or other." And turning to the piano she softly ran over the dances, whilst the mother gazed into the fire with unresigned sadness, which the bright music seemed to deepen.

"Well, there'll be no trouble about *that*," said Paula, with comfortable assurance, having ended the last waltz. "There's nothing here to tempt me into flights of originality; there'll be no difficulty in keeping to the hand-organ effect."

"Don't leave me with those dreadful impressions, Paula; my poor nerves are on edge."

Wiser Than a God

"You are too hard on the dances, mamma. There are certain strains here and there that I thought not bad."

"It's your youth that finds it so; I have outlived such illusions."

"What an inconsistent little mother it is!" the girl exclaimed, laughing. "You told me only yesterday it was my youth that was so impatient with the commonplace happenings of everyday life. That age, needing to seek its delights, finds them often in unsuspected places, wasn't that it?"

"Don't chatter, Paula; some music, some music!"

"What shall it be?" asked Paula, touching a succession of harmonious chords. "It must be short."

"The 'Berceuse,' then; Chopin's. But soft, soft and a little slowly as your dear father used to play it."

Mrs. Von Stoltz leaned her head back amongst the cushions, and with eyes closed, drank in the wonderful strains that came like an ethereal voice out of the past, lulling her spirit into the quiet of sweet memories.

When the last soft notes had melted into silence, Paula approached her mother and looking into the pale face saw that tears stood beneath the closed eyelids. "Ah! mamma, I have made you unhappy," she cried, in distress.

"No, my child; you have given me a joy that you don't dream of. I have no more pain. Your music has done for me what Faranelli's singing did for poor King Philip of Spain; it has cured me."

There was a glow of pleasure on the warm face and the eyes with almost the brightness of health. "Whilst I listened to you, Paula, my soul went out from me and lived again through an evening long ago. We were in our pretty room at Leipsic. The soft air and the moonlight came through the open-curtained window, making a quivering fret-work along the gleaming waxed floor. You lay in my arms and I felt again the pressure of your warm, plump little body against me. Your father was at the piano playing the 'Berceuse,' and all at once you drew my head down and whispered, 'Ist es nicht wonderschen, mama?' When it ended, you were sleeping and your father took you from my arms and laid you gently in bed."

Paula knelt beside her mother, holding the frail hands which she kissed tenderly.

"Now you must go, liebchen. Ring for Berta, she will do all that is needed. I feel very strong to-night. But do not come back too late."

"I shall be home as early as possible; likely in the last car, I couldn't stay longer or I should have to walk. You know the house in case there should be need to send for me?"

"Yes, yes; but there will be no need."

Paula kissed her mother lovingly and went out into the drear November night with the roll of dances under her arm.

II

The door of the stately mansion at which Paula rang, was opened by a footman, who invited her to "kindly walk upstairs."

"Show the young lady into the music room, James," called from some upper region a voice, doubtless the same whose impossibilities had been so summarily dealt with by Herr Engfelder, and Paula was led through a suite of handsome apartments, the warmth and mellow light of which were very grateful, after the chill out-door air.

Once in the music room, she removed her wraps and seated herself comfortably to await developments. Before her stood the magnificent "Steinway," on which her eyes rested with greedy admiration, and her fingers twitched with a desire to awaken its inviting possibilities. The odor of flowers impregnated the air like a subtle intoxicant and over everything hung a quiet smile of expectancy, disturbed by an occasional feminine flutter above stairs, or muffled suggestions of distant household sounds.

Presently, a young man entered the drawing-room,—no doubt, the college student, for he looked critically and with an air of proprietorship at the festive arrangements, venturing the bestowal of a few improving touches. Then, gazing with pardonable complacency at his own handsome, athletic figure in the mirror, he saw reflected Paula looking at him, with a demure smile lighting her blue eyes.

"By Jove!" was his startled exclamation. Then, approaching, "I beg pardon, Miss—Miss—"

"Von Stoltz."

"Miss Von Stoltz," drawing the right conclusion from her simple toilet and the roll of music. "I hadn't seen you when I came in. Have you been here long? and sitting all alone, too? That's certainly rough."

"Oh, I've been here but a few moments, and was very well entertained."

"I dare say," with a glance full of prognostic complimentary utterances, which a further acquaintance might develop.

As he was lighting the gas of a side bracket that she might better see to read her music, Mrs. Brainard and her daughter came into the room, radiantly attired and both approached Paula with sweet and polite greeting.

"George, in mercy!" exclaimed his mother, "put out that gas, you are killing the effect of the candle light."

"But Miss Von Stoltz can't read her music without it, mother."

"I've no doubt Miss Von Stoltz knows her pieces by heart," Mrs. Brainard replied, seeking corroboration from Paula's glance.

"No, madam; I'm not accustomed to playing dance music, and this is quite new to me," the girl rejoined, touching the loose sheets that George had conveniently straightened out and placed on the rack.

"Oh, dear! 'not accustomed'?" said Miss Brainard. "And Mr. Sohmeir told us he knew you would give satisfaction."

Paula hastened to re-assure the thoroughly alarmed young lady on the point of her ability to give perfect satisfaction.

The door bell now began to ring incessantly. Up the stairs, tripped fleeting opera-cloaked figures, followed by their black robed attendants. The rooms commenced to fill with the pretty hub-bub that a bevy of girls can make when inspired by a close masculine proximity; and Paula not waiting to be asked, struck the opening bars of an inspiring waltz.

Some hours later, during a lull in the dancing, when the men were making vigorous applications of fans and handkerchiefs; and the girls beginning to throw themselves into attitudes of picturesque exhaustion—save for the always indefatigable few— a proposition was ventured, backed by clamorous entreaties, which induced George to bring forth his banjo. And an agreeable moment followed, in which that young man's skill met with a truly deserving applause. Never had his audience beheld such proficiency as he displayed in the handling of his instrument, which was now behind him, now over-head, and again swinging in mid-air like the pendulum of a clock and sending forth the sounds of stirring melody. Sounds so inspiring that a pretty little black-eyed fairy, an acknowledged votary of Terpsichore, and George's particular admiration, was moved to contribute a few passes of a Virginia break-down, as she had studied it from life on a Southern plantation. The act closing amid a spontaneous babel of hand clapping and admiring bravos.

It must be admitted that this little episode, however graceful, was hardly a fitting prelude to the magnificent "Jewel Song from 'Faust,'" with which Miss Brainard next consented to regale the company. That Miss Brainard possessed a voice, was a fact that had existed as matter of tradition in the family as far back almost as the days of that young lady's baby utterances, in which loving ears had already detected the promise which time had so recklessly fulfilled.

True genius is not to be held in abeyance, though a host of Engfelders would rise to quell it with their mundane protests!

Miss Brainard's rendition was a triumphant achievement of sound, and with the proud flush of success moving her to kind condescension, she asked Miss Von Stoltz to "please play something."

Paula amiably consented, choosing a selection from the Modern Classic. How little did her auditors appreciate in the performance the results of a life study, of a drilling that had made her amongst the knowing an acknowledged mistress of technique. But to her skill she added the touch and interpretation of the artist; and in hearing her, even Ignorance paid to her genius the tribute of a silent emotion.

When she arose there was a moment of quiet, which was broken by the black-eyed fairy, always ready to cast herself into a breach, observing, flippantly, "How pretty!" "Just lovely!" from another; and "What wouldn't I give to play like that." Each inane compliment falling like a dash of cold water on Paula's ardor.

She then became solicitous about the hour, with reference to her car, and George who stood near looked at his watch and informed her that the last car had gone by a full half hour before.

"But," he added, "if you are not expecting any one to call for you, I will gladly see you home."

"I expect no one, for the car that passes here would have set me down at my door," and in this avowal of difficulties, she tacitly accepted George's offer.

The situation was new. It gave her a feeling of elation to be walking through the quiet night with this handsome young fellow. He talked so freely and so pleasantly. She felt such a comfort in his strong protective nearness. In clinging to him against the buffets of the staggering wind she could feel the muscles of his arms, like steel.

He was so unlike any man of her acquaintance. Strictly unlike Poldorf, the pianist, the short rotundity of whose person could have been less objectionable, if she had not known its cause to lie in an inordinate consumption of beer. Old Engfelder, with his long hair, his spectacles and his loose, disjointed figure, was hors de combat in comparison. And of Max Kuntzler, the talented composer, her teacher of harmony, she could at the moment think of no positive point of objection against him, save the vague, general serious one of his unlikeness to George.

Her new-awakened admiration, though, was not deaf to a little inexplicable wish that he had not been so proficient with the banjo.

On they went chatting gaily, until turning the corner of the street in which she lived, Paula saw that before the door stood Dr. Sinn's buggy.

Brainard could feel the quiver of surprised distress that shook her frame, as she said, hurrying along, "Oh! mamma must be ill—worse; they have called the doctor."

Reaching the house, she threw open wide the door that was unlocked, and he stood hesitatingly back. The gas in the small hall burned at its full, and showed Berta at the top of the stairs, speechless, with terrified eyes, looking down at her. And coming to meet her, was a neighbor, who strove with well-meaning solicitude to keep her back, to hold her yet a moment in ignorance of the cruel blow that fate had dealt her whilst she had in happy unconsciousness played her music for the dance.

III

Several months had passed since the dreadful night when death had deprived Paula for the second time of a loved parent.

After the first shock of grief was over, the girl had thrown all her energies into work, with the view of attaining that position in the musical world which her father and mother had dreamed might be hers.

She had remained in the small home occupying now but the half of it; and here she kept house with the faithful Berta's aid.

Friends were both kind and attentive to the stricken girl. But there had been two, whose constant devotion spoke of an interest deeper than mere friendly solicitude.

Max Kuntzler's love for Paula was something that had taken hold of his sober middle age with an enduring strength which was not to be lessened or shaken, by her rejection of it. He had asked leave to remain her friend, and while holding the tender, watchful privileges which that comprehensive title may imply, had refrained from further thrusting a warmer feeling on her acceptance.

Paula one evening was seated in her small sitting-room, working over some musical transpositions, when a ring at the bell was followed by a footstep in the hall which made her hand and heart tremble.

George Brainard entered the room, and before she could rise to greet him, had seated himself in the vacant chair beside her.

"What an untiring worker you are," he said, glancing down at the scores before her. "I always feel that my presence interrupts you; and yet I don't know that a judicious interruption isn't the wholesomest thing for you sometimes."

"You forget," she said, smiling into his face, "that I was trained to it. I must keep myself fitted to my calling. Rest would mean deterioration."

"Would you not be willing to follow some other calling?" he asked, looking at her with unusual earnestness in his dark, handsome eyes.

"Oh, never!"

"Not if it were a calling that asked only for the labor of loving?"

She made no answer, but kept her eyes fixed on the idle traceries that she drew with her pencil on the sheets before her.

He arose and made a few impatient turns about the room, then coming again to her side, said abruptly:

"Paula, I love you. It isn't telling you something that you don't know, unless you have been without bodily perceptions. To-day there is something driving me to speak it out in words. Since I have known you," he continued, striving to look into her face that bent low over the work before her, "I have been mounting into higher and always higher circles of Paradise, under a blessed illusion that you—care for me. But to-day, a feeling of dread has been forcing itself upon me—dread that with a word you might throw me back into a gulf that would now be one of everlasting misery. Say if you love me, Paula. I believe you do, and yet I wait with indefinable doubts for your answer."

He took her hand which she did not withdraw from his.

"Why are you speechless? Why don't you say something to me!" he asked desperately.

"I am speechless with joy and misery," she answered. "To know that you love me, gives me happiness enough to brighten a lifetime. And I am miserable, feeling that you have spoken the signal that must part us."

"You love me, and speak of parting. Never! You will be my wife. From this moment we belong to each other. Oh, my Paula," he said, drawing her to his side, "my whole existence will be devoted to your happiness."

"I can't marry you," she said shortly, disengaging his hand from her waist.

"Why?" he asked abruptly. They stood looking into each other's eyes.

"Because it doesn't enter into the purpose of my life."

"I don't ask you to give up anything in your life. I only beg you to let me share it with you."

George had known Paula only as the daughter of the undemonstrative American woman. He had never before seen her with the father's emotional nature aroused in her. The color mounted into her cheeks, and her blue eyes were almost black with intensity of feeling.

"Hush," she said; "don't tempt me further." And she cast herself on her knees before the table near which they stood, gathering the music that lay upon it into an armful, and resting her hot cheek upon it.

"What do you know of my life," she exclaimed passionately. "What can you guess of it? Is music anything more to you than the pleasing distraction of an idle moment? Can't you feel that with me, it courses with the blood through my veins? That it's something dearer than life, than riches, even than love?" with a quiver of pain.

"Paula listen to me; don't speak like a mad woman."

She sprang up and held out an arm to ward away his nearer approach.

"Would you go into a convent, and ask to be your wife a nun who has vowed herself to the service of God?"

"Yes, if that nun loved me; she would owe to herself, to me and to God to be my wife."

Paula seated herself on the sofa, all emotion seeming suddenly to have left her; and he came and sat beside her.

"Say only that you love me, Paula," he urged persistently.

"I love you," she answered low and with pale lips.

He took her in his arms, holding her in silent rapture against his heart and kissing the white lips back into red life.

"You will be my wife?"

"You must wait. Come back in a week and I will answer you." He was forced to be content with the delay.

The days of probation being over, George went for his answer, which was given him by the old lady who occupied the upper story.

"Ach Gott! Fräulein Von Stoltz ist schon im Leipsic gegangen!"— All that has not been many years ago. George Brainard is as handsome as ever, though growing a little stout in the quiet routine of domestic life. He has quite lost a pretty taste for music that formerly distinguished him as a skillful banjoist. This loss his little black-eyed wife deplores; though she has herself made concessions to the advancing years, and abandoned Virginia break-downs as incompatible with the serious offices of wifehood and matrimony.

You may have seen in the morning paper, that the renowned pianist, Fräulein Paula Von Stoltz, is resting in Leipsic, after an extended and remunerative concert tour.

Professor Max Kuntzler is also in Leipsic—with the ever persistent will—the dogged patience that so often wins in the end.

Alice Walker

Beauty: When the Other Dancer Is the Self

Alice Walker (b. 1944) is a prize-winning writer, African American studies scholar, teacher, and activist. In her writing, Walker fuses the personal and the political; her many works—poems, essays, short stories, and novels—express her views on spirituality, sexuality, and the abuse of power. Walker, who describes herself as a "womanist," has, like The Feminist Press itself, been devoted to restoring lost voices: It is due in part to her efforts that Zora Neale Hurston was rediscovered and has been granted her due place in twentieth-century American literature.

"Beauty" first appeared in 1983 in Walker's essay collection *In Search of Our Mothers' Gardens*, and was reprinted by The Feminist Press in 1987 in *With Wings: An Anthology of Literature by and about Women with Disabilities*, edited by Marsha Saxton and Florence Howe. The piece recounts how Walker finally made "peace with herself" long after a childhood "accident" blinded and disfigured one of her eyes. In it, she remembers her years of shame and of self-imposed isolation from others—and recalls the remarkable moment when she learned the true definition of beauty.

It is a bright summer day in 1947. My father, a fat, funny man with beautiful eyes and a subversive wit, is trying to decide which of his eight children he will take with him to the county fair. My mother, of course, will not go. She is knocked out from getting us ready: I hold my neck stiff against the pressure of her knuckles as she hastily completes the braiding and then beribboning of my hair.

My father is the driver for the rich old white lady up the road. Her name is Miss May. She owns all the land for miles around, as well as the house in which we live. All I remember about her is that she once offered to pay my mother 75 cents for cleaning her house, raking up piles of her magnolia leaves, and washing her family's clothes, and that my mother—she of no money, eight children, and a chronic earache—refused it. But I do not think of this in 1947. I am two-and-a-half years old. I want to go everywhere my daddy goes. I am excited at the prospect of riding in a car. Someone has told me fairs are fun. That there is room in the car for only three of us doesn't faze me at all. Whirling happily in my starchy frock, showing off my biscuit polished patent leather shoes and lavender socks, tossing my head in a way that makes my ribbons bounce, I stand, hands on hips, before my father. "Take me, Daddy," I say with assurance, "I'm the prettiest!"

Later, it does not surprise me to find myself in Miss May's shiny black car, sharing the backseat with the other lucky ones. Does not surprise me that I thoroughly enjoy the fair. At home that night I tell all the unlucky ones about the merry-go-round, the man who eats live chickens, and the abundance of Teddy bears, until they say: that's enough, baby Alice. Shut up now, and go to sleep.

It is Easter Sunday, 1950. I am dressed in a green, flocked, scalloped-hem dress (handmade by my adoring sister Ruth) that has its own smooth satin petticoat and tiny hot-pink roses tucked into each scallop. My shoes, new T-strap patent leather, again highly biscuit polished. I am six years old and have learned one of the longest Easter speeches to be heard in church that day, totally unlike the speech I said when I was two: "Easter lilies/pure and white/blossom in/the morning light." When I rise to give my speech I do so on a great wave of love and pride and expectation. People in the church stop rustling their new crinolines. They seem to hold their breath. I can tell they admire my dress, but it is my spirit, bordering on sassiness (womanishness), they secretly applaud.

"That girl's a little mess," they whisper to each other, pleased.

Naturally I say my speech without stammer or pause, unlike those who stutter, stammer, or, worst of all, forget. This is before the word "beautiful" exists in people's vocabulary, but "Oh, isn't she the *cutest* thing!" frequently floats my way. *"And got so much sense!"* they gratefully add . . . for which thoughtful addition I thank them to this day.

It was great fun being cute. But then, one day, it ended.

I am eight years old and a tomboy. I have a cowboy hat, cowboy boots, checkered shirt and pants, all red. My playmates are my brothers, two and four years older than me. Their colors are black and green, the only difference in the way we are dressed. On Saturday nights we all go to the picture show, even my mother; Westerns are her favorite movies. Back home, "on the ranch," we pretend we are Tom Mix, Hopalong Cassidy, Lash LaRue (we've even named one of our dogs Lash LaRue); we chase each other for hours rustling cattle, being outlaws, delivering damsels from distress. Then my parents decide to buy my brothers guns. These are not "real" guns. They shoot "BBs," copper pellets my brothers say will kill birds. Because I am a girl, I do not get a gun. Instantly I am relegated to the position of Indian. Now there appears a great distance between us. They shoot and shoot at everything with their new guns. I try to keep up with my bow and arrows.

One day while I am standing on top of our makeshift "garage"—pieces of tin nailed across some poles—holding my bow and arrow and looking out toward the fields, I feel an incredible blow in my right eye. I look down just in time to see my brother lower his gun.

Both brothers rush to my side. My eye stings, and I cover it with my hand. "If you tell," they say, "we will get a whipping. You don't want that to happen, do you?" I do not. "Here is a piece of wire," says the older brother, picking it up from the roof, "say you stepped on one end of it and the other flew up and hit you." The pain is beginning to start. "Yes," I say. "Yes, I will say that is what happened." If I do not say this is what happened, I know my brothers will find ways to make me wish I had. But now I will say anything that gets me to my mother.

Confronted by our parents we stick to the lie agreed upon. They place me on a bench on the porch and I close my left eye while they examine the right. There is a tree growing from underneath the porch, that climbs past the railing to the roof. It is the last thing my right eye sees. I watch as its trunk, its branches, and then its leaves are blotted out by the rising blood.

I am in shock. First there is intense fever, which my father tries to break using lily leaves bound around my head. Then there are chills: my mother tries to get me to eat soup. Eventually, I do not know how, my parents learn what has happened. A week after the "accident" they take me to see a doctor. "Why did you wait so long to come?" he asks, looking into my eye and shaking his head. "Eyes are sympathetic," he says. "If one is blind, the other will likely become blind too."

This comment of the doctor's terrifies me. But it is really how I look that bothers me most. Where the BB pellet struck there is a glob of whitish scar tissue, a hideous cataract, on my eye. Now when I stare at people—a favorite pastime, up to now—they will stare back. Not at the "cute" little girl, but at her scar. For six years I do not stare at anyone because I do not raise my head.

Years later, in the throes of a mid-life crisis, I ask my mother and sister whether I changed after the "accident." "No," they say, puzzled. "What do you mean?"

What do I mean?

I am eight, and for the first time, doing poorly in school, where I have been something of a whiz since I was four. We have just moved to the place where the "accident" occurred. We do not know any of the people around us because this is a different county. The only time I see the friends I knew is when we go back to our old church. My new school is the former state penitentiary. It is a large stone building, cold and drafty, crammed to overflowing with boisterous, ill-disciplined children. On the third floor there is a huge circular imprint of some partition that has been torn out.

"What used to be here?" I ask a sullen girl next to me on our way past it to lunch.

"The electric chair," says she.

At night I have nightmares about the electric chair, and about all the people reputedly "fried" in it. I am afraid of the school, where all the students seem to be budding criminals.

"What's the matter with your eye?" they ask, critically.

When I don't answer (I cannot decide whether it was an "accident" or not), they shove me, insist on a fight.

My brother, the one who created the story about the wire, comes to my rescue. But then brags so much about "protecting" me, I become sick.

After weeks of torture at the school, my parents decide to send me back to our old community to my old school. I live with my grandparents and the teacher they board. But there is not room for Phoebe, my cat. By the time my grandparents decide there *is* room, and I ask for my cat, she cannot be found. Miss Yarborough, the boarding teacher, takes me under her wing, and begins to teach me to play the piano. But soon she marries an African—a "prince," she says—and is whisked away to his continent.

At my old school there is at least one teacher who loves me. She is the teacher who "knew me before I was born" and bought my first baby clothes. It is she who makes life bearable. It is her presence that finally helps me turn on the one child at the school who continually calls me "one-eyed bitch." One day I simply grab him by his coat and beat him until I am satisfied. It is my teacher who tells me my mother is ill.

My mother is lying in bed in the middle of the day, something I have never seen. She is in too much pain to speak. She has an abscess in her ear. I stand looking down on her, knowing that if she dies, I cannot live. She is being treated with warm oils and hot bricks held against her cheek. Finally a doctor comes. But I must go back to my grandparents' house. The weeks pass, but I am hardly aware of it. All I know is that my mother might die, my father is not so jolly, my brothers still have their guns, and I am the one sent away from home.

"You did not change," they say.
Did I imagine the anguish of never looking up?

I am twelve. When relatives come to visit I hide in my room. My cousin Brenda, just my age, whose father works in the post office and whose mother is a nurse, comes to find me. "Hello," she says. And then she asks, looking at my recent school picture which I did not want taken, and on which the "glob" as I think of it is clearly visible, "You still can't see out of that eye?"

"No," I say, and flop back on the bed over my book.

That night, as I do almost every night, I abuse my eye. I rant and rave at it, in front of the mirror. I plead with it to clear up before morning. I tell it I hate and despise it. I do not pray for sight, I pray for beauty.

"You did not change," they say.

I am fourteen and baby-sitting for my brother Bill who lives in Boston. He is my favorite brother and there is a strong bond between us. Understanding my feelings of shame and ugliness, he and his wife take me to a local hospital where the "glob" is removed by a doctor named O. Henry. There is still a small bluish crater where the scar tissue was, but the ugly white stuff is gone. Almost immediately I become a different person from the girl who does not raise her head. Or so I think. Now that I've raised my head, I win the boyfriend of my dreams. Now that I've raised my head, I have plenty of friends. Now that I've raised my head, classwork comes from my lips as faultlessly as Easter speeches did, and I leave high school as valedictorian, most popular student and *queen*, hardly believing my luck. Ironically, the girl who was voted most beautiful in our class (and was) was later shot twice through the chest by a male companion, using a "real" gun, while she was pregnant. But that's another story in itself. Or, is it?

"You did not change," they say.

It is now thirty years since the "accident." A gorgeous woman and famous journalist comes to visit and to interview me. She is going to write a cover story for her magazine that focuses on my last book. "Decide how you want to look on the cover," she says. "Glamorous, or whatever."

Never mind "glamorous," it is the "whatever" that I hear. Suddenly all I can think of is whether I will get enough sleep the night before the photography session: if I don't, my eye will be tired and wander, as blind eyes will.

At night in bed with my lover I think up reasons why I should not appear on the cover of a magazine: "My meanest critics will say I've sold out," I say. "My family will now realize I write scandalous books." "But what's the real reason you don't want to do this?" he asks.

"Because in all probability," I say in a rush, "my eye won't be straight."

"It will be straight enough," he says. Then, "Besides, I thought you'd made your peace with that."

And I suddenly realize that I have.

I remember:

I am talking to my brother Jimmy, asking if he remembers anything unusual about the day I was shot. He does not know I consider that day the last time my father, with his sweet home remedy of cool lily leaves, "chose" me, and that I suffered rage inside because of this. "Well," he says, "all I remember is standing by the side of the highway with Daddy, trying to flag down a car. A white man stopped, but when Daddy said he needed somebody to take his little girl to the doctor, he drove off."

I remember:

I am thirty-three years old. And in the desert for the first time. I fall totally in love with it. I am so overwhelmed by its beauty, I confront for the first time, consciously, the meaning of the doctor's words years ago: "Eyes are sympathetic. If one is blind, the other will likely become blind too." I realize I have dashed about the world madly, looking at this, looking at that, storing up images against the fading of the light. *But I might have missed seeing the desert!* The shock of that possibility—and gratitude for more than twenty-five years of sight—sends me literally to my knees. Poem after poem comes—which is perhaps how poets pray.

ON SIGHT

I am so thankful I have seen
The Desert
And the creatures in The Desert
And the desert itself

The desert has its own moon
Which I have seen
With my own eye

There is no flag on it

Trees of the desert have arms
All of which are always up
That is because the moon is up
The sun is up
The stars
Clouds
None with flags.

If there were flags, I doubt
the trees would point.
Would you?

But mostly, I remember this:
I am twenty-seven, and my baby daughter is almost three. Since her birth I have worried over her discovery that her mother's eyes are different from other people's. Will she be embarrassed? I wonder. What will she say? Every day she watches a television program called "Big Blue Marble." It begins with a picture of the earth as it appears from the moon. It is bluish, a little battered-looking but full of light, with whitish clouds swirling around it. Every time I see it I weep with love, as if it is a picture of Grandma's house. One day when I am putting Rebecca down for her nap,

she suddenly focuses on my eye. Something inside me cringes, gets ready to try to protect myself. All children are cruel about physical differences, I know from experience, and that they don't always mean to be is another matter. I assume Rebecca will be the same.

But no-o-o-o. She studies my face intently as we stand, her inside and me outside her crib. She even holds my face maternally between her dimpled little hands. Then, looking every bit as serious and lawyerlike as her father, she says, as if it may just possibly have slipped my attention: "Mommy, there's a *world* in your eye." (As in, "Don't be alarmed, or do anything crazy.") And then, gently, but with great interest: "Mommy, where did you *get* that world in your eye?"

For the most part, the pain left then. (So what if my brothers grew up to buy even more powerful pellet guns for their sons. And to carry real guns themselves. So what if a young "Morehouse man" once nearly fell off the steps of Trevor Arnett Library because he thought my eyes were blue.) Crying and laughing I ran to the bathroom, while Rebecca mumbled and sang herself off to sleep. Yes indeed, I realized, looking into the mirror. There *was* a world in my eye. And I saw that it was possible to love it: that in fact, for all it had taught me, of shame and anger and inner vision, I *did* love it. Even to see it drifting out of orbit in boredom, or rolling up out of fatigue, not to mention floating back at attention in excitement (bearing witness, a friend has called it), deeply suitable to my personality, and even characteristic of me.

That night I dream I am dancing to Stevie Wonder's song "Always." As I dance, whirling and joyous, happier than I've ever been in my life, another bright-faced dancer joins me. We dance and kiss each other and hold each other through the night. The other dancer has obviously come through all right, as I have done. She is beautiful, whole and free. And she is also me.

CREDITS

Rediscovered Classics of American Women's Writing
from The Feminist Press at The City University of New York

Allegra Maud Goldman (1976) by Edith Konecky. $12.95 paper.
Brown Girl, Brownstones (1959) by Paule Marshall. $10.95 paper.
The Changelings (1955) by Jo Sinclair. $8.95 paper.
The Chinese Garden (1962) by Rosemary Manning. $12.95 paper, $29.00 cloth.
Daddy Was a Number Runner (1970) by Louise Meriwether. $10.95 paper.
Daughter of Earth (1929) by Agnes Smedley. $14.95 paper.
Doctor Zay (1882) by Elizabeth Stuart Phelps. $8.95 paper.
Fettered for Life (1874) by Lillie Devereux Blake. $18.95 paper, $45.00 cloth.
The Little Locksmith: A Memoir (1943) by Katharine Butler Hathaway. $14.95 paper.
    $35.00 cloth.
*I Love Myself When I Am Laughing . . . and Then Again When I Am Looking Mean and Impressive:
    A Zora Neale Hurston Reader* edited by Alice Walker. $14.95 paper.
Life in the Iron Mills and Other Stories (1861) by Rebecca Harding Davis. $10.95 paper.
The Living Is Easy (1948) by Dorothy West. $14.95 paper.
The Maimie Papers: Letters from an Ex-Prostitute by Maimie Pinzer. Edited by Ruth Rosen and
    Sue Davidson. $19.95 paper.
Now in November (1934) by Josephine W. Johnson. $10.95 paper, $29.95 cloth.
Streets: A Memoir of the Lower East Side (1923) by Bella Spewack. $10.95 paper, $19.95
    cloth.
This Child's Gonna Live (1969) by Sarah E. Wright. $10.95 paper.
Unpunished: A Mystery (1929) by Charlotte Perkins Gilman. $10.95 paper, $18.95 cloth.
Weeds (1923) by Edith Summers Kelley. $15.95 paper.
The Wide, Wide World (1850) by Susan Warner. $19.95 paper, $35.00 cloth.
The Yellow Wall-Paper (1892) by Charlotte Perkins Gilman, $5.95 paper.

To receive a free catalog of The Feminist Press's 180 titles, call or write The Feminist Press at The City University of New York, The Graduate Center, 365 Fifth Avenue, New York, NY 10016; phone: (212) 817-7920; fax: (212) 987-4008; feministpress.org. Feminist Press books are available at bookstores or can be ordered directly. Send check or money order (in U.S. dollars drawn on a U.S. bank) payable to The Feminist Press. Please add $4.00 shipping and handling for the first book and $1.00 for each additional book. VISA, Mastercard, and American Express are accepted for telephone orders. Prices subject to change.